Wakefield Press

The Hands

Stephen Orr is the author of five previous novels. He contributes essays and features to several publications. A fascination with the dynamics of families and small communities pervades his fiction and non-fiction. Stephen Orr lives in Adelaide.

Praise for Stephen Orr's *One Boy Missing*

'In *One Boy Missing*, [Orr] realises the slow rhythms of country Australia, its language and landscape ... skilfully ... It is great holiday reading, whether at home or abroad.' – *Australian Bookseller & Publisher*

'Orr creates an evocative landscape, the characterisations are truly wonderful, and because of that, the resolution of the crime at the heart of the novel is less important than seeing how these three can find some kind of peace with who they are and what life has done to them.' – *Hoopla*

'[Stephen Orr] is adept at partnering highly charged associations with emotionally arid landscapes.' – *Advertiser*

'The novel is not so much a typical crime novel but a more contemplative exploration of the relationship between fathers and sons.' – *Sun Herald*

'Two of Orr's novels are complex variations on the themes of loss, isolation, the difficulties of putting a self back together. His prose is measured and eloquent, his imaginative reach considerable, and his next novel worth the wait.' – *Sydney Morning Herald*

'Stephen Orr's detective is sunnier than Kurt Wallander, but his talkative characters and bitter realism stands comparison with Henning Mankell. He's a sincere storyteller with a flinty eye for the landscape and the sadness that drives good stories forward.' – *Weekend Press*

'Stephen Orr spends time drawing out his characters' foibles and the novel is all the better for his attentions.' – *Sunday Examiner*

Praise for Stephen Orr's *Dissonance*

'Orr's portrait of the controlling mother is the main attraction. He keeps the character in magnetic equipoise, attracting as much as she repels.' – *Age*

'Stephen Orr writes a story with great tension and momentum. The emotional and psychological layers of *Dissonance* prompt us to ponder the deep nature of familial relationships and their hold over one's life.' – *Good Reading*

'Orr brings us a cast of characters that are wholly believable. The first hundred pages alone would make a fine novella. As it stands, the entire novel is an accomplished work.' – *InDaily*

'This is an intelligent, beautifully-wrought novel. Its finely nuanced characters intrigue and move because of the complexity of their motivations and identities.' – *Australian Book Review*

'Orr is a no-nonsense, vivid storyteller. He punches out exchanges between his characters in a pragmatic way that transmits jealousy and heartbreak without sentiment.' – *Australian*

Praise for Stephen Orr's *Time's Long Ruin*

'*Time's Long Ruin* is Orr's eloquent, unusual, bold but responsible retelling of a veritable urban nightmare that still haunts the Australian imagination.' – *Sydney Morning Herald*

'The writing is accomplished, the imagery beautifully evocative ... despite the distressing subject matter at its core, this is a deeply affectionate novel.' – *Age*

'It is Orr's cleaving of the ordinary to the unspeakable that gives the novel its potency and brings it within the margins of the Australian Gothic.' – *Big Issue*

'Every now and again, you open a book that is so richly evocative, so poignant and haunting that the characters leach into your subconscious and you are caught in an intricately spun web of emotion, scent and feeling.' – *Sunday Tasmanian*

'*Time's Long Ruin* is a fine novel, thoughtful and unsentimental, convincing without being predictable.' – *Australian Book Review*

By the same author

Attempts to Draw Jesus
Hill of Grace
Time's Long Ruin
Dissonance
One Boy Missing

The Hands

An Australian pastoral

STEPHEN ORR

Wakefield
Press

Wakefield Press
16 Rose Street
Mile End
South Australia 5031
www.wakefieldpress.com.au

First published 2015
Reprinted 2016

An earlier version of the cowards' list story appeared
in *Meanjin* 4 – 2008

Cover designed by Liz Nicholson, designBITE
Edited by Margot Lloyd, Wakefield Press
Typeset by Wakefield Press

National Library of Australia Cataloguing-in-Publication entry

Creator: Orr, Stephen, 1967–   , author.
Title: The hands / Stephen Orr.
ISBN: 978 1 74305 343 0 (paperback).
Dewey Number: A823.4

Government
of South Australia

Arts SA

CORIOLE

McLAREN VALE

Australian Government

Australia Council
for the Arts

Publication of this book was assisted by
the Commonwealth Government through the
Australia Council, its arts funding and advisory body.

Part One

2004

1

Part Two

2005

95

Part Three

2006

287

For most of us, there is only the unattended
Moment, the moment in and out of time,
The distraction fit, lost in a shaft of sunlight,
The wild thyme unseen, or the winter lightning
Or the waterfall, or music heard so deeply
That it is not heard at all, but you are the music
While the music lasts.

T.S. Eliot, 'The Dry Salvages' (from *Four Quartets*)

In what way were we trapped? where, our mistake?
what, where, how, when, what way, might all these
things have been different, if only we had done otherwise? if only we might have known.

James Agee, *Let Us Now Praise Famous Men*

Part One

2004

Part One

I

Trevor Wilkie knelt in front of the fence. He pressed and released the top wire and it vibrated before settling. A sea of haze faded in the offing, and if he dropped his head the wire settled on the horizon. He looked up at a boy in the distance and called, 'You okay?'

His son waved back. 'What is it?'

'Nothing.' He stood, gathered a roll of wire and a strainer and headed back to his ute.

The fence line was straight, diminishing towards a distant corner where it spread out to form yards. Posts, perfectly spaced every twenty metres, single box, four wires and the spacers he trusted his son, Harry, to insert. As a fence, it was a marvel, but he guessed it didn't help him make money. It didn't put protein in the grass; it didn't find water, and if it did, it didn't pump it up; it didn't make it rain; it didn't make the price of beef any higher.

'All done?' he asked his son.

'Yep,' the eleven-year-old replied, wiping his hands on his trousers.

'We better get you home. What time's your lesson?'

'Mr Anderson said it didn't matter.'

He looked at him suspiciously. 'Yeah?'

'It's just history. Egypt. I don't care about Egypt.'

'So he said: You, young Harry Wilkie, don't bother about tomorrow's lesson?'

They stood and looked out across their farm. A light breeze moved through the grass. Trevor could sing its song through his cracked lips, feel it in his ears, his nostrils, on his face. He pushed his dog-chewed hat onto his head. Looked at his son, his expression full of an understanding that this was a place to be tamed, made to yield, more than his own intuition that it was nothing more than a sensation, the feel of sand in his boot.

He pointed to the canola meal on the ground. 'They're gonna trample that,' he said. 'You should've put it in a straight line.'

'It doesn't matter.'

'At two hundred dollars a tonne, it matters.' He noticed two of his big steers trampling meal into the soil-sand that made up most of Bundeena. 'Did you sweep out the ute?'

'Yep.'

'Well … we better get you back to King Tut, eh?'

'Dad.'

'Yer mother will be waiting.' He noticed his son's pants were too big, worn on the knees, ragged around the cuffs. He looked at his boots. 'When was the last time you polished them?'

They returned to the ute. Bundeena was marginal country. It could carry cattle, sparsely. To Trevor, this was where Australia became desert, where man – following the east-west railway, before it seriously set its sights on the Nullarbor – had given up on agriculture. Most men, at least. Except for them: sixth-generation Beef Shorthorn producers who'd wrestled with the land for 130 years. This was country that hadn't asked for farmers but had got them anyway. On the southern edge, the railway line, and to the north, nothing. They had neighbours to the east and west, but they might as well have been living in New Zealand.

They drove along the fence line. 'Did you notice that animal's eye?' he asked.

'What?'

'Pardon. That cow, eating the canola?'

Harry stopped to think. 'She looked okay.'

'Yeah?' He slowed through a gate. 'Cancer eye.'

Harry's teeth were bone-white and there was a space between the top incisors, just big enough for a toothpick. 'I didn't look.'

'There are too many old girls out there.'

'What'll happen to her?'

'What happens when you get cancer?'

'You die?'

'Not always.'

They drove, silently.

'But she will.'

Harry wiped dust from his lips and cheeks.

'Too many old girls,' Trevor repeated. 'I can't afford to waste any more feed.'

He screwed the knob onto the stick and changed gears. Slowed around a clump of acacia. 'What I don't get,' he said, taking off his hat, letting his hair fall down over his forehead, 'is why they'd teach a kid, living on a station, six hundred kilometres from the nearest town, about Egypt.' He looked at Harry, and he shrugged.

'What about something relevant?'

'Like what?'

'You know, explorers. Sturt, Stuart … even Burke and Wills. But Nefer-bloody-titi.'

'We've learnt about them too.'

'Yeah?'

'And how they only survived because of the black fellas.'

He looked surprised. 'What about the white fellas?'

'Most of them didn't know what they were doing. They got sand blindness. They followed their compasses, not the creeks, the birds, the songlines.'

'The songlines?'

'The way the black fellas went.'

Trevor was tired of songlines, and explorers. They weren't real – anymore, at least. An afternoon of welding in the sun: that was real. Numbers, too. Solid and reliable. Maths didn't lie. No one was teaching his son anywhere near enough of that. Liabilities, post spacings, humidity, days since last rain, protein percentage in feed – all real, knowable, helpful. Not like Ramesses II, rooting his sister.

Real: the fact that he'd worked out he was carrying 1800 less cattle since the drought had started; that their mortgage was taking on water, and sinking; the price of diesel; groceries; labour. As the voice on the radio droned about Howard Carter.

As they drove the broken clock rattled in its too-big receptacle. His eyes settled on a pocket of ground peeling away from the earth in the mid-distance. He felt himself falling, until he wasn't in his ute. This place – the fences, the cattle, their hunger, their thirst – seemed to have nothing to do with him. All he had to do was keep his foot on the accelerator. That would lead to arrival, eating, sleeping, vaccinating, ranting about government and stock agents driving Jaguars. But beyond all this, he felt smaller than a spider. 'You need a haircut.'

Harry ran his hand through his dusty blond hair. 'The snippers again?'

'I'll do it. Don't let your mother.'

'I'd rather just have it shaved.'

'I don't think so.'

Trevor turned onto the road that led to the house. He drove up a gentle incline, lined on both sides with native pines. On long, hot evenings the shade provided an escape from the house, sitting proudly on the hilltop, soaking up the last of the day's sun. He'd come down with Harry, and when he was home from boarding school, Aiden. They would spread out on a rug to read, or talk.

Then Carelyn would come down from the house, asking him to unblock the toilet or speak to his dad, Murray, who lived with but apart from them in his east-facing sleep-out. He'd complain, but go back in and tell his father to stop playing his Bing Crosby so loud it shook the walls.

He stopped in front of the house. Their old dog, Yanga, lifted her head, but didn't think it worth getting up.

'You better clean up for lunch,' he said, and Harry went inside. He could hear Carelyn calling him, something about lessons and helping Chris with his sudoku. Sitting in his ute, he tried to lift himself out of his seat. Took a deep breath, held it, and let go.

It didn't help. He had to convince himself to go in, to face the dozen details that would have accumulated since his departure. There would be technical tasks – things involving wires and gap-filler and two-inch nails – but there would also be matters of words, something Fay (Murray's older sister, who shared a room with her disabled son, Chris) had said to Murray; or a look she'd given Carelyn; or the way Carelyn had crossed her arms as she watched Chris walk, naked, to the back line to fetch his singlet.

He looked across to the machinery shed: a trailer with portable yards; the boys' trail bikes; the brick walls, burnt black, from when he'd left a pile of greasy rags on the bench. A hot day, and night, waking up to Yanga barking and an orange flicker through the bedroom window. 'Fuck.'

As Carelyn stirred, and managed, 'What?'

As he pulled on his shorts and ran from the room, followed down the hallway by his two young sons. 'Aiden, get the hose.'

'Where?'

'Christ, I dunno.'

Now, Carelyn stood at the back door of their old bluestone villa. 'You comin' in?' she said. 'Lunch is on the table.'

He stepped out of his ute. 'Just puttin' me gear away.' Took his roll of wire and strainer and walked across the compound in front of the house. Went into another, smaller, shed. It was built from leftover stone from the house, its roof supported by old wooden beams. It was his favourite spot, dark when he closed the door, musty, away from the business of the house and its various dramas. It had its own bench, three inches deep with wood shavings and tools and almond husks left behind by his great- and great-great-grandfather. He pulled a string and yellow light splashed across the bench. Hanging his wire from a hook, he added his strainer to the mess of tools and looked at a photo of the boys (Harry still in his nappy) above the bench.

'Trevor,' he heard his wife call. 'Come on.' Some job, some piece of bad news he was missing. He looked out of a small, ill-fitting window above the bench. Could see the yards in the distance and the crush, waiting for his welder.

A rack held tools which reflected light back into the shed. Polished chisels waited for pine blocks sitting in a basket on the bench. He heard the shuffle of feet and his dad, standing in the doorway. 'You comin' in?'

'Yeah, just cleaning up,' he replied, noticing what looked like dried jam on his father's whiskers. 'There was a whole fence down,' he continued, referring to the north paddock, stretching from the house to distant, desert reaches. 'It's a miracle none of them wandered off.'

'All fixed?'

'Yes.' He smelt his father's breath, heavy with coffee and the cheap tobacco he kept in his pocket.

Murray came further into the shed, grasping the bench, trying to straighten his back. 'Aiden rang.'

'Yeah?'

'Says he wants to come home on the weekend.'

He took a moment. 'Why?'

'That's what I said. Why? Stick to the exeats.'

He wiped his hands on a rag that only made them dirtier.

'Probably in trouble again. Does he want me to call back?'

'Didn't say.'

Murray Wilkie – the seventy-four-year-old patriarch of Bundeena, the old fella who could calm a bull just by looking him in the eyes, by singing to him (... *drifting down to dreamland, underneath the mellow moon* ...) approached his son's carving bench and picked up the beginnings of a hand. 'Who's this?'

'Harry.'

He held the length of pine, turned it over, smelt it, and felt each of the four still-unformed fingers and a thumb. 'You pick the hardest bloody thing.'

'Why?'

'Well ... y' got bones and nails and wrinkles.' He studied his own hand. 'And no one can agree on which finger's the longest, or how they bend.' He looked at his son. 'You should stick to fruit.'

'Trev ... Murray,' Carelyn called again. 'Come on.'

Trevor pulled the string and the shed darkened. They went out and he closed the door. 'I can't get him this weekend,' he said.

'Of course not. He can just stop there and do some study. It won't kill him.'

They walked across the compound. Trevor avoided looking at the salt damp and stone crumbling around the foundations of his house. Avoided thinking about how long he could put off repairs. Imagined Bundeena's walls collapsing, the roof falling in, Harry crushed, Carelyn dead, a dust-caked Murray crawling from the ruins. Then, as if telling him to stop, Yanga started sniffing and licking his pants. He scratched her head.

'You getting deaf?' Carelyn asked, standing at the door.

'Among other things,' he replied, as he went into the laundry, kicking off his shoes and washing his hands in the concrete trough. 'Aiden rang?'

'Don't worry, I told him ... we haven't got the time or money.'

'What was the problem?'

'Nothing. Just thought he'd try it on.'

'Probably got someone pregnant.'

Carelyn used her foot to push his boots into the mountain of RMs, sandshoes and thongs under the trough. She stood looking at him, her arms crossed. 'All fixed?'

'Yep … tight as a …'

Harry, sitting inside listening, already knew his dad's catalogue of sayings. Life in simple snatches. And probably the way it really was, he often guessed.

Carelyn smiled. 'Good.'

Trevor grabbed her hair and gave it a tug. She had it in her stay-wet, slicked-back, I've-got-work-to-do mode. The style highlighted her forehead, cut by a single wrinkle; a nose that was always red, and peeling, despite the fact she never went out in the sun. And her eyes, black-rimmed and tired; always tired. Full of expectations. For renovations. Forty days and nights of rain.

He looked at Chris's yellow bed-sheets, soaking in antiseptic. 'I told him to hang them out,' he said.

'They're stained.'

'Disgusting,' he muttered, but Carelyn just waited.

They went into the main living-dining area of the house – a room with twelve-foot ceilings and mortar walls, cracked in a dozen places from top to bottom. He'd managed to repair and paint one wall before losing interest in renovations. Before he'd really thought about whether he, and his family, would be here much longer. Murray, of course, was always on at him to keep up the work – the wiring he risked his life repairing, new floorboards – but enthusiasm, harder to muster every day, was the real problem.

Fay George, Murray's older sister, was already sitting at the table pouring tea. Still wearing her nightie and dressing gown. He wanted to say something, but didn't. Never did. Murray would just start in on him: *Unless it needs to be said, don't say it … or, Who made you the model of perfection?*

'Morning, Fay,' he said.

'Trevor …' She looked up, and spilt the tea. 'You were off early this morning.'

'Thought I'd beat the heat.' Although it was more about beating the early morning dramas of Bundeena. 'Morning, Chris,' he continued, looking at the forty-six-year-old man-boy, buried in a rug on the couch eating spaghetti.

'Good morning, Trevor,' Chris replied, spelling out each word. 'Have you been mustering?'

'No. It's too early for that. You should know that, Chris.'

'I do.'

'So when do we have calves?'

Chris stopped to think, still watching a threadbare tape of *The Battle of Britain*. 'Spring.'

'Yes. You gonna help with the muster this year?'

But Chris was caught up in a dog fight, his mouth open, spaghetti hanging from his fork.

'Careful, Chris,' Fay called, as she placed the tea cups in front of the plates.

They all sat down to cold ham, lettuce and pickled onions; Murray's bread thrown across the table.

'How are you feeling today, Fay?' Trevor asked, and she looked up, managing to pull her shoulders back.

'So so …'

'You seem better.' He realised this was probably not what she wanted to hear. 'Maybe I can help you with some gardening this arvo,' he continued, but her shoulders and head had dropped. 'Didn't you want some weeds sprayed?'

After a while she said, 'Yes, they need doing.'

He noticed his son's seat was empty. 'Harry!'

He waited.

'Harry!' He looked at Carelyn.

'I don't know,' she replied, slicing the last of the boiled eggs.

'Harry!'

'He's probably in his room with his headphones on,' Murray said, stuffing his mouth with bread.

He stood, walked from the room, down the semi-papered hallway and looked into his son's room.

Empty.

Then he went out through the sliding doors to the front of the house with its view from the hill, down the slope of old blood-woods. 'Harry!' he called, but there was no response.

He stood on the wide porch which, although at the front of the house, was really the back, away from the chaos of the compound. Broken tiles. A bull-nosed verandah that leaked, although they knew where to sit to stay dry. There were several old chairs – wicker, tube-steel, a fluffy stool from Carelyn's ABBA days – and an old tranny, although there was no signal for it to pick up.

This is where they'd come on hot evenings to escape the house, to watch distant freight trains or the Indian Pacific, scurrying between oceans. They'd watch them come into view and, an hour later, disappear. They'd follow their every painful inch, as if it was the first time they'd ever seen a train.

'Harry!'

Nothing.

He'd warned him so many times: *stay within calling distance of the house*. He could remember a night when Harry was three or four, when it was pelting down (the first time in years), the fork-lightning picking up the glint of the railway tracks, strobing the cattle-eye desert. And there he was, standing in this same spot, calling out, 'Harry, where are yer?'

Searching the sheds, the roads, the tracks, down among the

bloodwoods, out onto the flats, their rain-soaked outdoor lounge room; Chris cowering under a rug; Fay, still in her nightie, poking about in long grass with a broom.

Until Harry emerged from Murray's sleep-out, from under the canvas stretcher the old man slept on, saying (words like), 'I knew you wouldn't find me.' Smiling, laughing, wondering why his dad was covered in curry-coloured mud.

'Dad.' Harry was at the door.

'Christ,' Trevor said, turning. 'Where were you?'

'I left my iPod in the ute.' He was gone, back to the table, the thick slabs of cold ham and beef and pickled onions.

Trevor followed him in. 'Didn't you hear me calling?'

'Sorry.'

'It's probably those headphones, makin' you deaf.'

'Dad, it's not.'

They both sat down.

Fay's chin was nearly on her chest. *'Give us this day our daily bread.'*

They all looked at her, then at each other.

'What, you wanna say grace?' Murray asked his sister.

Fay took a deep breath and looked up. 'No, of course not.'

'You wanna say the Lord's Prayer?'

'No, I don't.'

'You were sayin' it.'

She shook her head. 'No, go on, get on with yer lunch. You want more tea? Anyone want more tea?'

They ate silently: nothing but the roar of Spitfires and Messerschmitts.

Half an hour later, Harry stood in the machinery shed wearing gloves, gumboots and overalls. Trevor looked him over and said, 'Fifty mils.' The hazel-eyed boy carefully measured fifty millilitres of herbicide into a cylinder and tipped it into a spray-pack. Then used a bigger cylinder to fill this with water. Took a stick, stirred the mixture and screwed the lid on tight. Primed the tank and started spraying around the sheds – coating every weed, every blade of grass with herbicide. He'd stop, prime the pump, and start again, following fence lines, in and around Fay's garden.

At one point, Carelyn stuck her head out of the door and called, 'Watch the washing.'

Trevor, following behind, just mumbled, 'There's not a breath of wind.'

Chris appeared from the house wearing his spaghetti singlet and boxer shorts and started singing *The Battle of Britain* theme. He conducted with his right hand as his head flew about in incomplete orbits. Finding the exact centre of the compound, he came to attention, saluted and started marching around the perimeter. Each step was in time with the music. He stopped, turned and was off again. Stopped, turned, marched.

Harry smiled at his father. Trevor just raised his eyebrows. 'Go on, get on with it.'

'Shouldn't we tell Aunty Fay?'

'No.'

He continued along the fence line, saying, 'Dad, what's gonna happen to Uncle Chris?'

'He'll get tired …'

'No … later? Will we have to look after him?'

'We already do.'

'No … by ourselves?'

Trevor saw he'd missed a spot, but he didn't say anything. It wasn't like you could get it all. Or, for that matter, stop it re-growing. No matter how careful you were the weeds would win. 'Maybe there will be somewhere he can go,' he said.

'Where?' Harry asked, pumping with the palm of his hand.

'A home.'

'A nursing home?'

'No, some sort of … well, perhaps a nursing home.'

Harry wasn't happy. 'But they're for old people.'

'Not always. Just people who need … nursing. Hence the name, numbat.' He knocked on his son's head. '*Nursing* home.'

Chris stopped and waited.

'What's wrong?' Trevor called.

And then thrust his arm out. '*Sieg Heil!*'

They had to stop themselves from laughing.

Chris was hot; he took off his singlet and stood at ease. Then, having received some sort of order, was off again, this time launching into a vocalise of the *Colonel Bogey March*.

Harry continued. The herbicide was running out; it was frothing, drifting in the chemical breeze. 'If he needs a home, we should start looking,' he said.

'Why?'

'Aunty Fay …' He didn't really know how to say it.

Trevor took a moment and said, 'I suppose you're right.'

'Are you gonna look?'

'Soon.'

This didn't seem the least bit sensible to Harry. 'Don't they have waiting lists?' he asked, finishing the poison.

As they marched back to the shed, Chris stopped and waited silently. Then he said, 'Fall out.' He walked towards the house, wiping his red flesh with his singlet, drying his armpits and the skin that formed a pouch between his belly and pubic triangle.

'We could always look after him,' Harry said.

'We could.'

'Will we?'

'That's up to Pop, and Mum.'

They arrived back in the shed and Harry unscrewed the top of the spray-pack. Trevor handed him the measuring cylinder. 'This time we'll do twice as much.'

Harry was opening the poison. 'I could do more, to help him.'

'We'll see. A lot could happen. He might need more help than we can give him.' He looked up and saw the yellow sheets hanging on the line.

Harry was just about to measure the herbicide when he heard the back door open. 'Harry, time for your lesson,' Carelyn called.

'Mum!' he complained, loudly.

'Now.'

Aiden Wilkie, seventeen, summer-tanned and red-nosed, waited for the singing to finish. The organ huffed and McIlwain, the chemistry teacher, switched it off. Brother Adlam stood and approached the lectern. 'Brother Giles left Mercy in 1971,' he read, using his right hand to settle his glasses on his nose. 'He'd helped redevelop school facilities and was always a positive presence …'

Aiden stretched his long, brown legs and compared them to the boy (a local, the son of a cop) sitting next to him: pale-skinned, none of the scars or discolourations of real life. And the Brother, completely removed from reality: 'He'd been a member of the Mercy staff since the early days …'

He guessed he had to be here, had to suffer, but felt that some good should come of it: book-keeping, letter-writing, physical education, even what passed for agriculture (a flock of sheep, a few calves, a few pigs). But not this.

'During these years two more Brothers passed on …'

He could see there was strength in his legs and he felt he was wasting it. He could see his dad digging a hole for a fence post, and his brother, trying to help him, although there were only a few jobs he was good for. Anyway, Harry had seven years of his own bullshit to wade through. Education in the ether: webcams and the faces of distant teachers, their lips refusing to synchronise with their words. King Henry the Fifth, Pontius Pilate, salmon swimming upstream, the importance of an opposable thumb, Mozart dead at thirty-five. Three times a day, despite what *really* needed doing around Bundeena. As he heard his father light the welder.

Now, Aiden, which of these is not a mammal …

Or, a long, hot afternoon, and 300 head to castrate. Looking at his mother, eyes pleading: 'I'll do twice as much tomorrow.'

'No.'

'Dad will be going for hours.'

As the baby (the pest, Harry-shit-arse) cried in the corner and Aunty Fay peeled potatoes. 'No, Aiden, Bill's helpin'' … they're nearly done.'

'Catholic laity began to assume responsibility for schools from various religious orders …'

He saw Mrs Dale pointing to his un-tucked shirt. He fixed it; just enough to keep her quiet.

'Examination results were invariably good: Latin, Classics, Geometry …'

He looked down at the school-crested carpet, discoloured by the light from the stained-glass windows. Noticed the dozen or so pairs of boots, and his were the most polished; legs, and his were the longest; hands (some clutching hymnals), and his were the strongest – and most frustrated (squeezing, rubbing, tapping). Then he looked through a window with the word 'Eucharist' in gold along the bottom. A leadlight showed a long table, chokers with disciples, each with their own pink beard. There was a white-whiskered Jesus, too old, too fat for Messiah-as-Catholic-school-leadlight.

It is, he thought, staring at him. Father Christmas. What year? I must have been eight or nine.

It was the same face: high forehead, and eyelids that covered most of his eyes; a small mouth, few words, dented chin.

It is, he thought.

An hour's journey in the family car: him, Shit-for-breath,

Trevor, Carelyn and Murray. He could remember stopping at the siding and getting out and waiting, his parents refusing to tell him why they were there. Remember wearing his new Akubra, a clean shirt and too-tight moleskins coming up above his gristly ankles. Murray grinning. 'They used to do this when I was a kid.'

'What's that, Pop?'

'Wait and see.'

Then the train: a pair of locos pulling a long, silver slug. The Indian Pacific stopping at Bundeena siding (the first time in twenty years, Murray pointed out, as the train slowed towards them). It stopped and waited and hissed. Then, Father Christmas descended the six steps from the front loco.

He could still see him in the leadlight, reaching for his chalice.

He was back in the desert. Harry was crying (because Santa had asked to hold him, to give him a small gift they'd stopped a hundred tonnes of train to share). He could remember waiting his turn, watching as Santa handed Shit-for-brains back to his mum; as the old man opened his arms and embraced him; as he knocked his Akubra to the ground; as the old man said, 'I've got a gift for you too,' and gave him a present that turned out to be a totem-tennis set.

He remembered telling Santa what he wanted, and Santa saying something like, 'Well, I'll do my best, but it's a long way for my reindeer to carry so many presents.'

And he remembered thinking, So what, you silly old bastard. Looking at the costume, and seeing that it barely covered the engineer's overalls, the beard doing little to disguise his coffee breath, his boots covered in oil.

He remembered looking at his parents and thinking, Thanks anyway.

Brother Adlam was still going. 'Handball calls into play every muscle of the body.'

He realised, not for the first time, that it was all a big put on.

'Let's keep it relevant,' Mrs Amery, Harry's teacher (captured in a small box in the corner of his screen, cigarette smoke drifting across her face) said to him.

Harry couldn't see how German was relevant – a clunking language giving everything labels that didn't fit. And why German? When was he going to Germany? Did they even have cattle stations in Germany?

'*Der Stier*,' she said.

'*Der Stier*,' he repeated, staring into the small camera on top of his computer.

'Which means?'

'A steer?'

He didn't really care. It was either this or Japanese and he had no idea what that was about. He could remember sitting, listening, as Aiden struggled with the words. He could see his brother now, looking down at him, rolling his eyes. And his father, standing in the background: 'Why on earth would they waste their time?'

'*Der Traktor*,' Amery continued.

'*Der Traktor*.'

Murray was sitting on the lounge rolling cigarettes, licking and lovingly sealing the seams. He had five lined up on the coffee table. '*Ich rauche jetzt eine Zigarette*,' he said.

Harry's classroom had colonised the corner of the lounge-dining area. His computer sat on a desk beside a bookcase made from old floorboards. There were posters – tables, the world, even Gandhi, as if (Carelyn had once supposed) this might inspire some sort of global consciousness in her trail bike-riding, cattle-branding sons.

Murray lit a match, placed it at the tip of his cigarette and inhaled.

'Not in here,' Carelyn said.

'I was going out,' he replied, standing.

She watched him go. He opened the sliding door and walked out. He could see low cumulus spreading to the north. The heart of the clouds was grey, but he knew they wouldn't drift any further south. Never did. Just along their fence line, before breaking up in a sunset of broken promise.

'*Die Gans*,' he heard Harry harping.

He noticed his nephew, further down the hill, harvesting lavender heads from bushes his sister had planted years ago. Chris moved on his knees, picking flowers, placing them in a shopping bag and moving along. Murray studied his body, his movements: careful, like he might be assembling a diesel engine or contemplating a line of calculus.

He knew why Fay had planted her lavender crop: their mother, always smelling of the stuff, making potpourri and lavender sachets to sit in drawers and under pillows. Thirty years later Fay's lavender was still there, prospering in full sun and bad soil. French, English and Italian, watered daily, pruned (Chris, manic with the shears) three times a year. Fay out of an evening walking between the rows, pulling a spike of *angustifolia* and smelling it, dropping it in the sand, passing on.

He watched and inhaled as Chris worked. He felt like this boy (for he was still a boy, really) had been at Bundeena forever; as he had been, for most of what amounted to a lifetime.

It was a cold day, July or August 1964. He could remember working with his dad in the yards, then the sound of a car in the driveway. It came up to the compound and there was Fay and her six-year-old son climbing out of an EH Holden. He could remember his sister getting out of the car, and immediately crying. 'Barry, he's run off.' As the boy ran down to the yards.

'Chris, careful!' he'd called, but he was gone.

'What do you mean, run off?' his dad had asked his only daughter.

'Left a note saying he's had enough.'

He'd noticed the suitcases and clothes in the back of the EH.

'What are you gonna do?' they'd asked, and she'd just shrugged.

Chris was poking a bull with a length of rubber tubing.

'Get away from that animal,' his father had shouted.

'I've come a long way,' Fay had answered, and there was silence.

'You wanna stay here?' his father had asked.

'Can I?'

'How long for?'

'A few weeks?'

Becoming months, years and decades. As the lavender grew, pushing its roots into soil that couldn't stand rain, not that they ever got any. As the EH was moved into one of the sheds, its motor seizing, its panels rusting.

'How much more you got to do?' he called to Chris, as he sucked his rollie back to his fingertips.

'A few more.'

'You should have a hat on.'

Chris looked at him as if he wasn't sure what he meant.

'Fucking idiot,' he whispered, focusing on the boy's big ears, burning deep red as he worked.

The Wilkies had found a room for them but after six months it was a very full house: Trevor in his first Akubra and boots always running away from Chris, forever wanting to hug and kiss him. Fay, always in tears, locking herself in her room for days on end as everyone fed, educated and entertained her not-quite-right son. Then there were the whispers and grumbles across the tea table. 'Of course no one minds that you're here, but if you're gonna stay, you gotta help out.'

'It's all Barry's fault.'

At first he'd been protective, telling his father to be patient, but by late 1964 a consensus had formed: enough was enough.

Then, as if by magic, Barry appeared on Christmas Day 1964. When Fay crawled out of bed at ten o'clock (the others having taken care of Chris, and his presents) he was sitting on the lounge assembling some of his son's new Meccano. 'G'day, Fay.'

'Barry ...'

As everyone watched, anxiously.

'What are you doing here?' she asked.

'I've come to see me son, for Christmas.'

'Oh.' She just stared at him.

'I thought you might be glad to see me.'

Her face hardened. 'Yeah? You thought? After just pissin' off?'

Someone said, 'Go easy, Fay, he's done the right thing.' But she just glared at them, turned and stormed into her room.

Barry shrugged. 'Give her a couple of days, she'll come around.'

As a voice called from behind solid wood, 'I'm not comin' out till he's gone.'

The family was torn. Yes, Barry could stay (that was their best, and only, hope) but what if he then settled and became part of the problem? Man and wife, living separately in the same house? How long could anyone put up with that? No one was entirely sure what Barry was thinking. They suspected he didn't like work, and as for the conductress he'd run off with – where was she? Were they willing to wait days, weeks, before the frost thawed, if indeed it ever would?

Still, some hope was better than none. So, they made up a bed in the sleep-out and Barry moved in. They fed him and provided a radio and magazines and a comfortable couch to sleep away the long, hot afternoons. Boxing Day. New Year's Day. A full week into one of the hottest Januaries on record. As he kept repeating, 'I really appreciate your hospitality.'

As they tried to draw Fay from her room. 'Come on, darls, he just wants to have a quiet word with yer.'

'No.'

'I'm sure he'll say he's sorry.'

'I don't care.'

Soon Fay was writing notes and sending them, via Chris, to her husband. *Please leave; you are not welcome here; I have no intention of talking to you* … As she thought, Once Strayed, Will Stray Again.

Chris was happy to have his dad around. Fay insisted he stay with her, but he wouldn't. She'd hold the door closed but he'd kick her leg. She'd only leave the room to go to the toilet, but only after she'd asked someone to check if *he* was around.

Early January, February, as Barry told the others there was no way he could go out and work in hundred-degree heat.

So, eventually, in a machinery shed conference, the Wilkies decided their experiment was a failure – that two rotten carcasses were preferable to three.

It was time.

Murray volunteered to tell Barry. Waking up one hot February morning, he looked over to the bed where his brother-in-law had lain for so many weeks and said, 'Hey, Bazz, you awake?'

No response.

He'd gone. Packed his few things and left, leaving nothing except a note on his wife's bedroom door.

> That sort of makes us even, I guess. Good luck with the boy. I don't know that I'm up to a lifetime of all that, anyhow. Also, if you've had concerns, I suggest you see a doctor. Me and Trish had started up before I'd finished with you. Then it turns out she was full of it. A few pills and I was all better anyway.

Luckily, Fay found the note first. She knew he was lying. She'd never had so much as an itch. Still, that's the sort of man he was, she concluded. Bad. Led through life by the tip of his purple donger.

The Wilkies feigned disappointment for a few hours before settling in for the long haul: life with Fay and Chris, still out picking lavender, as his shoulders burned and blistered and Murray tried to call him back in. 'Did you even bother with sunscreen? Idiot.'

'Murray!' Fay called, from somewhere deep inside the house, although she was used to this sort of talk.

'Look at him,' he called back. 'He's like a bloody lobster.'

'Chris!' Fay tried to shout. 'Listen to your uncle. Come inside, please.'

'I'm not finished.'

'Now!'

Chris kept picking. Murray lit another cigarette. 'Listen to your mother,' he said.

Nothing. The sound of Fay shelling boiled eggs.

'Hey, Fay, you gonna come out here and deal with this? He doesn't listen to me.'

'Well, he doesn't listen to me.'

'He'll end up in hospital. He's not all there.'

'Do you mind?'

Carelyn was at the door, glaring at her father-in-law, holding a dessert bowl half-full of his old cigarette stubs. 'What's this?'

'What?'

'This is for eating food, Murray.'

He looked at the bowl and shrugged. 'Looked like an old one to me.'

'It's not.'

'You told me you were sick of seeing my butts in the – '

'Not in a bloody bowl, Murray. It's a filthy habit.'

No response.

'And in the toilet. I told you not to smoke in the house.'

'It's my bloody house.'

She glared at him.

'The toilet's not inside, is it?'

'Of course it is.'

He took the bowl and emptied the butts in front of the house. 'There,' he said, returning it, 'just gotta soak it for a bit … good as new.'

She sniffed it. 'You'd eat from this?'

'When it's clean.'

He inhaled, but she took the cigarette from him, put it out in the bowl and said, 'Keep it.'

He shrugged again. 'It looked chipped to me.'

Then she looked over at Chris. 'Chris, get in here now. You should know better.'

This time Chris seemed to understand. He stood, gathered his bag and walked towards them.

Carelyn looked at Murray. 'What were you thinking, leaving him out there?'

3

Trevor drove along the edge of the road. Grass and bullock bush scratching the ute. 'We need to talk about the loan,' he said to his father.

'You needn't worry about that … it's manageable.'

'It's not.'

Again, a silence of rattling panels and exhausted shock-absorbers as he prepared for the same, almost daily, argument. 'It's not what we owe today … it's the future.'

Murray couldn't see the problem. 'My old man went fifteen years without a drop of rain. As long as you keep the pumps running. There's enough water …' He trailed off, his words diluting like a tea-bag he'd been using for years.

Your old man, Trevor thought, studying a forest of shoak bending in the wind: the one who got us into this mess in the first place. And his old man's old man, buying a dud property while so much green, productive land went begging across the rest of the state. 'As long as the repayments are heading south.'

'They're not gonna do that, are they?'

'Then we're gonna have to ask for more.'

'Bullshit.'

'Well, this afternoon, you ring Mercy, you ask 'em if they'll take another term of half fees; ring Elders, ask 'em – '

'Don't be so bloody dramatic.'

Trevor listened to the land breathe. Eremophila, in clumps, and growing over the track, spreading sacrificial limbs; attempting to reclaim the land, *his* land, although Murray (for now) held the deed. 'It was somewhere near here, wasn't it?'

'Eh?'

'God-man?'

Murray almost smiled. 'Bit further back, I think.'

They both remembered a hot day in 1992, coming across an abandoned bike saddled with two pouches of clothes, a Bible and empty water bottles. They'd got out and examined it and Trevor had said, 'Do you know anything about this?'

They'd tried to remember if they'd received a letter from a bike club, a lone trekker, a survivalist, anything.

'Buggered if I know,' Murray had replied, and they'd thrown the bike into the back of the ute and continued.

Then, another three or four kilometres on, they'd found the rider: a Canadian fireman cycling around Australia. He'd been attempting to cross the Nullarbor, but when he'd ridden past the turn-off to Bundeena, God had said to him: *Here, the Wilderness, enter this place* (or words that that effect).

'You would've killed yourself,' Murray had said to him, but he'd just replied, 'No risk of that, sir. Jesus was lookin' out for me.'

No, he was fuckin' not, he'd wanted to say. Instead, explaining, 'Do you know where this track goes?'

'I've lost a lot of weight,' the Canadian had explained, 'but I only ran out of water yesterday.'

'Another two hundred clicks and you're in the desert.'

God-man had just smiled, taken off his cap and wiped his matted hair, forehead and raw face.

'I'm sorry, but if you'd kept going, Jesus wouldn't have helped you,' Trevor had explained.

'You just keep driving, we'll see.'

Murray had shaken his head. 'That would be the same as us allowing you to die.'

No response.

'I'm not gonna have that on my conscience.'

'You've just gotta trust, sir. He's watching us at this very moment.'

Murray had been tempted to leave him there. 'Go on, get in the ute.'

The man had just stared at him. 'I think I might walk.'

'I think you might get in the ute, before we put you in.'

Trevor had stood with his arms crossed, for once, agreeing with his father. 'This is private property. Ours.'

Their visitor had yielded, climbing into the back of the ute. 'I appreciate you picking up my bike. Can you take me back to the road?'

Father and son had climbed in; Trevor had said, 'Eventually, after we shoot a few roos.'

Trevor pulled into a clearing beside the road. A marker showed the location of buried water containers. This is where they'd stop for the night if they were out working on the edge of their bluebush galaxy. Where they'd open their swags and slide the esky off the back of the ute, wash blood from their hands and light the primus.

They got out and made their way over to a long, concrete trough.

'As I suspected,' Murray said, noticing it, and the bore's storage dam, was dry.

The bore itself was capped by a metal ring bolted onto a square of concrete. There was a pump. PVC pipes led into the trough and down to the dam.

'Righto,' Trevor said. He fetched his tool box from the ute and started fixing the pump. Murray moved to the trough, sat down, produced another rollie and lit it. 'Old God-boy. I wonder what happened to him?'

'You really care?'

'Might still be out here somewhere.'

Trevor started wiping fine sand from the lubricated parts. 'It was his choice. There's only so much you can do to help some people.'

Murray studied the distant hummocks. 'He mighta made it to Mount George, perhaps … with a bit of help from Jesus.'

As they both remembered the night, in 1992, cutting up a roo, looking up to see the stranger dancing in the bush before disappearing into the mid-distance. 'Where the hell are you going?' Murray had called, but all they could see was scrub, and all they could hear were branches snapping. 'Christ … a complete bloody idiot.'

'You're gonna die,' Trevor had shouted.

He tried to start the pump. Nothing. Murray finished his cigarette, walked over and squeezed the fuel line. Milked it as if it were some type of mechanical cow. 'Go on.'

Trevor tried to start the pump, two, three times, and eventually it spluttered to life. He looked at his father and tried to smile. 'Well … very good.'

As they waited for water, Murray said, 'See, I'm not completely bloody useless.'

They drove to outstation 'Number one' (although, except for a pair of wooden rooms built by Murray's grandfather, Bill, in the 1890s, it was their only outstation). The old shack measured thirty by twenty feet, four bunks, what passed for a kitchen and a spot in the middle to sit and eat and talk about the day. It still had its original floorboards, part-iron, part-wood walls, a pressed-tin ceiling and iron roof.

Number one was used until the late 1960s. Murray could still remember staying with his dad and the older men during the horseback musters. He could remember beef and damper and sweet black tea, and nothing else, for days on end. Playing cards and drinking beer that was kept cold in a rainwater tank that was kept full from a bore. He could still see and hear the men farting their way through an unsleepable night. And remember how they smelt after the fourth or fifth day.

Trevor stopped the ute in front of the old shack and looked at his dad.

'Go on,' Murray said.

'You won't come in?'

'No.'

'That's stupid.'

Murray glared at him. 'Hurry up.'

Trevor got out and fetched a jerry can full of fuel from the back of the ute. He carried it towards the shack. His feet sank and he put it down, lifted it, walked a few more paces and stopped again. He went in, sliding it along the floorboards. Then he left it beside a table covered with a dozen or so rabbit traps. Looked up at the ceiling. It was held in place (mostly) by two lengths of right-angled redwood, cut to fit into each other. Someone had wrapped an electric wire around one of the beams.

He wondered where. Studied the beams but there were no clues.

Outside, Murray sounded the horn. 'Come on, what yer doin'?'

'Hold on.'

No rope marks, no notches, from where his great-grandfather, Bill Wilkie, had passed a rope around the beam, tied it off, managed a rabbit-trapper's knot as a noose, climbed onto the table and mumbled a few words. From where he'd jumped, unsuccessfully attempting to break his neck. There was no sign of where the rope had rubbed on the beam, no indication of the smell (after hanging undiscovered for six days), no signs of where his son, Morris, and two stockmen had taken him down.

And nothing, in this room at least, of the story behind it all.

'What are you doing?' Murray called, again.

This time Trevor didn't respond.

No newspapers (September 1916) with a Cowards' List – and the names of local men who had 'shirked their duty'. No indication of what his wife, Mary, had said or thought when they brought his body back to the house. No explanation of how John Wilkie, their eldest son, born as a fat-cheeked baby in 1895, had gone missing on the Western Front (although his parents knew their son was no deserter).

Still, this is where Bill, father of Morris, grandfather of Murray, great-grandfather of Trevor, had come to kill himself. To keep everything neat, and private, to bury his shame in a thousand square miles of sand. To leave his body, as it left the world (seeing how the list had been made public, and had become a sort of unofficial gospel) in the little dog-box of a house he'd built.

'Christ,' Murray shouted, holding down the horn. 'It's getting warm out here.'

Trevor returned to the ute. 'How long since you've been in there?'

'A long time.'

They drove towards Bundeena.

'Not since I … found out,' Murray said.

'Maybe it's time.'

'It doesn't need discussing.'

They drove silently.

'It was just too much for him,' Trevor dared.

'That doesn't excuse anyone. He was a coward.'

4

Harry stood on the edge of the compound holding his stock-whip. He lifted his arm, flicked the tongue, moved his wrist back and forward in a fraction of a second and listened to the crack. It echoed and settled around the sheds and garden, on the house and down the hill towards the lavender. He smiled. 'Dad,' he called, but he didn't know where he was.

He searched the horizon. Noticed a rusty gidgee tree in the distance. He often wondered why there weren't others: perhaps there'd only been a single seed, a drop of water. Why it was there, what purpose it served, how it could survive apart from other gidgee trees. It couldn't be shaded, or give shade, make other trees, even provide wood – because who, really, would have the heart to chop it down?

There were more trees at the back of the compound where their little world opened up to the road. One dead sheoak had become a bottle tree. An actual bottle tree, with old cans and bottles and jars placed over the dead tip of each branch. Some of the newer bottles and cans were still recognisable – spaghetti, creamed corn, Sno-Top – but most had lost their labels, rusted, clouded up and sand-blasted over the forty years Trevor had been decorating his desert Christmas tree. Since, aged six or seven, he'd found an old beer bottle on the ground. Every few days he'd come out with bottles and cans (and at Christmas, tinsel and other decorations).

Until, later, his sons had taken over. Until each of the branches were full, at which time Harry went to the kitchen drawer, found a roll of twine and started hanging the bottles, like baubles, along the length of each of the branches.

Now it was a giant wind-chime. No one really minded. Most evenings it made music. A few branches had fallen off and Harry had used more twine to reattach them. To him, the bottle tree was more than just decoration.

He turned to face it, lifted his hand and cracked his stock-whip. A beer bottle dropped and shattered. 'Yes,' he sang, running towards the tree, looking at the broken glass sitting in ankle-high compost.

'Harry,' he heard his father calling, from inside his shed.

He gathered his whip and ran across the compound. Felt the temperature rise as he went into his father's shed. Smelt a hot globe burning fine sawdust from the pine.

'Is that you smashing bottles?' his father asked, looking up from the hand in his lap, clutching a piece of folded sandpaper.

'Yes,' he replied, closing the door.

'I need your help.'

Harry sat on a stool beside his father, placed his hand on the bench and spread it out. Trevor looked at it, and back at the piece of wood sitting in a singlet in his lap. 'Right,' he said, studying the two hands, using the edge of his sandpaper to help sculpt the knuckles.

It wasn't a hand yet, he thought. Whatever made a hand a hand, it still wasn't there. There were fingers, with the right amount of curve; each fattened by blood vessels, and wrinkles, and nails he'd polish so finely they'd shine. There was the meat of the hand, with its tendons and more arteries and veins, and there was a thumb, of course, coming up past the bottom of the first finger. But it still wasn't there.

He'd followed the usual steps – chiselling, refining, sanding – but he hadn't got the usual result. Like his wife's and dad's hand, sitting on the shelf above the unused fireplace. Seven hands, in all, and these were only the successful ones.

He had five photos pinned above his bench: side views, finger-tip, wrist and palm. These were what he'd use for his sculpture. Mostly, apart from calling Harry in every few days to lay his small hand (sauce-smeared, his ring finger calloused from his pen) on the bench, to sit for an hour as he studied his fingers, felt them, moved them closer together, further apart.

'I've got a better idea,' Harry said.

'What's that?'

'Make 'em in clay?'

Trevor didn't reply. He used a pencil to lift his son's finger-tips, leaving the fingers curled like a claw. Then he said, 'No,' and pushed them down.

Harry studied his father's face. 'You should measure the fingers and thumb.'

'Perhaps.'

They sat together thinking separate thoughts. Trevor: how the little bits of fat in each finger bulged; Harry: how his father was slow and careful, content to wrestle with small things.

'You wanna be careful with that whip,' Trevor said, without looking up.

Harry just looked at him.

'When I was your age it came back at me.' He showed him the scar, just below his left eye.

'You keep telling me,' Harry said, moving his hand.

'Still!' Trevor growled, returning to his pine hand. 'Look, half-an-inch from my eye. Cos I was showing off.'

'I'm not showing off … I'm careful.'

'Good.'

'I could do this at the Show.'

'Why don't you?'

'I might.'

Trevor smiled. 'You'll make a good stockman one day.'

Harry waited for more, his hand lifting and dropping.

'One day?'

'You're still young. Patience.'

Harry wasn't happy. 'Old enough to help with the muster.'

'Yes, but ... school ... that's what's most important now, eh?'

'But you reckon it's a waste of time.'

'When did I say that?'

'Every time you walk past, you say to Mum, what's he need to do that for?'

'That's not because I don't think education's important ... it's just because ... it doesn't seem relevant.'

'To us?'

'No, to ....' He stopped to think. 'Education allows you to do whatever you want with your life.'

'Like being a good farmer?'

'Not necessarily.'

'But that's what you want me to do?'

Trevor placed the hand on the bench. He wiped his own hands on the singlet. 'That'd be nice. It's not the sort of job I can put an ad in the paper for. But ...' and he turned his face to him, 'if you or Aiden wanted to do something else.'

Harry wasn't sure about this. 'You wouldn't mind?'

'For instance, if you wanted to be an airline pilot ...'

'But I don't want to be an airline pilot.'

'*You're only young.*' He ruffled his son's hair, and indicated his hand. 'You can have that back now.'

'Harry!' Fay called from the house.

'Go on,' Trevor said.

Harry left the shed and met his aunt halfway across the compound. The sun was above their heads and there was almost no shadow. He could see her threadbare dressing gown; her slippers, open around the sides and on the toes; her legs, covered with fine hair and scabbed patches of what he assumed was old age.

'Here you go,' she said, handing him a small basket.

He went into the chook yard, with its nine Rhode Island hens, and into the laying shed. As he collected eggs from each of the straw-lined boxes, Fay said, 'You shouldn't need reminding.'

'I was just about to do 'em,' he replied, but she said it again, like she always did: 'You shouldn't need reminding.'

After he'd collected the eggs she made him weed the vegetables while she picked tomatoes. Then, he filled a watering can and wet the straw he'd spread around the base of the cucumbers, peas and beans. Kept studying his aunt, butterflied on her knees, her dressing gown open past the white fleshy meat of her thighs. If he looked he could see more. He wanted to say, Could you adjust yourself, please, but knew he couldn't. So he just studied her bony fingers as she picked spent leaves. 'Aunty Fay?'

She kept working, her face set hard.

'Can I ask something ... about Uncle Chris?'

Meanwhile, Trevor closed the door of his shed and called, 'How many eggs?'

Fay slowly lifted her head and replied, 'Eleven, although they're a lot smaller now.' She waited. 'Why do you think that is?'

Trevor walked past them. 'They're getting lazy.' He looked at his son. 'Give 'em a good drink.' Turning and walking towards the house.

'About Uncle Chris?' Harry repeated.

Fay looked at him.

'Will he always live here with us?'

She shifted onto her knees, picking peas and throwing them into the bucket.

'Me and Aiden, we'll always look after him.'

'I can look after him.'

He returned to the tank, refilled and came back to the garden.

'Just cos it's done one way, doesn't mean it always was,' she told him, as he started watering.

'What do you mean?'

'Like washing your clothes.'

He waited.

'Once, what we'd do,' she explained, searching for pods, 'was put all the clothes in a drum, like that one.' She pointed to the drum of chicken feed. 'We'd fill it with soap and water, and rocks, and drive around with it on the back of the ute for a few days.'

Harry had heard the story before, but couldn't see what it had to do with Chris.

'Got 'em beautifully clean,' she said. 'Then we'd tip all the dirty water on the vegetables.' She held a pea pod, remembering, perhaps, how peas used to be bigger and greener in the days of improvised washing machines.

Harry kept looking at her, waiting for her to explain, to make the connection.

'Nowadays we just use that thumping big machine.'

Harry thought and thought, making his brain work harder, attempting to solder a solution. 'So we could look after him?' he asked.

But she just said, 'I was always interested in Egypt.'

He was out of water, again.

'They used to have a black pharaoh. You knew that?' She looked at him. 'From Sudan. There are pyramids all across Sudan ... but they never mention that.'

Then there was a waltz – tinny, thundering across the compound. And with it, a voice, crooning:

Once more I hold you to my heart,
As thru' the waltz we sway ...

'Christ,' Fay mumbled, standing, dropping her bucket, peas and beans spilling across the soil. The sound of the sliding door and Chris, done up in Murray's suit, embracing a phantom partner as he waltzed into the compound.

'Chris!' she called.

Chris turned in graceful circles, tight in, then larger orbits, his arms raised at exactly the right angle. Fay was soon across the compound, pulling on his arm, trying to bring him back to the world of washing machines. He turned and almost slapped her across the face and she staggered back. She looked at him, accusingly. And then the boy-man was singing:

> *When you and I were seventeen,*
> *And life and love were new ...*

Harry could see his grandfather standing at the door to his sleep-out, smiling, then retreating a few steps back inside.

The waltz stopped but Chris kept dancing, caught up in the music in his head. Trevor emerged from the house wearing nothing but a towel around his waist. He smiled but stopped when he saw Fay standing alone. 'Chris!' he called.

Chris stopped moving, closed his eyes, lifted his head and took a deep breath, savouring his last few moments. He opened his eyes and walked towards the house. As he went inside Trevor stopped him. 'You shouldn't do this.'

Chris was breathing deeply, tasting the air.

'Do you hear me?'

'He's alright,' Fay managed.

'No,' he said. 'Look how all this business upsets your mum.'

'*Trevor.*'

'No,' he called to her. 'Look.' Turning his cousin around to face his mother.

Chris moved, but closed his eyes.

'Look!' Trevor shouted.

'Trevor,' Carelyn warned, from the door.

'It's all over,' Fay said, walking back towards the garden.

Harry looked from one person to the other, worried that his question, somehow, might have triggered all this. He noticed the sleep-out but Murray had gone inside and shut the door.

'Go,' Trevor said to Chris, and he went inside.

Harry watched his aunt kneel and gather the vegetables. Heard her mumble, 'If they'd just let him go,' and noticed she was struggling for breath, as though she was avoiding crying. He picked up the basket of eggs and said, 'I'll take these in,' and Fay replied, 'Make sure you put the can away first.'

Trevor returned to his steamy bathroom followed by his wife. He slipped off his towel, turned on the shower and stepped back in. 'Someone will have to start thinking about him,' he said.

Carelyn leaned on the doorway. 'I've tried.'

'We'll need to try again.'

She studied the parts of her husband she could see: his hairless chest with its sagging, pink-nippled tits; his stomach, bulging from his otherwise slender frame. 'You're getting fat,' she said.

'Getting?'

'Fatter.'

'Every fucking problem,' he muttered, soaping his legs.

She waited for the inevitable.

'Whatever needs solving; everyone else just stands back.'

'I do what I can.'

'Fay can't leave it all to us.' He waited until the thoughts multiplied. 'If it's not Dad it's …' Put his head back and let the warm water soak his face.

Carelyn could see his legs were sticks, screwed onto the bottom of his body. His arms, too, like a doll's, hanging loose, unremarkable. He didn't look like he could jump a bull, but she knew he could. It was all in the hands, he'd often explain. The will. The bloody mindedness. His little triangle, a full afro, like someone had run a line-trimmer around the fuzz; his little button cock, retreating into a forest of disuse.

He looked out through the steamy glass. As if he wanted to say, So, what is it? As if he was afraid, even now, of her seeing too much. Of the physical man and not the father-fixer-peacemaker he'd become. Even his wife, he guessed, had lost interest in the body-minus-its-clothing: moleskin man, castrating a hundred beasts an hour, welding pipes, controlling children.

He turned off the shower and stepped out and she'd gone. Dried himself and put on the fan and lay naked on his bed, airing the cracks and crevices, the dampness of his scrotum, the undried water in the creases of his fingers.

Then she returned with a slice of beef on a fork. She held it to his mouth. 'Taste this.'

And he did. 'Nice.'

She sat beside him. 'You okay?'

'I bet Dad gave him that suit.'

'No,' she replied, placing her hand on his leg. 'He's had it in his wardrobe for years.'

'Why?'

'*Why? Chris?*'

He sighed, aware of her eyes on his skin. 'Could you give me a hand with that spreadsheet tonight?' He could see his stomach, and leg, and the hand that wouldn't move. 'I can't get it to add up. If I could just do it on paper.'

She ran her hand up his leg and side, and retreated. 'Wait for Aiden,' she suggested, hovering between two worlds.

Then he thought, Now, now's my moment, but for some reason,

couldn't move. Maybe, he thought, he had to deal with this issue too. He had to hold her down and tear at her clothes. Instead, he sat up. 'Right, what's next?'

5

The next morning it started to blow. A north-westerly at first, smelling of dry grass, and Murray telling them they were in for a blasting. 'You should put the ute in the shed,' he told his son.

As they sat drinking tea the wind picked up, gusting, gently sandpapering their windows and bluestone walls. Trevor could hear the bottle tree; he went to the laundry door to look. A few plastic bottles skidded across the compound before tumbling down the hill onto the flatlands. Two or three beer bottles dropped and smashed and a few shattered on their strings, hanging like broken limbs. Trevor saw that it blew flat and fast. 'Harry!' he called.

Harry came out. They ran across the compound into the chook yard and chased the hens into their house. Trevor fastened the latch and tried to secure a plastic tarp over the windows.

'Washing,' he said to his son, and Harry walked, leaning into the wind, towards the line. As he went he shielded his eyes and spat sand from his lips. He wasn't tall enough to un-peg the clothes so he pulled on them and pegs went flying. He looked down the road and saw his father chasing Yanga, cornering her and carrying her in.

They stepped into the laundry, shaking sand from their hair and clothes, and Harry asked, 'Do you reckon it will be a bad one?'

Trevor shrugged, using his foot to keep the dog away from the door. 'Probably.'

They went back into the living room and Chris watching a war movie. Trevor just looked at him, then at Fay, and settled for the smallest shake of his head.

'Someone sealed the doors?' he asked.

Carelyn emerged from the hallway carrying a couple of wet towels. 'All done.'

Murray, still out on the porch, finished his cigarette and came in. Sat on the lounge and looked at the movie. 'This isn't gonna help,' he said.

'What?' Carelyn asked, sealing the kitchen window with a wet tea towel.

'Young steers.' He didn't say any more, didn't need to. He was out there with them, standing in the blue-bush, his eyes closed and his legs tense against the gale. He could feel the sand in his ears and on his skin. I'll just stand here until it blows over, he was thinking. Two days, three, whatever it takes.

'Oh, Christ,' Fay moaned, as she lay back in her chair. 'I gotta get to the shops before they close.' She sat up, leaned forward and rocked back and forth.

'What is it, Fay?' Carelyn asked, looking at Trevor and Harry.

'The shops.'

'What shops?' Trevor asked.

But she didn't seem to know.

'I can see now,' she said, 'he's starting to put things away.'

'Who is?' Carelyn said.

But again, she didn't seem to know.

'There's no bloody shop,' Murray explained. 'She's off with the fairies again.'

Carelyn wasn't so sure. She came over and felt her forehead. 'She's hot,' she said. 'Harry, get the thermometer.'

Harry came back and they took her temperature. A few minutes later Carelyn said, 'Nearly thirty-eight.'

'And she's dreaming,' Murray said. 'Is it Sauers, the baker?' he asked her, but she just continued rocking.

'Are you feeling sick, Fay?' Carelyn said.

'No, there's nothin' wrong with me.'

They put her to bed. Chris didn't notice she was gone, or even know there was a problem. He was busy digging a tunnel under the wires. He knew, from his dozens of viewings, that he'd come up short. At one point, he looked out the window and noticed the sandstorm. 'Wow, that's bad,' he managed, looking at Trevor.

Who, by now, had consulted the satellite image. He'd seen the front moving east, darkening everything in its path; Bundeena descending into days of blight; day turning to night, and the generator taking over from the solar panels (themselves sand-blasted clean); moods darkening, supplies of DVDs taken out of the cupboard and most of all, like Murray, he'd seen his stock sheltering beside the skeletons of gidgee trees, waiting.

By evening the storm was shaking the eaves, coming in and under the house and up through the gaps in the floorboards. Trevor stood looking out of the front window and saw sheets of iron blowing across the flats. Waited, consulting his watch. Saw the hazy, dot-dash yellow lights of the Indian Pacific. Watched it moving, consumed and spat out by the storm until it was gone, in the dust.

They went to bed and fell asleep to the accompaniment of rattling iron. 'I should go look,' Trevor said to Carelyn, as they settled into bed.

'Leave it,' she replied. 'We'll pick it all up tomorrow.'

And still, the sound of *The Great Escape* from the lounge room.

During the night they were woken by Fay. 'Mr Whitmore,' she was saying. 'I'm over here.'

Trevor and Carelyn went in to her. In the next bed, Chris was still asleep. Carelyn took her temperature, looked at Trevor and said, 'She's still hot.' Then gently shook her. 'Fay, have you got any pain?'

Fay just looked at her. 'Gee, I need a pee.' They helped her to the toilet. She sat and waited but nothing came. Carelyn stood beside her. 'Can you go?'

'Soon,' Fay said.

She didn't go, and they helped her back to bed.

'You alright now?' Trevor asked, bringing in a glass of water.

'Fine. Go on, everyone back to bed.'

Then Murray was behind them, hovering in the dark. 'She still going?'

'She's got a temperature.' Carelyn glared at him.

'She's just confused. She's getting old ... aren't you, Fay?'

They all crawled back to bed, to fading thoughts and visions that chased them through the storm. Murray watched as sand blew in under his sleep-out door. Lying in bed, Trevor asked his wife, 'Should we give her something?'

'Let's wait and see how she is in the morning.'

The next day it just kept blowing. The wind dropped then returned, dragging the morning and early afternoon towards a premature dusk. Trevor could see from the satellite that the storm was nearly over, but it didn't feel that way. He returned to his front window and watched the landscape ebb and flow towards and away from the railway line. Went out and saw the bottle tree was nearly bare. Sand had banked against nearly every wall and door. He made it out to feed the chooks but returned and told his son, 'Your veggies are all gone.'

'The lot?' Harry asked.

'Well, you can see the top of the tomatoes.'

It continued blowing during the afternoon. Sand had climbed halfway up the outside of the windows. The laundry door had blown off its bottom hinge and a four-metre length of gutter hung loose from the sleep-out. Fay started off better but by mid-afternoon she was hot again. This time Murray helped her back to bed, saying, 'You just gotta sweat it out.'

Around five o'clock the wind dropped and dragged its belly across the desert. Harry and Trevor put on their boots and went out to fix the shed roof. As they were finishing they heard Carelyn call from the house. 'Trevor!' They went in to find Fay back on the lounge, a rug across her lap, calling out above a soundtrack of Bruce Willis machine-gun fire. 'Steady,' she was saying. 'Steady so it doesn't collapse on yer.'

Chris was sitting beside her; he didn't seem concerned. At one point he blocked his ears. Murray just said, 'Come on, old girl, wake up, you're having another dream.'

'It's not a dream,' Carelyn said, kneeling beside her. 'You alright, love?' Her lips dry despite the fact she'd been sipping water all day.

They put her back to bed and returned to the lounge room. Trevor made a coffee and noticed Harry snuggled into the lounge.

'You might need a shower,' Trevor told him.

But Harry had entered the world of the hijacked office tower.

'Harry,' Trevor barked. 'Shower.'

'Now?'

'Yes.'

Harry stood and left the room, dragging his feet.

'She's still hot,' Carelyn told her husband.

'Right,' Trevor replied, stirring his coffee. 'I suppose we better call in.'

'Why?' Murray asked.

'She's ill,' Carelyn said.

'It's just the storm. The weather affects her, you know that.'

'Dad, you don't run a fever because of a dust storm.'

'It's old age.'

'It's not.' Trevor stood looking through the front windows. The topsoil had settled and he could see beyond the railway line. The air looked smoky. It was the light stuff, he guessed. He knew it would settle in a few hours. Still, he would have to check the bores – all of them.

Murray found the satellite phone and dialled. He sat in a nook beside Harry's lounge-room classroom. It shared the same chairs and desk but had a different purpose. There was a poster on the wall: an asexual human with dotted lines dissecting its body into small, meaty parts. Like the chart of beef cuts on a butcher's wall. And inside these segments, numbers 1–63, defining every part of the bilateral carcass that needed diagnosing. So they could call and speak to a doctor and say, Yes, Doctor, number thirteen ... a shooting pain that comes and goes.

Trevor waited and eventually spoke to a registered nurse. He told her about his aunt and explained her dreams and how she always needed the toilet.

'Does it burn when she pees?' she asked.

'Does it burn when you pee?' he called to Fay.

Fay looked at her brother. 'What's he saying?'

'Does it burn when you pee?'

'Yes.'

'Yes,' Trevor told the nurse, who explained that it was probably a urinary tract infection.

'A urinary tract infection,' Trevor said aloud, so they'd all know. 'Right ... how do we deal with that?' He listened as she took a few minutes to move papers and fiddle with her computer. 'She's not allergic to penicillin?'

Trevor asked Fay, who asked Murray, who asked her again, before she said, 'No.'

Trevor told the nurse.

'Good. Trimethoprim, three times a day, for ... seven days should do it. If she's not better after two or three days, call back.'

Trevor found a pad and pen and asked, 'What number's that?'

'Sixty-two.'

'Sixty-two, three times a day, for seven days?'

'Yes.'

'Okay, thanks.' He hung up.

Carelyn already had the medical kit out. She was sorting the ointments, dressings and plastic vials full of dozens of types of pills; checking the bold numerals designed to make sure no one gave the wrong medication. She found the pills: 62. 'Right.' After checking the name with Trevor she closed the box, relocked it and put it back in the cupboard. Went to the kitchen, filled another glass of water and sat beside Fay. 'The nurse thinks you have a urinary tract infection.'

Fay just shrugged. 'How did I get that?'

'You just get it. Here, take this.' She handed her the first of the yellow pills. Fay placed it in her mouth and Carelyn helped her with the water.

'Yes, I'm feeling better already.'

'You will.'

And Trevor said, 'It's just as well the storm's gone, Fay, cos that probably caused it.' He looked at his father.

'What?' Murray said.

'Nothing.'

They pumped diesel from a drum to the ute. Harry worked for twenty minutes, until fuel spilled from the tank. 'Dad,' he called, and Trevor came out with a small esky full of food.

'Thanks, old boy,' he said, ruffling his son's hair, and Harry asked, 'Why can't I come?'

'You need your beauty sleep.'

'Please?'

'No.' He climbed in behind the wheel. 'Your mother needs your help.'

Harry retreated, convinced, but not happy. What would be

more fun? Bush-bashing or wiping dishes? Cleaning out troughs or mopping piss from the toilet floor?

Trevor drove north. The track was all sand but he knew if he stayed on the ridges he wouldn't get bogged. Bore number one, an hour and a half from home, the water in the trough warm and soupy but the pump still working. He unscrewed the bung and cleaned the trough before refilling it. Kept going: numbers two and three, the same story. Now he was nearly three hours from home.

He took out his swag, unrolled it and sat eating chicken and drinking warm Coke. Sand was blowing over from a dry turkey nest dam. As he napped, the desert, his farm, was still and silent. It'd had enough of blowing. He was woken by kangaroos coming close then jumping off into a distance of small, nocturnal spirits. He sat up and ate biscuits and drank the rest of his Coke; then shook out his swag and rolled it up.

He drove towards number four. Passing a big group of steers, his heart sank when he saw ribs and hips and loose skin. Although he saw them as animals (with fear, and pain, reflected in their big brown eyes) they were also meat, living kilograms, dollars and cents per unit, Dry Sheep Equivalents. He could only start paying his mortgage and school fees when they stood on the scales at the abattoir.

After lunch, six hours of driving, thirteen bores, he headed home. On and on, as one of Carelyn's talking books read itself out and he retreated into his own thoughts, again. Late in the afternoon he started drifting off and the ute wandered into soft sand and bogged itself. He gunned the accelerator but realised he was just digging himself in. 'Fuck.' He got out, removed the tailgate and slid it under one of the back wheels. Getting back in, he started the engine and slowly inched out of the sand. The clutch shuddered and he stalled; his ute rolled back, settling, deeper, as if the land was alive, and hungry.

He got out. 'You bitch!' Kicked the tyre, and felt his toes crushing in his steel-capped boots. 'Christ!' he growled, leaning on the cab, noticing the sun settling on the western horizon.

It was after 11 pm when he came through the back door. Murray was the only one still up. 'How are you?' he asked.

He didn't see the point of answering. 'How's Fay?'

'She's cooled down … and she's stopped rambling.' He looked his son over. 'Problems?'

'An hour to dig myself out of sand. Then I had to refill three times.'

'The whole drum?'

'Yes.'

'Well, go get showered. I'll make you some eggs and bacon.' He pulled himself up out of his seat.

Trevor was too tired to talk, argue, think. Murray watched as he shuffled across the room. Watched his shoulders, slumped, and his head, looking at the ground; saw how he dragged his feet and how his hands and fingers hung heavy and lifeless. 'You okay?' he called.

'Yeah.'

'You're getting too old to do that by yourself.'

'Who else is there?'

6

Aiden lived in a converted storeroom on the second floor of Mercy's halls-of-residence. It looked out across a memorial garden, surrounded by dead lawn, lined by black-spotted roses that shed their little bit of perfume in the early evening, taking him back to Bundeena, and Fay, fiddling in her garden. It was a small room with a divan and no-nonsense mattress, cupboard, wardrobe and desk. There was an old aluminium lamp with a ring of little stars cut out of the shade. He often studied each of the five-pointed constellations and wondered how they'd been punched so clean.

He was sitting at his desk, reading a slab of words on his laptop; words he'd put there; words that made less sense the more he looked at them. *As the volume increases the surface area increases too. But at some point the volume gets bigger quicker …*

He studied these last few words: *gets bigger quicker.* Or should it be, he thought, gets bigger faster, at a faster rate, quicker rate, increases more, grows much faster? Do I, really, care?

He looked at the ring of stars and counted them. Nineteen. Shouldn't they have added up to an even number? *The volume increases at a faster rate than the surface area.* That's it, he said to himself, re-reading the sentence.

His eyes drifted out to the roses. Brother Symes was sitting on a bench, reading. He noticed his gold crucifix, and his Jesus hands and face and voice, blessing them like he really cared. And if it wasn't God's songs for his people and prayers and A-fuckin'-bide with me it was the perfect surface area-to-volume ratio. *If the discolouration can be calculated carefully …*

He stared at his laptop and the little camera watching him, still. Smiled. Good morning, Mrs Lawrence, he said, as he returned to the living room at Bundeena.

What are we working on this morning? Mrs Lawrence, his old School of the Air teacher, asked.

A practical report.

Go on.

He started reading but she interrupted by saying: Third person, past tense.

He shrugged. The thing is, I don't really care, Mrs Lawrence.

Aiden …

I'm nearly old enough to leave school.

What would that achieve?

I could help Dad.

You'll be able to help him soon enough. But if you neglect –

So what?

Aiden pressed backspace and his words (some he'd spent days sweating over) disappeared. When he was finished and the screen was blank he looked at Mrs Lawrence and said, That's what I think of Biology.

You'll have to do it all again, she said.

No, I won't.

He looked up at the Brother, pulling his undies from his arse.

I can keep failing, and they can keep nagging, he explained. Eventually they'll get sick of it and let me leave.

He looked at a few small stars floating above his desk. Leaned forward, opened his window and called out, 'What's up, Bro?' Then shot back behind the curtain.

Harry was still sitting at his classroom computer. Carelyn had made him dress for school, as she had Aiden, every day of his primary school years: his SOTA polo shirt, navy pants, socks and shoes. Lessons wouldn't begin until teeth were brushed and hair combed. And the background was always carefully controlled. No ironing piles or unwanted television. Chris was kept outside, mostly, and Murray was banned from singing or playing music.

It was morning assembly and Harry's year level (sisters from another station, a boy half an hour from Port Augusta, another from a wheat-sheep farm on the Eyre Peninsula) was running the assembly. Harry had taken charge. The others (he told his parents) weren't good for much. The sisters were always in their pyjamas, sucking ice-blocks, despite the fact that Mrs Lawrence was always on at them. The other boys just seemed to stare at the webcam and occasionally nod. Murray thought they were all inbred.

One of the sisters was having a birthday. Harry led them in a round of *Happy Birthday* and said, 'So, Shakina, could you tell us what gifts you got?'

The little girl smiled into the frame that contained their five faces. 'What?'

'What gifts did you get?' Mrs Lawrence repeated.

'Oh … Mum's made me a dress, and a couple of CDs, and Aleisha,' and her sister sat forward so her head took up the whole frame, 'she got me a thirty dollar gift card.'

'Are you having a party?' Harry asked.

'No.'

Then he read out his weekly quiz: the questions Carelyn helped him write every Wednesday night. 'Number one,' he said, as the others scrambled for their books and a pen. 'What is the second-biggest city in Queensland?'

The sisters looked at each other but the boys just stared at the screen.

'Well, what's the biggest?' he asked, and Shakina said, 'Perth.'

He turned and looked at his mum, sitting only a few inches

away. She rolled her eyes and said, 'Don't tell them. Move on.'

'Number two,' he continued. 'List the highest common factors of 24.'

Silence, again.

After the quiz they shared their news (Shakina's dad due an operation on his knee, the latest from *Australian Idol*), then he closed the assembly and Mrs Lawrence played a clip of the national anthem (complete with sheep flocks, a one-legged Aborigine and a Bondi lifesaver with a tattoo of the Queen).

Later, after a morning tea of Fay's re-warmed scones, Chris joined Harry at the computer. It was the weekly 'Meet My Family' session. Harry had worked through each member of his family three, four times, always avoiding his cousin, until one day Carelyn said, 'What about Chris?'

Mrs Lawrence got things started. 'Mr George ... perhaps you could tell us about some of the jobs you do at Bundeena?'

Chris just looked at Harry.

'Go on,' Harry said. 'They just want to know a bit about you.'

'Well,' Chris began, hesitating, 'I help out around the house.'

Silence. The two girls and the farmers' sons watched him. Shakina managed to keep her mouth closed. What is he, she was wondering, a retard? Around the house? What about the farm, the animals?

'I help Harry with the chooks and the veggies.' He indicated in case they were unsure who Harry was.

Silence, again. And then Shakina, unable to hold it in any longer. 'What do you do during the muster?'

Chris stopped to think. 'Sometimes I do the counter, so they know how many they've loaded onto the trucks.'

But Shakina wasn't happy with that. That was something you got a kid to do, not a man. 'So you don't do the rounding up?' she asked.

'No.'

'Why not?'

Everybody felt the awkwardness: Mrs Lawrence and Harry, the other kids and their mums; Murray and Fay, sitting on the lounge, and Carelyn, sewing a button on a shirt.

'It's sorta hard for him,' Harry told Shakina.

'Why?'

'He got a … injury, when he was a kid.'

Shakina still wanted to know. 'What, kicked by a cow or something?'

'Everyone does what they can on a farm, don't they?' Mrs Lawrence said.

But Shakina just stared at the oldish-looking man, unsure.

Chris bowed his head. He could feel them staring at him, thinking, deciding. This, he remembered, is why he'd given up on the School of the Air after only six months. In those days it hadn't been so bad. Just the radio, and the school books he couldn't make any sense of. But his fellow students (and back then there'd been twenty in a class) had somehow been able to tell. Although he was hundreds of kilometres away from them, they somehow managed to tease him. Not with actions, or words, but pauses, and questions they knew he wouldn't be able to answer.

Chris, what sort of tractor's your dad got?

Eventually, he'd retreated from the radio they'd set up for him and Trevor. Murray and Morris had said to Fay, 'Go on, make him do it,' but no matter what she said, Chris had refused to go anywhere near the black box. 'I don't understand what she's talking about,' he'd tell them.

'You just gotta sit and listen and answer a few questions,' Murray had said, but it didn't make any difference.

Miss, Chris reckons he's got a dozen girlfriends.

I didn't say that.

And he's kissed them.

No.

Chris looked at the small black eye. 'I have 187 videos,' he said. 'I've watched them all at least ten times.'

Harry gently bit his lip.

'What sort?' Aleisha asked.

Chris's face lit up. 'War movies ... and thrillers, like *Mission Impossible*.'

Silence.

Fay took a deep breath. She stood and walked over to her son. Mrs Lawrence and the other students watched her growing bigger in the background. She put her hand on his shoulder and said, 'Well, kids, Chris is gonna come and help me now.'

As they all thought the same thing. As they watched, as Fay led Chris out, towards the laundry.

And Shakina said, 'Is that his wife?'

Trevor returned to the shed. He went inside and studied his newly repaired roof. 'Right.' Turned to a pile of old timber, took out his tape and started measuring. Most of them were too short, but there was a piece of pine that looked long enough to replace the rotten eaves that supported the busted gutter. He secured it in his vice and started sawing. Moments later he stopped and sat down, looking at the pictures of Harry's hand. Looked at his own hands: liver-spotted, freckled, wrinkled; the pink, splotchy undersides marked with impossibly short life-lines. 'I'm so tired,' he said, leaning forward so his head almost touched his knees.

'Right!' Realising action was the only solution, he jumped up. Grasping the saw, he started working but stopped before he was half-way through. Placed his body in the darkest corner of his shed, sliding down until he was sitting on the floor, curling into a familiar tight ball. Breathing deeply, once, twice, before repeating: 'I'm not feeling so good.'

There, in the darkness, he was nine years old again: 'Well,' Murray was saying to him, 'the first thing is, you gotta learn to drive.'

'Now?' he asked.

'Yes, now. What if we're on a bore run and I have a heart attack, or slice me leg open?'

Trevor just looked at him.

So they climbed into Fay's EH and he settled in behind the wheel, watching and waiting for his dad. 'I can't see.'

Murray went around to the boot and found a rug for him to sit on. When they were ready, he said, 'Start her up.'

He turned the key and the motor crunched and growled.

'The clutch!' Murray said.

'I can't reach it.'

Murray shook his head and pulled the rug out from under his son's arse. 'There, how's that?'

'Now I can't see out.'

Trevor, curled in his dark corner, could still see his dad's face. Angry, of course, but he knew it was all show, and bluff, and even gladness that he was still too small to reach the clutch. He wiped a single tear with his sleeve.

'We'll give it six months,' his father was saying, 'or maybe we'll try on the tractor.'

He remembered wanting to talk to his father, to touch him, to hold him; on the hard, meaty part of his arm, perhaps. He wondered why they only talked about castration, and practical issues like clutches and molasses.

The hands were young, and always would be, and he would be reaching out for his dad, willing him to lead him across the paddock that stretched to their private horizon. Harry, too, who, he suspected, was thinking much the same thing.

The crew's hut had taken a battering over the years. The walls had been made from lengths of pine, but these had dried and peeled in the sixty years since Bill Wilkie had put them up. Tired of the muster team's complaints (up until then they'd slept on the porch), he'd spent three weeks (with a little help from Morris) building it. It had an iron roof, which had rusted, but stayed in place over the sixty winters and summers it had sat, mostly empty, between musters.

The box sat at the bottom of the hill at the end of a dolomite path that snaked down, between more native pine trees, from Fay's garden. It was away from the business of the house, so both the Wilkies and the team could maintain their own routines, keep their own hours and have somewhere to go when the disagreements became arguments.

Harry was sweeping it out. Someone had left both doors open and sand had blown in and gathered around the walls. The gaps between the floorboards were so big that all he had to do was sweep and the sand would fall through. Chris had joined him, and he'd sent him back to fetch the shed broom. As Murray often explained, the most important thing was to keep Chris busy. He only made problems when he had time to think.

He used a shovel to scoop the piles of sand and throw them out the front door. 'Mum said I shoulda kept the doors shut,' he said to Chris. 'I can't see how it's my fault.'

'It's not your fault.'

'Every time something happens. *Harry, why did you leave it there?*' He studied Chris's actions, his big arms, his slow strokes, the way he had to think about every movement.

'Chris?' he asked.

'Yes?'

'How did it happen, when you got hurt in the muster that time?'

Chris didn't walk to talk about it. How he was standing behind a steer, prodding its rump with a length of hose, when it kicked him in the face. How he fell to the ground clutching his broken jaw with its four shattered teeth and a mess of blood covering his hands. How Morris and Murray had shouted at him, called him *stupid boy* and *simple fool* before wrapping his face in someone's shirt, driving him back to the house and, in the middle of a muster, when they could least afford to, driving him all the way to Port Augusta hospital.

'I've showed you my scar, haven't I?' Chris asked, lifting his chin and showing him the faint line.

'I didn't know it was from that. I bet they were pissed off.'

Chris looked up. 'Murray, mostly,' he said, remembering sitting beside his shit-smeared, over-ripe uncle as they drove. He could still see his red eyes, clenched jaw and bit lip. And Fay, sitting in the front, looking back at them. 'Hold on, Christopher, it's only a few minutes.' The corrugations threw the car in the air; the suspension gave up trying. Chris muffled his groans so Murray might stop staring at him.

'What's worse,' Chris continued, 'was when they took me to Adelaide, he had to come too.'

'In the middle of a muster?'

'He was so angry.' Chris guessed that Murray had never really forgiven him – for the broken jaw, and a hundred other things. He still saw it in his eyes: the look he had when an animal needed to be culled.

'He's never liked me.'

'He does.'

'He never talks to me nice, and no matter how many times I've tried ...'

'It's just him,' Harry said. 'Old men are all grumpy.'

Harry guessed there was probably something in what Chris was saying. He knew the look, the tone, the distance. 'You've just gotta ignore him,' he said. 'You shoulda learnt that by now.'

They took the brooms and went back up, past the old drop toilet, and stopped at the bottle tree. They replaced the fallen bottles and jars and Harry went to his dad's shed to fetch his whip.

Then he spent an hour trying to teach his cousin (for the hundredth time) how to crack the whip so he'd break a bottle.

7

The land was crusted, drying before it was used, or presented as some sort of offering to the humans and small animals who attempted to live on it. Trevor drove, his hands held tightly ten-to-two on the steering wheel. He tried to imagine this land as a map: its blue-line-major-roads, black-hatch-highways, small-dot-towns and red-spot-cities; tried to imagine how it had been scrawled upon, bi- and dissected, measured and claimed in the name of civilisation.

Carelyn was sitting beside him, staring across the highway.

'Where do you want to stop?' he asked, but she told him to keep driving towards Port Augusta.

Harry was sitting in the back listening to headphones, singing and saying, *'Mein Vater hat ein grosses Auto.'*

Trevor looked at him in the rear-vision mirror. 'Eh?' Although he knew what it meant, knew each of the dozen or so phrases he kept repeating when he was bored.

Harry met his eyes and took off his headphones.

'What?'

'Mein Vater …?'

'Mein Vater hat ein grosses Auto.'

'My father has a big car?'

'Ja.'

'Is that all you know?'

'Ich habe keine Schwester, aber, ich habe einen älteren Bruder.'

Trevor studied the long, grey strip in front of them. He followed it half-way to the horizon before it was consumed by haze. By then it was blood red, pulsing and shifting across the desert. He could tell it was alive, held in place by nothing more than a million distance markers. There was saltbush and bluebush and dead shrubs that looked the same as the living ones; a rest-stop with a single bin, but nothing else, as if this too was some forgotten skeleton.

He reached over and turned up the radio. *'There were smaller numbers of vealer steers with most selling to feeder activity.'*

Carelyn looked at him. 'Christ, do we gotta listen to that?'

Harry stared at the road up ahead. *'Was it das?'* he asked, but they were already over the dead roo.

Trevor turned down the radio and looked at his wife. 'It's how we make our living,' he said.

She didn't reply; just found a magazine in the glove-box, opened it and pretended to read.

'We've never been careful enough with prices,' he said.

'What do you mean?'

But he just ignored her, turning up the radio again. *'Yearling steers sold mainly from 190 to 256 cents ...'*

'Timing,' he explained. 'Market fluctuations; we should be looking at the long-term. Still, perhaps I don't give a shit.'

'What?' She looked at him.

'We're never gonna become millionaires, are we?' He ground his hands into the wheel. 'Although it'd be nice to get out of debt.'

'We will.' She put the magazine down as a sign of solidarity.

'Perhaps we could find a buyer.'

'Who's gonna buy us out?'

'Someone ... one of these capital companies.'

But they both knew there was no point having this discussion again; at least as long as Murray was alive.

'So ... in the meantime?' he asked.

'You worry too much.'

'Someone has to.'

She pulled a baby-face. 'Snookums.'

'Fuck off.' He switched off the cattle report.

'Sell the place, then.'

'Yeah, it's that easy.'

He could remember how, one time, it had been much easier. How he'd visit her at work, two or three times a month, waiting beside the vitamin pills and energy drinks as she served. Then, with the smell of menthol and eucalyptus strong in his nose, approach her. He'd use Bundeena (and his prospects) as a selling point. Saying things like, 'I won't be able to come in much over the muster,' and, 'Dad said I should invite you out ... and you could stay a few days.'

The land and the animals gave him solidity, power, the look and smell of at least potential wealth. And he'd been happy to propagate this image. 'We prob'ly got three hundred heifers to move, maybe more. Dad's hiring a big team this year. Two cooks,' as he grinned, searching her eyes for approval.

Back in the car, Harry pulled off his headphones and said, 'You promised.'

'On the way back,' Trevor replied.

'No ... Aiden won't want to stop.'

Trevor indicated and pulled over. They stopped in a clearing. There was an old transportable on stumps. It'd been left to sink into the desert. Its windows had been smashed and wall panels kicked in. But it was still a strange miracle, stranded beside the highway, its thousands of nailed-on hub caps, rims, bumper bars and door panels glistening in the sun. It was a shell of spare parts, a hot iron organism roasting in the sun, protected by a skin of nailed-on licence plates.

Harry got out, produced his phone and started taking photos. 'It's cool,' he said to his dad, sitting on the bonnet watching him.

The roof was shingled with more car doors and a ring of old

tyres hung from the eaves. They knocked against each other in the little bit of wind. Whole exhaust systems had been attached to door and window frames, intertwining like bougainvillea as they snaked their way up drainpipes.

Trevor had never stopped at the car-house before. For years, as they'd passed it, he'd always made some comment, but left it at that. Once, there'd been a car parked out front, but that had long gone. He'd seen the house grow over the decades; marvelled at how its colour always changed depending on what new parts had been added.

Harry went into the house and Trevor followed him. 'Where do you suppose they went?' he asked.

'Maybe they were taken by aliens.'

'Do you think?'

'It's not like they were trying to blend in.'

The horn sounded.

'Come on,' Trevor said.

They continued for another hour, mostly silently; asphalt, rubber, steel and aluminium, petrol, plastic and glass; a hundred little bits and pieces, turning, lifting, opening and closing, growling, rubbing, expanding and contracting. At one point, Carelyn looked back at her son.

'Weren't you gonna vacuum the car?'

He took off his headphones.

'Weren't you gonna vacuum the car?'

'I'll do it when I get home.'

'But I asked you last week.'

'I'll do it.' He retreated into a shadow.

'Not much point,' Trevor said.

They returned to the road. Two, three minutes, but Carelyn couldn't let it go. 'It's funny the things you forget,' she said, turning around.

'Sorry?' he asked, removing his headphones.

'It's funny the things you forget.'

'What?'

'Don't worry.'

Trevor shook his head. 'Is this really achieving anything?'

She looked at him, and he knew she was accusing him too.

'What?'

'I asked him weeks ago.'

'Does it *really* matter?'

They arrived in Port Augusta mid-afternoon, slowing into suburb, drifting along the four lanes of chicken-shop-highway that marked the transition from country to town. There were servos and blocks of shops selling home-brew kits and bags of kitty litter. Small, semi-detached homes, their red bricks baking in the methylated sun of early summer; and bus stops, leaning where their concrete had lifted. The few people they saw were very old, or very young, shuffling along in wafer-thin thongs.

They drove through the gates of the college, parked and found Aiden alone, again, caught up in music, sitting in the memorial garden. He managed a hug for his mum and a handshake and slapped shoulder for his dad, but when he saw his little brother he just put him in a neck-hold and ran his knuckles from ear-to-ear. 'Three weeks, and you've grown, you little shit.'

'As if you could tell,' Harry replied, but he could see that his brother, too, had changed. More pimples around his lips and razorback nose.

They sat on two wooden benches, and Trevor asked, 'So, you all packed?'

Aiden indicated his case, sitting in the shade of an adjacent doorway. 'You said three.'

'Sorry, your brother slowed us down.'

Carelyn was studying her son's clothes. 'I didn't think you had to wear this in summer,' she said, straightening his tie.

Aiden wrestled her hands, and fixed it himself. 'That comes from his Holiness, Pope Prickmeister the Seventh.'

Harry smiled. He loved to look at his brother's tie, his school shirt (with its amateur-ironer scorch marks), a Mercy coat-of-arms above the pocket; he loved his khaki pants and his leather belt and he especially loved his socks, pulled up just beneath his knees, folded down to reveal green and blue stripes; and his leather shoes, although he hadn't polished them since the last exeat.

He could see himself as a proper gentleman, playing chess and cricket, spending his evenings in the left-open library. Could imagine his own small room, but he wasn't so sure about the sharing arrangements for Years Eight and Nine; the showers (and he'd seen them) that were only separated by translucent curtains of cows-over-the-moon.

Still, the smell of disinfectant in the halls of residence and incense in the chapel were more than enough compensation. Even the routines, the bells, the prayers, seemed to promise a world of things beyond the bulldust and cowshit of Bundeena; a different meal every night; dessert: a bowl of fruit that even now seemed tempting.

An old piano sat in the sun on a mover's trolley in the middle of the garden. Someone had written SCRAP on the side. As the Wilkies watched a boy wandered over, lifted the lid and tried a few keys. The piano sounded clunky, but in tune. After a few scales he squared up to the keyboard and started playing.

Harry watched and listened. As he did, he felt he wanted to be this boy; wanted his uniform, his musical fingers, his piano lessons. He felt (as he heard each of the careful notes) that this, perhaps, was a more satisfactory life. Surely these sounds, meshing like windmill gears, indicated a more logical and promising future than the vagaries of learning by radio, of living a million miles from anywhere, of relying on a few wandering cattle to provide a living.

'Little show-off,' Aiden said.

'He's very good,' Harry replied.

'Looks like a little brat,' Trevor said.

Harry looked at his father, although he said nothing. Then, he returned his gaze to the boy.

'So, how did it all go?' Trevor asked Aiden.

'The maths exam was … well, for a start, he hadn't taught us half of it.'

Carelyn *tcht*ed. 'Is it that …?'

'Mr Marsh. Everyone was complaining, even Tom, who's top of the class.'

'We'll have to go and see him,' Carelyn said.

'Let's just wait,' Trevor replied. 'Exams are generally never as bad as …' He trailed off, remembering. He'd sat in this garden thirty years before. It hadn't been such a different place. A generation had passed with nothing more than a little paint, a new statue of Mary and agapanthus where the rosemary once struggled. Murray, and his mum, had been here, too, quizzing him, and he'd given them the bad news: failed exams, and forgotten assignments.

'Maybe there's no point starting Year Twelve,' Aiden suggested, looking at his parents.

'Why not?' Trevor asked, not entirely surprised.

'Not if I'm gonna fail things.'

'Why are you going to fail?' Carelyn asked.

'Maybe not fail, but get through with Cs.'

She crossed her arms. 'You're not a C student.'

'It's getting harder.'

'So? You work harder. Year Twelve is a minimum for anyone now.'

'But what's the point if – '

'You. Will. Continue.' She decided against the lecture. How he (Yes, you, look at me when I'm talking to you) was, for seven years, the best student in his School of the Air class; how he used to finish his maths worksheets in minutes and spend half-an-hour waiting for the others; always scored an A on tests and had a spelling age five years above his actual age.

'It's only another year,' Harry said to his brother.

Aiden gave him his *shut up, Shit-for-brains* look. 'It's none of your business.'

'You're meant to set a good example.'

A tall man wearing jeans and a white business shirt approached them. 'Mr Wilkie, is it?'

'Yes, Trevor.' They shook hands.

The man hitched his pants and surveyed the group. 'Mrs Wilkie?'

'Carelyn.' A sort of finger-to-finger handshake.

And looking at Harry. 'Little brother, I assume?'

'Harrison Wilkie.'

The man introduced himself as Mr Owen-Smith, Jeff, your lad's tech teacher. Explaining, much to Aiden's disappointment, 'He's done brilliantly this semester.'

'Really?' Carelyn asked, turning to her son. 'That's funny, because he was just telling us how *poorly* he thinks he's going.'

'Not in tech. You got a moment?'

The Wilkies followed Jeff Owen-Smith towards the main building. As they went, Harry said to his brother, 'We had this huge sandstorm.'

Aiden just looked at him.

'Two days – and you couldn't even see the sheds.'

'Right.' He took out his iPod.

'No,' Carelyn said.

He looked at her, scrunched it into a ball and shoved it into his pocket.

'Do they hire movies?' Harry asked his brother.

'Does who hire movies?'

'In the boarding house?'

'Of course they do. What's that got to do with anything?'

'MA?'

'How would I know?'

Meanwhile, Trevor was walking beside the tech teacher. 'Still running metalwork?' he asked.

'Yes. Your son's very handy with an arc welder.'

'He's been welding since he was ten. There's always something needs doing, isn't there, Aiden?' He turned to him.

'Yes, Dad.'

'I did my Matric here in 1974.'

'Really?'

'Yes, very different then. It was, let me think, Mr Kristie running tech studies.'

'I've heard of him.'

'Old school, you know, no nonsense. You talked out of turn a piece of wood'd come flying across the room.' He smiled, remembering. 'I got clocked in the head a few times, but you learnt to listen.'

As they walked, Trevor studied the walls, covered with hi-gloss saints, Christ, Mary and the others, busy with dramas that filled every hallway, science lab and dining room. There were plinths, too, with statues that had been knocked over and glued together. Jesus, mostly, in the arms of Mary, or holding his hand out pleadingly to the 600 boys who walked past every day.

Around a corner, beneath a set of stained-glass windows, he noticed the honour board: block names reaching back to the college's foundation. And there, among the crowd:

ATHLETICS

1917	Morris Wilkie
1946	Murray Wilkie
1974	Trevor Wilkie

He could see the gap, still there, for 1911, where John Wilkie had once had his name. Before his public disgrace. Before his removal with mineral turpentine.

Owen-Smith led them into the workshops: tools on shadow racks and lathes sitting fat and solid in the sunlight. Around the welding bays, past the plastics' oven into the storeroom.

'Aiden tells me you like to work with wood,' he said to Trevor.

'Yes, sometimes.'

'Well, that must be where he gets it from.'

Trevor was lost for words. Kristie had been an old cunt, and when he thought about it, he'd never liked tech, or school. He'd hated the boarding-house food, the long hours of Latin, the commandments, the whispered prayers. He looked at his son. 'You okay?'

But Aiden was too ashamed, partly of the story the teacher was spinning, but mostly of himself, for going along with it.

'Look at this little beauty,' Owen-Smith said, retrieving a small coffee table from a shelf, finding a rag and wiping it down.

'Nice work,' Trevor agreed, running his hand over the stained pine.

'I gave him an A. Look at those joins … and every cut, neat and clean.' He lifted and turned the table, so they could see what he meant.

Carelyn took her son around the shoulders. 'See … and there's you saying you're not good at anything.'

Aiden wanted to pull away from her but knew he couldn't. 'I didn't say that.'

'You did.'

'He thinks he should skip Year Twelve,' she told Owen-Smith. 'Thinks he can only get Cs.'

'Nonsense. From what I hear …'

She returned to her son. 'See?'

Aiden wanted to argue, wanted to say, No, you don't understand. Why should I spend another year learning about matrices and mitochondria?

Harry looked at his brother but knew better than to say anything, at least now. He knew what he was thinking. *Why don't you all shut up and leave me alone?*

Trevor, too, was watching his son, wondering. 'It's a nice bit of work,' he said.

'Commercial quality,' the teacher explained. 'Someone would pay good money for that.'

'It's all in your head,' Carelyn continued. 'Whatever you set your mind to.' She ran a hand over the table's legs.

Trevor looked at Jesus on his cross, hanging above the door. He noticed how He'd been carved from wood. 'That leaves my stuff for dead,' he said to Aiden.

A few minutes later they were heading back to the garden, Trevor carrying the table. 'Weren't you gonna bring this home?' he asked his son.

'I forgot.'

Back at Bundeena, Murray seemed immune to the responsibility he'd inherited. He lay on his stretcher in his sleep-out smoking cigarettes, singing along to the record he'd left playing in the lounge room:

> *Tell me, darling, that you love me,*
> *While the moon is shining bright!*

He'd smoke each rollie, then snuff it out in the old jar that was more butt than sand. He'd wait, taking his time, then give in to the boredom, picking up his next cigarette, striking his lighter and slowly tempting the tobacco to life. More smoke, exhalation, the room filling with its usual port-flavoured fog.

He studied the pine beams supporting the ceiling. One had two small letters carved into it: PR. Paul Rice. He'd been one of Bundeena's few visitors – a rough-bearded, red-faced young man who, one day in 1916, had come walking up the front drive carrying a duffle bag. He'd knocked on the back door and Mary, wife of Bill, father of Morris, father of Murray, had greeted him with floury hands.

'You Mrs Wilkie?' he'd asked.

She'd wiped her hands on her apron and studied the stranger's face. 'Yes. You after my husband?' As she'd searched the yards for his horse.

He'd said, 'I walked.'

'From where?'

'The train. I come from Perth to tell you something.' He'd tried to smile but only revealed a few broken teeth. 'Name's Paul Rice.'

Mary had brought him inside. Made him a cup of tea and sat watching as he sipped and slurped, wiping his lips with the back of his hand. Although Bill was off with his rifle she didn't think this stranger, with his sun-bleached hair and dry lips, meant trouble. Why would you come so far to rob a farmhouse that wouldn't have anything more than a few old clocks?

'How long you been walkin'?' she'd asked.

'I got off last night,' he'd explained. 'I was too tired to walk, so I slept in some grass.'

A short silence. Eventually she'd looked at him and asked, 'So, what have you come to tell us, Mr Rice?'

He'd studied the china cup then met her eyes. 'It's about John. I was serving with him.'

Mary had sat forward, her breath halved, stolen, her heart racing. It was the first time she'd heard her missing son's name for months – since he'd been shamed on the Cowards' List in the 7 September 1916 edition of the *Port Augusta Chronicle*; since, a month before that, when they'd received a letter from the army:

Dear Mr and Mrs Wilkie,

It is with regret that I write to you regarding your son, Private John Wilkie, 2419387. At evening roll call on 21 July 1916, Private Wilkie was found to be missing. Enquiries with his officers and NCOs revealed nothing. Dozens of infantrymen from his battalion were interviewed but none had seen him since the previous evening ...

She'd remembered the way the words were arranged into paragraphs, how the typewriter (with a fading ribbon) dropped its k and how there was a finger smudge on the bottom right hand corner of the letter.

The battalion was involved in heavy fighting on the 19th, but a survey was taken of the Fallen, and your son was not among them. Mr and Mrs Wilkie, I must inform you that John had been recorded as a deserter ...

Later that day, after Bill had returned from his shooting, he'd sat with Mary and Paul and asked him about their son.

'I last saw him when we attacked,' Rice had told them. 'He was right into it, and took the charge.'

'He did?' Bill had asked.

'Yes ... he was no shirker, Mr Wilkie.'

Then Bill had gone to a drawer and found a copy of a letter they'd sent to the army.

He lives for his mates and would die for them. John is no coward. Surely what you mean is 'missing'? Maybe he is dazed, confused, lost, captured? We don't like to think of it, but perhaps he is dead?

'That's about right,' Rice had told them. 'The army's got it all wrong. I told our captain, but he wouldn't listen.'

Bill and Mary had just waited, barely breathing.

'John was no coward,' he'd said. 'I think the noise, the shells, and what he saw, just got to him. I'd often see him crying at night. Like he'd reached some sort of ... end.'

Mary and Bill had looked at each other.

'I think he was shell-shocked. He'd curl up in a ball. He wouldn't talk to anyone, even me.'

There'd been a meal and an evening around the fire. Then they'd offered him the sleep-out.

'That'd be nice, folks,' he'd replied. 'I got sent home because of my kidneys.'

'Your kidneys?' Bill had asked.

The stranger had showed them the scar where the shrapnel had hit him and cut deep into his belly.

Murray hadn't known the stranger, of course. But the overheard whispers had been enough for him to reconstruct the story, to make the connection between his uncle, the sense of bitterness and regret that lingered in the family, and the body hanging from a rough beam in Number one. There'd always been a feeling that this tragedy had somehow finished the Wilkies. Not as a catastrophic collapse, but as a crack in the prism through which they viewed the world.

He noticed a puddle spreading from under the walls, soaking his rug, flowing under his bedside table. 'Christ.' He heard running water from the bathroom and knew it was Chris. Dragging himself up, he went into the house and down the hallway to the bathroom. 'Chris. Where are yer?'

The bath had been left on. Water was overflowing onto the tiles, into the hallway, under doors, soaking into a pile of books on the floor of Trevor and Carelyn's room. He went in, turned off the tap and called again. 'Chris!'

Nothing.

So he went into the room the boy (for he always thought of him this way) shared with his mother. And there he was, naked, stretched out on his bed, listening to the iPod Fay had bought him. 'What the hell are you doing?'

Chris sat up and took out his ear-pieces. He made no attempt to cover himself. 'I'm gonna have a bath.'

'Bloody idiot … there's water everywhere.'

Chris just looked at him, confused.

'Get a mop and clean it up.'

He stood and started to walk from the room.

'After you get some clothes on,' Murray growled. He remembered the books. Returned to his son's room, picked up the pile and laid the volumes on the bed. When Chris reappeared he said, 'When yer done you can get the hairdryer and start on these.'

Chris went to the laundry and returned with a mop.

'Where's yer bucket?' Murray asked, emptying the bath. 'What are you gonna put the water in?' Again, Chris stopped, looked at him and returned to the laundry.

'Bloody idiot,' Murray grumbled.

'I am not,' Chris replied, turning.

'Get the water.'

'I just forgot.'

'Yeah, I know, you always forget, that's why you're a bloody idiot.'

'Mum!' Chris howled. He dropped the mop and ran out, looking for Fay.

A few minutes later she came in to find Murray mopping the hallway.

'You can't call him an idiot,' she said.

Murray didn't respond. He started on the bathroom.

'Did you hear me, Murray?'

'He was lying on his bed, fiddling with himself.'

'I was not,' Chris said.

'Looked like it to me.'

'I was waiting for the bath to fill up.'

Murray almost laughed. 'How long were you gonna wait?'

Fay looked at her son. 'What were you gonna do in there?'

'Nothing,' he said, and Fay tended to agree. She'd trained him well enough, early enough, to do that sort of thing over the toilet.

'He was just waiting,' she said to her brother.

'Really?' Murray asked.

'I was,' Chris insisted.

'Well, either way.' He handed Chris the mop.

Fay glared at her brother. 'You've never understood how hurtful your words are.'

Murray shrugged. 'They're not hurtful, they're facts.'

'Calling people idiots?'

Murray was having none of it. 'You gotta say it as it is,' he told his sister. 'Otherwise, where would we be?'

'We'd be getting along.'

'The world doesn't work like that.' He wondered how they'd tolerated such weakness for so long. He looked at his sister. 'You startin' tea soon, or do I gotta do that too?'

8

With a predicted top of thirty-nine degrees they decided to start the School of the Air picnic early. A couple of dozen mums and dads and fifty or so kids gathered on the dead lawn of the 'Scooter' Haraway Memorial Park and within fifteen minutes the competitions had begun.

The egg-and-spoon race. Harry the number one runner, using his often practised walk-run, the spoon held at chin height. He was the second to cross the line, passing his spoon to Carelyn, who fumbled it, dropped the egg and looked at him. 'Quick!' he said, pulling his hair.

Carelyn picked up the egg, replaced it and walked slowly. 'It won't stay there,' she said, and the crowd (some of whom had started an improvised chant) laughed.

'Keep your eye on the egg,' Harry called.

'I am.' She looked back at him and the egg dropped again. By now the second member of every other team had finished. She carried on, handing over to Aiden, who managed to sprint the twenty metres without looking at the egg; handing it to his father who, having seen they'd lost, took his time, slowly sauntering towards the line. He stopped a few feet from the finish, feigned a twisted ankle, turned to the crowd and said, 'I don't think I can make it.'

'Lame,' Harry called.

'Get on with it,' Carelyn said.

'Dad,' Aiden sang, above the voices.

He turned, tripped, and the egg fell, shattering on the ground.

They rewarded him with applause and he looked at them as if to say, Such is Life.

There was music on a tinny PA and the group broke into families and clans: the wheat-sheep group, the cattle group, the roadhouse kids, and Shakina and Aleisha, hanging off a set of old monkey bars. The Wilkies drifted back to their table, their bottles of Coke and lemonade, half-eaten chicken and a pair of dips that had hardened in the morning sun. Aiden sat beside his brother and said, 'You told me you'd been practising.'

'I have,' Harry replied.

As he recalled his relays around the compound with Chris – three, four broken eggs on the ground and him saying: 'You gotta keep your eye on the egg.' As Chris just looked at him, dropping another one. Until Carelyn came out, saw what they'd wasted, and said, 'No more.'

Back in the park, Harry was glad to be sitting beside his brother. 'I was trying to teach Uncle Chris,' he told him. 'I thought he might come this year.' He studied his brother's face. Noticed his pale skin, probably from too much study. But the changes looked far more dramatic, and final, in a way, he guessed, that would affect everything that had always passed between them. 'I can help you with your car.'

'What?'

'Finish painting it.'

Aiden shrugged.

'How often do you shave?' Harry asked.

'Mind your own fucking business.'

'Aiden,' Carelyn growled.

'Well, tell him to stop crapping on.'

'I'm not crapping on,' Harry replied. 'I just wanted to know.'

Silence, as Aiden gave him his shit-for-brains look and then almost smiled. 'We gotta get some paint,' he said to him.

Harry looked at Carelyn.

'What?' she asked.

'Can we get some paint?'

She poured herself a glass of wine. 'Ask your father.'

The park was a concession to civilisation: old play equipment and thin-on-the-ground pine chips; concrete tables with cast-iron shelters whose shadows hardly ever fell across burnt skin. A few dead trees, with a banner strung up: 'SOTA Xmas Picnic', the date painted out and updated. Someone had set up their barbecue in an old pond beside a brick construction with a plaque: 'In Memory of "Scooter" Haraway, AO, who played in this park as a child. His contribution to the local' – (and someone had scribbled 'porn') – 'industry changed many lives and impacted the history of our town. A' – (and someone had added 'gay') – 'man in a big world'.

'Pity if they watered the lawn,' Carelyn said to her sons, watching her husband caught up in a conversation with an old friend on the other side of the park.

'Can we get some paint?' Harry asked.

She thought of the holidays, the lean hours, the empty days; the lack of real or virtual education; the claustrophobia. 'Okay, but you can contribute.'

'Some,' Aiden said.

'Half.'

They noticed a small elephant harnessed to a wooden cart pulling half-a-dozen kids around the park. It plodded across the grass and continued into the carpark, stopping to wait for a reversing Fiat.

'Where did they get an elephant?' Harry asked.

'It's here every year,' Carelyn replied. 'Poor bastard … it's probably wishing someone would shoot it.'

Shakina was soon over, pulling Harry's arm. 'Come on, they're doing a treasure hunt.'

He resisted. 'No, I'm too hot.'

'Come on.'

'Go on,' Carelyn said.

'She won't bite you,' Aiden added.

He stared at his brother, stood and followed Shakina towards the briefing, looking back and pulling a face.

'No kissing,' Aiden said, and he turned to come back.

'Go on,' Carelyn insisted, shooing him, gulping her wine, watching her husband laugh and slap his friend's shoulder.

'Who's he?' Aiden asked, noticing.

'Your father used to play football with him.'

'Football?'

'When he was your age,' she explained. 'I remember … we went to his wedding.' She squinted to see if this man was who she thought he was. 'Gary … Gareth … who knows?' The rope on the banner came loose and one end fell in the dirt. 'I wonder if anyone's gonna fix it?' she said.

'Maybe I should.'

'No, let it go. Someone's just gotta take it down anyway.'

She studied the children. There were two types: town (in thongs, with shoulder-length hair, seeking shade) and country (in polished boots and ironed shirts).

'It's all a bit sad, isn't it?' she said.

'What?' Aiden asked.

'How all these people never meet, then have to be friends for a day.'

'They don't have to be.'

'Try to be.'

Aiden sat back in his chair. 'What choice have they got?'

But she didn't reply. Harry ran past holding a small Christmas-wrapped gift. 'Look.'

'Keep going,' Carelyn said.

Aiden waited a few moments. 'You know, you and Dad could save yourselves a lot of money.'

She knew where he was going. 'How's that?'

'If I didn't do Year Twelve.'

She thought for a moment, sat up and looked at him. 'Your argument assumes you want to spend the rest of your life ... fiddling around with cattle.'

'I do.'

'You might change your mind.'

'No.'

'You never know.'

'But it's what we *do*.' He couldn't grasp what she was saying. 'We always have.'

'Doesn't mean we always will.'

Dust, in a little tornado that passed onto the road.

'Look at your father,' she said.

'What?'

'It's a lot for one man.'

'It's not just him.'

'It is, mostly.'

Aiden wanted to argue the point, but suspected she was right.

'All that weight hangs off a man,' she said. 'Day and night. It's not healthy.'

Again, nothing but the sound of kids' voices and a soft ball striking a hard bat. 'It hangs off you,' she repeated. 'And things only get harder, every year.'

'That's why you do things *differently*,' he said.

She guessed her son couldn't be told. Not now, at least. Later, when he'd learnt the lessons that defied explanation. That problems were the inability to change things, to start again. She watched Trevor shaking his friend's hand before walking back towards them. He sat down, smiling. 'You remember Jeff?'

'Jeff,' she said. 'Of course.'

'He asked me to a reunion.'

'You should go.'

'I'm not coming back before Christmas.'

'You two used to be quite friendly.'

He opened a beer and drank as a sand-shoed Saint Nick walked across the park ringing his bell. The kids shouted and ran towards him.

'Go on,' Trevor said to Aiden.

'You gotta be kidding.'

Carelyn was still studying her husband's face. She knew he'd given up everything for them. 'You should go,' she repeated. 'You should stay in touch with your mates.'

'What's the point, if you only see them every ten years?'

'You don't have anyone …' He watched his son receiving another present, this time from the budget Santa. Carelyn looked at Aiden. He met her eyes. 'What?' he asked.

After tea they drove west through a suburb of gravel lawns, broken fences and oleander. Only a few gardens had enough colour to break the semi-detached gloom of an unweeded, industrial dusk. A boy, slightly older than Harry, was pushing a girl in a shopping trolley. Wrestling with it, he managed to keep it on a footpath of cracked concrete.

There were factories and empty blocks full of rubble and flat, lifeless plains where the city gave way to what was already outback. And the highway, again, proudly dressed in fresh white paint, cooling in the early evening.

Harry was still looking at his three laminated certificates: 'Presented to Harry Wilkie, 2004, Excellence in Spelling'; 'Harry Wilkie, Mrs Lawrence, 2004, Most Improved, Creative Composition'; 'Awarded to Harry Wilkie for Attention to Detail and his Willingness to Help Out and Encourage Others'.

At the end of the afternoon they'd stood listening to Mr Runkorn talk about how unique and special they were; how nowhere else in the world do kids learn like you learn; how you show that shared education can really work (as he thanked all the mums, dad, brothers, sisters and grandparents); how you are part of one of the great social experiments, an Australian icon, like lifesavers or the Sydney Opera House.

As Harry thought, How are we like the Opera House?

Dusk became night. Trevor drove in an almost straight line towards Bundeena. He ran parallel with then moved away from the train track; crossed low hills, a bridge, then back towards the east–west line. He felt himself tiring, drifting, jumping back to life. Winding down his window, he turned up the music.

The desert was dark, gone from sight. The only world they could see was the one their lights created: asphalt, the monotony of distance markers. There were stars but they were just a blur through dusty windows. The only sound in their movable world was *Human Nature*, tyres, and the occasional muttered comment.

'Mr Runkorn looks like he's been 'round a while,' Trevor said.

'He crushed my hand,' Harry replied, as he remembered his principal's sweaty palm and wedding ring.

'Did you say thank you?' Carelyn asked.

'Yes.'

'Show me.' She took his certificates and read what she could in the dark. *'His willingness to help out?'*

'What?'

'I think this belongs to that *other* Harry Wilkie.'

Aiden was caught up with his iPod. He took off his headphones and looked at his brother. 'You been ridin' my bike?'

'No.'

'Mum, has he?'

The car drifted. Trevor suddenly woke, unaware of where he was. He grabbed the steering wheel and they shot off across the road. Carelyn and Harry screamed as their fast-moving world of clothes and books and half-eaten chicken and paint and certificates tumbled once, twice, three, four times across the desert, crushing, settling, bushes, grass. The car balanced uneasily on its left side. It started to move and fell back, flat.

'Dad!' Harry screamed. He could feel metal wrapped around and entering his right leg.

No one replied.

Back on the highway, a road-train stopped. Two men jumped from the cab and ran towards them.

'Dad!'

'Get out,' Aiden said, undoing his and his brother's seatbelt.

'I can't.'

The truck drivers were looking in. 'Everyone okay?' one of them asked.

'The boys,' Trevor managed.

'You alright, boys?' One of the truckies tried Aiden's door. 'No, it's crushed shut,' he said, before running back to the truck. 'I'll call for help.'

Trevor looked at the cold liquid on his arm. He touched it and studied his blue and green fingers. Looked over at his wife. She seemed to be asleep, still clutching Harry's certificates. 'It's okay,' he said to her. 'We landed feet first.'

The second driver came around to her. He opened the door and could see, straight away, from the way her head rested too perfectly on her shoulder. He looked at Trevor. 'Stay still,' he said. 'They'll be here in no time.'

'Carelyn?' Trevor called.

'You boys okay?' the truckie asked.

Aiden was getting out through the window. 'I can help,' he said.

The driver stood back, overcome, thinking what to do, his eyes caught up in the dilemma of the dead woman.

Aiden had come around to his brother. 'Shit,' he said, trying the door. 'Listen, Harry, it's just yer leg's caught, eh?'

'Yes.'

Aiden felt the paint on his face, and it went into his eyes. 'Shit,' he said, rubbing them, collapsing to his knees. 'I can't fuckin' see.'

And Trevor, sitting up, replied, 'Come 'round to me, son.'

Trevor rolled out of the car and onto the ground. He felt as though every muscle in his body was burning. Nothing was broken, he could tell. Could remember the time he'd come off his trail bike, tumbled, and mashed his leg into a fence post. Aiden (at thirteen) had driven him back to house as he'd told him how to work the gears.

He sat staring into the darkness, saying, 'I can help,' as the voice of the fatter of the two truckies came back, 'Stay there, let the ambos work out what's wrong.'

He heard sirens and, in the distance, doors slamming and feet on bitumen. There was a short silence. When he looked into the sky, with its lines and circles and scattering of stars, there was a figure beside him saying, 'Nothing broken … do you think you can stand up?'

'Yes.' He sat up, splayed his legs and stumbled to his feet.

'Steady,' the paramedic said, helping him.

'I'm okay.' He reclaimed his arm and looked at the car, mostly intact, its edges and corners crushed smooth. 'Everyone's alright?'

'You should go with your son.'

'Righto.'

The man led him towards the road. He looked back at the torches poking around inside the car. 'What have I done?' he asked.

'Don't worry about that. Your son needs you now.'

'Carelyn?'

'Come on. We got him out, but his leg's smashed up.'

He felt the road beneath his feet. He was blinded by the light inside the ambulance – clean, white, drugged and bandaged, electrical equipment packed into bays; a spot for the sheets and a shelf for the rugs; little blue boxes full of dressings packed in plastic; a drip stand, a bag of clear fluid and a tube leading to his son's arm; a catheter and his boy, bare-shouldered and flat-chested, lying on a chaotic bed of linen and torn plastic.

'Christ, Harry,' he said to him, climbing into the ambulance, sitting on a seat that was half as wide as his arse, squeezing in beside a second paramedic. This man smiled at him and said, 'Relax, it's just his leg.'

Trevor met his eyes. Right, he wanted to say. Nothing serious? But he looked at his son and wasn't convinced. The paint on his arms and hands, his hair, wet with sweat, pushed back off his face by one of these strangers; the rug across his belly and the red cast clamped around his leg.

He leaned forward and ran his hand across his face. 'Harry, can you hear me?' he asked, but the paramedic just said, 'He was awake … but we've given him a sedative.'

The back doors closed and they drove off, quickly picking up speed, switching on their lights and siren and hurtling down the highway.

'You the father?' the driver called back.

'Yes.'

'What happened?'

'I don't know.'

He held his son's hand and stroked it. It was warm, and he could feel the bones and knuckles. He looked at his small lips, redder than usual, and his ski-jump nose with its little beads of sweat. His eyebrows, rising as they met in the middle of his face. 'Christ … sorry,' he said.

The world had stopped. There was nothing beyond the ambulance, the road, the two little tabs stuck to Harry's chest, the monitor and the numbers that meant nothing to him. 'Christ.' He cried, placing his son's hand on his knees, dropping his head down onto it, smelling him, gasping.

The paramedic touched his shoulder. 'People have accidents. He'll come good.' He indicated the trace that described the boy's will to live.

Trevor took a deep breath. He wanted to thank him. To say, Enough of this and you might make me believe. Instead, he said, 'What about my other son?'

'He went in the other ambulance. Seemed okay, but he'd knocked his head, so they put him in a brace.'

Harry opened his eyes and saw his father. He smiled.

'It's just your leg,' Trevor said.

'Again,' the paramedic said to Harry. 'One to ten.'

'Nine.'

'We're nearly there,' Trevor said, and Harry closed his eyes and took a deep breath from the mask over his nose and mouth.

'My wife?' Trevor asked.

The paramedic looked at him, thinking, deciding. 'There was another ambulance.'

'So?'

'They've got her.'

'But she's okay?'

He shrugged, slowly. 'Let's just worry about the little fella's leg.'

Trevor stared at his son's closed eyes.

'Where were you headed?'

But he couldn't answer.

Trevor stood at the hospital window, third floor, high dependency, watching 3 am Port Augusta struggle through another night. An ambulance pulled into Emergency. *Their* ambulance, most probably, tasked with someone else's disaster, driving from one nightmare-avoided (or realised) to the next, as if it were delivering bread.

He went into Harry's room – small, stripped back, full of plugs and buttons and gas vents; monitors singing above the hum of the air-conditioning. He sat beside him, took his hand and studied his face. 'I'm sorry,' he repeated. 'I'm sorry.' He wondered if his hand would hold a whip again, or pluck lavender from its stem; if he'd ever jump back on his trail bike (and now he studied his trussed-up leg) or run around a paddock.

No, he told himself. He'll come good. Two days, a week, a month, a year; small bones had a way of fixing themselves; skin, of healing, hiding its history of trauma.

A nurse entered.

'When's the doctor due?' he asked.

'He's still downstairs,' she replied. 'I think they're busy in Emergency.'

'No one's told me anything about my wife.'

'The doctor will know. He's the one you've got to talk to.'

She checked Harry's pain relief – dripping one clear, cold millilitre per minute – and adjusted a red knob. 'He looks comfortable,' she said, but he didn't respond. He stood and walked across the hallway into Aiden's room. There were two beds. Another young man was listening to music through headphones. He sat beside his sleeping son, his eyes padded with gauze, bandaged, the paint still visible on his cheeks and neck. The young man slipped off his headphones, looked at him and said, 'He woke up for a while.'

'How long ago?'

'Half an hour, perhaps. Said he'd been in an accident. Nothin' too bad?'

'No, I don't think so.'

'Told me he got some paint in his eyes.'

'Yes.'

'That'll come good, if that's the worst of it.'

He just wanted to say, Shut the fuck up, and perhaps the young man sensed this. He slipped the headphones back over his ears.

Trevor reached out and felt the bandage, soft and tight around his son's skull. That'll come good, he thought. The eyes too, he guessed, could handle their fair share: acid, diesel, metal splinters from grinders, Harry poking him with a stick, a face full of drench.

Anyway, they had to come good. Aiden himself had explained that he wanted, needed, to be a farmer. His eyes and hands would be his livelihood. There was no alternative, no other way to get around the problem.

'Aiden, you awake?' he asked. He heard the response in his son's breath, saw it in his jaw, opening and closing.

'Can I take this stuff off now?'

'No, wait for the doctor.'

'I can see light ... and the bandage.'

'That's good, but you're gonna have to wait. Is there any other pain?'

'No ... my arse and backbone's sore, but I can move.' He wriggled his hips to show him. 'How's Shit-for-brains?'

'He's banged up his leg, but he's okay.'

'Is it broken?'

'Several places.' And he saw the door, crushed on Harry's leg. 'There were some gashes but they've fixed 'em.' He could see crushed metal hanging from the car and fragments of Harry's pants blowing in the breeze.

'And what about Mum?'

'Still trying to find out.'

There was a long pause. The prospect of bruises or a broken collar bone, concussion, or maybe, maybe she'd just walked away from the wreck? Of course; maybe it was worse; maybe she was dead; maybe the doctor was just waiting to tell them. Or nearly dead, strung up with a million wires and tubes? Maybe she was holding on, waiting for them, desperate to tell them how much she loved them.

'I'll go find out,' Trevor said, standing.

Aiden reached for him. Trevor took his hand and squeezed it. 'I know it seems bad ...'

Aiden, blinded by the bandages, didn't know if he could trust his father's words. 'Harry's leg will heal?'

'Yes.'

And then he asked, 'Did we hit something?'

Trevor waited. 'There was a roo on the road.'

Silence; nothing except the cymbals and bass drum from the second bed.

'I must have swerved to avoid it.'

As Aiden thought, You should've hit it. You knew to keep going, Dad. Instead he said, 'It's just instinct, I suppose.'

Trevor leaned forward. 'Get some sleep.' He moved closer. 'I'll be back as soon as I can.' He went out and stood in the middle of the hallway. 'Hello?'

Nothing. There was a radio, somewhere, busy with country music. He approached the nurses' station but there were just piles of unfinished paperwork, a half-eaten yoghurt, and charity chocolates. 'Hello?'

He walked along the hallway, looking into each room. Darkness. Green and red light. A television left on. Someone smiling at him, asking when breakfast was due. He checked his watch. 'It's only three-thirty.'

Eventually he came to the television room. He slid the door open, went inside and a middle-aged man, wearing a singlet and pyjama pants, said, 'How are yer?'

'You haven't seen the nurse?' He sat down beside him.

'Ha! Good luck.'

The man was watching a black-and-white movie, John Mills, a few London gangsters, and the inside of a bank vault. 'Warren,' he said.

'Trevor.' They shook hands.

'Absolute shit at night,' the stranger explained. 'It's either this or how to flatten yer fuckin'... abs.'

'Can't sleep?' Trevor asked.

'Sleep all day. Night time's better: no one to bother you.'

'I need to find a doctor.'

'What, y' sick?' He smiled.

'I wanna find out where my wife is.'

'What happened to her?'

'I rolled the car. They took her in a different ambulance.'

'You should go down to the main desk and ask. Decent roll?'

'Sorry?'

'Your car?'

Trevor shrugged. 'I suppose. We ended up in ... the bushes.'

The man massaged the stubble on his chin. 'I've rolled me car a couple of times. Dirt roads ... I mean, y' start off slow, don't yer, but the next thing yer doin' eighty and there's a bend and bam, over you go.'

He watched an ad: a ladder being assembled, broken down and put back together.

'I just ducked, as we tumbled,' Warren said, remembering. 'I's sure it was gonna crush me, so I ducked ...'

Trevor saw his lips moving and heard sound but didn't really know what he was saying. He wanted to stand, find his wife, but something was stopping him.

'So, who was in the car with you?' Warren asked.

'My sons ... my wife.'

'Right.' He was watching the movie. 'Boys okay?'

But he didn't want to answer.

'I'm off to bed. You want this on?'

'Why not?'

Warren hitched his pyjama pants and was gone. Trevor was left with no excuse. 'One's fucked up his leg,' he replied, to the empty room. 'The other one's blind.' And then he cried, dropped to the ground and drew himself into his usual tight ball. Five, ten minutes. The storm of tears receding and overtaking him. Fence posts; distance markers; describing his journey towards darkness.

'Mr Wilkie?'

It was a doctor, but not the reassuring, tweed-jacket, John Mills type. A young Indian in jeans and sandshoes.

'Yes,' Trevor said, realising there was no escape from this room. He sat up, took a deep breath and looked at the doctor who, having put on his solemn face, sat opposite him. 'You have been in a motor vehicle accident?' he asked.

'Yes.'

There was silence; nothing, except a strangely out-of-place chase sequence.

Part Two

2005

Part Two

9

It had been a moderate summer. There'd only been a few days when they'd had to retreat indoors, switching on the backup generator, re-watching movies, staying out of each other's way. January had rolled towards its conclusion; the two month anniversary had come and gone (like some stranger waiting on their doorstep, never knocking). Then, a storm had arrived. Low, grey clouds spread across Bundeena. Sand had blown around the compound, filling the empty jars and bottles that had fallen from Harry's tree. Trevor had picked them up, once, twice, but had decided to leave the rest for now; he'd wait until Harry came home.

The muster crew's hut had filled with sand again. Chris had asked Trevor if he should sweep it out, but he'd just shrugged and said, 'If you feel like it.' Murray had overheard them and taken Chris and a couple of brooms and swept it out anyway. Chris had been surprised at how easy-going, how helpful his uncle had been. Something had changed.

Chris knew the old man had liked Carelyn. He'd often help her. More than Trevor, who was his son, which made it different. Fathers and sons had to be at odds, he guessed. Which perhaps was why Murray didn't like him. Maybe he'd become his son, somehow.

Fay and Chris had worked on the veggies and tended the chooks through this first part of summer. To Fay, it was important that when Harry returned everything was normal. He would want to come out and fill his tin with grain and sprinkle it; he would want to collect eggs and, she thought, it might be good for a laugh if he dropped a few, and said something like shit or fuck, looking at her apologetically, and of course she'd say (she could hear herself now), 'Not to worry, Harry.'

She'd often think about her grand-nephew. How she loved him. More (she felt) since she'd visited him at the Children's Hospital; since she'd seen him, sitting up in bed eating ice-cream and jelly; since she'd heard him say, 'It's already better, Aunty Fay. They reckon I'll be back on my bike by September.'

At which point Aiden had just looked at him. 'Highly unlikely, dickbrain.'

Aiden hadn't forgotten his brother. He'd cleaned and oiled his bike; emailed his teachers and friends with regular updates ('Yes, unfortunately, he is just as annoying as ever'); given him his spare mattress so he wouldn't have trouble getting in and out of bed; bought posters and put them up around the room.

He, like Fay, and all of them, had realised how much he missed Harry. After Aiden's own week in hospital, and after the bandages had come off, the first thing he'd said to Murray (who'd been left in Port Augusta) was, 'What time's the bus for Adelaide tomorrow?'

Carelyn was gone, and he'd spent most of the days since in agony, with a sore jaw from trying to stop himself crying. But now, he sensed, his thoughts should turn to the living.

'Bill Clarke's comin' to drive us home,' Murray had explained, but Aiden was having none of that. 'Can he drive us to Adelaide, or should we get the bus?'

So he'd caught the bus, or been driven to town by Trevor, every week over those first two months of holidays. He'd slept beside his father in his brother's room on a couch they made up every night. He'd spent his holidays telling his brother to get off his arse and hobble down to the cafeteria with him; to walk across to the gardens; to keep on with his physio, despite feeling like he didn't care about anything anymore.

Trevor – his thoughts split between house, farm and black-dog hours spent sitting on a shitty public toilet (until the cleaner moved him on) – had been there for the first two weeks. He'd watched the nurses remove his son's cast, adjust the metal pins, clean his skin, treat an infection and try to humour him. Helped him with his pain, and he'd cleaned his arse. Grown close, so that they were really just the same being. Washed him and dressed him and read to him, and played games that bored him shitless. Dealt with the voices telling him he'd had enough.

And later, he'd helped him with exercises; two, three, four times a day, telling him the more he did the faster he'd be home.

After Christmas and New Year he'd realised how much needed doing back at Bundeena. So he'd asked him if he minded if Murray came to stay.

'I suppose,' he'd agreed.

Murray, with his unsmokable cigarettes and transistor, had set up on the couch. At first Harry wasn't happy. 'Pop, can we play Scrabble?'

'No.'

'Pop, they got *Mad Max* on tonight.'

'Well … you go.'

Then Murray would disappear for hours at a time, sitting on a bench just beyond the yellow line at the entrance, chugging away, making friends with every stray father and uncle he could find. Anything was better than *that* room, trapping him all day, every day (mostly). Just because his son hadn't taken out the roo. He couldn't stand the antiseptic smell, the nurses' fake smiles, the small servings of lean beef and mixed veg. The walls, closing in on him. 'Harry, I'm just off for a smoke.'

'But, Pop, I got physio in a minute.'

'The nurse can take you. That's what she gets paid for.'

Harry felt like a chunk of his world had been surgically removed:

the bottle tree, his whip and trail bike. Even his responsibilities: vacuuming his room, making sure his homework was packaged and addressed ready to be sent off to SOTA. And his rewards: building jumps with Aiden, helping his mum spoon mixture into patties. This is why he was lost – lying staring up at the ceiling of square tiles; watching, but not watching, the plasma in the television room. Looking at Murray and thinking, What have you got to say? What are we going to do?

Even the afternoon of his mother's funeral, as he sat trussed up in bed, reaching out through the air, the walls, the city, the hills, along the hundreds of kilometres of railway track. 'What time does it start?' he'd asked Murray.

'Two.'

As he'd looked at his grandfather, and asked with his eyes, Will it be better afterwards? Murray's face replying, Not necessarily.

Back at Bundeena, Aiden had retreated to the shed. To Fay's old Holden, its windows sitting loose in their slots, a heavy green tarpaulin pulled back to reveal an unfinished artwork along the body of the car: a house and a field of purple lavender; a bottle tree; a yelping dog; and a herd of stick-legged cattle wandering across the bonnet. There were people too: round-headed, big-bodied; a mum and dad, boys, an old man, a woman, a blur of paint disappearing into the wheel well.

Chris was drawing more flowers – hibiscus, and lavender.

'Not too small,' Aiden said to him.

Chris knew how they could paint them: olive-green stems, the florets, the small serrated leaves. His hand made long, flowing lines as his head tipped from side-to-side to follow his own music. 'It's quiet now.'

Aiden said, 'Well, it's gonna be, isn't it?' He wondered how much Chris really understood. 'She's not coming home.' Dipping his brush, starting on a rose with a stem the size of a gum tree.

'No one says much anymore,' Chris continued.

'I do. Dad does. Pop's always grumbling.'

But Chris was thinking about it differently: how they used to form groups and laugh or discuss cattle prices; how there was always a buzz; how Carelyn always seemed to be the centre of everything: cooking, SOTA, arguing with Murray, keeping the boys in line. He wondered who would do these things now; who would make Aiden polish his boots, remind Trevor about air filters and ordering diesel; who'd make Murray take his cigarettes outside. 'We need someone to take over,' he said.

'Take over what?'

'The house.'

Aiden scraped the bottom of the tin for the last of the paint.

'Someone to take Mum's job?'

'Yes.'

'Who's gonna do that?'

Chris stopped to think. 'Maybe it should be you.'

'I've got school.'

'Maybe you should quit.'

'I'm not allowed to.'

Aiden dropped his brush into the empty tin, placed it on the bench and wiped his hands on an old singlet. 'That's the last of it,' he said.

Chris stopped half-way through a flower. 'Should we buy some more?'

Aiden couldn't answer. There'd been enough in the car to finish the mural. 'We should,' he replied. 'Perhaps we can ask Dad.'

Chris couldn't see the point of drawing stems and leaves no one would ever paint. 'I can pay for it.'

'How much you got?'

'Two hundred and ... fifteen dollars.'

Aiden smiled. 'Well, if you'd like. You could choose the colours.'

Chris thought again. 'No, we gotta keep it the same.' He stood, gathered the empty cans and said, 'I'll write down the names.' Then he turned and walked from the shed. Threw the brush back at Aiden. 'Aren't you gonna clean it?'

'Yes,' Aiden replied, holding the brush, studying it.

It was khaki. He could still see it, dissolving in his eyes; the following few days, on his face; even a week later when the dressings were removed. A translucent green, filtering every object he saw in his room, as his new roommate (a tyre-fitter named Sterry) said, 'Good as new, eh?'

'Sort of.'

'Still not clear?' the specialist had asked.

'Clear enough.'

The doctor had looked at Trevor. 'It'll fade over the next few weeks.'

Aiden hadn't been too concerned. He was studying his good pants and jacket, lying across his bed. He'd looked at his father and asked, 'What time does it start?'

'Two.'

'Do we gotta get there early?'

'I suppose we should.'

Although he really wanted to ask, Do we gotta go at all? Do we have to make a public display of all this? Why? What will it achieve?

Trevor, already in his own suit, had ironed his son's clothes. 'You'll feel better when it's over.'

After everybody's watched us, with false pity, Aiden wanted to say. When they've seen us blubber, and break down.

He looked at the brush, ran the bristles over his hand and threw it across the shed. He wondered why he was bothering. The mural, by necessity, would have to remain unfinished. He picked up the singlet and smeared the fresh paint across the door.

Trevor was standing beside him. 'You okay?'

He looked up without speaking.

'Could you help Fay get tea started?'

Then studied his mural.

'Well?'

'Okay!'

Trevor stood his ground. 'There's only one of me,' he said.

'I know.'

'You know that Chris is next to useless.' He reminded him of the day he'd asked Chris to hang out washing and found him, an hour later, carving flowers out of cheese slices, sticking them onto windows and watching them melt and peel off. He turned and walked away, stopped and looked back. 'Come on then.'

'I'm coming.'

'You got the shits on?'

Aiden just stared at him, thinking, You are the reason. You.

'Well?' Trevor asked.

He dropped his head into his hands. 'Fuck off,' he whispered.

'What?'

Don't make me say it, he thought.

But Trevor was gone, into his ute, throwing up gravel and dust as he disappeared down the hill.

'Fuck!' He stood, kicked the side panel of the car, two, three times and stared at it. Some of the paint had flaked off but the scene was mostly intact, remade with new hills and valleys. He kicked it again, this time on the passenger door. 'Fuck you!' he shouted.

He walked to the front of the shed, sat on his trail bike and started it. Then he revved the engine and drove off, almost immediately at full speed. Fay came out of the house, calling something to him.

He rode down the hill onto the main bore run. Then, travelling on the verge, opened his throttle and shot across the desert. He squinted, but there was no wind, no sand. He knew there wasn't any danger; knew he'd be fine. Accidents only happened to the old, and soft, and stupid. He leaned forward and, for the first time in months, felt good. Angry-good. Dropping his head he worked the throttle and rode the bumps and clumps of bluegrass gently in his saddle. The horizon kept receding, as he hoped it would. There was no limit to this world, to its sand and gidgee trees, its bushes and dried bores. It just accepted him as he went further, but no further, into it. It had no life, no death, no love; no under-standing and no forgiveness; it had nothing; no morals, values, compassion. It didn't like him, it didn't hate him; it refused to know anyone or anything.

He saw a few kangaroos and set off into the grass, chasing them. They fled then stopped and looked back at him. He kept moving. Full throttle. They jumped away. He closed on them. They stopped. He kept moving. They started again, but he was up to them.

There was a single juvenile at the back, by itself. As he caught up to it he kicked it in the back of the head and it tumbled. He stopped, turned and went back to it. The other roos stood watching. 'Fuck off,' he shouted. He got off his bike, killed the engine and let it fall into the sand.

The juvenile had just got to its feet, but he kicked it in the head again and it fell over. He stood watching, detached, unaffected by the animal's plight. It kicked its legs, making a long, deep arc in the sand, unable to stand up.

He took a deep breath, found his knife in his pocket and opened it. Then he knelt down beside the animal, grabbed its scrotum and cut into it. The roo struggled and made a series of low, guttural moans. Only wanting to finish the job, he castrated it, stood up and threw the warm, bloodied sac onto its body.

He waited for a moment, satisfied. Saw it bleed from the wound, and noticed how the sand welcomed the blood. How it stopped moving, mostly. Breathed deeply; seemed to be asleep.

He looked at the other roos. 'Well?'

They turned and hopped off, occasionally stopping to look back.

He saw that the animal was still moving, but didn't care.

Harry, sitting in bed, sick of his own thoughts, looked down the hallway. 'Pop,' he called, but there was no response. Picking up his phone, he messaged him: *Pop where r u?*

Send; and received, by Murray, sitting across the road in the Cathedral Hotel. He read the message and muttered, 'Christ,' thinking how it hadn't been more than an hour, wondering why Harry couldn't entertain himself for such a short time; draining his schooner, wiping his mouth and saying to his newest mates, 'Gotta get back.'

'The boy?'

'Yes, the boy.'

Meanwhile, Harry was busy with his usual Friday visitors: Dr Feelgood and Dr Diamond, clown doctors (or, according to Murray, just clowns). Diamond, with his polka dot bandana, pink hair and Groucho Marx nose/glasses combination, playing his ukulele, attempting a Tiny Tim falsetto; all fluorescent wig and exploding bow-tie, improvising a hornpipe that started at the door and finished at the window.

Harry tried to smile. He thought they needed his approval and encouragement. Felt himself laughing, but then thinking, Go away.

Diamond used a tube and a wand to blow bubbles. 'Harry, do you know what I hate most about hospitals?'

'No.'

'All those blocked passages.'

There were balloons, blown up and twisted into a dachshund which, at least, was an improvement on last week's misshapen monkey. After this, Diamond went over to an empty bed beside Harry's and said, 'Well, he seems to have lost a lot of weight.'

'He's as white as a sheet,' Dr Feelgood added.

'I think he's had a nip-and-tuck,' Diamond observed, returning to Harry, taking his wrist and looking at his watch. *'Eins, zwei, drei,'* he began, *'vier, fünf* ... hold on, it's stopped.'

Feelgood raced over to Harry's side. 'Is the patient still alive, Doctor?'

'He's okay, it's my watch.'

Murray walked in, saw the clowns and said, 'Oh, it's you two.'

Diamond looked at him with a spark of recognition. He could remember him from the previous Friday, sitting, falling asleep in the armchair. 'Which one's this?' he asked Feelgood.

'Sneezy,' she replied.

'You sure?'

'Grumpy?'

'I think he likes your card tricks,' Murray grumbled, sitting in his well-worn seat.

Diamond stared at him, momentarily stumped. 'Right.' He took out his cards and sat on the bed beside Harry. Meanwhile, Dr Feelgood lined up a Polaroid. 'Does Sleepy want to join in?' she asked.

'No, Sleepy does not,' Murray replied.

Doctors and patient smiled, Feelgood took the photo, waited for it to dry and wrote the date on it. Then she put it with the other five beside Harry's bed.

Diamond guessed Harry's card.

'I know how you do it,' Harry said.

'Do what?'

'The trick.'

'Uh uh …' Diamond sprayed Harry with water from a plastic sunflower in his lapel. 'It's magic.'

'No, it's not.'

'It is. Don't you believe in magic?'

'I think you're barking up the wrong tree,' Murray said.

'Why's that?' Diamond asked.

'He's just lost his mother in an accident.'

Diamond stared at him.

'The fairies and pixies seem to have deserted us this year, *Doctor.*'

Diamond shrugged. He looked at Harry, smiled, picked up his ukulele and tried again.

I'm like a man demented,

Oh, it is a burning shame …

As Diamond played, Murray studied his grandson's face; he grinned, and Harry grinned back; he rolled his eyes, and Harry nearly smiled.

When Diamond finished, Murray applauded. 'Do you take requests?'

'I only know three songs.'

So, Murray took Diamond's ukulele, strummed an E chord and began.

My wife has run away from me,

And I forget her name …

When he was finished the three of them applauded. Harry said, 'I didn't know you could play, Pop.'

Murray returned the uke. 'I can play,' he said. 'The ukulele, that's idiot-proof.' He smiled at Diamond, squeezing his arm and saying, 'Next week I'll teach you another one, eh?'

10

Chris sat spinning a knife on a placemat. He leaned forward so his chin was only an inch above the table. 'You could get everything in there,' he said to Aiden. 'Choo-choo bars, chocolate frogs ...'

'And food,' Fay added, stirring the bubbling stew.

'Chips,' Chris continued. 'Every flavour.' He stopped to remember, visualise the lollies, washing powder and Gravox lined up on the shelves of the Tea and Sugar, a supply train that once traversed the Nullarbor, stopping at sidings, work camps and one-pub towns. As farmers' wives and their brown-skinned kids waited with their wheelbarrows, eager to fill them with flour and sugar and pork from the butcher's van.

'Sparklers and humbugs,' Chris remembered. 'And the man used to give you peppermint leaves.' He paused to smell them.

'Fuck,' Trevor said, slamming the computer keyboard. 'I've done exactly what it says – costs in one column, deductions in the other – but it won't work it out.'

Aiden stood, approached him, studied the screen and changed a single value. 'Try that.'

Trevor pressed Enter. Smiled. 'That's what I did.'

'Obviously not.' Returning to his seat, tearing a chunk of bread from a loaf and slipping it in his mouth.

They all sat at the table. Fay moved the four bowls into position, leaned over the bread and started slicing. Threw them each a slab. 'They had bread on the Tea and Sugar,' she said, taking her first forkful, 'but it was always as hard as the hobs of hell. Remember, Trevor?'

He looked at her, wiping gravy from his lips. 'Not really. I just remember Mum saying she'd only buy what she really had to.'

'The butcher always had choice cuts,' Fay recalled. 'Nothing fancy, but good for stews and braising. When Carelyn got her crockpot ...'

It'd be far easier if no one mentioned her, Trevor thought. Two months. Surely it's time to get on with things.

'She made a beautiful beef burgundy,' Fay continued.

Aiden looked at the empty chair and wondered why no one had moved it. It wasn't his job, of course, but it looked so lonely, so obvious, so wrong. A chair was no memorial, just a reminder of something, someone, inconveniently lost.

'Remember the Nullarbor Cliffs?' Fay said.

'What?' Trevor.

'That holiday, when the boys were little?'

He wasn't interested; he knew where it would lead.

'We were up on those high cliffs, remember? And I was scared one of the boys would topple over.' She stopped. Nothing but the sound of forks on cheap china; the computer, humming, guarding the columns of numbers that described their lives.

Aiden ate, stopped, looked at his father, turned away, wanting to say, Yes, Dad, you can say it. You can think it.

'And remember, when we saw the whales?'

'I remember that,' Chris said. 'Five or six of them. We watched for hours.'

Aiden could remember. Sitting beside his mother, staring out across the Southern Ocean, indifferent, bored with whales. Saying, 'Do I gotta sleep with Harry tonight?'

'Of course you do.'

'Can't you? Can't I sleep with Dad?'

He could still see her face: soft, covered with fine hairs, a couple of freckles on her cheeks and around her eyes; her pink-tipped ears; two crooked teeth.

'I'll sleep outside,' he'd said to her.

'Fine.'

'He farts.'

'We all fart.'

'Not as much as him – for a four-year-old.'

No, he thought, as he played with his stew, someone should move the chair. Not far, just against the wall, so she's not there every time we eat.

'I remember the tiger snake,' Chris said.

Trevor had finished; he sat staring out of the window.

'That's right,' Fay said. 'Do you remember, Trevor, how you went and got the shovel and took off its head?'

He nodded.

'And you boys,' and she looked at Aiden, 'were screaming, and Carelyn was growling at you. *Stop goin' on like a couple of girls!*'

'Okay,' Trevor said.

'Then Carelyn said she refused to sleep in the tent that night.'

Aiden was watching his father.

'And she slept in the car, remember?'

'Yes,' Trevor managed.

'And when she woke the next morning she was screaming, cos you, wasn't it, Aiden, had laid the dead snake across the windscreen?'

'It was Harry,' Aiden said, still watching his father.

'Yes, and he went and picked it up, and Carelyn was screaming loud enough – '

'Right,' Trevor said, and she stopped.

Chris was still giggling, but he soon worked out that he should be quiet. Then, for a few moments, there was silence.

Fay gathered the plates, took them to the sink and returned with four bowls of chocolate mousse. Aiden kept studying his father, as though he were some not-quite-dead specimen squirming under the lens of a school microscope. Eventually he said, 'What's wrong, Dad?'

Trevor started his mousse. 'Nothing's wrong.'

'They sold this on the Tea and Sugar,' Chris began.

'No, they didn't,' Fay replied, sensing the new mood in the room.

'They did.'

Silence; spoons in bowls.

'We're allowed to talk about her,' Aiden said.

'Who said you couldn't?' Trevor shot back. He worked on his mousse: slowly, methodically, scoop by scoop.

'It wasn't your fault.'

'What?'

'The accident.'

Silence. Chris started licking his bowl. 'Don't be so disgusting,' Trevor thundered.

'It was a kangaroo,' Aiden said.

'So?'

'You seem – '

'Enough!' Trevor stood, pushed his chair in and looked at Aiden. 'You should leave people to themselves.' Before turning and storming out the back door.

Harry sat in his wheelchair, his leg sticking out at an uncomfortable angle. The television flickered flower-people and pots-with-legs scampering across green pasture. Murray was asleep on his couch, his head on his shoulder, his chest rising and falling to the in-sync rhythm of a distant monitor. He had nine cigarettes lined up on the table, the last two rolled from newspaper.

Harry studied him, angrily. He knew the old man was running out of patience. The little things: the hours with his head in a newspaper; the reluctance to make or follow up conversation; the way he'd seek fresh company in the television room.

Even that morning, while he was in physio. He'd worked hard, holding the bars, moving one foot in front of the other; walking back and forth as he sweated and felt his arm muscles aching.

And then he'd sat down.

'Come on,' Murray had said. 'You gotta keep at it.'

'I'm resting.'

'You got all day for that.'

He'd looked at the physio, and she'd turned to Murray and said, 'We gotta take it slowly, Mr Wilkie.' He'd just looked at her, thinking, If we waited for you …

The evenings had become lonely. Murray would make his way to the Cathedral Hotel after the news, settling in for the evening, ringing every few hours to make sure he was okay. One night, after he'd staggered up drunk, he'd woken Harry and said, 'Listen, it might be best if you don't mention this to your father.'

'Why?'

'He's got a lot on his mind.'

He studied the old man's nasal hairs. Disgusting. Why didn't he cut them? This was a hospital, there were scissors everywhere. And what about his ears? The rabbit-fur fluff and glowing yellow wax?

Murray shifted, raised a finger, scratched his nose and drifted back into his musty (Harry thought, if it smelt anything like his clothes) dreamworld.

The smallest things. Once, at the beginning, he'd lay out his meal, open his orange juice and watch him eat. Maybe even help him cut tough meat. Now it was just the girl bringing it in and plonking it down. He wasn't even interested in the leftovers – he was buying his meals at the hotel. He'd wheeled him across to the park, but no more. Now there was just television, the activities' room and, since the start of term, lessons. Two hours every morning: worksheets, corrections in red, colouring (although Harry explained he was too old) and, on the previous Friday, an afternoon in the art room making a collage. So, he thought, why not? Enough was enough. At the rate Murray was spending money on himself he wouldn't miss it anyway.

He manoeuvred his wheelchair around the room. Quietly moving a drip-stand, he brushed past his grandfather's leg. Then, without running over the old man's feet, he approached the fat wallet beside the cigarettes. Opened it and took out a five-dollar note. Replaced the wallet, and set off down the hallway.

'Where you going?' a nurse asked, and he showed her the money. 'Pop said I could get chips, as a treat.'

He glided across the glassed-in walkway between the two main buildings. Arriving at the lifts, he stopped, reached up and pushed the button. He travelled down with a doctor who looked at his leg and asked, 'How did you manage that?'

'It was my first parachute jump,' he said. 'The main chute wouldn't open so I had to use the reserve.'

The doctor looked at him. 'Truly?'

'Truly. It was a rough landing.'

The doors opened. He wheeled himself out. He knew which machine he wanted, and the number: K2. The money-slot sucked in his note but spat it back out. Shit, he thought. Maybe it knows. Maybe Pop's woken, found his wallet, reported the money missing, and maybe the hospital has put out some sort of bulletin. Maybe there are security guards searching for me?

He tried again. The money slid in and stayed there.

K2.

The metal spring twirled and his Crunchie dropped into the pit. He moved closer and got it out. Took the change, found a quiet spot beneath the stairs, across from the florist, away from the gaze of anyone coming or going from the hospital. Then he began, slowly, determined to make every mouthful count.

When he returned to his room, Murray was awake. He wheeled himself in and said, 'Hi, Pop.'

'Where you been?'

'The telly room.'

'They set you any homework?'

'No.'

He checked his hands for chocolate and cleaned his lips with his tongue. 'You goin' to the pub?' he asked.

'Yes,' Murray replied, fixing him in his stare. 'When you give me my change.'

Morning and evening always happened in the distance. Every day was the first day; always had been, always would be. A butter-smudged horizon leaking light onto a land of gorse, and shingles, and bluestone ruins. So that every fold, and exalted valley, welcomed its next dose of day. Flooding wombat holes and filling turkey nests. Heading towards another equinox of sweat-soaked socks. Birds shredding shade in native pines. High, trailing clouds (that made Trevor feel good). No breeze; excellent flying weather. As he offered his head to Fay, and listened for the helicopter.

The extension cord ran from the laundry, under the fly-door into the compound. He sat on an upturned crate, his body covered with a sheet. Fay switched on the clippers and started on his collar-line. He could feel chunks of hair against his skin, dropping onto his shoulders and down his back.

'How much?' she asked.

'Number two ... stubble,' he replied.

Soon she'd done the back of his head, the sides, the front. It felt good. He took a deep breath and tried to smell the morning.

'You got red patches,' she said. 'You need to stop scratching your head.'

'I don't.'

'You do. I see yer.'

He heard the distant chopper and within a few minutes it was on top of them, slowly dropping into the compound. He stood, kicked the crate away and waited as his part-time manager landed. Clumps of hair scattered; Fay's dead petals flew around the compound. He heard Harry's bottles and jars working against each other, and one smashing; the chooks, squawking, as a cloud of dust consumed them. Fay smiled, waved at Bill Clarke and went inside, dragging the extension cord.

Bill touched down and allowed the rotors to slow. Then he motioned to Trevor, who came over and opened the door. 'Wanna cuppa?'

'When we get back.'

Trevor climbed in, settled into his seat and slipped on his headphones. 'How are you?'

'Good ... and you?' They shook hands.

Without looking, Bill slowly pulled the collective and the Robinson lifted into the air. Trevor noticed Chris and Fay watching from the laundry door. He waved but they didn't respond. Fay was shaking her head, as she did every time there was a helicopter.

Bill climbed, banked and said, 'Where do you reckon?'

'West,' Trevor replied, indicating. 'Then we can try an arc ... to the north.'

Bill gained height, selected a course and settled into his seat. 'You been out lookin'?' he asked, although he guessed he would've had other things on his mind.

'Yes, some small herds, but I don't know how spread out they are.'

The census was twice yearly – summer, and before the muster. With the cattle spread so thinly, and distantly, this was the only way to know where the herd had wandered. Trevor opened a map and studied his farm: a million brown dots that indicated nothing; a black cross here and there for a bore; a dotted line for a track; a few contour lines where the land managed something dramatic.

Bill looked over. He used a finger to trace their approximate course. 'How far out, do you reckon?'

Trevor shrugged. 'Thirty, forty kilometres.'

They kept flying, their machine gently pulsing through the air. 'How you been?' Bill managed, looking at him.

Trevor knew what he meant: since the funeral. Since Bill, and his whole team, had arrived at the church in Port Augusta, done up in their best (what passed for) suits. Their hats held across their chests and their faces nicked by blunt razors; dropped shoulders and a look of, I'm not sure what to say.

But trying anyway. 'I don't know, mate. She was … a good person, eh?'

They'd sat through the ceremony, the hymns and a generic homily from a minister who'd been roped in at the last minute. But at the hotel afterwards things had come good. They'd taken off their ties, put an arm around Trevor and said things more simply. 'Fuck, mate, whatever you want, just say, and we'll be there. Right? Just get on the phone. Anything.'

'We just gotta get things back to normal,' he'd replied, and they'd nodded their heads, taking off their jackets and unbuttoning their shirts, one of them sneaking Aiden a beer and saying, 'It might seem hard now, but things will come good.' Asking, 'How's young Harry coping?'

'Good.'

'Yeah? He's a fuckin' marvel on a bike, eh? And you, too, you're a fuckin' marvel.'

Eventually Aiden had started feeling good, aware, for the first time in days, that life might go on.

Moving above the desert, Bill asked, 'How's Harry's leg?'

'He's hobbling around.' Noticing a few cattle and writing a 2 at their approximate location on the map.

'So, we gonna get him back on the bike?'

'Of course. Young bones heal quick. That's what they said.'

Bill looked at him, trying to work out if he believed this or if he was reciting some sort of prayer. 'He's a tough little bastard,' he said. 'Although ... the leg might not be the problem.'

Trevor saw another bunch. 6. 'What do you mean?'

'You know ... emotional issues.'

'He'll be okay.'

Bill wasn't so sure. 'Just gotta keep an eye on him, eh?'

'Na ...'

4, Trevor wrote, as they flew over a dry waterhole. 'Should we start heading north?' he asked.

Bill banked, slowly. 'What about you?'

'What about me?'

'How you goin'?'

Trevor looked at him and shrugged. 'She's dead. What can I do? I've got a bloody farm to run.' He looked into the distance and saw a big group of animals. 'Hold up.'

Bill flew around them as he counted.

27.

Resuming the journey, Bill said, 'You should come into town more often.'

'Why?'

'You know, stuck out here: kids, Fay and Chris. Sometimes it's good to have some ... adult company.'

7.

'I haven't got time.'

'You gotta make time. Alcohol, that's the key.' He smiled.

'It'll be hard, when Aiden's at school – having to leave Harry with Fay and Chris.'

Bill pointed out another group. 'It's the isolation that gets people,' he said. 'You gotta make an effort, old man.'

They kept on for another ten minutes but there were no more cattle, around here at least. As the conversation stalled, Trevor descended into the landscape. The Mitchell grass had thickened and he felt he might drop from this machine, this loud thing-of-dials-and-flickering-green-numbers, this airborne dialysis ward, into the bed of soft vegetation.

'Over there,' Bill said, indicating.

3.

Or perhaps it could end more suddenly. All he needed to do was take the cyclic, push it forward, hold it down. Bill would fight him, perhaps, but at this height it wouldn't make any difference. The nose would drop, they'd tumble from the sky. There'd be a loud shattering and twisting of metal and perhaps the fuel would leak and ignite. But then it would all be over: a little mess, two dead bodies, and no more worry.

4.

'Sandra often mentions her,' Bill began.

'Who?' Trevor asked.

'Carelyn. There's a book of photos of them together. Like the time they went shopping in Melbourne.'

Trevor stopped to remember; the trip to town; the over-priced airport parking; the girls laughing, sucking on miniature bottles of brandy as they lined up to board the plane.

'She said when yer in town next, she'll cook yers a roast.'

Trevor could see them, giggling, as they walked the length of the aerobridge.

'That'd be nice.'

'She was upset she didn't get a chance to speak to you at the funeral.'

Trevor couldn't remember whether he'd seen her or not. 'They gave the credit card a workout that weekend,' he said.

'Eight?'

'Yes.'

As he descended, again, into a landscape of lost cattle.

11

It was time. The doctor called on a Thursday night and the following morning Aiden and Trevor were packing the car, checking the tyres, wrapping Fay's sandwiches in plastic and planning what they'd say to Harry.

'He'll be a hobbler for another few weeks,' the doctor had explained, 'but then he should be able to go solo.'

Father and son set off into an already warm morning. Fay was standing in her nightie at the back door, making them promise to drive carefully, to bring her little boy home safe. Chris was busy squeezing a handful of tissues, wiping his nose, squeezing again, as Fay picked the white fluff from his lips and nostrils.

Trevor guided his new car along the dirt road towards the highway. He slowed, riding the corrugations, and drove into the bush to get around a puddle. Then he sped up and coasted down the hill, watching the purple road grow closer, seeing in it (for the first time) a new beginning. 'So,' he said to his son, as he quickened through the soft sand, 'the four nucleic bases?'

Aiden looked at him. 'Not now.'

'Yes, now. There's never a good time, is there?'

It was only a week until school returned. Trevor had received and paid for the book list. On their last trip to town he'd stopped at the uniform shop and bought the Year Twelve blazer and a new pair of pants. He'd signed off on his son's five subjects; planned the day and time he'd return him to his glassed-in room. He'd said to him, 'This is gonna be a good year,' and Aiden had replied, 'That's yet to be seen.'

Now, sitting next to him, he guessed it was time to start getting serious. 'Come on.'

'Adenine.'

He slowed, stopped and looked both ways. 'All clear,' he said, and half-asked his son, confirming there wouldn't be another mistake.

'All clear,' Aiden dutifully replied.

He pulled onto the highway and accelerated. Soon they were cruising at a hundred. He was sitting up, head erect, windows open. Eyes welded to the road. When he couldn't see over a hill or around a bend he'd slow, almost stopping, as Aiden said, 'There's no point being paranoid.'

'I'm not.'

The car jumped across road grates and passed the remains of truck-struck cattle. 'The other two?'

'Cytosine.'

'And?'

Aiden shook his head. 'I don't know. What's it matter?'

'Thirty weeks, then you can do what you want.'

'Why can't I do it now?'

'You'll regret it.'

They passed a B-triple carrying prime movers and Trevor gripped the wheel. He wondered why he'd lost control. It was all so simple: accelerate, steer, indicate, turn ... stay awake. There was only one road, and all you had to do was keep left.

'You need me now,' Aiden continued, still looking out.

'I'll get by.'

'Who'll run the house? Who'll help Harry?'

'We'll work it out.'

As the car just growled.

'Bill's offered more help,' Trevor said. 'He's not going back to the Territory.'

'But he's not there every day, is he? For whatever needs doing.'

'Thirty weeks,' he half-sang.

'I'm not going back.'

'Yes, you are.'

'You can't make me.'

'I can. I've just paid your fees.'

Aiden looked at him. 'I'll pay them back.'

Trevor took his time, but eventually said, 'Thirty weeks.'

'Fuck thirty weeks.'

And as if attempting to avoid the inevitable, he said, 'I'll help you, the whole way. I'm not entirely stupid, you know.'

Trevor was enjoying the ride. Their new Commodore seemed to fly, or at least hover above the road. Inside they were oblivious to the pistons and fan-belt, the changing of gears and rotation of wheels. It was luxury, but not deserved, he guessed. A consolation, but no consolation, really. Still, he couldn't help but enjoy it. With only 3000 kilometres on the clock it promised a replacement future.

For a moment he took his eyes from the road. 'One day you might even thank me.'

Aiden just looked at him.

'What if you lost interest, and drifted away from the farm?'

'What else would I do?'

'That's the whole point. You're not to know ... not at seventeen.'

'So, *you'd* rather be doing something else?'

'Yes, some days I would.'

'Like what?'

Trevor almost shouted in frustration. 'That's what I'm saying. How do I know? I never got the chance.'

'You love the farm.'

'*Some days*. Others ...'

Silence. They passed a roofless cottage, its walls three-quarters buried in sand. 'See, that'll be Bundeena in a hundred years' time,' Trevor said, indicating.

Aiden just shook his head. 'You're the one should be encouraging me to stay on the farm.'

'If that's what you want.'

But Aiden wasn't happy with this. 'Who else is gonna take over? If not me ... and Harry?'

'Well, that'll be it.'

Aiden studied him, caught up in a confusion of matrices, meiotic division, the causes of the Russian Revolution in 1000 words. Why was he talking this way? Why was he so willing, so eager, to risk losing Bundeena? 'I'm not going back.'

'Yes, you are.'

'You can't make me.'

'I can ... I will.'

Trevor thought of Harry's hand, sitting half-finished on his bench for the last two months. He wanted to get back to it. Could see how it would finally look, each of the little wrinkles and tendons sandpapered into pine, varnished, hung on the wall, a reminder. But now he felt tired. He sat up, shook his head and took a deep breath. Switching on the radio, he said, 'So ... adenine?'

'No.'

'Come on.'

He came up behind a truck but then dropped back, twenty, thirty metres.

'You're not gonna hit it,' Aiden said.

'Leave the driving to me, please.'

Aiden remembered the day they'd picked up their new car from the dealer in Port Augusta. Remembered how carefully Trevor had driven from the lot, waiting for a woman to back out, checking distances between vehicles; indicating for a full thirty seconds before turning; checking, re-checking corners; cruising slowly down suburban streets; parking in empty corners of carparks.

Things had improved, he guessed, but not enough. 'That's why people have accidents,' he said.

'Why?'

'You're too cautious.'

'Rubbish.'

Once, he remembered, on their way home from visiting Harry, his father had pulled over as he approached a B-triple. Aiden had said, 'You're losing your nerve.'

'No, I'm not.'

He was still looking at him. 'You've gotta put it out of your head.'

Trevor approached the truck, checked for oncoming traffic and pulled out. The car growled and flew past the soft-sided trailers, ever-lengthening, refusing to yield. 'He's speeding up,' he said. Soon he was up to the cab, shaking his head at the driver. When they were back in their lane, Aiden said, 'See.'

They stopped at Port Augusta for lunch. Trevor parked in Gladstone Square and they walked to Commercial Road. Fay's sandwiches were deposited in a bin and they found a chicken shop on Tassie Street. Then, as the sun peaked, they sat on a bench on the foreshore and each worked their way through a yiros, shedding yellow lettuce and soft tomato. 'We should make these,' Trevor said, allowing the mess to fall between his legs.

When they'd finished, he stood, put his dripping bag in the bin and said, 'I'll meet you back at the car in twenty minutes.' He searched his pockets for his keys and handed them to Aiden.

'Where you going?'

'Elders.'

'I'll come.'

'No … why don't you find a video for Chris?' He took his wallet and handed him a twenty-dollar note.

'He needs more videos?'

'It shuts him up.'

Aiden took a short cut through a three-lane drive-thru and watched a forklift load pallets of beer onto a truck. Walked along hot footpaths with their stray chips and gummy concrete. There was nothing worth watching at Country Target so he returned to the car, settled in the passenger side, switched on the radio and reclined his seat. Adjusted the rear-vision mirror so he could sit watching the locals pass; big clans of bare-footed, footy-shorted bodies drifting from one shop to the next. He saw an old man pushing a shopping trolley full of bags of cans. Hunched, but determined, leaning into the little bit of wind that tunnelled between the shops and over the dead lawns.

Then there was his father, two blocks away, talking to a brown-haired woman who was wearing some sort of uniform. He sat up, turned around and watched them through the back window. His father spoke, smiled and laughed. He watched as he moved closer to the woman, held her arm and then released it. And laughed again, rolling his head back, stepping forward and whispering something in her ear.

They seemed to say goodbye. Trevor waved at her then turned and headed back up the hill towards the car. The woman watched him go then went back inside the shop. He tried to see what it was. A bank? A chemist? Yes, a chemist. He watched his father approaching, crossing the road, almost skipping along the pavement, moving for an old couple and greeting them.

Trevor got in and looked at him. 'Any luck?'

'Nothing. What about you?'

'Yes, drench … but I'm gonna pick it up on the way back.' He started the car and, without his usual caution, backed onto the road. 'I have this vision of it splitting open, and ruining another car.'

'You worry too much.'

Trevor noticed his expression. 'What's wrong?'

'Who was that woman?'

He drove off, carefully. 'Old friend of your mother's.'

'Who?'

'Gaby ... Sacrow, I think.'

Aiden studied the narrow road ahead. 'How did she know Mum?'

'I don't know ... just knew her, somehow.'

Aiden wasn't happy with this. What would he say next? I was just walking along? I just ran into her?

'I popped in to say hello.'

'Did she come to the funeral?'

'No.'

'Why?'

'How do I know?'

They drove out of town, back to the highway. Trevor was silent, caught up in his own thoughts. Aiden was reading him; through the words he didn't speak, the way he held the wheel, the number of times he searched for a station on the radio.

Gaby, he thought to himself. He'd never heard of a Gaby. 'She works at the chemist?'

'Yes. Were you watching me?'

He shrugged. 'Maybe she didn't know.'

'What?'

'About the accident.'

Trevor shook his head. 'She found out later.'

It was a long drive to town. Beyond the gulf, as they headed south, the vegetation changed to eucalyptus, shelter-belt wattles and rest-stops littered with melaleuca and fresh nappies cooking in the sun. There were plenty of skid marks and shredded tyres, reduced to their steel belt. A few wrecks, left in the scrub, over-grown with sheoaks. There were fatality markers, too – black with a red cross. Although they hadn't placed one, yet, at the site of their accident, Trevor guessed it was just a matter of time. Before some arsehole decided to rub their nose in it.

He kept his eyes on the road.

Aiden was looking at his face. 'I suppose it'll be good to have Shit-head back,' he said.

'Yes.'

'He does have his uses.'

'How's that?'

But Aiden didn't know.

They crossed the road and started walking towards the centre of the park. There were several boys in wheelchairs, one in his hospital gown. Another had his legs covered by a rug, his feet protruding. The walking wounded: a dozen or so boys and girls, one with only a few strands of hair, a broken arm, a gauze-covered face and neck. There were a few nurses, talking, laughing, one with a cigarette, joking with Murray as he dragged his feet across the lawn. A doctor wore a stethoscope as a sign of authority. Trevor and Aiden cracked jokes with a six-year-old from Penola who'd crushed two vertebrae in a riding accident. And out front, struggling through the thick grass: Harry.

'You okay, Harry?' one of the nurses called, but he ignored her, unwilling to be the cripple any more.

They arrived in the middle of the park. Harry stood beside a big stone with a brass plaque commemorating a child who'd spent his entire life in and out of hospital. He'd already read it, weeks earlier, when he'd been pushed here by Murray; left in the sun as the old man retreated to a bench, and a cigarette. And when he'd asked, Murray had said, 'It'll do you good.'

'Why?'

'It just will.'

Harry showed his friends and carers where to stand. They did as they were told and one of the nurses took out her phone, ready to film him.

'Okay.' He let out his whip. 'It might scare the little ones,' he explained, and one of the boys replied, 'I've heard one before.'

Harry looked forward and grasped the whip, just as Murray had shown him. For the last several months he'd been telling his new friends about his farm, his animals, adventures along the bore run, trail-bike races with his brother; his virtual school, his chooks, his mental dog, and his whip. In the end, he felt, he needed a demonstration of his outback idyll; something to bring the sounds and smells of the desert to ward 5B. He'd held them in awe, these city kids, but now he needed to prove himself.

He took a deep breath. In one quick movement he lifted and flicked his hand. Crack! He turned, smiling, to the group. Again. Crack! A chorus of voices mumbled in admiration. 'You see, you've just gotta send it forward, but then pull it back on itself,' he said, showing them. 'Neat, eh?'

At last he felt vindicated: farm boy in the Park Lands. 'I have this tree with lots of bottles hanging on it,' he said, 'and I try to break them, don't I, Dad?' He looked at Trevor.

'Yes, lots of mess to clean up.'

The cracks continued ringing across the park. Soon there was a small crowd, stray children, and a team of council workers. The nurse with the phone came closer. 'Once more, from this angle.'

Crack!

Then one of the boys ran up to him. 'Can I have a go?'

'I don't know …'

'It's dangerous if you don't know what you're doing,' one of the nurses warned.

'He's okay,' the boy's mother replied.

'Well, if he wants,' Trevor said, looking at the mother.

Harry showed him how to do it. The boy tried but the whip just snaked around on the grass. Soon all of the kids were having a go but none of them managed a crack. Still, there were phones and photos, and everyone got to look the part. Harry was left with the feeling that this was *his* specialty.

The novelty wore off and the group started crumbling – wheeling, limping and even running back across the park towards the hospital. Soon the Wilkies were alone. Harry gathered his whip. Aiden placed his hand on his shoulder. 'Let's see them beat that,' he said.

They walked back across the grass. Murray lit up a half-finished cigarette.

They gathered the three bags of Harry's and Murray's gear and said goodbye to the staff. Trevor had bought a box of chocolates and distributed them to anyone in uniform (including the ward clerk, and a cleaner who'd once helped him with one of Harry's accidents), shaking hands, kissing cheeks, saying things like, 'This has meant a lot to us,' and, 'Harry won't soon forget.' Although, of course, that's exactly what he wanted to do.

As they walked from the ward, one of the nurses handed Murray a new ukulele, its price tag still attached. 'I almost forgot,' she said. 'Doctor Diamond left this for you, Murray.'

Surprised, Murray took the instrument. A note had been threaded through the four strings: 'Dear Grumpy. So you can come up with your own act. Yours, Ted H. (aka Dr Diamond).'

'He was looking for you yesterday,' the nurse said, 'but I think you were at the Cathedral.'

Trevor looked at his father. 'The cathedral?'

'No, not that one.' He walked on, unwilling to explain, taken by the only real gift he'd had in years.

Ten minutes later, Trevor was reversing from the spot in the carpark he'd been in and out of since the first few days; his hands trembling on the wheel, visions of flesh and bone and the small metal rods that had held his son's leg in place. He moved back, straightened the car, and a ute came around the corner, closing on him. The driver braked and held down his horn. Trevor put down his window, put up his finger and said, 'Fuck you.'

Aiden, sitting in the back beside Murray, smiled. 'Nice work, Dad.'

'What a prick. What's the limit in here? Ten, twenty?'

Soon they were on city roads. Trevor was still driving slowly, over-indicating, waiting for anything that looked like a pedestrian. When they were on a clear stretch he asked his son, 'How does it feel to be going home?'

'Great,' Harry replied. 'Although it wasn't all bad.'

Silence; late braking; the radio avoided, for now. Then Harry said, 'So, you got a surprise party planned for me?'

Aiden laughed. 'Yeah, the surprise is, you move out into the shed and I get my own room.'

But they all knew Harry was a good guesser; was probably aware that Fay had hung streamers and balloons; Chris had made a 'Welcome Home' poster; that there was chicken, hot dogs, chips, Coke, and chocolate. '*I* should get my own room,' Harry said. 'I'm the cripple.'

'You're not a cripple,' Trevor growled.

'Injured.'

Harry looked at his brother. '*You* should be in the shed.' And then at Murray. 'He can move in with you, can't he, Pop?'

'No bloody way,' as the old man finished tuning the ukulele, and started singing, '*Tell me, darling, that you love me, While the moon is shining bright …*'

'Very good,' Trevor said, 'but I don't want to have another accident.'

'I've got my L plates,' Aiden said, leaning forward.

'Not in town.'

'Come on?'

'No.'

'I just want to get home in one piece,' Harry added.

'You're lucky I gotta be nice to you,' Aiden replied.

'No, you don't.'

'I've been told.' He looked at his father. 'What if we find a back street?'

'No.'

'Why today?' Harry asked.

Aiden looked at his brother, but stopped himself.

'Didn't you come to bring me home?'

Aiden shook his head. You weren't the only one in the accident, he wanted to say.

They all sank into their seats. Murray played one final chord, just to make it known he wouldn't be told. They travelled in silence for a few minutes. Trevor provided a critique of the local drivers. 'That's it, don't indicate, I can read your mind.' Then, glaring at the driver of a van in the rear-vision mirror: 'Nice work. Could you get any closer?'

'Hey, Harry,' Aiden said. 'Dad's agreed to let me leave school and become your full-time tutor.'

Harry looked at his dad.

'He's bullshitting,' Trevor said.

'He said I'd be more use at home,' Aiden continued. 'Helping out ... especially with you hobbling around.'

'I won't be hobbling around much longer.'

'Anyway, that's what's gonna happen, isn't it, Dad?'

'No.' He came to a stop in the middle of the road and turned to his son. 'Do you bloody well mind?'

'What?'

Trevor undid his belt, got out and walked back to the van. 'Are you completely stupid?' they heard him ask the driver.

'Oh, no,' Harry said. He glared at his brother. 'Look what you've done now.'

'What?'

'Dad's pissed off.'

'It's your fault.'

'What did I do?'

The van sped off, almost collecting Trevor. 'Prick!' they heard him call, as he returned to the car.

'Trevor!' Murray growled, although his window was up.

'It's *your* fault,' Harry said to Aiden. 'You could see Dad was stressed.'

'Fuck off.'

'Aiden!' Murray barked.

'He hates city driving,' Harry continued.

'Shit-for-brains. I was having a nice bloody time until ...'

'Should I go back to the hospital?'

Aiden just sat with his arms crossed. Murray shook his head. 'You need to grow up. Don't you think your father might need a bit of – ' He stopped, as Trevor climbed in and put on his belt.

'What a prick,' he said, starting off, as a few angry drivers sounded horns and drove around him.

Aiden knew what his grandfather was about to say. Help. Understanding. Cooperation. And a little less silliness.

Trevor glared back at Aiden.

'What?' the older boy asked.

'Thanks.'

'Sorry. I was only kidding.'

'You need to ...'

'Sorry.'

Murray placed his ukulele on the floor. It would be a long trip home.

.

12

The following morning Harry was already at work. Out in the lavender patch. *Lavandula angustifolia*, *spica*, *dentata*, purple flowers plucked from their stems, thrown into buckets hiding between rows. Chris had fetched him a chair and set it out close to the plants so, according to his wishes, he could make himself useful. He leaned forward, harvested and launched each of the flowers in a perfect parabola he'd practised throwing a tennis ball into a bin in the corner of his hospital room. Murray had kept saying, 'Enough,' and he'd replied, 'What else am I meant to do?'

'Read a book.'

He'd looked at the pile beside his bed. 'I'm bored.'

Harry smelt his fingers. Lavender was okay. It was better than the stink of Betadine and the antiseptic they used around his room; the smell of Dr Diamond, with his wet underarms, or cabbage floating across his plate. Lavender was Aunty Fay, tisane, furniture polish, potpourri and scented water sprayed in the toilet after one of Murray's sessions. 'How much does she want?' he asked.

Chris stopped to think. 'All the buckets.'

'All of them?'

Chris was bent over, caught up in the task. Harry could see confetti on his scalp, stained by the poppy oil Fay combed into his hair every morning. 'That was a nice party,' he said, but there was no response.

It had already been cleared. Fay, up at six o' clock with her old Hoover, vacuuming the rugs and carpet, tearing down streamers and removing cards from lengths of tinsel. And, of course, Deepest

Sympathies, and all the other rose and carnations spreading their cursive grief across book shelves and venetian blinds.

Fay was always the efficient one. The casserole dishes and oven trays put away, the beer returned to the drinks' fridge, the flat dregs of Coke and Fanta tipped down the sink. There was no point drawing it out – they'd had their celebration – now they just had to get on with things: white sauce for the silverside, the boys back to their old routines, churchy-silence during the news headlines.

It had been a good party. Confetti, as Harry came through the door, Chris playing the *Mastersingers* overture, Fay dutifully presenting her cheek for kissing, Harry ushered to the table, a party hat slipped onto his head, bon-bons left over from Christmas, and lids lifted from steaming bowls of chicken and tuna mornay. Eating, jokes (at his expense), Chris with his fists clenched and then, inevitably, silent gaps.

'It's good to be home, I bet?' Fay had asked.

'Of course,' Harry had replied.

'I've made up your bed with new sheets, straight from the pack.'

'Thanks.'

'No point thankin' me. You've just gotta get better. Get that thing off your leg.' She'd looked at his cast.

'Not much longer,' he'd replied, but she'd just stared at it, as if it were something she couldn't understand.

'It doesn't hurt,' he'd said.

'No?'

Aiden had grinned. 'It's gonna stink when it comes off.'

'You always find the positive,' Trevor had said.

Back outside, Harry smiled at Chris and said, 'I had to wake Aiden up during the night.'

'Why?'

'I had to go to the toilet and couldn't get out of bed. It sinks in the middle. Do you think Dad could put something under it?'

'Yes,' Chris replied. 'I do think Dad could put something under it.'

Harry looked at him. 'He's not your dad.'

'Trevor,' he said.

Harry thought it strange how he'd barely mentioned the accident, and nothing at all about Carelyn. 'It's sad, what happened,' he said.

Chris just kept working.

'Were you sad?'

He dared to look up. Didn't know what to say. She'd gone, and hadn't come home. Like his own father. Sometimes, apparently, people just did this. It was hard to say why. One thing led to another; arguments to unhappiness; anger to weeks in the wilderness. Carelyn wouldn't come back. She was dead. 'I couldn't understand,' he said.

'What?'

He fell silent.

'Anyway, we have to keep going,' Harry said. He grabbed a handful of lavender heads and pulled them from their stems. Then he smelt them and threw them into the dust.

'Not there,' Chris said.

'You can say it,' Harry continued. 'You can say you miss her.'

Chris was biting his lip. Why was Harry going on about it? Why couldn't he just pick the lavender? 'I miss her,' he said, mechanically.

Then Harry leaned forward. 'Wanna know a secret?'

No, Chris thought. No secrets. They always meant trouble. More arguments. More anger. 'Yes,' he made himself say.

Harry took a moment. 'I still speak to Mum.'

'When?'

'At night … in the toilet … when there's no one around.' He

waited for Chris to ask him more, but he didn't. 'I tell her what I've been up to.'

He only stared at him.

'Like, I might say, the surgeon took out the screws and he says my leg's nice and strong. Or, I've finished another Specky Magee.' He sat back and continued picking. 'Anyway, it's not like I'm … praying,' he said. 'I don't believe in all that. It's just like she's listening … in case she's listening.'

'She is listening,' Chris replied.

'You think?'

'Yes.'

'I don't believe in Heaven.'

'She might be in Heaven,' Chris said, but this time Harry didn't know what to say. Eventually he managed, 'Maybe it's like that, but Aiden reckons all that Catholic shit they teach him …'

Chris smiled.

'It's all just to keep people …' He couldn't see the point of the thought. Not now, anyway. 'Yesterday on our way home, I asked her if she could help Aiden pass his driving test. But then I thought …'

'What does she say back you?'

'Ah … nothing.' He sighed, slowly dropping his head. 'I wish we hadn't gone to that picnic. If it wasn't for my lessons.' He looked at Chris. 'It was a stupid party anyway.'

'It wasn't because of the party.'

'It was.'

'It could've been – '

'It was! Don't be so stupid, *Christopher*. You shouldn't talk about what you don't understand.'

Silence, as Harry looked down, and immediately felt bad, looked back and said, 'I'm sorry.' Pausing, listening to the morning. 'I say some dumb things now.'

But Chris couldn't understand what the problem was. To try and make things right he said, 'I do miss having Carelyn here.'

'Really?'

'Yes.'

'I wish she was still here, Uncle Chris.' He could feel his eyes well up and he wiped them with his lavender fingers.

Chris wasn't sure how to react. So, he took a full bucket inside and returned with it, empty. He knelt down on his cushion and recommenced the harvest.

'I bet it was good without Murray,' Harry said to him.

Chris didn't look up. That was only inviting trouble.

'He was painful,' Harry continued. 'Can you imagine, all those weeks, in the same room?'

Chris giggled. His shoulders jumped about.

'He'd take off his socks and cut his toenails and gather all the scraps in his hand, like this.' He demonstrated. 'Then he'd just think about it ...' He showed how Murray threw the clippings over his shoulder. Chris was laughing, his eyes squeezed shut. Harry sat forward in his chair, half-remembering, half-inventing. 'He has these corns, like lumps of dead skin on his feet. So he gets out this little grate thing and starts to sand them, right beside my bed, and when he's finished he just blows all the dead skin away and it goes over my sheets and the floor and when you get up you walk through it all.'

Chris put his head back, still laughing.

'And the cigarettes. He'd just sit there, fiddling with them for hours, and spitting on them, and you could smell his spit. Man, you were so lucky.'

'It was nice and peaceful,' Chris agreed.

'I bet it was. He'd come back to my room smelling of beer and crawl into bed, and fart all night.' He blew a few raspberries on his arm for good effect.

Chris fell to the ground, laughing. Harry just watched him. It felt good to be home. 'And the worst,' he said. 'You know his potato sack undies, and the holes in them? He started wearing them around my room. His singlet and undies!'

Trevor came out and walked into the shed. He started the ute and drove into the compound. Looked at his son and asked, 'Coming?'

'Where?'

'I gotta fix some fences.'

Harry abandoned the lavender, climbed in and they set off. He was surprised to see it was clean – no wire, elastrator rings, tools, no dried-out chicken bones. It had even been vacuumed. 'What happened in here?'

'Fay,' Trevor replied. But it hadn't been Fay. It had been him, on a lonely day without his son, moping around the house, finding something to do and willing himself to do it. 'How are you feeling this morning?' he asked, as they drove along the bore run.

'Fine.'

'Any pain?'

'Not really.'

'Cos the doctor told me what combinations, how much, how often.' His eyes searched the land and all of its disappearing fences. 'He said it was important to stay on top of it. He said you might try and … ignore it.'

'No pain at all,' Harry replied. He moved his leg about, to demonstrate.

'He said he can send it through the mail, or – '

'Dad.'

They drove silently. Harry savoured every oomph of the shock absorbers, the rattle of the strainer in the tray, the clunk of the post-hole digger; the hiss of the radio, minus its signal, always switched on, hopeful, waiting.

'And your exercises,' Trevor continued. 'He said you'd know what to do, and show me.'

'I will.'

'Half an hour, three times a day?'

'I know … I'm not a cripple.'

'I never said you were.'

'Like you think …' He stared at him.

'What?' Trevor asked, as he veered into the sand, but then gunned his way out of it.

Like you feel guilty, Harry thought. 'Like you think you've gotta fix everything,' he said.

'I just want to …'

'You don't have to do anything. I can look after myself.'

Trevor looked at his son; his forehead, with a long scar; the dozen or so freckles beneath his eyes, fading, still, as they had been since he was a baby; his cracked lips; a partly yellow incisor.

There's no point saying sorry, Harry thought. I've worked out I can't get her back. 'It wasn't your fault,' he said.

'Well, perhaps.' But he didn't see the point of taking it any further. 'Hold on.' They shot off into the bush. The ute jumped, dropped, slid down an embankment and stopped. Trevor was out, running towards a steer that was caught in the fence. He looked back. 'Careful,' he said.

The animal was all rib and hip, a well-muscled rump and legs. Its head was caught between four lengths of wire and a run of rusty barbs that cut into the back of its neck. 'Careful,' Trevor warned, watching it kick, imagining a hoof contacting his son's skull.

Harry managed to come around, to stand beside it. He studied how the four wires had wrapped around its neck. He saw how they were twisted and how they might be undone. 'If you could hold his head.'

'No,' Trevor replied. 'I'll cut the wires.'

'No, it's easy.' He moved forward and started pulling the wires.

'Harry!' Trevor growled, but he was already halfway there. 'Hold his head, Dad.'

Trevor stepped forward and put an arm around the steer's head. The animal flailed and the barbs cut deeper into its flesh. Then, as if sensing what the boy was trying to do, it settled. Turned its brown eyes to him. Harry lifted a wire, pulled another out from under and motioned for his dad to let go. The steer's mouth and nostrils dripped with milky saliva. It reversed, waited, then turned and ran away.

That night, Aiden was woken by his brother's crying. 'What is it?' he called across the room, and the noise seemed to stop. He got out of bed and sat beside him. 'What's wrong?'

'Nothing,' Harry managed, but Aiden could hear his voice cracking. He lifted the shop-new sheet and crawled in beside him. 'Remember what she used to say?' he whispered.

'What?'

'I'm sick of your sarcastic tone, young man!'

Harry laughed, and sniffed again. Then for a full minute there was nothing. Finally, he said, 'Some nights, in the hospital, I just wished I wouldn't wake up in the morning.'

Aiden took his time. 'Well ...' But he couldn't find words.

'I miss her,' Harry said, and he descended into tears again.

They could hear Murray's tape deck, old music, high violins. And Yanga in the hallway, scratching fleas.

'I didn't even get to say goodbye,' Harry said.

Silence. The iron roof cooling, contracting.

'What were we talking about when it happened?' the small voice asked. 'School certificates? Or had she just asked you a question?' He looked at his brother.

'What's it matter?'

They heard Murray's stretcher moving as he lifted his arse and farted.

Then Harry was laughing. He thumped the wall. 'Fart arse!'

'Get to sleep!'

The balloon had somehow survived from the party. It sat beside Aiden's feet on the floor of the new car. He studied its wrinkles and how it spread across the carpet like a small, overweight arse. He wore polished shoes (Fay), ironed pants and shirt (Harry) and a new watch Carelyn had bought him for Christmas. Placing his foot on the balloon, he gently pushed down.

'What time's it start?' Trevor asked.

'Six.'

'It doesn't matter if we miss it.'

'I'm supposed to go.'

It was the boarders' mass, held at 6 pm every Sunday before the new term. Starchy, oven-warmed religion, held in the red-light, cracked-wall chapel, packed full of mutton-chopped farmers and their big families – mums in summer frocks, little brothers and sisters done up in suits and sandals. Aiden was familiar with the drone of the electric organ, the crackling PA and the smell of old paper from the hymnals. Voices raised in praise, but straining and cracking; mumbled complaints; St Luke cut short for the evening meal.

He pressed down on the balloon; it split open, emptied and sat small and lifeless like a stillborn calf.

'I'll give it a term,' he'd agreed, finally, with his father. Ten weeks. Don't pay any more fees until I say.

Taking this as a good sign, Trevor had agreed.

I'll bring you home every fortnight, he'd told his son, as a sort of peace pipe he'd placed in his hands along with cash, a carton of Coke, chocolates and lollies, the plasma screen from his own room and the box of new text and exercise books.

If I can't handle it I'm gonna tell you, straight off, Aiden had explained.

Fine.

I'm not gonna be made to stay.

Okay ... understood.

Aiden was staring at the balloon. 'I really don't feel comfortable.'

Trevor looked at him. 'Why?'

'I'm nearly eighteen and I'm still wearing this shit.' He indicated, studying the monogram on his shirt, pulling at his knee-length shorts with their precise, Harry-made creases.

'Your brother spent an hour doing that for you,' Trevor said.

'So?'

'You look very smart.'

'We shouldn't have to wear all this, like we're still ten years old.'

Trevor shrugged. 'You're still a student.'

'They should treat us like adults.' His eyes drifted across the familiar landscape. There was a stretch of road, a kilometre, maybe more, where all of the white distance markers had been removed from their holes.

'Remember this?' Trevor asked, indicating.

'Yeah.'

It'd been a late summer afternoon. They were heading home from town. They slowed as they approached a lane of cars and trucks waiting behind a police car with its lights flashing. They got out and joined a small crowd. Further along there was an injured man, his wife and a few others gathered in a protective semi-circle. A police officer, and another man who might have been a doctor or nurse.

'A heart attack,' someone said. 'The Flying Doctor's gonna land on the road.'

Then one of the officers had come over and asked for a volunteer. 'The pilot wants the markers removed,' she explained. So there was Harry and Aiden, running beside the highway, loosening each of the markers and pulling them from the ground as the plane circled overhead. Then, when they'd gone far enough, the officer waved at them and they ran back. The plane lined up, descended, roaring towards the asphalt only metres above their heads, and landed on the too-thin ribbon of grey.

'Remember how you wanted to be a pilot?' Trevor asked.

'I still might.'

'Yeah?' He gave him his you-know-what-I'm-thinking look.

'A chopper pilot, for the farm,' Aiden explained.

'But you were interested in the Flying Doctors.'

Aiden shrugged, as if this might or might not be true.

'So, if you want to be a pilot you gotta study maths.'

'Not necessarily.'

'You do.'

Aiden could still see the pilot – a tall, wide-shouldered man who flew the plane with the same ease he rode his trail bike.

'Doesn't mean you can't try,' Trevor said.

'What?'

'You can't just sit back and not work and then say, Oh no, that was way too hard.'

'Why would I do that?'

Aiden could see his brother, soaked with sweat after he'd pulled his twenty or so markers from the ground. He could remember saying something like, Good effort, Shit-for-brains. 'Have I ever ... stood back?' he asked.

'No.'

'Well?'

Trevor couldn't understand why the markers hadn't been replaced. It wasn't his or his boys' job, surely? 'I can help you with most things,' he said. 'Year Twelve, as I remember, is a hard slog. Lots of late nights.'

'I said I'd give it a go.' And what he wanted to say: You should be grateful. With everything that's happened, I could've just refused. 'As if I wouldn't try,' he said.

Trevor looked at him.

'So, you're assuming I'm going back just to keep you happy?'

Perhaps, Trevor thought, but then said, 'No.'

'I don't really want to dress up like a three-year-old, but I can see that ...'

They passed the site of the accident again. Noticed a black marker, with a red cross painted onto it. 'Fuckin' amazing,' Trevor said. 'It doesn't take them four years to do that.'

Aiden was caught up in his own thoughts. The uniform was too tight, and too itchy. He pulled his undies from his arse and said, 'How far ahead was it?'

'What?'

'The roo.'

There was a long silence. 'How should I know?'

'You can't remember?'

'Twenty metres.'

'And it was definitely a roo?'

'Yes.'

Aiden took his time. 'You shoulda just hit it.'

'I know. I should've.'

'You've hit plenty of others.'

Murray had been left to watch Harry. Instead, he retreated to a seat just outside the laundry. Sat down with his ukulele and started playing, trying to remember rhymes, bawdy and otherwise: a mother and her three chaste daughters, and something about one of them heeding the calls of a randy butcher.

Harry came out of his dad's shed with his whip. He stood in front of the bottle tree and managed to smash half-a-dozen long necks. Then, without turning, he said to his pop: 'Aiden reckons you won't go into that outhouse.'

Murray stopped playing. 'It's not that I won't – it's that I don't need to.'

'He reckons it's because of your granddad.'

Murray waited. 'He does, does he?'

'Yeah. Cos he hung himself in there.'

'*Hanged* himself.' He strummed his ukulele. 'Your brother doesn't know everything, young man.'

'But he did, didn't he?' Harry asked.

'Who? What?'

'Your granddad? He hung himself?'

'*Hanged* … yes.'

'Why?'

'How should I know? I didn't get to ask him.' He started to sing. '*Mrs Hill had three plain-looking daughters …*'

'Your dad must have told you?' Harry said, destroying another bottle. 'I mean, it was his father?'

'He never talked about it, and you don't need to either.'

'He never said?'

'No.'

'What are you scared of?'

'Christ!'

Harry kept working his whip. He felt he'd lost form, and needed to improve.

'*… and they all wore plain-looking clothes.*'

'Do you think his ghost is in there?' Harry asked.

'No, I don't think his ghost is in there.'

'Then why – '

'Listen! There are some things a child doesn't need to know.'

Harry turned to him. 'I just thought it was strange. How you won't go in there. I go in Mum's room. I'm even reading one of her books.'

'You don't understand *why* he killed himself.'

'And you do?'

'Yes … no. Christ, sometimes you can be so bloody annoying.'

Harry shrugged. 'He must have been depressed.'

'No.'

'That's why people hang themselves.'

'There are other reasons.'

Harry stared at him, trying to work it out. 'Did he accidentally kill someone?'

'No.'

'Did his wife leave him?'

'No.'

'Did his child die?'

Murray glared at him.

'That happened a lot back then,' Harry explained. 'Diphtheria? Flu? Remember all those graves at the Moonta Cemetery? Thirty, forty kids every week. And they couldn't dig the holes fast enough.'

'No one had dip-fuckin'-theria,' Murray growled.

'It's just that you're not scared of anything,' Harry said. 'So I guessed there must be a good reason.'

'I just don't want to.'

Harry knew it was all a lie. It was only a room, filled with dust, and old furniture.

They were too late for mass so they waited in the car trying the five or six gristly radio stations, each sounding like a hair dryer. Then Aiden said, 'Should we practice my parking?'

'Here?' Trevor asked.

'I wanna book a test before I come home.'

Trevor found two bins and set them out near the kerb. Moved them apart, but Aiden complained, so he put them back. Aiden climbed into the driver's side, belted up and attempted a reverse parallel park. He entered too sharply and ended up against the gutter. Trevor moved the front bin and he pulled out. 'Forty-five degrees,' he said.

'I know.'

He tried again as Trevor watched, stopped him, moved the bins and refined his lecture. 'Nice and tight, and when you're in, straighten.'

And again. This time his foot slipped and he shot back. He knocked over the rubbish bin, mounted the kerb and clipped a car parked five metres behind. 'Shit,' he said, getting out.

'What happened?' Trevor asked.

'I was barely touching the pedal ... then it just ...'

They examined the damage: a dented front fender, a few crumbling flakes of paint. And on their own car: a barely noticeable scratch. Trevor looked around. 'No one's here.'

'Should we leave a note?'

'How about you put the bins back and I ...?'

'Dad.'

'It's nothing ... they probably won't bother fixing it anyway.'

Trevor studied the carpark, and the front of the chapel, the raised voices venting across a struggling rose garden. As he moved the car, Aiden shifted the bins. Then they walked towards the chapel. 'We could go in and ask for forgiveness,' Trevor said.

Aiden shook his head. 'You're not much of a role model.'

Trevor shrugged. 'Well, I'm the only one you've got.'

13

The weeks passed with only an occasional word from Aiden. Trevor took it as a good sign. There were a few phone calls about cash and mitosis but his tone was calm, considered, so Trevor knew he was on the job. Like, for instance, when they stood around discussing what to do with an animal with a broken leg, before Aiden returned to the ute and fetched the rifle.

Late afternoon, Friday. Trevor was in charge of cooking the roast. Fay had put the meat in the oven before retiring to her room, saying, 'I can feel the start of another headache.'

Earlier, Chris had been in one of his moods. He'd returned to the compound, mouthing Puccini, a not-so-waif-like Mimi moving in rhythm with the breeze and the sheoaks that sang back to him. He'd used his hands, as though it was Tai Chi, and he'd used his lips to suffocate every word. Fay had come out and started shouting at him. 'You're determined to put me in an early grave, aren't you?' She'd taken him by the arm and dragged him back in as Harry, at his computer, watched and grinned.

With Fay in bed, it was down to Trevor again. He'd put on an apron and secured it around his globular belly; taken a knife and started slicing the cabbage; asked Harry to set the table, and Murray to slice the bread.

Yes, the roast would get cooked, but it would all be up to him. No one would volunteer their time or show any initiative. At one point he'd said, 'How about I put my feet up and you lot do this?' No one had replied. 'If I waited, we'd all go hungry, wouldn't we?' But again, nothing.

Murray had managed four slices before stopping; Harry had

set the placemats before sitting down to listen to his grandfather.

'The stranger slept in the sleep-out,' Murray said. 'He told Mary and Bill that he'd served with John, and that John was a good soldier.'

'Did he know what had happened to him?' Harry asked.

'Wait, yer jumpin' the gun,' Murray said. 'The stranger told them John had been fine until this one particular battle. A big push from the Germans – heavy artillery, machine guns laying down a carpet of fire.' He paused to remember, or at least imagine. 'He told them John had just, how would you say, flipped. He told them he'd found a hole and curled up inside, crying and shaking.'

'Harry,' Trevor growled, and he returned to the kitchen, fetched the knives and forks from the drawer and started setting the table. 'Haven't we heard this a hundred times before?' he asked his father.

'The boy wants to know,' Murray said. 'It's *your* family history.' He looked back at his grandson.

'When's tea?' Chris asked, from the couch.

Trevor slammed down his knife. 'When you get off your arse and help.' But this wasn't enough to convince him to venture beyond the guns of Navarone.

Murray managed another slice of bread before laying down the knife. 'So,' he said to Harry, 'the stranger told them John had become a sort of child, not talking, too scared to move about. You know what it was?'

'No,' Harry pretended, although he did.

'Shell shock. His mind had just shut down.'

'*Dad.*'

'Sorry.'

Harry returned to the kitchen and Trevor handed him the peeler. 'That lot,' he said, indicating potatoes in the sink.

There was machine-gun fire and Chris sat up, fisting his hands.

'So,' Murray said, louder, 'to cut a long story short, one morning they woke up and John had gone. Wasn't at roll-call; they couldn't find him around the camp. They looked in town, everywhere, nothing. So they said he was missing – deserted. And that started all the trouble for Bill and Mary.'

'Dad,' Trevor insisted, 'if you've finished, can you butter it and cover it?'

'Calm down.'

'I'm very calm.' He glared at his father. 'If you want to eat some time tonight.'

Murray started buttering. 'Then Mary and Bill got the letter, then the *Argus* published the Cowards' List. They refused to believe he was a coward. When the stranger arrived they latched onto him, and what he was saying. They wanted to believe. They *needed* to believe.'

Trevor looked at the half a potato his son had peeled. 'Can you work any faster?'

'No.'

'Give 'em here.' He took the peeler and started attacking the potatoes.

'I can do them,' Harry said

'I'll do them.'

'What did I do wrong?'

'Nothing. You did nothing wrong.'

Murray didn't care. His story was a chop, and there was still plenty of meat on it. As he continued buttering, he said, 'Mary and Bill complained to the *Argus* but they wouldn't apologise. Said, This is what the army told us. Bill said, Well, the army is wrong. And it went on like that.'

'Butter's too thick,' Trevor warned his father.

'It is not.'

'You'll go through half a tub.'

'So, we'll buy more.' He stared back at him. Then he rewarmed his burley-blended voice. 'No, these were not good days,' he said to Harry. 'Neighbours were talking, shopkeepers ... even at church. So Mary and Bill started taking the stranger places with them. They'd get him to explain, to tell people what had really happened to John.'

Trevor shook his head.

'But it got worse,' Murray continued, to his audience of one. 'John had gone to Mercy, and he'd got his name on the honour roll. Athletics, wasn't it?' he asked his son.

'Yes.'

'One day Bill was talkin' to this fella, and this fella said, Hey, Bill, your boy, they've taken his name off the roll.' He sat back, as if it was the first time he'd told the story. 'What year was it?' he called to Trevor.

'Nineteen eleven.'

'Yep.' He returned to Harry. 'They just scraped it off; you can still see the gap.' He let his words settle, as though Harry might actually be shocked. He finished buttering the bread, covered it with plastic and leaned forward. 'Shame,' he whispered. 'The worst thing that can happen to a family, isn't it?'

Harry shrugged. 'I suppose.'

'Believe me, it is, isn't it, son?' He looked at Trevor.

'If you say so.'

'So, Bill Wilkie wasn't going to live like that. He went to town and demanded a meeting with the principal. Insisted they replace John's name. He took the stranger with him, and got him to explain. Demanded an apology from the school.'

'Did he get one?'

'No.'

'And they refused to replace his name?'

'They believed the army over the stranger. That's what it was like back then. Everyone was very patriotic. If there was even an inkling ...'

Trevor put the potatoes into the pot. He placed it on the stove and lit it. 'I still gotta fill the cars,' he mumbled, mostly to himself.

'I can do them,' Harry said.

'No.'

'He can help me,' Murray added.

Trevor ignored them. He opened the oven door and checked the meat.

'Go, go, go,' Chris chanted, like a machine-pistol, as the giant doors of the fortress closed. 'They're in,' he said, turning.

'Another half-hour,' Trevor said, closing the oven.

'What, I've never filled a ute?' Murray said to his son.

'*I'll* do it.'

'You got shit on the liver.'

'Yeah, that's it.'

'If you wanna sulk.' He turned to Harry but this time he was in no mood for the familiar story. Still, he continued. 'For the next few months the stranger helped out with odd jobs. The cattle. Bill would always be asking about John. Did he look pale, sick? Did he shake? Did he talk about us, the farm, his brother, Morris? Could he look you in the eyes? Did he laugh? Did he make jokes? Did he talk about his school? His athletics? His awards? Did he ever say he'd had enough?' He stopped for breath. 'Or, I suppose, he'd help Mary around the place. I suppose he sat right here, talkin' with 'em. Eatin' the eggs he'd helped gather, the veggies he'd helped grow.'

'Bit of an odd jobs man?' Trevor asked his father.

'Yes,' Murray replied. 'He was a good builder too; helped Dad with the old yards.'

'Probably stood here, cookin' a roast,' Trevor said. 'Although blokes didn't do those sorts of things back then, did they? They were too busy tryin' to run the farm.'

Murray took Harry's hand. 'Come on, we'll go fill the cars.' As he went he said, 'Yer just diggin' yerself a bigger hole.'

Yanga kept scratching the hotspot on her cheek. Her skin was raw, bleeding. 'Stop it, you stupid mutt,' Murray said to her, digging his foot in her side.

'She can't help it,' Harry explained. 'We should take her to the vet.'

Murray couldn't see the point of a vet; not for an old dog. After the eczema came the limp, the cataracts, the loose bowel, the rotten teeth. Vets just delayed the inevitable. 'What?' he said to her, as she kept staring at him, accusingly. Then she scratched herself again. 'Stop it.' He kept prodding her with his foot. She stood, moved a few feet and sat down on the far end of the porch.

He was smoking, watching his hot tip eat away another rollie. He studied the distant line of steel and noticed a train. Picking up his binoculars, he squinted into the cold eyepieces. 'NR25 and 26,' he said.

'Ladies shoes. Where does the apostrophe go?' Harry asked.

'Wherever you want it to go,' he replied, studying the carriages, the windows, the plastic-looking forms behind the glass.

'I think it's after the *s*,' Harry continued.

'Silly bastards.'

'Who?' Harry asked, looking up at the train.

'Why would you take a train to Perth, for Christ's sake? Why wouldn't you get on a plane?'

'They want to see Australia.'

He wiped his eyes and returned his binoculars to the table.

'What's to see on the Nullarbor?'

'Us.'

'Yeah.' And returned to his cigarette.

'Childrens Hospital?'

'What?'

'The apostrophe?'

Murray wasn't happy. How the hell was he meant to know about apostrophes? They just went where they fit, where they looked right. No one knew what to do with an apostrophe. It wasn't like anyone was going to check. 'Don't they give you some sort of … rule?' he asked.

Harry shrugged. 'I think it's after the *s*.'

'Your father should be here. He knows all about this stuff.' He waved his hand above the assignment.

'I wanna get full marks.'

'Well …' He looked at the dog, looking at him. 'Ask Fay.'

'I did.'

Murray wasn't sure it mattered. He'd survived his few years of wireless, his Nefertiti and geometry, attempted with Morris's or Bill's unforgiving HB pencil. He'd sat where his grandson was sitting, throwing random apostrophes at the ends of words he didn't understand; he'd practised his copperplate and added rows of figures. In the end, there wasn't a lot they could teach him that he needed to know. Two years at Mercy. Before he'd stood in the middle of a lesson, walked from the room, the school, and jumped on a flat-top. Getting off, somewhere in the distance, in the stretch of cattle country that he was staring at now, and walking to the little house on the distant hill. Telling his dad, 'That's enough of that.'

'We've paid till the end of the year.'

'I'll pay you back.' Going to his room, and changing into his workpants.

The train was still moving across the desert. 'Sittin' in there with their fuckin'… riesling and clean sheets,' he said. And their air-conditioning and plate of prawns, he thought. 'They wanna see the outback they should stop off here for a few weeks.'

'With us?' Harry said.

'Yes.'

'I could rent out my room.'

Murray looked inside the house at Chris, sitting on the lounge helping his mother sew lavender bags. 'Yeah, real bloody outback experience.'

Harry scratched his head. He looked at the next question and bit his lip. '*I am unsure to who, or whom, I send the letter.*' He looked at Murray.

Murray glared at him. 'Ask your bloody father. He brought you into this world, he should be …' He trailed off again, wondering where his son had gone. His second time to Port Augusta in a week. Second time he'd shaved and ironed his clothes and said to them, 'I should be home before tea.' Second time he'd planted a kiss on Harry's forehead and almost skipped out the front door.

He noticed a small herd of wandering cattle, picked up his binoculars and studied them. 'All bloody bone,' he said, spitting tobacco from his lips.

The phone rang. Fay stood to answer it but he called out, 'Leave it, I'll get it.' He flicked the last of his cigarette into his sister's lavender and went inside.

'Yes?' he said.

'Howdy.' A woman's voice.

Howdy? 'Who's this?'

'Is that Murray?'

'Yes, who's this?'

'My name's Gaby … a friend of Trevor's. Is he there?'

'No.'

There was a break, and static. 'I thought he'd be back by now,' she said.

'From where?'

'Here. Port Augusta.'

'Right ... he's been with you, Gaby?'

Silence, then, 'Yes.'

He waited for an explanation.

'He left his wallet here,' she said.

'Where?'

'You're Trevor's dad?'

'Yes.'

'Well, Murray, if you could tell him? I thought he might need it.'

'I'll tell him.'

'Nice to speak to you,' and Murray thought, Why? Who are you? But then, in a moment of grace, he managed, 'Yes, Gaby, I'll pass the message on. Maybe he can call you back?' He could hear shop sounds – a sliding door, a cash register. 'Where at?'

'The chemist.'

'Right.' He hung up and returned to Harry, and the dog, still scratching herself.

'Who was that?' Harry asked.

'Bill.'

Harry looked down at his work. 'Personal pronouns?' he asked.

'What?'

'Do you know?'

'No, I don't know,' as he cursed Trevor, again, for sniffing around in a chemist when he should've been home with his son, explaining grammar.

'I think they're words – '

'Just work it out,' he growled, standing, pacing the porch, using his foot to stop Yanga scratching.

Harry was watching him. Something had happened, he knew.

'What's wrong?' he asked.

'Nothing's wrong.' Murray was gone, through the lavender, around the back of the house. He walked across the compound and down the access road, stopping under sheoaks and lighting another cigarette.

Another woman? Trevor?

Not that he thought his son incapable. Just caught up with other things. She sounded reasonable, he guessed. But, if he was friendly with her, he was probably *more* than friendly.

A shop girl? Or maybe a pharmacist? That'd be useful, he told himself. But then he did the maths. It was April 2. When was the accident? December 2, 3, 4? Four months. That he knew of. Four months. And why hadn't he said anything? Unless, of course, he'd just left his wallet at the pharmacy. That did happen. People left their wallets places.

He stood on his road savouring the silence, kicking a pile of bricks salvaged from a shed Bill had built with the stranger. That he, and his own father, another stranger, of sorts, had pulled down. Then he saw his son slowly coming up the road. He stood where he could be seen. Cocking his head, he looked down at the figure in the car.

Trevor stopped and put down his window. 'What are you doing out here?'

'Exercising.'

'Everything okay?'

'I been helpin' your son with his grammar.'

Trevor smiled. 'Right.' He went to drive off but Murray stepped forward. Put his hand on the roof of the car. 'Maybe you could spend a bit of time with him. I don't know much about apostrophes.'

'I'll help him tonight.'

He just stared at him. 'Get your insurance sorted?'

'Yes.'

'Good.'

Trevor shook his head. 'What is it?'

'Gaby called.'

'Yeah?'

'Said you left your wallet at the chemist.' Then the thought occurred to him: What if it was somewhere else? Her flat? A motel unit? He could see his son pulling on his pants, strapping on his watch, slipping on his boots.

'She was one of Carelyn's friends,' Trevor said. 'I popped in to say hello.'

'And you had to buy something?'

'No … yes, I did.'

Murray realised his cigarette had nearly burnt itself out. 'So, you gonna tell me?'

'What?'

'Don't be so bloody clever.'

Trevor took a moment. 'We had lunch. There's where I must have left it.'

Murray just looked at him.

'Okay, I've seen her a few times.'

'So when were you gonna tell me?'

'When you asked.'

'Don't be clever.'

Trevor took off his sunglasses. 'Can we talk about it later?'

By mid-April the desert had cooled; naphthalene skivvies and flannelette shirts salvaged from the bottom of drawers. The days wilted like so much forgotten fruit. All this was good news for Murray, whose sleep-out was the only uncooled part of the house. Now he could cover himself with rugs and get to sleep easily, lying in his little gully with his face frozen white. Fay, too, who loved to strip the beds and fit electric-blankets. Life was warm, forever breathing, sustaining; except on the other side of her nephew's bed, destined to remain cold and tightly tucked.

There was the woman, of course, Murray had mentioned her, but she couldn't see a time when *Gaby* was sleeping here.

Easter had come and gone. Trevor had taken Harry to town to buy eggs. They'd come home with a bag full of chocolates he'd placed on top of his wardrobe. But Chris had sniffed them out, attacking a bunny – so that by the time he noticed there was nothing but a foily set of lower limbs. 'Chris?'

'I just had a taste.'

Anzac Day, the whole family gathered around the telly; tea and sultana cake, and John's battalion, minus any sign or memory of a Wilkie. Ninety years of history hidden in a cupboard, as Murray said, 'Bill had a fight with them too.' As everyone just stared at the shuffling warriors, filling in the blanks: Bill catching the train to Keswick for a meeting with some brigadier. But in the end there was no Anzac Day for those on the Cowards' List.

Aiden, home for the holidays, emerged from the laundry carrying four tins of paint. The wire handles cut into his fingers and he stopped and knelt in the middle of the compound. He noticed the sunset and red flare that coated the undersides of the big, scalloped clouds. He picked up the cans and went into the shed. Harry was waiting, sitting on a stool in front of their EH mural. 'What should we do first?' he asked.

'Wait,' Aiden replied. He put the cans down, picked up a hammer, opened the front passenger door of the car and started flattening the dents he'd made with his foot.

'Are we getting more?' Harry asked, checking the colour of the paints.

'That'll do. Mix and match.' He tapped a dent and it magically popped out.

'There aren't as many colours as we had before.'

'So?'

'It won't look as good.'

'Bullshit.'

Harry loved to look at their unfinished mural: the house with its green roof and red walls; the black path leading down to the road, which crossed the railway line, although it didn't; the whole family standing in front of the house; Carelyn, still smiling, holding his hand, her feet obscured by Yanga and her twenty hot spots.

This was still the real world, Harry guessed. Paint on metal. There was nothing he wanted to change – not the oversized bottle tree, reaching into the sky, or Murray smoking a cigarette twice the size of his head. He used a screwdriver to open the red and sat stirring it with a length of wood. As he found his rhythm he looked at his mum. He'd given her a red dress, because she had a red dress. But he hadn't finished painting it. 'Did you meet Gaby?' he asked his brother.

'For a minute.'

'What was she like?'

'I don't know … okay.' He used the claw of the hammer to smooth more dents.

'Man, you've got a temper.'

'I'm fixing it.'

Harry looked at his unfinished mum. The margins rough, the shape absurd. 'You shouldn't have kicked it,' he said. 'You should've kicked a lump of wood or something.'

'Or you.'

'You can't kick me, I'm a cripple.'

'My arse.' He continued working the metal.

Harry studied his own balloon portrait, his two good legs. 'You drew me too short and fat.'

'You are short and fat.'

'I'm disabled, you should have some respect.'

'Would you shut the fuck up?' He closed the door, stood back and looked at it. 'That'll do.'

'Can we start?'

Aiden fetched the brushes. They stood looking, trying to think of objects that might be red. Harry painted his mum's dress as Aiden started the undersides of his cotton-wool clouds. They worked silently, savouring the moments, each stroke, each breath. If Harry's foot got in Aiden's way he'd just kick it. If they brushed against each other there'd be a sharp, unforgiving elbow. At one point Aiden said, 'Mum didn't have a red dress.'

'She did ... does.'

'I can't remember her having one.'

'She did.'

Soon, all of Aiden's clouds were bleached twilight. He stood back and looked at them. There was nothing end-of-the-day about them, he thought. 'Shit.'

'What?'

'It's meant to be a sunset.'

'Well ... none of it looks real, does it?'

It annoyed Aiden how the little shit always made sense. As he studied his brother's small, glazed nose, he wondered what would've happened if he'd been killed: another empty bed, the quiet hours, the lack of words. But then he spat out the thought and looked at the family portrait. 'Yeah, I remember the dress,' he said.

Harry stopped painting. 'I wish she was here,' he whispered.

'Well, what are you gonna do?'

Harry flicked the excess paint off his brush. 'There's no point worrying, is there?'

Aiden smiled. 'Come on.' He took his brother's arm and led him over to the biggest of the trail bikes.

'No,' Harry said.

'Get on.'

Aiden slid onto his taped seat, kicked out the stand and angled the bike so Harry could get on. 'Come on.'

'Dad'll kill me.'

'Dad won't know.'

'What if I come off?'

'Get on!'

Harry slipped his good leg over the seat. Then he held on to his brother, feeling ribs and muscle.

'Ready?' Aiden asked.

'Yep.'

Aiden started and revved the bike. He put it into gear, edged the nose from the shed and set off down the road. He switched on his headlight. 'Hold tight.'

'I am.'

He worked his way through the gears. They moved silently through the dark desert. 'Good, eh?'

Harry was beaming, the breeze cold, and real, on his face. He saw the way forward. The road. The corrugations that threatened, every moment, to throw him from the bike.

14

Murray sat on an old sofa. It had been exiled from the house when Carelyn had bought an all-leather number (since worn down to the flesh under Chris's angry arse). It had been placed against the house, perhaps to disguise the damp and un-mortared bricks, or maybe just because it was the best spot, in the sun. Here it got rained on and sand-blasted, slept on by Yanga, used to store bags of fertiliser and rolls of wire.

He sat back, savouring every sun-warmed breath. Without looking, he reached over to a small table and picked up Dr Diamond's ukulele. He strummed a few chords. Then played a song he'd always liked but never known how to play (Harry had downloaded the chords for him).

> *We were comrades, comrades,*
> *Ever since we were boys,*
> *Sharing each other's sorrows,*
> *Sharing each other's joys ...*

He savoured the last note. '*We were comrades, comrades ...*' There was a rattle from the junkyard behind the shed. 'Hello?'

Nothing.

He could see the rusted-out water tank with its shards of peach- and gravy-coloured iron flaking off. Yanga appeared from a rust hole with a mouse in her mouth. She dropped it at his feet. 'Go on, get out of it,' he said, kicking it away. She looked at him, tilted her head, returned to the tank and went back inside.

He could remember when the tank had sat at the bottom of the hill, not far from the crew's quarters. Could remember sitting one morning, in this spot perhaps, when the hands had started calling, 'Bertie, what the hell are you doing?' Remembered running down the hill (as a twelve- or thirteen-year-old) and standing in the bushes, staring into the overflowing tank.

Bert (who'd suffered from depression) had climbed into the tank fully-clothed. He was thrashing about – his body agitating as his head disappeared below the water. One of the men had said, 'He's fuckin' well drowning,' and another had replied, 'Someone get in and save him.'

He could remember seeing Bert stop, tread water and start to remove his clothes. Wring them out and hang them over the edge of the tank as the rest of the crew watched. Could remember Bert looking at them and smiling and asking, 'What's wrong?' and someone replying, 'We thought you were drowning,' and Bert laughing, and replying, 'No, it's just how I clean me clothes.'

And he could remember, years later, after the tank was empty, ten or more men pulling it up the hill with a series of ropes fed through the rust holes. Dragging it to where it was now. All this, and everything in the junkyard, just because it was easier to keep stuff than throw it. Throw it where? You could make your own dump, of course, away from the house, but what would that achieve?

Harry came out of the house and stood waiting for something.

'*Old Pew!*' he called, closing his eyes and walking blindly across the compound. He felt with his feet, step after slow-and-careful step. When he came to the shed he stopped. Turned around and started back, still blind, still groping. '*Old Pew!*'

'Who's he?' Murray asked.

Harry opened his eyes. 'The blind pirate.'

'Which blind pirate?'

'From *Treasure Island*. I've just finished it.' He closed his eyes and continued. '*Tapping up and down the road in a frenzy ...*' He stopped and looked at his grandfather. 'I need a cane.' And found a stick sitting in leaf litter. *'Old Pew was groping, calling out for his old comrades …'*

'How about your exercises?' Murray asked, strumming chords. 'Will this do?'

'Ten minutes of walking. Make sure you lift your legs.'

Harry continued his groping, this time in a circuit around the edge of the compound. Murray underscored his mutterings with music, occasionally singing a line. *'Comrades when manhood was dawning …'*

'Don't leave me here,' Old Pew groaned, leaning forward, searching the air with his free hand, tapping in a telegraphic frenzy. *'Wasn't I there for you, when there was a knife at your ribs?'*

'Can you feel your muscles working?' Murray called.

'Aye, and me knees bending, and me flesh mending!'

'Just keep going.'

Tap, tap, tap. Yanga dropped another mouse at Harry's feet.

'Eh, Pew,' Murray said. 'Someone's come back for you.'

Harry opened his eyes. 'No, Yanga.' He thrust his stick at her and continued. *'I could walk to the ends of the earth and just fall off. Into a river. And how would you feel, dogs?!'*

Yanga started barking at Pew. She couldn't work out why the old pirate didn't want her mouse.

'Ssh,' Harry growled. 'Go away.' But she stood looking. *'Curse you, Blackbeard!'* The old pirate leaned forward, almost falling over, shouting. *'Old Pew!'* Spit hung from his mouth and clung to his chin. Then he straightened up and threw the stick away. 'I'd rather do my stretches now.'

'What happened to Pew?'

'Still going, I suppose.'

The phone rang inside.

'Shit!' Murray said, standing. 'Keep going.'

Harry continued, walking the way the physio had showed him. When Murray was gone, he went to the shed and fetched his whip.

Inside, Murray picked up the phone and slumped forward on the kitchen bench. 'Yeallo?'

'Dad?'

'Where are yer?'

'Still in town.'

'Still?' He checked the clock. 'You were meant to be back an hour ago.'

There was a short silence. He could hear the crack of Harry's whip, and glass breaking. 'Harry, exercise!' he called, but the noise continued.

'Listen, I think I might stay over,' Trevor said, cautiously.

'Where?'

'Port Augusta.'

'*Where?*'

Another long pause.

'Gaby's got a spare room.'

'Has, has she?'

'It's getting late and I'm too tired to drive home. It's safer.'

He could see them in bed together, and he could hear them fucking. 'How's that gonna look to the boys?' he asked.

'I'm just stayin' here … in a spare room.'

'Well, no one's gonna think that are they?'

'You want me to drive home and have another accident?'

Murray looked at the uncooked chicken on the bench; the raw vegetables, the unopened jar of sauce. 'Well, I'll cook tea I suppose.' Outside, he could still hear the whip. 'Harry!'

'The boys can help.'

'Fay's got another bloody headache … she won't come out of her room. And I haven't seen Chris for an hour. He's probably off drowned somewhere.'

166

'Okay, I'll come home then.'

He could hear the girlfriend in the background: *What's wrong?* And his son, covering the phone. 'No, he's not complaining …'

'I'm not complaining,' he growled. 'Stay. I don't need you dead too.'

Is it that much of an inconvenience?

'No, it's not,' he barked down the phone. 'Tell your lady it's not.'

'Pop!'

He heard Harry's cry and the back door slam as his grandson came in. 'Shit,' he said.

'What is it?' Trevor asked.

'Your son's cut himself.' He studied the gash, an inch or so below his eye.

'It just came back at me,' Harry said, holding his sleeve over the wound, which continued bleeding.

'He's caught himself with his whip,' he told Trevor.

'Is it bad?'

'Hold on.'

He put the phone down and found a clean tea towel in a kitchen drawer. Handed it to his grandson who put it over the gash.

'Aiden!' he called. Then he picked up the phone again. 'It's under his left eye.'

'Is he okay?'

'Yes.' He spoke to Harry. 'Press down, tight!'

'Is it gonna need a stitch?' Trevor asked.

'Show me,' he growled, and Harry showed him. He returned to his son. 'Yes.' Called out again. 'Aiden!' Turning to Harry. 'Where's your brother?'

Harry shrugged.

Chris was watching them, but he guessed there was no point asking him. 'Jesus, you're …' he said to Harry, but trailed off.

Harry knew what he almost said: clumsy, accident-prone, stupid. He could see it in his pop's eyes. Wanted to cry, but stopped himself. Wouldn't let the old man see.

'Aiden!' Murray called. 'Fay!'

No one appeared.

'I can come and get him,' Trevor said. 'I can bring him back. Or you could drive him, in the ute.'

Murray waited. 'There's not much choice, is there? Has it got petrol?'

'Yes.'

'I can't find Aiden.'

'He won't be far. I'll meet you at the hospital.'

He sighed. Wanted to say it: this is what comes from neglecting your responsibilities. It falls to someone else. Which makes *you* the selfish one. 'Righto, I'll see you in a couple of hours.'

'Don't rush,' Trevor replied.

The air was sucked, with a little hum, into the void. There was nothing – no trees, no shrubs, no shredded tyres; no wrecks; no parking bays. There were stars, of course, but they were just a blur. The ute didn't growl like the new car; it had a mechanical wheeze, like it had to push itself across every inch of asphalt. There were only two seatbelts, so as Murray drove Aiden sat in the middle holding the dashboard. Harry sat beside him, clutching his cheek, studying the glass and plastic world lit up around him. 'I could've waited,' he said.

Murray glanced at him. 'You can't wait – it's gotta be sewn.'

'I didn't mean to.'

Murray just drove. He was leaning forward, his chin above the wheel; his back arched, his bottom lifted off the seat. Aiden noticed he was squinting. 'Can you see okay?' he asked.

'I'm not blind.'

But he wasn't so sure. 'I can drive,' he said.

'Not at night.'

'I can drive at night.'

Murray didn't acknowledge him. Harry bit his lip and dropped his head onto his shoulder.

'You okay?' Aiden asked.

'It stings.'

'You gotta be more careful,' Murray said.

'I've been doing it for years.'

'You coulda got your eye, and where would we be then?' He turned the thought over in his head. 'If your dad's gonna be off, and I'm gonna be running things …'

'What?' Aiden asked.

'You gotta do what I say.'

'He was just – '

'Without arguing!'

He turned up the radio but then thought better of it. 'I'm too old for all this.' Grain blew about in the back of the ute. 'How did you manage to get yourself?' he asked, looking at Harry again.

He shrugged.

'You're gonna have a nice scar.' Without slowing, he drove into a shallow bend that became tighter. Aiden could feel the wheels lifting. Slow down, he wanted to say, but dared not. Instead, he asked, 'Sure you don't want me to drive?'

'No … yes, I'm sure.' He drove off the asphalt, onto the gravel. For a few seconds he fought with the wheel before bringing the ute back onto the road. 'Jesus, they should fix that.'

Harry lifted his head and opened his eyes. 'There's no more blood,' he said, checking the tea towel.

'You're not having a good run,' Murray said.

'It wasn't his fault,' Aiden replied.

'Ten-year-olds need to be careful.'

'I'm eleven,' Harry growled.

'It's a dangerous age. Children are accident-prone.'

Harry wasn't happy with this. 'Accident-prone?'

No reply.

'*He* wasn't driving, Pop,' Aiden said.

Murray sat back in his seat, straightened his arms and said, 'If your father's not around …'

'What?' Aiden asked.

'I saw you two taking off.'

Aiden looked through the cracked windscreen, past the gaffer tape that seemed to be holding it in place. 'It was just a bit of fun.'

'Like I said, it's a dangerous age.'

'We gotta have a bit of fun.'

'Well, have it when your father's around.' He leaned forward, again, wrapping his arms around the steering wheel.

Aiden studied his grandfather's arms, his neck, his grey side-burns, and thought, Yes, it's all someone else's fault, isn't it?

The word was with Murray and Murray was the word. Not for the first time, he could feel himself starting to hate his grandfa-ther. There wasn't much love or compassion in him. He was a sort of farmer shell, a hollow man full of regrets and knowledge and skills he couldn't use any more, except as a sort of walking opinion that no one wanted to hear.

They approached and passed a B-triple.

Too close, Aiden thought, as Murray struggled to keep control. 'You're tired,' he said. 'I should have a drive.'

'I'm not tired. I'll tell you when I'm tired.'

Aiden could tell what he was really thinking: I didn't cut myself open; I didn't ask to be sitting here, dealing with you two.

'If it wasn't for his little … shop girl,' Murray said.

Neither boy spoke.

'I'm too old for all this … too old.'

'Well, let me drive.'

'I should be playin' lawn bowls.' He throttled the wheel. This time the ute got away from him. They moved onto the gravel and he braked hard. Then they were in the grass, and onto the sand.

'Fuck,' he said.

Aiden flew forward against the dash. They stopped; there was dust in the cabin and in their mouths. 'You okay, Harry?'

Harry was clutching the door. He dropped his head and started crying. Aiden put his arm around him.

'Jesus,' Murray said.

The engine was still chugging. A car flew past without stopping. 'Stop crying.'

'Is your leg okay?' Aiden asked his brother. Harry didn't reply; he was sobbing, turning away from Murray, desperate to escape the car.

'Christ!' Murray said.

'It's not his fault!' Aiden shouted. He climbed over his grandfather, opened the door and got out. 'Move over.'

Murray just glared at him. He waited before undoing his belt and moving into the middle. Aiden got in and pulled the seatbelt over his chest. He closed the door. 'You ready, Harry?'

Murray sat opposite the woman. Her arms were crossed, even her feet, tapping out the tune to the muzak that played, apparently, all night. *Quando, quando, quando.* He heard himself starting to hum, and stopped. His eyes surveyed the hospital foyer: the information board, holding painted slats with names like Haemaphoresis and Gynaecology, floor numbers, room numbers; posters telling you how to wash your hands; a teenage mums' clinic; a cleaner's trolley left out.

'It could've been a lot worse,' Gaby said to him.

Murray just looked at her. It could've been a lot better, he thought. If he hadn't done it; if I wasn't sitting here at 1 am talking to you.

A cleaner came out of the men's toilet, gathered her sign and pushed the collection of mops and buckets down the hallway.

'Four or five stitches,' Gaby continued, and Murray managed, 'We'll see.'

He'd already decided he didn't like her. He had this sense, he believed, of what a person was like, or at least of what they'd become. Maybe, he often wondered, it was something chemical, maybe the shape of the head, the cheek bones, the forehead; maybe the way a person talked, or looked at you. Maybe it was the false pity, the forced sentiment.

When she looked away he studied her face: flat, with big eyes, like they were being pushed out of her head; a man's forehead, trailing all the way across her skull; hair that was too short, and too cropped, and not its natural colour; wire and bone earrings that were too big, and holes that were too big for them; a passable neck, perhaps, but a long scarf wrapped around it. 'You knew Carelyn?' he asked.

'Yes.'

He waited for an explanation but it didn't come. 'How?'

'We used to play netball together. And we went to Melbourne a few times. *Cats.*'

'*Cats?*'

'Yes.' She stared at him.

'That's a show?' he asked.

'Yes.'

He sighed. 'My idiot nephew has the record.'

They both watched as a woman in a dressing-gown floated across the foyer, stopped in front of a vending machine and made a selection. The machine stirred and clunked but nothing dropped.

'Shit,' she said, pushing and then shaking it. 'Shit.'

'No one's gonna help you,' Murray said. 'You'll have to call the company.'

The woman tried shaking it again. 'Typical,' she said, before floating back to the lift.

He studied Gaby's dress: a sort of stripey parachute falling down around her ankles; her slipper-shoes, woven from rattan or coconut fibre. Her ankles, he noticed, were fat; her legs, not recently shaved. 'Didn't see you at the funeral,' he said.

She smiled. 'I didn't know, until later.'

No, you didn't know, did you? 'It was a very sad event, especially for the boys.'

'Yes?'

'They're the ones I worry about.'

'I could imagine.'

I could imagine. What does that mean? 'You got any kids?'

'No.'

No, of course not, fuck yer. He decided he wouldn't talk to her any more. She was all show, like wallpaper, or the Myer windows. She wouldn't let on who she was or what she was about. So fuck yer, he thought.

Then she said, 'The boys might have a hard year or two, but they'll come good.'

He glared at her. *How the fuck do you know?* 'Perhaps.'

'Especially Harry, but he's as tough as nails, eh?'

This time he decided not to respond. *Tough as nails?* How did she know, from the two minutes she'd been with him? How *could* she know about what made him cry and run away to hide in the shed?

'Still, Aiden seems to be a good big brother.'

He watched a few old men smoking out front and he wanted to go join them. But no, he'd given his word to Trevor. 'I'll wait here with her, if you like. You see to Harry.' There was no way he was going to watch a doctor sew up skin. He could handle bleeding scrotums and the smell of burning flesh, but as for anything human …

'That music's annoying, isn't it?' she said.

'Something to listen to.'

'Is this his first accident, with the whip?'

'Yes.' He looked at her, thinking, That's the sort of shit that happens when you live in the real world. Studied the four or five bangles around her wrist. 'It's useful to know how to use a stock-whip.'

Yes, she thought. You silly old prick.

She even smells like a pharmacy, he thought. Clean, menthol, with a spray from the testers at the front of the shop. Like she was off on a big night. *Cats*. Or some play with its head up its arse.

'I bet he was screaming,' she said.

'Who?'

'Harry, when he did it.'

'No, there's no point screaming. You just gotta fix the problem. He just came in and told me.' Then he reminded himself he didn't want to talk to her.

'Very brave of him.'

'Yes.'

'He's had a rough trot.'

'What?'

She sat back. 'I mean … with the accident.'

'Of course he's had a bloody rough trot.'

Nothing annoyed him more than people who stated the obvious. Conversation makers. Idiots with too much time on their hands.

'Has he sprung back?' she asked.

Sprung back? 'What do you mean?'

'In himself?'

Fuck.

'I mean, is he happy?'

'How the hell should I know? Ask him.'

He studied the carpet: the stains. He wondered where they'd come from. 'So, you knockin' about with Trevor?' he asked.

She didn't know what to say. '*Knockin' about?*'

'You know what I mean.'

'Well, I suppose I am.'

Great, an almost simple answer, he thought.

'Why do you ask?' she said.

'No reason.'

'No?'

'No.'

Silence.

'I'm entitled to know. If I wait for Trevor to tell me anything …'

'I think he's perked up.'

'What?'

'Since he's had someone to … talk to.'

He almost laughed. 'He does plenty of talkin' to us.'

'You know what I mean.'

He smoothed his trousers, sat up and pushed out his lower back. 'Well, he's a big boy, he can choose.'

'He's got his own dilemmas.'

'Dilemmas?'

Then they were there: the three boys.

'What you been sayin' about me?' Trevor asked his father.

'Five stitches,' Harry glowed, showing them the gauze across his face.

'Very nice,' Murray replied, standing up, running his hand across his grandson's forehead. 'You'll have a nice scar there. Women go for a scar.'

Gaby watched the old man. She could already feel him pulling his son, and boys, away from her. 'Does it hurt?' she asked, and Harry looked at her, unsure. 'Not much.'

Aiden was studying her too. 'This isn't unusual,' he said.

'No?'

Murray took his grandson's shoulders and steered him towards the door. 'Come on, it's a long trip.' He turned his back on the woman.

Trevor looked at Gaby. 'Thanks for staying. He wasn't too painful?'

'Well ...'

Although it was dark, Aiden could see the outlines of sheds and ruined cottages. 'Lot of them had trouble with calving last year,' he said to his dad.

'Not a lot.'

'A few.' Trevor could remember sitting in the ute, watching the cows with Murray's binoculars.

Harry had fallen asleep. He'd taken off his boots and laid himself across the back. Nuzzled his head into the gap between the door and the seat. Mumbled a few words ('I did it like I always did ...') before drifting off.

'You shouldn't let Pop drive,' Aiden said to his father.

'I didn't have much choice.'

He cracked his knuckles before thinking better of it. 'Hopefully I'll pass first time,' he said.

'You'll be okay. They go easy on the farmers' sons.' Trevor remembered his own driving test, once around the block, stopping at the deli so the man could buy some smokes. He checked his rear-vision mirror. Murray was still there, hanging on like grim death, one of the ute's headlights permanently stuck on high beam. He'd close on him and drop back, half a kilometre or more. Trevor would slow, Murray would catch up. Trevor would say, 'Can't you stick to one bloody speed?'

'Got all your assignments finished?' Trevor asked.

'No.'

'Why not?'

But Aiden was caught up with a difficult birth. There was nothing better than walking up to the animal, holding it, helping it.

'Why not?' Trevor repeated.

'I don't know.'

He looked at his son, who lifted his head and said, 'Gaby wears some … interesting clothes.'

'What's that got to do with anything?'

Harry moved about, seeking a comfortable spot for his head. 'How much longer?' he asked.

'Not long.'

'Go to sleep,' Aiden said. He stopped to think. 'I don't reckon Pop liked her much.'

'How do you know?'

'You can tell.'

Trevor had to agree. 'He doesn't like anyone.'

That may be true, Aiden thought, but he's gonna make your life difficult.

'So, what do you need to finish?' Trevor continued.

'Biology … English … everything.'

'Why haven't you asked?'

'Cos I don't want to go back. I failed the Biology trial exam.'

'Jesus … see, you didn't ask for help.'

'It doesn't matter. I don't get it. I don't want to get it.'

A long pause. Harry, too, was disappointed. He knew his brother was smart.

'You're wasting your money,' Aiden said.

Silence.

'I'd be more use at home.'

Trevor guessed that was it; that he could keep arguing, and pushing, for no reason. 'That's disappointing.'

'It's just how it is.'

'I keep thinking it's because of the accident.' He saw the blinded kangaroo in his headlights.

'It's nothing to do with that.'

It is, Harry was thinking. It is.

'If you remember, I was asking to leave a long time before that.'

'I wanted you to finish school. Mum wanted you to.'

'Don't say that.'

'She did.'

'She wouldn't want me to be … miserable.'

Harry had to stop himself from speaking. Don't be stupid, he wanted to say to his brother. And don't think that I need your help, cos I don't.

'What about English?' Trevor asked.

'Fifty-four, fifty-six, I can't remember.'

'We could work on that.'

'No. You said. One term. I tried.'

They continued, Murray closing and drifting, the conversation flagging, Harry falling asleep.

15

A few days before Aiden was due to return to school, father and son sat (with barely a word passing between them) in the front of the ute. Trevor was listening to an old tape he'd found under his seat. He was surprised it still played. Years of heat and dust had failed to dull Bach's *Goldberg Variations*. The music appealed to him: notes as footsteps trailing across the landscape. It was no-nonsense music. Farmers' music. Winding itself around his ears and brain like a too-tight fence snapping and unravelling.

'Hungry?' he asked his son.

'Not yet,' Aiden replied, searching the hummocks for cattle.

They'd driven an hour from home. Stopped in the middle of the track to watch a large herd approach from the west. Then Trevor had pulled in behind shrubs, killed the engine, and waited. The cattle had come close but stopped short, lifting their heads and watching them.

Trevor studied the tape turning inside the player. Never surging or slowing as fingers worked like tappets in a cylinder, a motorhead of motion that somehow pleased him. The little door to the slot had fallen off and Harry had spent years shoving chip packets and pencils inside the mechanism.

'That one there's about to drop,' Aiden said, pointing.

Trevor studied the cow. 'Yeah …' He looked at the sky, full of low, rolling cloud. 'She'd better get on with it.'

It was cold. Winter had arrived. The morning chill persisted all day. Murray would lead Chris to the shed to fetch wood; return, drop bark and dirt everywhere; make his boy-scout construction and light it; move his chair closer and cover his legs with a rug;

complain that he could feel his gout coming on. As Trevor said, 'It's not the cold brings it on.'

'How would you know?'

'Red wine, tomatoes.'

'When do I drink red wine?'

Trevor knew his father won every argument by default. There was nothing he didn't know. Once, he'd asked him, 'Where do you get all this information?'

'Books, and common sense.'

'What books?'

But he'd just tapped his head.

Back in the ute, Aiden had covered his legs with his coat to keep warm. 'Should we move on?' he asked.

Trevor was watching the cow. 'She's started.'

'How many are pregnant?'

'Seven, eight … that one on the edge perhaps.'

Although the desert was gale-swept, Trevor had rolled his window down. He could feel the chill on his face and neck. The clouds had taken the light. It was a grey-sludge day. But he liked this; it kept things neater, simpler, easier to comprehend. The trees and the cow piss in the cab with him. The oestrus and the damp bark, the smell of approaching rain.

'That's a good sign,' Aiden said.

'Yeah, perhaps.'

If this many cows were pregnant then it might be a good year: yards full of calves waiting for a tag; to grow old, gain weight and make money for them.

'There's not enough feed,' Trevor said.

'It's gonna rain all winter.'

'Perhaps.'

They waited. Aiden wanted to survey the other herds but Trevor needed to see this animal born. It would be a sign: life had interruptions but kept going, moving across the baked earth. The tempo persisted. Each small component fell in line. Nothing was greater or less than the thing that came before it. It just was.

He checked the cow. She was moaning, starting to push. A few other animals were standing close, watching, nuzzling her. 'She's off,' he said, sitting forward.

'Can we go now?'

'No, wait.'

The rain started to pepper the windscreen. There were little explosions of dust then trails of mud running down the glass. Trevor half-raised his window but he loved feeling the drops on his face and arms. He breathed the wet wood, and grass. It was the first smell he'd ever known (apart from the powdered scent of his mother) and it was the thing that made most sense to him.

The cow was bellowing, pushing harder, but there was no sign of a calf. 'Don't tell me ... first of the season,' he said.

'Give her a minute.'

The drops became a shower, exploding across the windscreen, leaking into the cab through the taped-up crack.

'Maybe we should head home,' Aiden said.

But Trevor wouldn't be drawn. He watched the struggling cow. Could see how hard she was working, and how impossible it had become. The torrent had consumed them: ute, cow and farm. Horizon diminished to hummock, hummock to road, road to cow.

'Come on,' Aiden said. He opened his door and walked into the rain. Trevor watched him for a moment then followed. He closed his door, but Aiden's was still open, and the Bach came tumbling out of the cab. As they approached the cow the rest of the herd drifted away. Aiden went around behind her and noticed how far she'd dilated. Trevor came up behind him. 'Go get your coat,' he said, above the howl, drawing his head into his body and wiping rain from his eyes.

'I can do it,' Aiden said.

'Go on then.'

He took off his windcheater. Within a few moments his T-shirt was soaked.

'Feel around,' Trevor said, leaning towards him.

Aiden slipped his hands into the pink and chocolate-brown opening and felt around. Trevor studied his determination; saw him close and open his eyes, lick rain from his lips and shake it from his hair. Stop to think. And then glide his hands in further, feeling. 'What have you got?' he asked.

'Breech.'

He waited, willing him to take charge, to show how the problem could be fixed. 'If you're gonna move it you need to watch the neck.'

'I know.'

'And the cord.'

'*I know.*' He just looked at the cow, standing on her little bit of grass, helpless in the driving rain.

Trevor saw his son's shoulders. He noticed how they moved together like strands of rough rope as he took hold of the calf's body and tried to move it. How he put his head back as he tried to imagine what was going on inside the uterus. How he bent and tensed the trunk of his body. But mostly, how he made this job the only job in the world; how he fell into a sort of trance.

'Fantastic,' Aiden said, smiling, as he guided the head through the birth canal, as the small brown eyes and velvet face appeared. 'Yes,' he said, reclaiming his hands and arms. 'It's coming.'

Trevor held his son's strong arm and squeezed it.

They took a few steps back. The calf's legs, tail and body appeared and slipped into the grass with a *glmph*. Aiden was still smiling, consumed by the moment, watching the small animal's every movement. Trevor wasn't looking at the calf. He was studying his son's square jaw (which had hardened, from the soft jaw of the past); his stony face, wet with little ponytails of hair; his bright eyes; the water on his eyebrows and the blood on his cheeks.

Aiden turned to him. 'What do you reckon?'

'Good work.'

'It's okay,' he said, indicating how the calf was moving and how the cow was already licking it clean.

'A nice strong one,' Trevor replied.

Now the chill had set in. Aiden was shivering. He picked a few clumps of grass, wiped the worst of the mucus from his hands and arms and they returned to the car. When they got in the Bach was still playing. He couldn't stand the distraction and ejected the tape. They wiped their faces and hair with their shirts. Trevor started the engine and turned on the heater.

'It's not so hard,' Aiden said. 'You just gotta feel what's what. And when I pushed it,' and he shook more water from his hair, 'it just turned.'

Trevor smiled at him. 'She just needed a bit of help.'

Aiden looked over and saw the calf trying to stand up.

They headed home on the hard part of the road. Aiden blasted himself with heat. As a joke, Trevor said, 'See, if you went back to school you could become a vet.'

Silence. Bach. Hot air. The rain, still, hammering down on their ute.

You had to bring it up, didn't you, Aiden thought.

'No, I can see it now,' Trevor said.

Aiden looked at him.

His hand was only guiding the wheel, letting it slip between his fingers. 'You warm?'

'See what?' Aiden asked.

He looked at him. 'If I let yer, you gotta pull your weight, okay?'

Aiden closed his eyes. He lifted his head and for the first time in a long time, felt happy. Since he'd stood beside his mum helping her peel potatoes. He looked back at his dad and met his eyes. 'I can deal with Harry,' he said.

Trevor almost laughed. 'I can deal with him.'

It rained all night. Just after two, Murray abandoned his sleep-out and moved inside. The rain had been coming through his tin roof, onto his rug, soaking its way towards his feet. The wind had worked its way through his louvered window, chilling his face. Yanga slept beside the couch, farting her way through another night, waking up, going into the boys' room, pissing on the carpet, returning, snoring.

The following morning the rain eased, allowing gutters to drain and the top few millimetres of soil to air-dry. There was time for Chris to feed the chooks and gather the wet shoes from outside the laundry, and for Murray to reclaim the porch for a smoke. The bottle tree was silent. Some of the bottles had filled and broken their strings, smashing onto the ground.

Trevor walked around the house, expecting the worst. It wasn't a wet-weather building. It had adapted to the sun but knew nothing about water. He noticed more of the mortar washed out from between the bricks and stonework. In some places there was nothing under the foundations of the house.

He went in, sliding the door closed. Harry was still in his pyjamas, sitting on a stool that Fay kept putting in the shed and Murray kept bringing inside. Aiden was standing beside him, a pair of surgical scissors in his hand, tweezers, dressing and Betadine on the bench.

'I want Dad to do it,' Harry said.

Trevor sat down on the couch. 'Aiden is much steadier than me.'

'I don't care.' He glared at his brother.

'Trust me,' Aiden said.

'What about Aunty Fay?'

Aiden imitated the tremor in her hand. 'It's either this or I'll have to drive you all the way to town.'

Harry shrugged.

'You won't feel a thing,' Trevor said. 'Will he, Aiden?'

'Of course not, Dad.'

'Aiden's an excellent doctor. Just delivered his first calf. A few stitches? Nothing.'

Aiden smiled in agreement.

'Why didn't you take me?' Harry asked.

'All in good time,' Trevor replied.

Aiden made his first two snips.

'Ow.'

'Bullshit.'

'Aiden!' Fay rang out, from the bathroom.

'You didn't even feel it.'

'Did so.'

'*Did so.*'

'Get stuffed.'

'Harry,' Murray growled.

'Well, he's – '

'Enough. Aiden, just get on with it, please.'

Aiden looked at his brother. 'Close your eyes.'

Harry refused.

'Little shit.'

'You could scar me.'

'*I will* scar you.'

'Harry,' Trevor said, and he closed his eyes.

Aiden snipped the rest of the thread. Harry sat still, wincing, repeating, '*Ich bin, du bist, er ist, wir sind ...*'

'I'm not removing your leg,' Aiden said.

Harry opened his eyes and looked at him. Closed them and continued. '*Ich arbeite, du arbeitest ...*'

185

Aiden picked up the tweezers and with a series of sharp, accurate jerks, removed the stitches.

'Christ,' Harry said, reaching for his head.

'All done.'

He opened his eyes. 'That hurt.'

'How about a thank you?'

'*Thank you.*'

'Right, you can put the rubbish in the bin. I'm cooking breakfast.'

That afternoon Trevor and Murray returned to check the cows. Aiden asked to come with them but Trevor said, 'No, Harry will need help with his lessons.'

'That can wait.'

Trevor just stared at him.

'Just for the calving?' Aiden asked.

And the look, again.

'Okay ...'

Father and son set off. The weather would clear but then descend again, settling low over the land. They'd find a herd and stop and watch. There were already a few calves hobbling around on stilt-legs, smelling grass, brushing up against their mothers. Once, when they stopped, Trevor said, 'He did a good job delivering that calf.'

Murray took his time before replying. 'So, you're happy he's leaving school?'

'Not happy ... but what else can I do?'

'Make him see it out.'

Trevor guessed his father was having a few bob each way. 'Well, you try and make him,' he said.

'You're the boss.'

'You know it's not that easy.'

Silence; then thunder rolling across the desert; photo-flashes picking up the hummocks, highlighting the empty, electric world in front of them. 'Shit,' Trevor said.

'Where's that comin' from?' Murray asked.

And the rain, easing, pushing against their ute. Neither of them spoke. Trevor knew there was no use trying to make conversation or discuss the weather. The worse things got the less you needed words. All disasters were accompanied by silence. 'I've got it,' he said.

Although the curtain of rain had destroyed any visibility he knew the outhouse was only a few minutes away. 'I'll stop … we can wait it out in Number one.'

Murray didn't reply.

'Dad?'

'I'll wait in here.'

'Don't be stupid.'

Trevor rose from the grass, cut across the road and followed it, parallel, towards the roofline in the near distance. When they arrived he killed the engine, gathered their lunch esky and looked at his dad. 'Come on,' he said. 'I'm hungry.'

Murray knew there was enough room to stay dry on the porch. Still, he could see Bill climbing the steps to the outhouse. He could see him standing, looking out across his farm, and he could feel (knew, exactly) what he was thinking. He could see him sighing, deciding, going in, dragging the rope behind him. 'I can wait here,' he said.

'Don't be so stupid.'

He looked at his son. 'What's it matter? I'll still be dry.'

Trevor shook his head. He got out, ran over to the porch and stood looking back at his dad. Then he waved for him to come in.

Murray took a deep breath. He got out and walked slowly through the rain to join his son on the porch.

'Come on,' Trevor said. He went inside.

And waited.

'Dad?'

Murray knew he'd see him hanging if he walked through the door. It would be real: the sound of the rope against the wood, the body gently swinging despite the lack of breeze; the scuff on his shoes and the scabs on his arms; his shirt done up to somewhere near his nipples. 'I'll stay here,' he called.

Trevor came back out. 'You're so superstitious.'

'That's not it.' And what he wanted to say: Would you disturb a grave? Would you upset a memory (a few yellowing photos of his grandfather herding cattle into a yard)? Could you face the most unpleasant facts of your own history?

'For a man who's up-front about everything.'

Murray glared at him. 'Don't talk about what you don't understand.'

But Trevor did. 'It's not like they didn't take him down.' He opened the esky and took out two foil-wrapped sandwiches. The sound of peeling foil was lost in the rain. He spoke as he ate. 'I was thinking of bringing the muster forward a few weeks.'

'Why?'

'It's better for Bill, and the crew.'

'Well, it's not better for us.'

'It might be, depending on the weather.'

Murray ripped at his sandwich and a slice of tomato fell on the floorboards. 'We've always started on the same day.'

'The date's never actually mattered.'

'It has. So we can plan.'

'That's what I'm saying. He organises the labour, the trucks, the abattoir ...'

Murray shook his head. 'No, just cos it suits him ...'

Trevor had had enough of being told. 'I'm the one running it.'

Murray looked at his son's face, the trespass upon his authority.

'You can stand back and have your say but I'm the one who's gotta make it happen.'

He was itching to say it: *It's still my farm. Look at the deed.*

'I don't just work for you.'

'You work for the family.'

'So I'll make the decisions.'

He gave him his *you-certainly-will-not* look. 'The oldest has always decided,' he said.

'That's ridiculous. If you want to know the truth …'

'What?'

'If you want to encourage me to stay and make this place work …'

'Why, where are you going?'

Trevor stumbled. 'What I mean is, there needs to be some incentive.'

'Or else you'll leave?'

'I didn't say that.'

'You did.'

'I didn't mean it.'

But Murray wasn't so sure. He'd never heard anything like this before. 'So you think I should sign the place over to you?'

'If I'm the one running the farm.' He was unsure if that's what he really wanted anyway. There were other lives – shacks, beaches, afternoons of fishing; a few acres somewhere near the coast, a dozen sheep and his hands, sawdust, and the smell of Gaby's carrot cake drifting into his shed. 'What would it matter? It's just a piece of paper.'

'Exactly, a piece of paper.'

He was retreating, aware that he was arguing with a rock. He threw his crusts into the rain. 'Bill asked me,' he said. 'So they can do Separation Well before Christmas.'

'So he can make more money.'

Trevor started on a muffin that Harry had cooked. 'So?'

'We have an arrangement.'

'We do not. It's just that he's always accommodated us.'

The rain started to ease. In less than a minute it had stopped. The run-off continued dripping from the roof and walls.

'He's got a dozen men to think of, Dad.'

'So? We've got a farm in drought.' He looked at the puddles surrounding them.

'I'm gonna tell him it's okay.'

'You will not.'

'I will.' He stared back. 'I'm running the muster.'

Murray moved his lips, but stopped.

'I'm running the farm, aren't I, Dad?'

Nothing.

'So, I'll tell him?'

'Do what you want.'

I'm not eight years old any more, Trevor wanted to say. I've just let *my* son make his own decision. 'Anyway, Aiden will be a big help this year.'

Nothing.

'I'm cold.' He picked up the esky and went inside. 'Coming in, Dad?'

Murray stood still, convinced this piece of choreography was for his benefit.

'Dad?'

He threw his sandwich into the mud. Then he walked down the few steps and returned to the ute. He got in the driver's side and started it and turned the heater to full. Inside, Trevor just stood waiting, listening. After a few minutes he opened one of the jerry cans and went out to fill his ute.

16

Aiden sat in an uncomfortable seat in the motor registry. He held a small card in his hand. He studied the number: 56; the equally sized and spaced numerals, the tight, crimped edges of the laminate. A digital queue on the wall counted down from 97. Every time the number clicked over he looked at it, willing it to hurry, unable to work out where these forty people were. His shins were crossed, his left foot tapping. When he realised he stopped, but soon started again. Then sat up and spread his feet flat on the ground.

96. He looked at his brother. 'What are you gonna do with that?'

Harry was holding a section of his freshly removed cast. It was wrapped in a plastic bag and tied up, as if it might be carrying some sort of superbug. 'Keep it as a souvenir,' he said.

'Why?' He started tapping his foot again.

'A reminder.'

It had been an eight o'clock appointment – Trevor, Murray and Aiden lined up beside the bed, Harry propped up on a mountain of pillows, the nurse with the electric cutter and a slightly-too-wide smile. 'Shall we get started?' She turned it on and it buzzed and Harry looked at his father.

'The sooner it's off the sooner you can get back to work,' he said.

The small teeth of the saw bit into the cast and white powder settled across the bed, the sheets, his pale skin. He winced, waiting for the pain, turning his head so he wouldn't see the blood.

'She's not gonna get you,' Aiden said.

'I hardly ever mess up,' the nurse added, smiling. She cut the cast down both sides. It fell away to reveal a small, bony leg, paler than the skin around it, still punctured where the pins had been inserted and removed. 'How's it feel?' she asked, brushing away the powder.

Harry tried to bend his knee. 'It still works.'

91.

'Christ, how slow are they?' Aiden said, looking through a booklet that had turned soft and sweaty in his hands.

'Do you want me to test you?' Harry asked.

'No.' He looked at the immovable digit. 'Okay.' He handed the booklet to his brother and Harry laid it across his cast. Then he studied the rules. 'A crossroad,' he said. 'You're turning left, the guy coming the other way is turning right. Who goes first?'

Aiden closed his eyes and squeezed his cheeks against his eyeballs. 'Well, I gotta give way to the right … so he goes first.'

'Good.'

87, 86 …

'Are you allowed to change lanes in the middle of an intersection?'

'No.'

'When exiting a property, is the driver required to give way to pedestrians?'

'Yes, of course. Give me some harder ones.'

Harry looked at him. 'There's no point, you know 'em all.'

Aiden reclaimed the booklet. He rolled it up, put it in his top pocket, took it out, flattened it, put it in his pants pocket, took it out again and handed it to Harry. 'Here, hold on to it, will yer?'

He took the booklet. 'You're nervous.'

'Of course I'm fuckin' nervous.'

'I was nervous when they cut this off.' He patted his plaster leg.

'It's a bit different.'

'How?'

'It is.'

'She could've cut my leg open.'

The pulsing number changed from 86 to 62. Aiden sat up and studied the box. 'What happened?'

Customers kept standing, approaching the counter and handing over their stubs. Aiden wasn't sure he liked all this progress. Every digital clunk, every screaming kid, every aborted argument brought him closer to his driving test. He watched a girl wait and smile and shake hands with her examiner. He studied the man: crew-cut, closely shaved, a tie cutting into his neck. 'I hope I don't get him,' he said. He watched the pair walk through the front door and heard the girl ask, 'Have you had a nice day?'

And the response: 'What type of vehicle will you be driving today?'

'If I get him I'm rooted,' he said.

Harry didn't know what to say. 'Don't look nervous.'

He stared at him. 'It's not something you can control.'

'If they see you're confident …'

He wanted to ask, What the hell would you know? But didn't, realising he meant well.

61, 60, 59…

Then, time slowed. One, two minutes. He couldn't see any staff behind the counter. 'Where is everyone?'

'What do you think of Gaby?' Harry asked.

He shrugged. 'I dunno.'

'She looks a bit … way out.'

'How can you tell? You've met her once.'

Harry wrapped the booklet around the cast. He smoothed it, asking, 'The speed limit in a built-up area?'

'Shut up.'

'I'm just trying to help. She had all those bangles, clattering together.'

Aiden glared at him, more confused than annoyed. 'So?'

'And that necklace with the shells on it.'

'*Fuck* … so what if she did?'

'It's okay, but Mum wouldn't have – '

'*Shut up!* Do you think I care, now? I've got a driving test.'

58.

'If you're like this you'll make a mistake. I'm trying to get your mind off it. I just thought, I couldn't ever see Mum wearing all those bangles.'

'Well, she's not Mum.'

'But she's nice enough, isn't she?'

'Yes.'

Harry imagined his mother hacking into a leg of lamb as a dozen bangles dangled in the grease. 'Do you think Dad likes her?'

'Of course he does.'

'Do you think he'll …' He trailed off, into the unimaginable, the neither pleasant nor unpleasant, the drift into an unknown future.

'I don't know what he'll do. But it's his life.'

He wasn't sure about this. 'So, you wouldn't mind …?'

'What?'

'If he …'

57. An old hump-backed cocky stood and approached a staff member who'd appeared from the back office.

'Would you?' he said.

'I don't know. I suppose not … if it came down to it.'

This response gave him cause to stop and think. *If it came down to it.* Which, the way things were going, it might. Aiden thought it was okay. So, maybe it was. 'That dress she had on,' he said.

'What?'

'Mum wouldn't have worn a dress like that.'

'What's that got to do with anything?' He tapped his foot.

'I don't know whether I like her … yet.'

'Jesus. It. Is. Too. Early.'

'I know.'

'Well, why are we having this conversation?'

Harry looked forward, and shrugged. 'I don't know what Mum would think.'

'Mum would want Dad to be happy.'

He stopped to think. 'I suppose that's right.'

'Yes, it is. It's right. I'm always right.'

'Mum would just want …'

'Give it time,' Aiden said, looking at him. 'It'll sort itself out.'

56.

He breathed deeply. 'Wish me luck.'

'You'll be okay.'

The examiner appeared from a side door. He had the same short hair, but hadn't shaved for days. There was no tie, and his shirt had come untucked at the sides. His gut hung over his belt and his pants were stained and un-ironed.

'See, *she'll be apples*,' Harry half-sang, poking his brother in the side.

'Aiden Wilkie,' the man called out. He coughed, searched his pockets for a handkerchief and spat into it.

Aiden stood and approached him. 'Hi,' he said.

'How are yer, Aiden?'

'Fine, thanks.'

Aiden could see phlegm on the man's lips and chin. The examiner used his sleeve to wipe his face. 'I'll just get you to pay your money to this lovely lady here.' He indicated the clerk.

Aiden bit his lip. 'Two seconds. My dad's got it.' He walked past his brother and winked. He went outside and found his father and grandfather (smoking) standing in front of an adjacent deli. He asked for the money.

'Good luck,' Trevor said, as he pulled the notes from his wallet.

After he went back inside, Murray said, 'If he gets his licence you'll never see him again.'

'He's not using my car.'

'Well, you'll have to buy him his own. A ute. Something reliable.'

'Where's the money for that?'

Murray stopped to think, and smoke. 'I won't have him doin' bore runs in a rust bucket.'

Aiden and the examiner came out of the motor registry office. Aiden looked at them and grimaced.

'Go easy on him,' Murray called out, and Aiden glared at him.

'He'll be fine,' the examiner replied.

Aiden opened the car, slipped into the driver's seat and waited for the older man to settle in and buckle up. Trevor watched anxiously as the car started; as his son slowly backed out; as he exited the carpark, indicating (thankfully); as he pulled into the flow of traffic and disappeared down the road. Then he said, 'I think I've got a solution.'

'What?'

'Money.'

'There's money.'

'There is not. There's debt.'

Murray took a moment. He knew the figures. He'd seen the spreadsheet; he'd seen the piles of bills, Trevor's hand-scribbled sums predicting what was going to come in and what needed to be spent; the bank statements, the totals of monthly and yearly interest; the rainfall gauge and the meatless ribs on his cattle.

'There's some off-farm work going,' Trevor said. 'Gaby's brother-in-law. Works for this salvage company. They've got a contract to rip up a heap of spur lines.'

Murray had never heard his son mention work that *other people paid you for*. 'What spur lines?'

'Apparently there's a whole heap of lines that were put in, used for a while, then abandoned. S'pose the iron's worth something.'

'Where?'

'West. Might be away for a few days at a time.'

'And meanwhile?' He flicked his cigarette to the ground, turned away and crossed his arms.

'Meanwhile, you and Aiden keep things ticking over.'

No response; just cars pulling up in front of shops.

'Me and Aiden?'

'You know what you're doin'. It's your farm, isn't it?'

Murray wouldn't be drawn. 'Meanwhile, we don't keep up with the work.'

'Six hundred dollars a day to drive a tractor?'

'Wait for the muster.'

'Wait, it's always wait. Things *never* get better.'

'They will.'

'How?' And what he wanted to say: Prices will go up? It'll rain, the grass will take off, the cattle will fatten, go forth and multiply? Make us millions? 'It's bloody good money, Dad.'

'It's not the same, workin' for someone else.'

'What, cos you actually make money?'

Nothing.

'So, it's agreed?'

'And I'll be the one left in charge?'

Harry came out of the office carrying his cast, searching the roads for any sign of his brother. 'How much longer?' he asked.

'Not long,' Trevor replied.

'Aiden reckons he's gonna drive me to town, to the pictures.'

'He doesn't have a car.'

'But he can use yours.'

'No.'

'You can buy him one?'

And looking at Murray. 'Perhaps. What do you say, Dad?'

'There's no point arguing with you.'

'With *me*?'

Meanwhile, Aiden was driving slowly along the highway that headed out of town. He was well under the limit; ten-to-two; straight back, keen eyes, watching for anyone who might pull out in front of him, kids on bikes, unexpected lane-changers.

'Farm boy?' the examiner asked.

'Yeah.'

'How many head?'

'Five thousand, just under.'

The examiner seemed impressed. He wrote something on the sheet in the folder in his lap. Aiden glanced to see what it was but dared not linger.

'What's yer place called?'

'Bundeena. A couple of hours west.'

'Yeah?' He wrote again.

'Everything okay?' Aiden asked, looking at him.

'Yep.' He looked up and smiled. 'What was that sign we just passed?'

'Sixty.'

'And what are you doin'?'

He checked. 'Fifty-five.'

'Good lad.' He wrote again. 'Mum and Dad both with you today?' He looked up.

'Dad is ... Mum died.' He wondered whether he should've mentioned it, whether it might look like he was casting about for pity.

'That's a bummer. What happened?'

'Car accident.'

'Well ...'

'Dad rolled the car.' Then he felt even worse. 'A kangaroo came out and he swerved …'

'That's the thing, isn't it? You can learn all you like …'

'Yeah.'

'So, you don't want to be comin' back to do all this again?'

'No.'

'Despite the fact that you just went through a stop sign.'

Aiden shook his head. 'Did I?'

'Pull over.'

He checked, indicated and pulled over. Then he sat back in his seat, cursing himself. 'Bloody hell, I've failed, haven't I?'

'Yes.'

'Shit.'

And the examiner asked, 'What have you got, Shorthorn?'

Aiden didn't get it. 'Sorry?'

'Well, there's no point comin' back, is there?' He started ticking a column of boxes on his sheet. Then he looked at him. 'Promise me you'll look next time?'

'Yes.'

'If a truck hada come along then …'

'Okay.'

'Right, so you can reverse parallel?'

'Yes.'

He ticked the box.

'Reverse around a corner?'

'Yes.'

He looked at him. 'No bloody grog, right?'

'Yep … no.'

'Not a drop. You wanna stay alive?'

'Yes.'

'Slow on dirt roads, and don't try to impress your mates. They're prob'ly a bunch of inbred farmers' sons anyway, present company excepted.'

Aiden smiled. 'I haven't even got my own car.'

'No V8s, no fat wheels, roll bars, all that shit. Keep it simple.'

'Yep.'

'And stop at stop signs.'

'Okay.'

'And yer better watch out for kangaroos.' He paused and looked him in the eyes. 'I bet she was a nice lady, your mum?'

'She was.'

'One death's enough. Got it?'

'Yes.'

'Good. Do a U-turn and stop in front of that shop. I gotta buy some smokes.'

When they arrived back at the office, Aiden pulled in and gave his dad the thumbs up. He parked, got out and swapped his L plates for Ps. Harry was the first to him, and he stared up as though he'd just returned from the moon. 'See, I told you,' he said, studying the piece of paper with the ticks. Trevor and Murray were soon over, shaking his hand, before Trevor turned to the examiner. 'I remember you.'

He was hitching his pants. 'Almost perfect,' he said. 'Forgot to check his mirror once, apart from that ...' Then he turned to Aiden. 'Come in and we'll get your licence.'

For the first time in a long time Aiden felt that life wasn't so bad, that it wasn't all weight, that there was something beyond the confusion. He turned to his dad and whispered, 'I went through a stop sign.'

Trevor smiled, remembering.

Late afternoon, long shadows. Aiden cruised the back streets of Port Augusta, stopping for pedestrians, giving way to cars that should've given way to him.

Harry was laughing. 'So you stopped at the deli for him?'

'Yep, and he came out and lit up a smoke and asked if I wanted one.'

Trevor sat in the back beside his stony-faced father. Remembered being offered his own smoke. He arranged a bottle of wine and Coke on the floor between his feet. Gaby had told him she'd cook a stir-fry, so he'd bought fortune cookies. He took one from the bag and broke it in half. *You will prosper in the field of wacky inventions.* He tried to think of one. His modified cattle crush? A cradle he'd welded together to help with the marking? Or maybe his hands, destined for greatness? He offered his father a cookie but he just shook his head.

'Go on.'

'I'll have one,' Harry said, and he offered him the bag. Harry took one, opened it and read his fortune. '*Hard work breaks no bones and fine words butter no parsnips.*' He looked at his dad. 'What's that mean?'

'Who knows?' He turned to his father.

Murray looked at him as if he were stupid. 'It means that a lot of talking gets you nowhere.' His eyes seemed to stay on Trevor, who was offering Aiden a cookie.

He was far too busy. 'Left or right?'

'Left.'

Murray was still staring at him, and his eyes said, You seem to know the route well.

'What?' Trevor asked, taking another cookie. He crushed it and it crumbled into the seat. '*Listen to life, and you will hear the voice of life crying: Be!*' he almost sang.

Murray was still looking at him. 'Be?'

'Yeah, get on with your life.' He leaned forward. 'Straight ahead at this roundabout.' He studied the scrap of paper. *Be!*

It sounded so simple: Be! Exist. Function. Live. Love. Eat. Fuck. Smile. Be happy. So simple but so difficult. He'd come to believe that every left turn was laden with guilt; every comment analysed and found wanting; every suggestion ignored, or at least discounted; every idea for a new way forward rolled tightly in his father's fingers, lit and smoked; every line of poetry lost in the generator's grunt. He flattened the fortune and placed it in his shirt pocket.

'Can I have another one?' Harry asked.

'After tea.'

Gaby's house was modest but inventive. It was Port Augusta dolomite, surviving in the sun with its red-tile carapace, bleached besser bricks and too-big windows shaded by torn blinds. But she'd imparted herself upon it: a little cactus garden where the grass had died, a few gnomes, one with his head glued on, a windmill made from beer cans. There was a hose dribbling onto a lemon tree and a football-sized Buddha resting between cane chairs on the verandah; wind chimes, a dreamcatcher and prayer flags, some worn down to a stub of threaded philosophy.

Aiden pulled into the driveway, careful to manoeuvre between the narrow fence posts. He stopped and they got out. Murray stood staring at a collage made from shells and leaves, hanging beside the front door. 'It's not Bundeena,' he said.

'Promise you'll try?' Trevor asked.

He shrugged.

'A couple of hours, okay?'

He didn't mind this, as such. It was more a case of what came next: the small wedding, in a small park; the moving van; the bathroom reclaimed by lavender soap and fresh towels; her, inserted into his life like a deep splinter; opinions floating through the air and settling on the floor like talc; *fine words butter no parsnips*; her laugh; bright dresses on the line beside their overalls and pyjamas. This woman, part of his family.

Trevor was still looking at him. 'A couple of hours?'

'Go on, get going.'

She met them at the door, took the wine and fortune cookies and kissed them all (even Murray) on the cheek. She ran her hand through Harry's hair but he just looked at her, unsure. Then she turned formal, shook Aiden's hand and said, 'I hear congratulations are in order?'

'I only lost one point.'

'Great.' She took his arm and squeezed it. He wanted to reclaim it but she wouldn't give it back. Instead, he said, 'Dad said I could have the car every Saturday night.' He smiled at his father, determined to take advantage of the moment.

'No, you misheard what I said,' Trevor replied. 'You can earn some money and buy your own.'

Murray was already finding it far too saccharine. Everyone was trying too hard. He wanted to turn and walk all the way back to Bundeena. Nothing, he guessed, came from dreamcatchers. The bangles, again, and this time, earrings made from loops of wire, banging up against each other like a scaled-down solar system.

'Come in,' she said, and they went into the house, smelling of incense and fresh basil in cold rolls in the middle of a coffee table in the middle of her small living room. 'Sit down.'

They all found a spot on one of her old couches. Murray sank into his plastic-covered cushion. *Why, why cover it? It's old. It's shit.* He watched as she offered the cold rolls to his family. 'No, thank you,' he said, when she came to him.

'Go on. You'll like them.'

But he was holding up his head, indicating she shouldn't continue.

He was worried about the crappy furniture. What could it mean? Earth mother with plastic sofa covers? A mean streak? He thought he could see it in her small, brown eyes. She was all for Gaby. Everything else was a hobby. That's why she didn't have a husband or children. She was some sort of monster, trawling life for its every giveaway possibility. He looked at a bookcase and noticed a picture of a young girl. 'She your niece?' he asked, indicating.

'Yes,' she replied. 'My sister's daughter.'

Trevor was looking at his father. I told you she's been married and divorced, he wanted to say. I told you the fella was a prick, and broke her jaw. I told you all of this, Dad, so why bring it up now?

She sat and looked at Harry's leg. 'How's it feel?'

'Good.' He showed her, moving it around.

'Back on the bike soon?'

'Yes.' Although he knew he should've been chattier, he couldn't force it. He didn't know who she was or what she wanted from him. He looked down the hallway into the bedroom and was even more confused. Had his dad been in there? With her? And what about his mum, what would she be thinking about all this? But he tried. 'You can see here and here, where the pins are.' He showed her.

'Nasty,' she said, leaning forward. 'Can you still feel them?'

He stopped to think. 'No.'

'You'll be able to show your grandchildren.' She stopped, realising. There was a few moments' silence. Murray sat back, folded his arms, stretched his legs and crossed his feet. Nice work, he thought, studying her face. Fairy fucking godmother, loved by all.

Trevor was looking at him. He could read the body language.

'We been out with the calves, haven't we, Dad?'

'Yeah.'

'I's telling Gaby all about it. She said she'd like to come and help out.'

'Yeah?' He studied her. 'Work in a chemist, do yer?'

'A pharmacy.'

'What's the difference?'

'None, really.'

Well, why fuckin' mention it.

'Big difference between cows and … cattle,' she said.

'Yes.'

'Still, I'd like to come and have a look at your station.'

'Farm,' he said, feeling himself sink into the couch.

Old prick, she thought, although she kept smiling.

'You might find something to interest you,' he said. 'Carelyn often slipped on her boots and came out to help.'

She guessed this was how it would be if she intruded any further. 'That's nice,' she replied, looking at Trevor for help.

'Carelyn liked to look the part,' he said, but stopped, turning to the boys with a slight smile.

'She was no good with a spanner,' Aiden added, but even he had to leave it there.

Gaby stared at Murray. He smiled back. 'You could always try a bit of branding,' he said.

She stood and went into the kitchen. Trevor followed her. She removed a tray of spring rolls from the oven and slammed them down on the bench. 'Why did you have to bring him?'

Murray heard her; the boys heard her. They looked at their grandfather. Harry wanted to say, You should make an effort, Pop. Aiden wasn't so subtle, but said it with his eyes.

'What?' Murray shot back, but Aiden just reached for another cold roll, dipped it and stretched back in his own plastic.

'Why's she got this stuff on her couches?' Harry whispered to his brother.

'Keep them clean.'

Then the kitchen door closed and all they could hear was mumbling.

Gaby was working with her head down, filling a finger-bowl with sweet chilli sauce. 'There's no point talking to him,' she said. 'He's an old prick.'

Trevor tried to come around, to meet her eyes. 'He just takes a while to warm to people. It took years before he even acknowledged Carelyn.'

'Well, you need to tell him to grow up. That's bullshit. No excuse for rudeness. Even old age.'

He didn't know what to say. She was right. But there was no quick fix with Murray. He'd have to teach her patience – the sort he'd perfected over many decades.

'What have you said to him?' she asked.

'You know.'

'What?' She glared at him. 'That's weak, Trevor. *You could always try a bit of branding.*'

'Ssh.'

Murray tipped his head back. 'Maybe she could put a pie on for me,' he said.

'Pop,' Aiden said.

'What?'

'You've eaten Mum's stir-fries.'

'And her cold rolls,' Harry added.

'Can't remember that.'

'You have,' Aiden said.

Gaby slid the spring rolls onto a glass tray. 'I wanted to come to the hospital.'

'Ten minutes and it was all over,' Trevor replied.

'I think I've hit it off with him, haven't I?'

'Of course. Harry's anyone's friend.'

'Thanks.'

'You know what I mean. He won't get bitchy, like that old cunt.' She smiled.

'That's the main thing, isn't it, the boys?'

'I guess.'

'And Aiden, he just deals with facts, you know?'

Meanwhile, Murray was cataloguing her living room: some sort of New Guinea or Polynesian mask; a wall hanging – an old rug that, he supposed, told some sort of story; a sideboard covered with happy and serious Buddhas; a bookcase full of books (he guessed) she'd never read. And even if she had, it just proved she didn't live in the real world: *Timon of Athens*, *The Power of One*. Shit. Nothing about anything real. All as phoney as the cubist self-portrait hanging above the door.

Harry liked the painting. He walked over and stood in front of it, trying to recognise the figure hiding in the lines. As she came in he asked, 'Is that you?'

'Yes.'

'I thought so.'

She put down the spring rolls and came up behind him. 'See, the nose,' she said, showing him her own. She put her arm around his shoulder and asked, 'You like art?'

'Sort of,' he said, stiffening.

Murray was watching them.

'I've got plenty of canvases, brushes and paints.'

'Aiden likes art,' he replied, turning to his brother and using this movement to loosen her grip. Murray could see what he was doing. He closed his lips and ran his tongue over the back of his teeth.

She sat down and smiled at Aiden. Guessed he would be the harder nut to crack. 'A farm boy who likes art?'

He shrugged. 'It's something to do.'

'He's good,' Harry said, sitting down. 'We're painting Aunt Fay's old car.'

'Does she mind?'

'It doesn't run any more. It's like a hundred years old.'

'Forty,' Aiden said.

'We're painting the whole farm on it. Aiden drew it.' He looked at his brother.

'I can't wait to see it,' she replied, turning to Murray. 'You've got some very talented grandsons.'

'Yes,' he said. 'Hopefully they end up being very talented farmers.' He looked at Harry, wary of his growing enthusiasm. He could see that she would trap him this way.

'It's modern art,' Harry said, and Murray wanted to tell him to be quiet.

'Have you tried watercolours?' she asked Aiden.

'No.'

'Before you go, remind me, I'll give you a set.'

He lit up. 'Great.'

'Try your hand. When I visit you can show me.'

When I visit … when I visit, Murray thought. He studied the way Aiden was looking at her and wanted to say, She's not your mother, boy.

'And you,' she said to Harry. 'I'll give you a canvas. You can try your own self-portrait.'

'What about me?' Murray asked.

'You paint?'

'I haven't got the time to paint.'

Trevor came in with three glasses of wine. He put them down on the coffee table. Murray said, 'I can't drink that.'

'Why?'

'My gout.'

One glass, Trevor wanted to say. One fucking glass. You would any other time.

'I'll have it,' Aiden said.

Trevor slid it across the table.

'He shouldn't be having that,' Murray said.

'One won't hurt him, he's seventeen,' Gaby said.

Murray glared at her. He could see his future, again, and he didn't like it.

'In France they're drinking at twelve,' she said.

'In France, children do what their *parents* tell them.'

'Dad, one won't hurt,' Trevor said.

Aiden sensed the dilemma. He lifted the glass and put it back beside his father's. 'I think I'd rather Coke anyway.'

Gaby looked at Trevor, and Trevor at his dad.

'What?' Murray said. 'The law says eighteen.'

'Since when do you …?'

Aiden stood and asked Gaby for a Coke.

'Of course. I put it in the fridge.'

'Want one, Harry?'

'Ta.'

Aiden went into the kitchen and there was silence. After a while Gaby picked up the spring rolls and offered them to Trevor, Harry and Murray. 'No, thank you,' he said. 'And I'm not sure about the meal. What are we having?'

'Cantonese stir-fry,' she replied.

'I don't suppose you got a chop or anything?'

'No, no chops.'

Trevor shook his head and looked at his father. 'Should we just go home?'

'I just asked if she had a chop.' He moved about in the plastic and wiped something from his lip. 'It doesn't matter … I can get something on the way home.'

Trevor said, 'Perhaps we should just leave it for tonight, Gaby?'

'Why?' Murray growled.

'Why?' Trevor shouted at him. '*Why?*'

'Fine.' He stood and walked from the house.

The Wilkies said their goodbyes, and apologies, and set off into the night. They found Murray a few blocks away. Trevor slowed beside him but he kept walking. 'Get in,' he said.

Aiden had had enough; he reclined in his seat listening to his iPod. Harry put down his window. 'Pop.'

Murray nearly tripped on the gutter. Then, he stopped and got in the car.

17

The following day the mood persisted: Trevor sorting his receipts, scribbling columns of numbers. 'How long did you have that sports top?' he asked Aiden, sitting beside his brother at the computer.

'End of last year.'

'Did you ever wear it?'

'No.'

He put the receipt aside, determined to ask for a refund.

Murray sat across from him reading a letter from an old friend who was offering the services of a stud bull. He wanted to tell Trevor, but wouldn't. Wanted to say, We can have him for a month, and apparently he's in like Flynn. But he wouldn't even do this.

Trevor said, 'Harry, do you need more stationery?'

'No.' He kept studying the chatter on the screen.

History. Now that Aiden was Harry's home supervisor he had to make him understand; to work hard. 'What's the three age system?'

Harry stopped to think. Looked at the screen; Aiden minimised it. 'You're meant to remember.'

'I do.'

'Go on.'

'Stone Age, Bronze Age, Iron Age.' He smiled a sort of told-you-so smile.

'And what are the three Stone Ages?'

Harry shrugged. 'Maybe we should do maths?'

'*I* decide now. Fifty minutes of history. The three Stone Ages?'

Trevor guessed it could work. Aiden knew more than enough to get him through. Of course, there was the problem of familiarity, the possibility of telling your teacher to get fucked on a regular basis. But Harry knew the part he'd have to play, and that he was only allowed to kick his brother after the computer was switched off. He knew Aiden wouldn't put up with any bullshit. The corner of the room was school and it had its own set of rules. It was home room and Saturday detention and what went with those places: listening, waiting to ask questions, avoiding distractions (Chris and his movies had been banned during school hours).

'Paleolithic,' Harry said. 'Mesolithic. Neolithic.'

Aiden checked his supervisor's notes. 'Good. And what do they mean?'

'Old, Middle and New Stone Age.'

'Excellent.'

Harry grinned at him.

'What?'

'You don't have to *sound* like a teacher too.'

'Would you say that to Mrs Amery?'

'She *is* a teacher.'

'And so's Aiden,' Trevor growled, looking up.

'He's not qualified.'

Aiden slapped the back of his brother's head. 'Concentrate.'

'You could get the sack for doing that.'

'So I *am* a teacher?'

'No … sort of, I suppose.'

'Time to work.' He opened his brother's exercise book. 'All of that information summarised … go.'

'Yes, sir.'

'Don't be so rude.'

Trevor came up with a total but decided it couldn't be right. He started entering the numbers again. Could feel his father looking at him, thinking of words, waiting, returning to his letter. He knew he was probably sorry, somehow, but would never say it. Hadn't said a word during the drive home; hadn't even looked at him the rest of the evening; hadn't acknowledged him all morning.

I'm the one who should be pissed off, he thought, glancing up at him, watching his clumsy fingers crushing the paper. *I'm* the one waiting for an apology.

Their eyes met. He shook his head but Murray wouldn't be drawn. You old misery, he thought. It'd never occur to you, would it? Just to say it? No, son, she's not so bad. A bit *different*, don't you think? But her heart's in the right place.

'*Prehistory was before stuff was written down*,' Aiden read, running a finger beneath each of his brother's words.

'What's wrong with that?' Harry asked.

'Before *anything* was written down.'

'Same thing.'

'No, it's not. And here … it should be n,e,a – '

'Rubbish! Neolithic: n, e, o …' He looked at Trevor, who confirmed the spelling.

'See,' Harry said. 'And you're meant to be the teacher.'

'Harry!' Murray barked. 'Don't be such a smart arse.'

'I'm not, but anyone knows …'

'Your brother's agreed to help you.'

Not agreed, Harry thought. It's because he can't hack school.

Aiden took a deep breath. 'I never said I's the world's best speller.' He laid a worksheet in front of his brother. 'Right, answer these questions. Full sentences.'

Harry started reading. 'You're meant to explain.'

'You're smart. Work it out.'

Murray watched his son working. What, he wanted to ask, are you hoping to achieve? The money's already gone. Stop fiddling with figures. Get a new bull and let's start again.

'Full sentences,' Aiden said.

'They are.'

Murray noticed his son's hand, and the pile of receipts. This woman, he thought. The ultimate distraction. You'd rather be with her and her Buddha, wouldn't you? You really think she's gonna come and live with you? Pull on a pair of boots and walk through all that shit? Then he said, 'She started it.'

'What?'

'*He can drink*. He's my grandson.'

Trevor had recognised this streak, but it was nowhere near as bad as his father's arrogance. 'She didn't mean it like that.'

'No?'

'She's just used to speaking her mind.'

The boys were listening. Harry had written the words, *History is* ... but all he really knew was that Murray hated Gaby. 'You can't do that,' he said to his brother.

'What?' Aiden replied, grabbing the mouse and minimising the screen.

'He's looking at utes,' he said. He took the mouse, maximised the screen and revealed a page of rolls bars, spotlights and fat tyres. 'See. If he's meant to be teaching me ...'

'I was just getting a few prices,' Aiden said.

'New utes?' Trevor asked.

'Second-hand, doesn't matter.' He reclaimed the mouse and got rid of the page.

'That was the agreement,' Trevor said. 'You're meant to be helping your brother.'

Aiden looked at Harry, who just raised an eyebrow, and continued working. Chris came in with a bunch of white chrysanthemums. He went into the kitchen, filled a vase and placed the flowers in the middle of the table. Murray said, 'Are you completely stupid?'

'Mum said to bring 'em in.'

He stood, took the flowers and threw them in the bin. Then he returned, sat down and continued the letter.

'They were nice,' Chris said.

'What are chrysanthemums for?'

'That's ridiculous,' Trevor said. Aiden and Harry were listening but neither turned their head.

'Ridiculous?' Murray glared at his son accusingly.

'They're just flowers.' He turned to Chris. 'That was a nice thought.'

'Mum said …'

'I know.'

Aiden knew; Harry knew. They'd harvested Fay's chrysanthemums every May, bringing in the variously coloured bunches, placing them in vases around the house in preparation for Mother's Day. There were more on the Sunday morning, in another vase, on the tray beside the burnt toast and undercooked bacon. But this year they'd forgotten, or not bothered. The flowers had still opened, of course, which proved that nothing was that different; that their mother would still have wanted chrysanthemums.

Harry stood, went to the bin and retrieved them. Put them in the vase on the table and faced his pop. 'They're just flowers,' he repeated. 'Mum liked them.'

Murray shook his head, dropped his letter and went outside for a smoke.

'What should I do?' Chris asked.

'Go cut the rest,' Trevor said. 'Bring them inside.'

He went out to his mum. Harry returned to his lesson and Aiden to his notes. Trevor said, 'What's the point?' He piled the receipts into the box. The boys ignored him. Harry asked Aiden if Homo had a capital h and he replied, 'You should know.'

But Trevor didn't hear. He threw the calculator in the box and sat back. Then he went out to his shed, closing the door and shutting out nearly all the light and noise. He stood in the near-dark for a few moments, but even now he could hear voices: Fay asking her brother why he put the flowers in the bin; Murray asking Chris why he was such an idiot; Aiden coming out and telling them all to be quiet; the door to Murray's sleep-out slamming; Fay telling Chris not to mind him, to come and help her pick the rest of the flowers.

He pulled the string and the light popped on. Shadows, long and angular, from the lumps of wood left lying around the shed; the softness of sawdust and shavings under his feet; the consolation of freshly oiled tools moving yellow light around the room. He sat down, picked up Harry's lumpy hand and studied it. Compared it to the photos; lifted it and looked at it from every angle. Then he picked up a piece of fine sandpaper and started working between the fingers and around the knuckles.

The photos showed fine hairs, but how could you sculpt them? You could stick something on but that would look stupid. You could even gloss the fingernails but then you'd be left with some sort of ... curiosity. Something Harry would give to his sons, as they examined it, and laughed, and put it in the bin with all the other junk they were throwing away. Before Harry said, No, you better keep it ... he spent months working on that.

Meanwhile, Murray was walking down the hill at the front of the house. He stopped and stepped on his cigarette and continued. Through the bullock bush and spinifex; his laces collecting burrs and seeds. He arrived at the graveyard: four generations of Wilkies asleep in the shade of a sheoak. The small mounds of earth were covered in a carpet of pine needles. There was an old broom that had been there since he was a child. He picked it up and used it to clear the graves.

A cast-iron fence around the plot was rusting and flaking.

One of its panels had broken from the concrete and someone had wired it in place. Nothing more permanent. Screwing, bolting and welding were for the living. The graves had been cleared of weeds. This was Chris's job, every few weeks, coming down with his hoe to take care of the grass. One of the headstones had cracked. Murray had repaired it with mortar.

IN THE ARMS OF GOD

MARY WILKIE

WIFE OF BILL

MOTHER OF MORRIS AND JOHN

A no-nonsense inscription; written by Morris on the back of an envelope and sent to the mason in Port Augusta. Then the drive to town to pick it up, to wrap it in a blanket and put it in the boot; to place it in a wheelbarrow and push it, on a hot day, down the hill. The good son checking his slab was dry, fetching his mum and carrying her through the little filigree gate. Prayers (although there'd already been a service) and silence; bowed heads, as the concrete started to dry, as Mary was permanently anchored into Wilkie soil. Morris avoiding tears, happy his mum no longer had to worry about his brother. Sad that John's plot would stay empty until Jesus came to gather the faithful.

Although perhaps he already had him. Perhaps the stranger was right. In the words of the letters he'd helped Bill write to the army.

Late night and kerosene lamps, and Bill saying, 'We'll go right to the top. Monash. Leave the address, we'll find that out later. Start off by saying how you're writing on behalf of me and Mary and how you fought with Private John Wilkie. His number was 2419387. Write that down.'

Bill watched as the stranger started scribbling.

'Then tell him what you saw – about John's mental condition. His shaking and crying and screaming. Go on.'

The stranger wrote. 'Slow down,' he said.

'And say we want an inquiry, with doctors, psychiatrists, experts. Tell him how we want John's name cleared.'

The stranger stopped and looked up. 'Bill, I'll write your letter but I need time.'

'If you do it tonight I'll take it to town tomorrow.'

In the end, the stranger stayed for weeks, helping Bill and Morrie with the muster and Mary with her vegetables and flowers. Every few nights Bill would say to him: 'Perhaps we need to write another letter' or 'Perhaps we need to go to Melbourne to see them.' But the stranger would always say, No, they won't listen to us, although he did suggest they contact their local MP.

But now, Bill too was asleep in the arms of the Lord, and it'd been years since he'd worried about his lost son.

WILLIAM JAMES WILKIE
'LISTEN TO ME, LORD, AND ANSWER ME,
FOR I AM HELPLESS AND WEAK'
(Ps. 86)

Murray knelt down and ran a finger across the faint letters on the headstone: W I L L I A M … Then turned to Morrie and Mary and the bit of land the whole family would at last be forced to share.

Then there was Carelyn, still in her urn, surrounded by a pile of rocks at the base of the tree. Trevor hadn't worked out what he wanted to do. Scatter her between the graves or in the park near the house where she'd grown up in Adelaide (she'd mentioned it, but they'd never thought there was any rush deciding).

But the spot beside Mary would always be left vacant. She'd told them that one day he'd be found and brought home to sleep in the sand.

18

Trevor rose at four. He was showered and dressed before the sun was up. He closed the door to his boys' and aunt's rooms and sat down to a breakfast of hot porridge. After a few minutes he stood, opened a drawer in the tallboy and sorted through the junk: cards, receipts, handkerchiefs and two Mother's Day cards. He studied Harry's: block letters, glitter, a cotton-ball flower he'd made in the secret cave beneath his bed. HAPPY MOTHERS DAY. There was a small hand-made envelope stuck to the card, labelled: COUPONS. He pulled out a pile of cardboard disks and read:

> 1 free movie about you
> 1000 free fetch food
> one free dishwasher unpacking
> 7 free hugs (1234567 free)
> 7 free back massages

He sat down and flicked the squares of card between his fingers.

> unlimited breakfast in beds
> free make my bed for 3 days (only)

Another card was more matter-of-fact: a big cursive greeting.

Dear Mum, I hope you have a wonderful day. I'll keep Harry busy so you can watch Pretty Woman. Thanks for all the things you do and putting up with us, lots of love from your son, Aiden XXX

There was no glitter, no colour, no drawings. It was like one of his father's receipts: simple, to the point; itemising what was owed by who to whom.

He looked out of the window. The sun was up. He didn't want to be beaten to the spoils of another day, especially at sixty dollars an hour. So he placed the coupons back in the envelope, returned the cards to the drawer and grabbed his backpack. He went out through the laundry, quietly closing the door, looking at Yanga in her basket and saying, 'No barking … got it?'

Harry was awake. He sneezed three times and rubbed his eyes. Then he sniffed and said, 'Shit.'

'Shut up,' Aiden said, turning towards the wall.

'I can't help it.' He sneezed again.

Aiden attempted to cover his head with a pillow. 'Go out.'

'It'll stop.' He snorted. 'I think it's hayfever.'

'Go out!'

'It'll stop!' He tried to make it stop. His nose was tingling and he could feel another sneeze coming. It arrived; two, three, and a full-faced, snot-tailed fourth.

'Fuck off,' Aiden said.

'That must have been Dad going.'

'So what? Go back to sleep.'

Harry got out of bed, walked down the hall to the toilet, pulled a few metres of paper from the roll and returned. He waited until the trickle started and blew his nose. 'How many days will he be gone?'

'Three.'

I hope he's okay, he thought. He imagined the crane and the long lengths of steel suspended in the air; the wheels of the tractor; and his father, without a hard hat, failing to predict or see the thing that might kill him. He blew his nose again. The paper shredded and there were fragments clinging to his nose.

'Stop sniffing,' Aiden said.

'He'll be okay, won't he?'

'You've got shit all over your face.' He turned back to the wall.

Harry wiped his nose and the paper crumbled onto the sheets. He lay back against his bedhead. 'Mum used to always tell me off, remember?'

'What?'

'I remember once, it was so bad she gave me a tea towel and said, That should last a few hours.' He remembered trying to do his lesson as Carelyn wiped his forehead with a wet flannel, as he dragged his tea towel across his red-raw nostrils, as she said, 'Just blow it all out, I'm sick of hearing you,' and he replied, 'It just keeps coming.' He remembered Mrs Amery saying, 'Perhaps we should try again tomorrow?'

'It's Mother's Day,' he said.

'I know.'

Silence, as they both tried to think how the gap might be plugged, for today at least.

'Now I don't feel so good,' he said, giving up on the paper and wiping his nose on his bed sheets.

Aiden looked up at him. 'There's no point going back over everything.'

He knew he was right. It just made you feel worse. But she was still there, sitting on the bed, talking about hayfever. 'Aiden, remember when I did all those coupons?' He kept wiping his nose on the sheet. 'I remember I had to keep unpacking the dishwasher.'

'You did it once.'

'More than that, and remember, the back massage?' As he remembered spreading cushions and laying his mum face-down on the lounge-room floor. He could still smell the menthol on his hands.

'You lasted a week,' Aiden said, giving up on sleep, laying back and staring up at the ceiling.

'What?'

'A thousand free fetch foods.'

He guessed he was right. It was only a few days before he'd decided he'd been over-generous: 1000? So one day when Carelyn was out hanging washing on the line he'd gathered all his coupons from around the house, put them back in the envelope and buried the card in the bottom of the tallboy drawer. 'I shouldn't have done that,' he said.

'What?'

He couldn't say it. Still, he knew now. It was a selfish thing to do. Carelyn had never mentioned the coupons again. Perhaps, he thought, she'd forgotten. Or perhaps she knew what he'd done and let it go. Forgiving him; blessing him with her silence. 'I don't feel so good,' he repeated.

'Well, there's not much you can do.'

'Why did Dad have to go … today?'

'He had no choice.'

He wasn't happy with this. 'Why would they work on Mother's Day?'

'It's just another day.'

'No, it's not.'

Seven free hugs. He remembered giving her all of these, crossing them off the card, offering more. That was easy. The thought of this redeemed coupon made him happy for a moment.

'We can't just forget her,' he said.

'I never said that. I just said …' Now he wasn't sure himself.

'I hid the coupons.'

'Well, that's the sort of thing nine-year-old shit-heads do. Don't feel bad.'

But he did. He felt his forehead: cool. His nose was clear and the tingling had stopped. He wiped the last few drops of mucus from his hands. 'I'm not sneezing,' he said.

'Good.'

Silence.

'Maybe we should cook breakfast anyway.'

Aiden looked at him. 'For who?'

'Aunty Fay. She's a mum. I don't think Chris is gonna do anything.'

Aiden smiled at him. 'That's it, Shit-for-brains. Useful ideas.'

Trevor drove west for three hours. Highway, with lunch at a rest-stop; dead wombat; a Rotary map that had been removed, or had never existed. After another hour he turned left at a pair of tractor tyres, consulted a mud-map and drove east.

This was the back of a forgotten beyond, good for nothing (Murray would say) except walkabouts and atom bombs. But Trevor liked it. At least the roads were hard; smooth and sun-baked, leading from somewhere to nowhere. The vegetation, hanging on around soaks and creeks, was mean and hardy: sandalwood and plenty of mulga, even a scattering of Mitchell grass across the low country.

He arrived at the base camp just after 1 pm. It had been set up beside an overgrown pile of old tracks. There was a maintenance shed full of bird shit, lumps of iron and a spaghetti of old signals and wires. A water tank beside a length of track that hadn't been ripped up. Nearby, a flat-top truck and on this, a transportable building with a set of steps leading up from an area all campfire and esky, swags and a tent-kitchen. He parked and got out.

'Hello?'

He walked over to the steps, climbed up and looked inside the transportable. 'Hello?' It contained an office and a collection of camp stretchers. He stood on a landing and studied the camp.

'Hello.' A short man emerging from behind a distant pepper tree, hitching his pants and smiling. 'You Trevor?' Approaching him, carrying a roll of toilet paper. They shook hands. 'James Turner. Nice to meet you.'

'Likewise.'

'I's expecting you this morning.'

Trevor was taken back. 'Ross said I'd be starting tomorrow.'

Turner shook his head. 'No, mate.' As though it wasn't up for discussion. 'Today. Sunday.'

'Well, I can get straight to it.'

'That's what I like to hear.'

They went into the transportable and sat on either side of a desk. 'We'll fill in the paperwork tonight,' Turner said. 'You're not plannin' on havin' an accident today, are you?'

'No.'

'Good.' He sat staring at Trevor. 'Ross said you run Shorthorn?'

'Yes.'

'Beef prices are shit, eh?'

'Very shit.'

'That why you're here?'

'Pretty much.'

'Okay.' He seemed happy with this. 'This track out here, it's a fifty-kilometre spur. We've done about ten clicks but the rain's set us back. That's where you come into it.'

Trevor was happy to listen. He'd never had a job interview and he didn't want one now. He'd offered his back, hands and brain, and as far as he was concerned they'd already shaken on it. And anyway, he was in no mood to feign enthusiasm. He was tired and didn't care about spur lines.

'Us few blokes often work together, we're a team,' Turner said.

'Good.'

'So, you're the … extra muscle?'

'Fine.'

'The rail's all fifty and sixty pounds a yard. Most of it's headed

up to Queensland for the sugar rail. Fishplates, bolts, the rest –
straight into a skip. We've got twelve-tonne excavators, a four-
wheel drive, rubber-tyre dozer, three semi-trailers, couple of utes
and this thing to live in … or yer swag, if you'd like.'

'In the car.'

'Good. I thought we'd start you on one of the excavators. You
happy with that?'

'Very.'

'Yeah?' He wondered why Trevor asked so few questions.
'One's fitted with a hydraulic rock breaker. We use it to shear off
the fishplate bolts.'

Trevor moved in his seat. 'Sounds easy enough.'

'We're workin' a couple of clicks up the track. I'll drive yer. You
wanna get changed?'

Trevor looked down at his boots, shiny with an hour of Chris's
spit and polish. 'I'm ready to go.'

Back at Bundeena, afternoon tea was Harry's scones – flat,
crumbling, chalky in the mouth. Sitting on the porch, waiting
for the Indian Pacific, Fay was happy. She was holding a card –
her son's. He'd spelt the words correctly (with a little help from
Harry) and coloured the paper so hard he'd made holes. He was
sitting beside her, looking where she looked, breathing when
she breathed, eating when she ate. 'I did the sifting,' he said, as
scone crumbled down his chin.

'Perfect,' she replied, placing her hand over his. 'This is the
best Mother's Day ever.'

'Really?'

'Of course.' She tried to recall a time when he'd even remembered, ignoring her in favour of Carelyn, apparently the only
mother at Bundeena.

She waited for the train but it wouldn't come. It was

overdue. 'Maybe there's been some sort of delay,' she said.

One year, she remembered, Chris followed the boys into their mum's room. He stood waiting for praise for the breakfast he hadn't cooked. Carelyn said, 'What about your mum, Chris?' He'd looked at her, unsure what she meant.

'Shouldn't you make her some breakfast?'

'Mum?' He'd stopped to think.

'Yes. What about a soft-boiled egg?'

Harry came out with a cup of tea and placed it beside her. 'Uncle Chris said they're your favourite.'

'Yes.'

'And he said he's gonna do all the dishes tonight, to save you.'

Fay looked at her son. 'He can help me.'

'No, by himself,' Harry demanded, looking at Chris.

'By myself,' Chris said.

And she patted his hand again.

Harry sat down and waited. He watched how she drank from the china cup (the only one she'd use) and dried her bottom lip with her handkerchief. He studied each of her yellow teeth and noticed how she kept moving her jaw in a slight circular motion.

'The train's late,' she said, looking at him.

'Is it?'

'The old days, the Tea and Sugar, that'd never be late.' And she was back on the gravel, climbing the steps to the post office, going inside the small, hot room; taking a stub and filling it out; giving it to the girl behind the counter.

'That all today, Fay?'

'Yes, please.'

Chris had filled out his own slip and handed it to the teller. 'Two hundred pounds please.'

She smiled at mother and son. 'It's dollars now.'

'Two hundred *pounds*, please.'

Shelves, with a dozen different forms that could be filled in; rubber stamps on a carousel; ink, in jars, on pads; wood veneer; posters of SA GOV Reg 3C PT 5; the smell of clean lino; flies (despite the wire); and a little fan, caged in the corner, with its precise grey blades slicing the air.

'What grade are you in?' the girl asked Chris.

'Seven.'

'No, you're not,' Fay said. 'He got to grade four, but we discontinued.'

Back on the porch, Fay studied the writing on the card. 'They were always on time,' she said.

Harry didn't understand the connection between his aunt, the card and the train. 'The Tea and Sugar?' he asked.

'Yes.'

'Did you have to be there, waiting?'

'That's right.' She put the card down. 'And if you weren't, there'd be a trip to Port Augusta.'

Chris could see his mum had given up on the scones. 'It's Mother's Day,' he told her.

'I know,' she replied, holding his hand.

That afternoon and into the grey of the evening Trevor worked ahead of the gang, using his adapted excavator with its rock-breaker to shear off bolts and remove the fishplates holding the sleepers in place. One, two, dozens, hundreds, as the sun collapsed onto the horizon. Again and again, the same movement of his hands, the same shifting in his seat, the same thoughts of home: Aiden arguing with Murray, Murray descending into one of his moods.

The interior of his cab was full of dirt and chip packets. There was a tape-deck: Dire Straits on a loop. By 5 pm he knew which song was coming next, where the tape had been chewed, each guitar solo and lyric. Turner would arrive and knock on the cab window and ask, 'You gettin' the knack?' and he'd think, Six hundred metres of cracked bolts. Does it look like I'm gettin' the knack? But he'd say, 'No problems, once you get the rhythm.'

'Good … when you get going you should be able to work a bit faster.'

'Really?' As he looked at what he'd done and wondered how that could be the case.

There was a late tea of cold chicken, strong coffee and thick slices of stale bread coated with jam. Then, a talk around a fire of old sleepers, the chill settling on their faces. Someone asked him, 'What would you rather? This, or mucking around with cows?'

'This is a lot simpler.'

'But not as much fun?'

They talked among themselves: a story about a monkey and an ape; Mick Reynolds gone back to Alice; and Turner, fiddling with papers and a calculator. 'We're not gettin' enough sticks on the trucks,' he said.

'How's that?' someone asked.

'There should be a hundred and eleven rails on each trailer. I calculate, a hundred and four or five.'

There was a pause as everyone waited for a solution.

'We'll have to work on that.' He looked at Trevor. 'How about you have a go tomorrow?'

'Sure.'

'I'll show you how it's done. If we miss five per load that's an extra trip every day.'

Turner stuck to his figures, but the others turned to politics. They formed a chorus of half-remembered song, unreliable memories and stories about their families. Trevor didn't feel part of this arrangement. He walked away from the fire and tried to call home but there was no coverage.

The next day he was on an excavator equipped with a hydraulic forestry claw. Another man, a young Irishman named Romona, put a chain around each of the loose sticks and he lifted them onto the tray. After he'd lowered them Romona released the chains. He worked slowly, constantly aware of the young man's head, the rails swinging in the light breeze.

Mostly it was just boredom, again. No variation on the theme of up, down, left, return, move, handbrake. By 11 am he'd ejected the tape. He'd thought of each member of his family and what they'd be doing.

He felt anxious: his body sweating, his heart racing. He didn't know why he felt this way. Things would be okay for a few days without him. There'd be arguments and muttered insults. Harry would tell him when he got home and he'd have to spend a few days sorting it all out. But they'd survive.

At 1 pm Turner arrived in his ute, watched them working for a few minutes and counted the number of rails on the truck. Trevor noticed how he moved his lips as he counted; how he lost track and started again. How, when he'd finished, he scribbled something on his sheet.

Turner called to him to stop working. He gathered this team of two and stared at them and shook his head. 'Ninety-three sticks.'

Trevor shrugged. 'So?'

'You could get another five or six on.' He waited. 'Ten sticks short. That's another truck.' Then he approached the end of the tray so he could see how they'd been stacking them. 'See, gaps, here and here … you haven't been careful enough.'

Trevor didn't respond. Turner was an unlikable person. Trying too hard to understand why they were seven sticks short and how the fuel had been used up so quickly.

'Here, see, the way I showed you this morning. With all the flats up close.'

Trevor nodded, mostly defeated. He tried to remember the last time anyone had talked to him like this. Murray, all the time, but that was different. The deputy principal at Mercy? For refusing to pick up other people's rubbish. He could remember saying, 'Fair enough if it was mine.'

'Walking past other people's rubbish is just as bad as if you'd dropped it yourself.'

'No, it's not.'

'Pardon?'

Although he remembered standing up to the Brother then he didn't feel the same way now. 'We've been working as fast as we can.'

'Precision beats speed, mate.'

Mate? What did he mean by that? *Mate?*

'We can work on that too,' he managed.

'Good. Even if you could get five or six more.'

He looked at him and thought, Could you get 111? Has anyone got that many? In the same way he'd said to the principal, when he'd been dragged in to see him, 'It was an old sandwich.'

'Yes?'

'Old meat and pickles.'

Just a pair of eyes sizing him up.

'I take responsibility for myself.'

He was shrinking, collapsing, in front of Turner. He thought of the money but remembered the debt and wondered if it would make any difference. 'Should we stop for a bit of lunch?' he asked.

'We've gotta get this load off, so you're gonna have to finish it first.'

'Does it matter? If we make it quick? Twenty minutes?'

Turner glared back. He could tell the troublemakers. 'It's better if we can all just agree,' he said.

'It is ...'

'So?'

Trevor took a moment, and returned to his excavator. Turner watched him go. He couldn't see why they were arguing over seven lumps of iron.

That night he decided to sleep inside the transportable shack. Here, he was safe from the cold on his face and the conversation and singing and laughing that dragged into the night. As he lay in his swag he thought of Harry. There hadn't been a day, he guessed, when they'd gone without hearing each other's voice. Even during the months in hospital there'd be a morning, lunch and bedtime call.

Still, he supposed, he'd be okay. He'd be running things, as usual, growling at Murray for leaving his loose tobacco on the coffee table.

He heard rats, but couldn't see them. He wondered how they'd travelled so far. Maybe they'd come with the building and settled in to make the best of things? Or maybe they were from the old machinery shed, already stripped back to its iron skeleton.

No, he thought. That's enough.

The thought came to him in an instant. *That's enough*. Like an unexpected breakfast, brought into his room on a tray, as Harry jumped up and woke him from a deep sleep.

That's enough.

He could have remained, and argued with himself, but he couldn't see the point. Life was too short. The pain in his left wrist, from where he'd wrestled for fourteen hours with someone else's hydraulic controller, was a prompt. He rolled his swag, gathered his few things in his backpack and left the building. Once he was at the bottom of the steps he stopped and looked at the sleeping faces. The fire was still burning.

He turned to go.

'You won't get any pay,' Turner mumbled.

'Shove yer fuckin' pay,' he replied. 'And yer sticks.'

There was a short pause, then Turner said, 'Can't hack it, eh?'

Trevor waited. He could still see the principal, grasping the cane, his jaw clenched.

19

Turkey nest. He could see it in the distance – full, less than a week ago, but now shrunk to a puddle. He could see the rest of his farm from halfway up the ladder: the old long-drop where Murray would sit with his ukulele; the trail-bike track where Harry and Aiden used to race each other; the scar, in the distance, where the earth had once been graded for a landing strip; a graveyard of old fence posts and wire; the neat square where his wife sat waiting.

The power had failed during the night following his return: the roads peeling away as he drove too fast, his tyres skidding on loose gravel. He'd wondered if it mightn't be for the best. The car, his head and body, perhaps, compressed; a fire, just to make sure; the wreck going unnoticed for a few days.

He arrived at the top of the ladder and checked the eight solar panels. The circuits were all switched on, functioning. There was a row of green lights but no sign of electricity. Fay was anxious, her washing machine full, her vacuum sitting idle in the lounge room. Chris was staring at the television, waiting for a miracle, trying to force a video cassette into the machine. Harry was more philosophical. Lessons could wait. Tuesday was year level assembly, maths, and another hour of the Mesolithic. Luckily, Aiden had already learnt to improvise: a page of homophones.

He crawled onto the roof, inched his way over to the panels and shook them. Secure. Examined the cables that ran from the silver boxes. Intact. 'Fuck,' he said, sitting down on the tiles.

'What?' Murray called up.

He moved to see him. 'They look okay to me.'

'They all read zero.'

'Must be a problem with the control panel.'

'You can fix it,' Murray said, farting and then lighting a cigarette.

'We might need an electrician.'

'Bullshit. You can fix it.'

Murray couldn't remember ever having had an electrician. Even when the house was wired (Bill up a ladder, shouting at Mary), rewired, fans fitted, extra power points added. It was all common sense: earth, live, neutral. And anyway, what electrician was going to travel to Bundeena?

'Where are the manuals?' Trevor asked, climbing down.

'In the desk.'

He jumped down the last few steps and walked towards the door. Murray followed him. 'You think I should start the generator?'

'No.'

'Fay wants to get on with it.'

'Tell her to wait.' He went inside. A few minutes later he re-emerged, flicking through the manual.

'It's full of diesel,' Murray said.

'What?'

'The generator. We've lost food before. It's a big job to replace it all.' He wanted to mention the time, seven or eight years before, when the power had dropped out during the night. When he, Trevor, whose job it was to fix that sort of thing, had taken most of the following forty-three degree day to deal with the problem. Then two trips to town for fresh food. The waste piled beside the bottle tree. Rabbits, rats and dingoes until he, Trevor, head of the house, found time to dig a hole and bury it. 'It's better to be safe than sorry.'

'Five minutes.'

'That's what you said two minutes ago.'

Trevor glared at him, then kept reading. 'The problem must be in the box.'

Murray looked out across the grass. 'So, they payin' yer?' he asked.

'Yes.'

'You won't see any money.'

'How do you know?'

'If someone walked out on me ...'

'I didn't walk out on anyone.'

'No?'

'He was a prick.'

Murray couldn't see the problem. 'He'd have to be, wouldn't he?'

'Why?'

'He's got some other fella breathin' down his neck.'

Trevor was confused. 'It wasn't *what* he said ...'

Murray spat tobacco from his lips. He was used to this argument. It didn't bother him anymore. It was just Trevor, unfortunately. Even as a child he'd act the same way, building half a table, wiring most of a fence, finishing the majority of his education. You can't afford to lose interest, he'd always say. Even if it's a mistake, see it through, otherwise people won't take you seriously.

His boy, he knew, could be trusted with the muster, mostly, but he still had to be there, watching, telling him to finish a mob when he wanted to leave them until the next day. This is why he believed he had to keep the place in his name for as long as possible. Family businesses were ruined by the weakest link. Like John, curling up in a trench somewhere, and Bill, living the bit of life he could handle before it all got too much. This was a shame they were still recovering from. 'We've got a lot of meat in those freezers,' he said to his son.

'He wouldn't even let us have a lunch break.'

'You do the same with the men, if there's animals waitin'.'

'That's different.'

'How?'

'These were lumps of metal.'

Murray was angry that his son couldn't see the world as it really was. 'He's runnin' a business.'

'So?'

Fay appeared at the sliding door. 'Chris is asking about his movie,' she said.

'Tell him it can't be repaired.'

'No?'

'Give us five minutes.'

Trevor knew he'd done everything he could to show his father he was capable. He'd done well at school, despite the indifference of his teachers and the irrelevance of the subjects. He'd put his own interests on hold. He knew he could've done something creative: art, sculpture, music. But all these things were just notions, not something anyone took seriously when there were troughs to clean and gates to weld.

So, he'd determined to become a good farmer. He clearly remembered Murray putting him in charge of the muster when he was nineteen. He remembered riding his favourite horse and finding big, angry mobs and moving out in front of the other men. Remembered talking on the radio, and Bill Clarke saying, 'If you head another mile east there's a couple of dozen more.' Finding them, and other herds, and bringing them all into the yards.

Murray threw the scraps to the chooks. There was a flutter of legs and feathers and the leghorns started trawling the leftovers. 'Go on,' he said, kicking one away from a lump of chicken schnitzel. He went into the chook house, searched the boxes and emerged with six shit-smeared eggs.

An old Toyota with dented panels drove into the compound. Gaby got out and looked around. 'Hello?'

He retreated into the darkness of the henhouse, careful not to give himself away. Watched as she opened her back door, retrieved a small case and a bag full of awkwardly shaped objects; as she tried to hold both and walk towards the laundry; as Chris came out and took the case from her.

'I'm Christopher,' he said, offering his hand.

She accepted it. 'Hello, Christopher, my name's Gaby.'

He couldn't work out what she was wearing: knee-high boots over a sort of riding pants arrangement; a plaid shirt and a vest – something the Queen might wear at Balmoral. He couldn't work out why she was dressed this way. Was she intending to work, and had she misunderstood the dress code? Or was this some sort of landed gentry fashion statement? Or was she just a snob, trying to create the right (wrong) impression?

She went inside, and he followed with his eggs, his stony face, his determination to retreat from their society-of-seven until she was gone. As he came in she stood, smiled, held his arm and kissed him. 'Murray, beautiful place, just like I imagined.'

'How are yer, Gaby?'

'Excellent. It's a nice straight drive, isn't it? Gives you time to think about things.' She stopped, realising the road was connected to other things.

Trevor was sitting on the couch, holding the bag she'd brought in, while Gaby sat next to him. Harry was on the floor and Aiden was perched on the armrest. Fay and Chris were at the dining-room table, and Chris looked unhappy, seeing how this woman had settled on his throne.

'I feel like Father Christmas,' she said, placing her hands on her knees, and searching each face. 'Right, children first.' She reached into the bag and produced two plastic-wrapped canvases. 'There,' she said, presenting one to each of the boys. 'As promised. I expect to see a masterpiece before I leave tomorrow.'

'We've only got three colours,' Harry said, and she produced two sets of acrylic paints. 'See.'

The boys took the gifts and smiled. Murray stared at her. He hadn't thought she'd try to buy them, yet. Even she'd be more subtle than that. She was feeding off their gratitude, using it to strengthen her resolve.

'I'm gonna try a landscape,' Harry said, and he stood and showed her the possibilities beyond the front door.

'There's not much to paint,' she said.

Murray sat on the edge of the table. 'It's just how you look at it.'

She knew he was trying to block her. 'Well, you paint whatever you like,' she said to Harry.

Trevor was staring at his father. 'Perhaps you should have a go, Dad?'

'I haven't got time for all that.' He could see from the grin on his son's face that these two were now a team. 'That generator's nearly empty,' he said to Trevor, reminding him of where, and who, he was. 'We can't use up all the diesel, if those panels don't work.'

'I'll get to them.'

Gaby knew she could get around the old bastard. Had to. She knew he could be a tornado, ripping through every landscape he didn't like. Trevor had already told her the stories – how he'd never liked Carelyn, either, but how she'd learnt to manage him by throwing every lie, every grudge, every inconsistency back at him. The way he loved steak and kidney pie one night but refused to eat it when he was in a shit with her. How Carelyn would just say, 'Fine, go hungry then,' and he'd reply, 'What am I gonna eat?' and she'd say, 'You sound like an eight-year-old.'

She produced a carton of cigarettes, handed them to Murray and smiled.

'What's this?' he asked.

'What's it look like?' Trevor said.

'Right ... I generally roll my own.'

'Oh, I didn't know that,' Carelyn said, pretending. She held out her hand to take them back. 'I'm sure they'll give me a refund.'

'Pop, you smoke those,' Harry said.

'Not this brand.'

'But you just said – '

'Okay.' And he glared at the small brown eyes. Then he looked at Gaby. 'I prefer rollies, but these'll do nice, thank you.'

'No worries,' she said, savouring the moment.

'You'll be through those in a week,' Trevor added.

'We'll see.' He knew what she was doing; the games she played. He wanted to ask her about her previous relationships – a husband, ground down beneath the heel? Or, more likely, a succession of boyfriends; managerial types, probably; more pricks that had no idea about anything; agreeing with her every tedious opinion until they couldn't agree any more; until the gifts and gushing and home-cooked Asian food weren't enough.

There was more: a box-set of Bruce Willis videos for Chris (although he had them all) and a book titled *A History of Lavender* for Fay. She was taken, searching the pages for French, Italian and English strains she knew but had never named: *Lavandula dentata* var. *candicans*; *L. stoechas* spp. *stoechas*. 'Beautiful,' she said, holding the book against her chest. 'I want to plant some new types.'

'They're all in there.'

'Yes, and my brother said he's gonna help me with a new garden.'

'I am?'

'Paved walkways, the lot.'

'Good on you, Dad,' Trevor said.

Murray looked at him. He wanted to ask: Can't you see how

she works? Instead, he said, 'Looks like you've been giving Gaby some ideas.'

'Well, I told her how you liked brandy.'

She fished around in her bag and produced the spirit. Handed it to Murray, sure that this would do the job. 'Aged,' she explained.

'Like you,' Trevor said, laughing. They all laughed.

Murray wanted to hit someone. 'Christ, it's almost like you're trying to buy our affection,' he said.

She waited, and wondered what to say. 'I could have a go … if you think it'll work.'

'It won't.'

Harry, meanwhile, had ripped the canvas from its plastic. He was looking at the blank and imagining what would go where.

'I'm gonna start,' he said.

'The shed?' Trevor suggested.

He was up, and out the door. 'Come on, Aiden.'

'No.'

'Come on.'

Gaby looked at Aiden. 'You've been told.'

He tried to smile. A canvas? Really? I'm seventeen, you know. I have my licence. He stood and followed his brother out. She squeezed his hand as he brushed past.

After lunch, and a tour of the house and its surrounds, Trevor and the boys took Gaby to the shed to show her the EH mural. There was a bull, and a boy pulling on its tail, and she asked Harry, 'Why's he doing that?'

'He's a bull-catcher.'

'A bull-catcher?'

'Yes, during the muster, when someone's gotta catch the bull.'

She inspected the brown blob of a bull and its triple-jointed legs; its tail, three times the length of its body; and the orange-haired, blue-faced boy struggling with the animal. 'So,' Harry explained, hoping his picture might make it clear, 'you ride your bike towards the bull and when you're close enough you jump off, grab its tail, tip it over and tie its legs.'

'That sounds very dangerous.'

'Aiden can do it.'

'Can you?' she asked.

'Long as it's not too big, or pissed off.'

'You ought to see him,' Harry said. 'This bull was charging and Dad was screaming to keep away from him, but Aiden just chased him.' He looked at his brother. 'You were going too fast.'

'Coulda been another accident,' Trevor added.

'Then he just launched himself from his bike, like this.' He showed her the action. 'And as he came down his hands grabbed its tail. The whole team was watching and cheering. Bang! Over it goes, and he's on top of it.'

'How long ago was this?' she asked Aiden.

'I was fourteen, fifteen perhaps.'

'We used to have bike races on the track,' Harry said, stopping to remember. 'And sometimes I won.'

'I let you,' Aiden said.

'Not always.'

'No, always.'

Harry was thinking. 'Dad?'

'No.'

'Please?'

'No.'

There was a short pause. Harry looked at the track he'd painted on Fay's car door: the figure on a trail bike throwing up a cloud of dust. 'That's me too,' he said, indicating. She studied the small shape, its arms and legs and orange hair. 'Isn't it safe?' she asked Trevor.

'I dunno.'

'Come on,' Harry said. 'You gotta let me some time.' He ran across to his bike, sitting fuelled near the door. Aiden was a few steps behind, warning about helmets and speed but then saying, 'You never have and you never will beat me.'

'Bullshit,' he replied, strapping on his helmet and starting the bike.

'Go easy,' Trevor called.

The boys were off, down the hill and through the grass towards the track. Trevor and Gaby followed them. Murray, standing on the porch, saw what was happening and headed down for a look.

On the way over, Gaby said, 'The leg doesn't seem to stop him doing anything.'

Trevor agreed. 'It's not so much the leg ...'

'You're a worry wart.'

He smiled. 'A *worry wart*?'

She took his arm and held it against her body. '*Your life will be a succession of good things.*'

'You reckon?'

Murray, walking behind them, noticed. It was the first real proof he'd had of their love, like, lust, or whatever it was. He searched his fag-pocket for a cigarette and felt one of the plastic-covered packets she'd given him. No, he thought, looking at her. No.

Trevor was aware of her arm, his father, his kids, already racing each other around the track. They arrived and Harry rode past and waved at them.

'See,' she said. 'He's fine.'

'I never said – '

'He was gonna fall off and break his neck and you were gonna be left feeling guilty for the rest of your – '

'Bullshit.'

'Bullshit nothing.' She nuzzled her head into his neck and kissed it and lingered. Murray stood back, watching. Harry and Aiden pulled up.

'You can be the starter,' Harry said, over the growl of the motors.

The boys lined up; nudged their wheels forward. Then they revved, and waited for their dad.

'Go!'

The bikes jumped forward. Harry, Aiden, Harry, as they closed and opened the gap. Aiden dropped his head, streamlining his body, leaning into the curve of the track. Soon he was ten metres ahead of his brother. But Harry wouldn't be beaten. He opened his throttle and almost touched his chin to the handlebars. It didn't matter. Aiden flew past him again.

Both boys returned to them and Harry demanded another go. Aiden agreed, but beat him again. Harry asked for the best of four, five, six. On the final circuit, as Harry passed his brother for the first time, Gaby stepped forward and reattached herself to Trevor. 'He's gonna do it,' she said.

But he just called to his son. 'Slow down.'

Harry ignored him. He wasn't going to be beaten. He flew past them and Trevor dropped his arm. Gaby jumped up and Murray just stood looking at her.

'See,' she said to Trevor. 'He's a marvel.'

'Yeah,' he managed. 'He's very competitive.'

'That's good, isn't it?'

'Sometimes.'

The boys pulled up in front of them. 'Gotcha,' Harry said to his brother.

'I let you have one.'

'Rubbish.'

'Good boy, Harry,' Gaby said, but he just looked at her. He noticed how she was clinging to his father, and how he looked stiff and uncomfortable. 'He doesn't let me win,' he said to her.

'I always have,' Aiden said.

Aiden shook his head. He, too, noticed their bodies. It was apparent she was trying to claim him. He turned to Murray for some sort of explanation, but he just stood there, avoiding eyes.

The boys returned to the track, revolving, again and again, in the thought of their father, the claws, and what this woman was really after.

20

It was close to midnight. Murray, lying on his stretcher, could hear his son and the woman talking in the lounge room. He could hear them touching glasses, and laughing, and long silences. Words, a blur, a phrase; the creaking of springs, a mug on the coffee table, and her voice, again. 'He came in and without so much as a thank you …' Before she hushed to a whisper.

He studied the wall of his iron-clad life; every dent, every lifted nail; an old snake skin on a wooden ledge. Left by the stranger, he often fancied. Lying in this same spot, thinking these same thoughts. He could imagine him waking in the morning, pulling on a dirty white shirt, an old suit jacket with its arms turned up, grey canvas pants and old boots. He could see him going outside, noticing Mary in the chicken pen and approaching her. Saying, 'Good morning … need a hand?'

Mary holding a knife. 'Bill usually does it for me.'

The stranger going into the yard, picking up the fattest chicken he could find and saying, 'What about this one?'

'She'll do.'

Murray could see Mary turning away as the stranger knelt down, put the chicken across his knee and removed its head with three passes of the blade. Standing up, returning the knife and saying, 'Finished.' Finally, holding up the twitching chicken and smiling.

Mary taking it by the legs. 'Thanks.'

The stranger picking up the chicken's head and throwing it out of the yard; wiping his bloody hands on his pants; picking up a bowl of scraps and scattering them about.

Mary saying: 'Can I ask a favour?'

The stranger telling her to be careful as blood dripped onto her shoes. 'Of course.'

Her putting the chicken on a nearby bench and saying, 'Could I ask you to talk to Bill?'

'About ... John?'

'Yes.' Mary stopping to think. Looking at the chicken, and back at his broad hands. 'I mean, we talk, but it's not the same coming from your wife, is it?'

'I don't know.'

'It's not. Maybe from ... someone he can talk to. The thing is, all of this business has hit him hard. John was his boy, he meant everything to him.'

'I could imagine.'

'He was gonna share the farm. They were mates, and these last few months ... Bill's been lost.'

The stranger had seen it – in the pictures on the wall, the way they'd left his room, full of old bears and zebras, tin soldiers and a golliwog she'd made. The way they talked about him like he was due home any time, and the way she always cooked an extra portion. He'd heard it in the stories – how Bill and Morris and John had built a raft out of old timber and a couple of 44-gallon drums. How Bill had bought a pirate's flag from a shop in town and flown it above the raft. How they'd stripped down to their underpants and sailed on the little bit of water in the turkey nest.

The stranger had seen the raft, broken up, overgrown with weeds.

The stranger saying, 'I can talk to him but ... what do you want me to say?'

Mary moving closer. 'I want you to tell him ... it's not worth it.'

'What?'

'I think he might kill himself.'

'Jesus ...'

'I think. When they published the Cowards' List ... you heard about that?'

'Yes.'

'John was no coward.'

'I know.'

'But Bill ... he's taken it to heart.'

The stranger shaking his head, taking her arm and saying, 'What was he gonna do?'

'He has ropes, in the shed.' Explaining: the knot she'd seen in a length of rough twine the day after the list was published; Bill's changing moods; his despair; his talk about selling the farm. 'A few years ago he had all these new ideas: fertilisers, machinery, new types of wheat. He was determined to improve things. But now he's just let go.'

'Maybe we should both talk to him?'

'No, you, please.'

Murray strained to hear what the woman was saying. *Give me time, I'll bring him around.* Or something similar.

And Trevor. 'You've gotta be kidding.'

Then there was something about memory, hypocrisy; someone refusing to face up to something. He moved his ear closer to the wall and pressed it against the cold brick.

Trix. Yes, he was talking about her. He wouldn't, would he?

He stood, went out, and watched them through the sliding door. Trevor was lying on the couch. She was nestled against his body, holding a glass of red wine, swirling it, looking up at him and down at the silent images on the telly. He was half-asleep. 'Not a word, ever,' he said.

'He's told you not to?'

'No, but she's never discussed. Never has been. If she comes up he just leaves the room.'

There was a short silence. 'Strange,' she said.

'Not really. If it gets discussed, then it turns to blame.'

'So what happened?'

'We used to have yards, a lot closer to the house. Dad had a bull tied up. I think it was on loan. Mum comes out, and she gets talking to him. Next thing, she drops something, leans over and the bull kicks her in the head. Dad's screamin' at her: Jesus, what were yer thinking? But she was already on the ground, with a big fracture, here.' He rubbed the soft spot on the side of her skull.

'That's terrible.'

'All I can remember is him shoutin' at her: Come on, get up. Shaking her.'

'You must have been horrified.'

'I just sat there screaming, watching Dad and thinking, Why are you doing this? It wasn't her fault.' He waited, remembering. 'Then the plane took her to town ... but she was dead before they got there.'

Murray opened the door and glared at his son. 'I don't believe it.'

Trevor sat up. 'What?'

'How can you – '

'Aren't I allowed to talk about her?'

Gaby also sat up. 'Murray, we were just – '

'It's none of your bloody business.' He wanted to slap her. Reclaim his story. Explain how it really was. But there was no point.

Harry was up early collecting a few eggs, cleaning out the tubs of water, coming inside and asking his father (sitting with Gaby, looking through a box of old photos) why chickens shat in their own water.

He stopped to think. 'Maybe they've just got a bad aim.'

Harry could feel his neck, and ears, cold. Even the skin on his scalp, freshly shaved with his mum's clippers. Gaby had done the job. He'd sat silently, feeling the buzz down his side, feeling goose pimples, feeling ashamed. It was a sensation that belonged to his mother's hand. It was an extension of her touch, her hold, her hug.

Aiden was lying awake in bed, listening. He didn't want to get up; couldn't see the point. Murray was off inventing jobs for himself. Gaby was dreading his return. As she studied photos of the old bastard she could see he was almost human. One image showed him and the boys in the overflowing turkey nest. They were all squeezed into an inner-tube, smiling, laughing. 'When was this taken?' she asked Trevor.

He looked at the photo, then his son. 'Four, five years ago, wasn't it, Harry?'

He studied the photo. 'Yes. Then we had hot weather and it all dried up.'

She could see the boy had remained a child – the clear eyes, the small nose, the thin lips – but now his hair was darker and his skull, perhaps, narrower. 'Are there yabbies in the dam?' she asked him.

'No.' As he thought, How could there be?

She could see Murray looked no different. Down to the white flab on his arms, the liver spots on his cheeks, the fine capillaries across his nose. But he was laughing. 'He seems happy here,' she said to Trevor.

'He has his days. He can even be quite funny, believe it or not.'

This was an image she didn't want to invoke. It was easier to think of him as a miserable old bastard. 'How cute,' she said, holding up an old photo.

It was the interior of one of the Tea and Sugar carriages. There was a screen at the front and wooden chairs set out in rows. A porter stood beside a poster featuring an unshaved Glenn Ford with gloves and a gun, too-clean denim and a sweat-soaked hat. Burnt letters proclaimed: *Heaven with a Gun*.

'Is that you?' Gaby asked, pointing to a small boy sitting in the nearly-empty theatrette, smiling back at the photographer.

Trevor squinted to see. 'Yes.'

Harry came around behind them. 'Look at your clothes.'

'I was made to wear them.' Long socks, polished shoes, a shirt and tie and his hair slicked back with poppy oil.

In contrast to the scene that Harry could make out on the screen. An old barn with a sign:

MISSION CHURCH OF THE GOOD SHEPHERD
J. KILLIAN – PASTOR

A ladder, horse-rails and two cowboys about to draw. He wanted to ask who got killed but realised there was no way his father would remember. To Gaby, it was her versus Murray – the bent legs, the hovering hands, the long shadows across the compound. Yanga might have even been there, and Fay, waiting for them to finish so she could hang out the washing.

Trevor looked at the photo. He was sitting alone. 'It was only a couple of times a year,' he said. 'If you didn't like the movie, bad luck. I remember once, Mum asked for a musical. They brought *South Pacific*. Grumble-arse just sat there with a scowl on his face saying, Why couldn't we have another Western?'

'Why's there no one with you?' Harry asked.

'They were probably sitting up the back. Maybe Dad was workin' the projector.' He explained how the Tea and Sugar butcher was also the projectionist and how, after he'd started the show, he'd return to his carriage to make up more orders.

'Pop still likes Westerns,' Harry said, thinking how the barn didn't look quite real, how someone, apparently, had ironed the cowboys' clothes.

'Well, he's living in one, isn't he?' Gaby said.

Harry took this to mean the cattle, the dirt, the weeks without showers, but Trevor knew this isn't what she meant.

There were other photos: a smiling Morris holding a cow skull, a fag hanging from the corner of his mouth; Morris and John as boys, leaning against the water tank, the crew hut half-built behind them; Murray as a teenager standing in front of a pub in Port Augusta, his tie crooked and his shirt untucked; the Wilkie brothers, again, John with his arm around Morris, pointing at the camera accusingly as Bill (perhaps) joked with them from behind the photographer.

Harry took a handful of colour photos and sat in Chris's spot.

Nineteen ninety-seven. He was standing beside this same couch, looking at Chris (watching a movie) with a puzzled expression. Aiden was sitting at the table, writing, biting his bottom lip as he clumsily clutched his pen.

'Look at me there,' he said to his dad, holding up the photo.

'One of your few quiet times,' Trevor replied, turning to Gaby. 'He didn't say a word for two years. Then one day he started talking, non-stop. Questions, twenty-four hours a day. *Daaaad, what makes the lights work?*'

Gaby laughed. Harry wasn't sure that this was her memory to share. He shrugged. 'I wouldn't say that.'

'*Daaaad, why do I gotta wipe my bum?*'

Aiden could hear. He smiled. He could remember his brother going through the pain-in-the-arse stage. Was still going through it. He was a creature, a *thing* that had to be tolerated – his voice, his face, his smell. He knew that soon he would be human, bearable, reliable. '*Daaaad, how do they make the peas green?*'

Harry returned to his photos. A trip to Adelaide, a cruise on the Port River, grey dolphins (although he didn't think they looked that interesting); in a carriage at the Railway Museum,

Aiden's head hanging from the window, him, bigger than a fish but smaller than a person, being thrown into the air by Carelyn, her arms strong, straight and ready; her face glowing, as if his return to earth was the only thing that meant anything to her, as if these few inches of air between them were too much to bear, the bits of seconds too long.

He studied her face. He didn't mean to, but he shivered, his eyes filled and he felt like he couldn't draw breath. The moment was gone. He'd fallen and she'd caught him. She'd hugged him before moving on to other things: the journey home, purée to feed him, his shitty arse.

Gaby could see all of this. She stood and moved beside him. Trevor realised this was his job but she was already there. He was unsure. He didn't know what photo it was, but guessed it might've been the one at the museum.

Gaby looked at the photo, and at Harry. 'You okay?'

He could feel her presence filling, but not filling, a void. She was like some sort of wall, keeping him from his old life. She put her arm around him. He winced. Tolerated her, but stiffened.

Trevor could see it coming. 'Harry?'

Then she squeezed and rubbed his arm. He grimaced; his face tightened. He let out a sort of growl. She felt this tension and released him.

'You're not my mother,' he said, looking at her.

'Harry!' Trevor said.

And then to his father. 'Why?'

'What?'

But he was up, across the room and out the back door. Aiden heard it all. He was quickly out of bed. He went into the lounge, still in his pyjamas. 'What happened?'

'He's upset,' Trevor said.

'Why?'

'He was looking at photos.'

Aiden looked at Gaby, and knew. 'Where?'

Trevor pointed to the back door.

He went out, stood in the compound and called, 'Harry, where are you, it's only me.'

No reply. He worked his way around the yard, checking the sheds and crew quarters. Nothing. He made his way back to the compound, and Yanga, sniffing about. 'Where are yer?' he shouted, studying Gaby's bomb, its balding tyres and Greenpeace sticker. He stopped to think then walked down the roadway searching shadows between the pines, the honey-brown litter shifting in the warm breeze.

'Piss off,' Harry said, jammed a few metres up between a trunk and branch.

He walked over to him. 'What's up?'

No reply.

'You got the shits on?' He climbed the same tree and found a solid branch opposite him. 'This better be good,' he said. 'It's sore on my arse.'

Harry handed him the photo and he studied it. He could remember the day – lunch in the old Tea and Sugar cafeteria car; climbing over dozens of trains. He could remember rides in the miniature carriage, the steam, the rumble of the rails through their feet and spines; and the driver letting them pull the cord for the whistle.

But, he could see, the photo showed more than this. It showed their mother, happy, starting out on a journey with them, and not so long ago.

'She'll never be our mum,' Harry said.

Aiden looked up the hill at the old car. 'Well, she's never actually said …' He trailed off, confused about what she wanted. 'All I can remember is Pop getting his rocks off,' he said.

'Why?' Harry asked.

'You wouldn't remember, but the Tea and Sugar was in a big shed and you could look in it. And he took me in, and he's saying: *Well, this is where you'd line up and wait for the butcher to serve you.*'

Harry could hear the old man.

'And this is where we'd sit to watch a movie. Had 'em all: South Pacific ...'

He could still see his grandfather picking the loose melamine on the counter of the provision store, saying, 'See, I started this, and no one ever fixed it.' As Trevor asked, 'What was that Western, with Gary Cooper?' And Murray shook his head. 'It wasn't Gary Cooper ... let me think ...'

He returned the photo to his brother. 'She thought the sun shone out of your arse.'

Harry didn't reply.

Meanwhile, back inside, Gaby was packing her few things into her case. 'It'll be best,' she said to Trevor.

'Rubbish,' he replied. 'It had nothing to do with you.'

'No?'

'Of course he's gonna miss Carelyn. He's only a kid.'

'We should let it settle ... longer.'

'Why?'

'Or maybe you could talk to them?'

He studied her face. This was something he hadn't noticed before. She had theories about grief, the words, even the experience, with the loss of her own parents at a relatively young age. But, somehow, she just didn't seem to get it. 'What am I talking with them about?'

'How they should make ...'

He waited – *make, make, an effort?*

'How would you feel if that was my daughter and she said that to you?'

She zipped her case and he took it from her. 'I'll go get him. Have a talk. Ask him to apologise.'

'That'd just make it worse.' She went out through the laundry, opened her boot and waited for him to load the case. 'How about this? We can take them away for a night somewhere? Before the muster?'

'Fine. Any ideas?'

'I'll ring you tonight.' She held his face, smoothed his cheek and kissed him.

Fifty metres away, the boys were watching. 'What did you say to her?' Aiden asked.

'Nothing.'

'Is that why she's leaving?'

'No.'

'Well, what you gonna do?'

Harry moved to get down but stopped. He looked at his father, alone, beside the house. The car started and drove off down the hill.

'Well?' Aiden asked.

He stared at him.

'He's gonna be so pissed off.'

He stopped to think. Looked at the ground, then at his father, then the car, disappearing down the driveway.

'I'm goin' in,' Aiden said, as he jumped from his branch. 'Coming?'

He turned away from him.

'Fair enough.' He walked up to the house, pulling his pyjamas from his arse. Harry watched him go. He doesn't understand, he thought. Doesn't see it. He studied the photo again.

Aiden passed his father. 'He's up that tree.' He indicated.

Trevor looked and eventually found the small figure in the branches.

'He's in one of his moods.'

'Well, leave him,' Trevor replied, but Aiden had already gone in. After a few moments he set off down the hill. When he arrived at the tree he said, 'You got the shits on?'

No reply. Harry pretended to look into the distance.

'She was only trying to … be nice.' He looked up. 'You gonna talk?'

'Yes.' He could see her car approaching Murray, in the ute, and noticed how close they seemed to pass.

'You gotta think about how she feels,' Trevor said.

Nothing.

'Okay.' He turned and walked away. 'I don't think your mother would've liked all this.'

Keep her out of it, he wanted to say. He watched his father go, slipping on the pine needles. 'What is she?' he called.

Trevor stopped and looked back. 'What do you mean?'

'Is she your girlfriend?'

'I suppose.'

He turned away. Trevor continued.

He felt safe in his little Y. Couldn't feel the indentation on his leg or the rough bark on his skin. He searched the trunk for spiders, as he'd done, sitting in this same spot, a year or so before. Carelyn, on her knees, holding an empty jar, searching the leaf litter.

What does she want? she'd asked.

Any insects or spiders, he'd replied.

Then what?

Then we gotta gas 'em and pin 'em onto some foam.

As they'd done, together, him neglecting the ether in favour of pinning them alive, watching them struggle for an hour or more: bugs, moths and a butterfly trying to rustle its wings. She'd said, That's just cruel.

No, it's not. They're insects. They haven't got brains.

They've got some sort of feeling.

Nothing … they don't realise what's happening to them.

She'd spent an hour on her knees, as he lifted every bit of bark and flicked every spider he found into his own jar.

What have you got, Mum?

A cockroach.

No … that's a slater.

He was still watching the car. But he could hear his mum in the pine needles. I gotta go back in and get the tea started.

A bit longer.

I got a few.

Please!

Delay, always delay, to keep her closer, longer. He closed his eyes and could still smell her, feel her arms around his body.

Then lights, tearing metal, the sensation of tumbling, cold paint on his skin.

Her breath on the back of his neck. It was his afternoon sleep and he was lying in his hot room. She was there beside him, holding him (it was the only way she could get him to go to sleep). Five, ten, minutes … Then he could feel her slipping from the bed.

Longer …

As she returned to him. A few more minutes, and she was trying again.

Longer …

I've got work to do.

But she returned to him.

His next memory was of waking an hour later and feeling the vacant hole in the bed. Feeling it.

Mum?

But he could hear her in the kitchen, talking to Fay.

He wondered how long she'd waited before reclaiming her arms and going out to finish the folding.

He looked at the house – the cold, stone box – and wondered.

They're all the same, his mother said, studying the bugs in the jar. Maybe you could look somewhere else? In the paddocks?

I could use Aiden's old collection?

No.

They'll never know. Still the same bugs, aren't they?

As she stopped to think and remembered all the jobs waiting at the top of the hill.

I can just rewrite the labels.

As he recalled the time it took for the car to roll and settle in the sand, like it had been there, that way, forever.

She was looking up at him. Perhaps you can use *some* of his.

He stayed in his tree until lunchtime, until hunger brought him back to the house. As he went in he heard them at the table; as he was taking off his boots they stopped. He moved closer and saw that someone had set his spot. There was a plate with pie and chips and a glass of cordial.

No one looked at him.

'Pass the sauce,' Murray said, and Fay passed it to him.

'Yer lunch is there,' Trevor said, without looking up.

He turned and went into his room. He was determined to stay hungry, to teach them, to show them that loss and grief shouldn't be a comfortable thing. Lying on his bed he found the photo in his pocket and placed it under his pillow.

There, that should teach them, he thought, seeing how they hadn't started talking again.

21

September. Winter had passed with almost no rain. Trees and shrubs had waited for water but given up, shedding leaves and pollen in disgust. With the end of winter, everyone agreed, it would stay dry for another year. The cracks in the walls would widen, and tempers fray around the edges. Yanga would find shade in the lowest, coolest part of the farm.

Winter hadn't even supplied cold mornings. Murray had woken, his sheets kicked off, his naked toes not the slightest bit numb. There was no frost and there was hardly any dew on the bit of lawn they tried to keep green. They'd had a few evening fires but these were a nod to winter: the memory of cold, rained-in nights, something to remind them of this equinox avoided. Short days that promised nothing but long nights.

With this dark quarter already complete it was time for the muster: this re-scheduled, argued over, barely planned, sap-sucking chunk of their lives. Trevor was hoping it would be over in a month but knew, with the cattle wandering further in search of feed, it would take longer. He was bracing himself, hoping the house and his family would be able to take care of themselves for the duration. It seemed unlikely. Fay and Chris left dangling like a couple of live wires; Murray everywhere and nowhere, generating stress; Gaby, still trying to find her place in the small gaps and widening cracks; the boys, torn between their bikes and the horror of lessons; Carelyn, gone, unable to hold it all together, to tell everyone why they should be somewhere else doing something they didn't want to do. That, now, would fall to him.

Although, maybe something good would come of it, he thought.

Maybe the absences would lead to a new dynamic. Maybe people would work out they needed to help. To cook, to clean, to put stuff away. Maybe not, he thought, sitting at his computer, reading an email, selecting Print and watching the words become real.

Dear Mr Wilkie,

I was given your name by the Elders stock agent in Port Augusta. I represent the Malboona Rural Equity, Investments and Partnerships Group.

He took the paper, held it by the tips of his fingers and re-read it. 'Once in a lifetime,' he whispered to himself.

'How's that?' Fay asked.

He looked up. 'Just thinkin', Fay.'

'Ah.' She continued stirring port-wine gravy.

Once in a lifetime. She wondered if he'd received some good news. Nothing much happened once in a lifetime – except birth (Chris's, drawn out, problematic), death (excluding other people's), decay, a rotten husband, the making and unmaking of a family. She could still see Chris, ten or eleven, walking naked around the house, and Murray looking at her. 'He shouldn't be walking around like that.'

'He's not hurtin' anyone.'

'It's not right!'

Family, she realised, was the most difficult thing of all. It never reached a point of completion and what was there never seemed satisfactory. But one thing, she realised: there was always a pivot, one person at the centre holding it all together. 'You lookin' after yerself?' she asked.

He looked surprised. 'What do you mean?'

'What I said.'

'I'm okay.'

'Yeah?' She looked like she didn't believe him. 'Sometimes it's worth goin' to the doctor, even if you don't think there's nothin' wrong.'

'Why?'

'A check-up: heart, sugar ...'

'No ... fit as an old mallee bull, Aunt.' He started re-reading the letter.

She guessed it would be a heart attack. Always was. Morris, dropping to his knees, telling them he couldn't feel his fingers; rolling onto his side, drifting off. Dead before anyone knew what was happening. 'Just to be sure,' she said.

He smiled. 'What, you know something I don't?'

'You got a lot of people relying on you now.'

'Fit as a fiddle.'

She wasn't so sure. It was his habit of leaving the toilet door open when he pissed; and her good ears, listening for his stream. She knew the plumbing was the first to go. Heard Murray two or three times a night, sliding the pot out from under his stretcher, or going out against the lemon tree; the piss that wouldn't come. 'You're nearly at that age,' she said.

'What age?'

'When you should have your prostate checked.'

'That's not till fifty.' He looked at her strangely. 'Why do you bring it up?'

'I thought it was forty.'

'No.' He stared at her, unsure.

'Anyway,' she said, turning off the gravy, 'as long as you feel well ... in yerself.'

'I do.'

'Sometimes it can be a bit much for one person.'

Now, he guessed, she was talking about something else. 'How's that?'

'As long as you keep talking.'

'Sorry?'

She knew that he knew – about how long he spent in his shed, and how quiet he was when he came in; how he'd started going for long walks in the desert paddocks; made less conversation around the dinner table; wasn't asking to check Harry's assignments any more. 'You gotta laugh sometimes.'

'I do.'

How he just sat staring at the television as everyone else laughed at Stan and Blakey.

'Keep talking,' she said. 'That's the main thing.'

'I'm okay … what, you think …?'

'Don't think nothin' … just sayin'.'

But he knew exactly what she was thinking. He knew it was always the woman who noticed, who'd help, intruding onto dark, unproductive land. 'You think I'm gonna jump off a cliff?'

Her face was blank. 'Well, look what happened to Bill.'

'Bill was sick.'

'No, he wasn't.' She knew the outstation walls had closed in on him until there was no room to move, until the noose (without him touching it) slipped over his neck, until the floor opened up beneath him, until he fell, through no fault of his own. 'He was just ashamed,' she said.

'Yes.'

'It was a situation he couldn't get out of.'

He didn't answer. He wasn't so sure – but then his thoughts turned from the outstation to his shed. 'It was how he looked at things,' he said.

You can only see things one way, she thought.

'He should've moved on.'

'It was his son.'

'Still …'

As he saw Carelyn's fingers, joints, nails.

'It was his choice,' he said.

'Perhaps. But maybe the Wilkies have got some sort of ... gene.'

'Perhaps,' he conceded.

He'd learnt that Fay didn't say much, and she certainly didn't like to interfere with other people's business (Murray had spent forty years warning her off). But what she did say was generally right. She would leave it at that for now, he guessed. Let the thought germinate and emerge into the sunlight. Then, in a month, or a year, if nothing had happened, she would return to it. She would work at it. Just a hint, a look.

'I'm okay,' he said. He folded the piece of paper and went outside.

Meanwhile, Murray was trying to instil some sort of order. Bill Clarke had arrived early and landed his Robinson near the crew's quarters. Harry and Aiden had stood watching, shielding their eyes from the dust, marvelling at the globular insect, spastic with enthusiasm. They'd noticed the spotter's seat and wondered when their turn would come. They'd asked Bill where he'd come from and he'd said, 'WA ... via the moon!' He'd shaken their hands. 'I'll take you up later if Dad says it's okay.'

Harry had gone with Bill to the smallest of the crew's trucks, parked along the road, full of panels for the stockyards they'd soon be moving across the desert. Aiden had brought up the ute and helped Bill roll two drums of avgas onto the back. Then he'd driven Shit-for-brains and the boss of bosses down to the helicopter. Bill had opened the tailgate and kicked the drums and they'd rolled and dropped onto the sand beside his machine. They'd lifted them, then pumped most of the first into the bowels of the chopper. When they'd finished, Bill had said, 'That's her ready to go ... what's next?'

There were three trucks, and back towards the highway, the

first of the road trains for the first of the cattle. Murray told each of the drivers where to leave his vehicle – half-road, half-scrub – so they could get their car and ute around. He stood in the middle of the road waving them forward, back, further, further, don't worry, it's not soft ground. Inside the cab of the second truck one of the men said, 'Fuck, not this old prick again,' and his friend replied, 'Don't worry, you don't see him once the work gets started.'

Murray greeted and escorted each of the men to their quarters. As he did every year he showed them where he'd set up their camp stretchers and they said, No, thanks, and rolled out their swags. Sat on old logs and lit smokes and started asking about the muster.

'Trevor has a map,' he told them. 'He knows where most of the mobs are.' He said it like Trevor was the most knowledgeable grazier in the country. 'Calves were down, but then again, everything's pretty poor, eh? And dry.'

A stockman named Walker said, 'It's only gettin' dryer.'

'I know,' he replied, sitting on a rock and finding his own cigarette. As he lit it the whole crew watched his hands shake.

Bill Clarke wasn't interested in small talk. 'We'll need to sit down and plan it. October ten. That's the latest we can stay.'

'Five weeks?'

'Gotta get up north before the wet.'

Murray wasn't fussed. He didn't want it dragging on any longer. 'That should be fine. We're all ready to go. How long was it last year?'

'About that. Five weeks. I's tryin' to be fair to yers.'

There was a long silence. Another man, Stephen Higgs (although the others called him Susan), flicked his cigarette into the cold fire, stood and walked a few metres. He unzipped and started pissing. 'You're right, Murray, that's dead-looking country.'

Murray wanted to tell him there was a short-drop but he guessed there was no point. 'This is our sixth year of drought.'

Higgs returned to the circle. 'Up Queensland it never stops pissin' down.'

'Well ...'

'Should be farmin' up there.'

Murray didn't understand. 'We've had worse.'

'Yeah?'

'In the thirties. Nearly killed my father. Whole place was de-stocked for nine years.'

'Well, maybe it will come to that.'

'No, it won't.'

Bill looked at Murray, then Higgs. The boss hardly ever said what he was thinking. 'It was worse in those days, wasn't it, Murray?'

'You bet it was.'

'How many bores back then?'

'Not many.' He looked at Clarke, unsure.

'Kidman always moved his animals,' Higgs said.

'He could,' Murray replied. 'He owned half the country. We just got Bundeena.' And he looked at each of them. 'That's all we got.'

'More than us,' Higgs said.

He remembered why he didn't like the man. 'Yeah, but I bet you got a nice place somewhere.'

'Double Bay ... and a yacht.'

Some of them laughed, and lit new cigarettes.

He stood. 'Right, I better get Trev, I suppose.' As he went up the road he heard them laughing. 'Prick,' he mumbled, as he came across his son changing the wheel of the ute. 'Is it flat?' he asked.

Trevor turned to him. 'Worn.'

'Bill wants to have a talk with you.'

'Two minutes.'

'October ten, he reckons.'

Trevor didn't seem to care. He took the printout from his top pocket, opened it and handed it to his father. 'Got that this morning,' he said.

> As you are no doubt aware we have recently purchased 'Preston', a property of 73,000 square kilometres lying along your west and north boundary ...

Murray looked up at his son. 'It's that same mob again.'
Trevor nodded. 'Read what it says.'

> Our group is attempting to consolidate holdings in your district. In the present economic climate, and considering the advantages of economies of scale ...

'Why are you showing me this?' Murray asked.
'Read.'
'Why? You wanna sell to them bastards?'
Trevor had been rehearsing his response. 'We've got so much excess land.'
'What?'
'We could sell a bit. Think of the money.'

> The details of our offer are outlined below. They are, of course, open to negotiation ...

Murray looked at his son. As he did he folded the sheet again and again until he was stopped by the seventh fold. 'Not an inch,' he said, defiantly.
'Dad.'
'Not a single grain of sand.'
He knew that one foot would lead to a hundred, a thousand, the lot. He pushed the folded note against his son's chest. 'Bill wants to talk to you.'

The next morning the team was up before dawn, rolling swags, emptying bladders, eating bacon and eggs Fay had brought down from the house. Black, sweet tea and the smell of deodorant on crusted armpits, powder in boots and more laughing around the glowing fire. Short, sharp scraps of conversation.

Murray was there, handing out the sausages. 'Excuse fingers.' Figuring the more they ate the more they'd work. 'Anybody hungry?'

'What's for lunch?'

'Wait and see.'

The swags and boxes of gear were loaded onto the trucks. The Robinson hummed and groaned to life. Bill Clarke said a few words to Trevor before taking off. Harry and Aiden, waiting beside their trail bikes, watched him go. He'd come good, taking them both up the previous afternoon. An hour-long circuit around Bundeena – cattle (as he told Harry to note the GPS coordinates), a low glide above the railway line, the highway (as he hovered, and cars slowed, wondering what he was doing).

The convoy – Trevor in his ute, the trucks, the boys, and a few other men on bikes – headed north. As they pulled away from the compound, Fay, Chris and Murray (who was going to fly back with Bill later) stood watching and waving. To Chris, the smell of diesel meant muster, the population of Bundeena tripling, more willing ears and weeks of chaos in the kitchen. Diesel meant an empty house, and a break from Murray.

Half an hour up the road the convoy stopped. Trevor pulled up beside the lead vehicle. 'What's wrong?'

'It's Bill … the first mob,' Chris Eccles, one of the new men, explained.

Trevor took the radio and told Bill how far they'd come.

'I can see you,' the voice came back. 'That's as good as anywhere. I'll start pushing them south.'

Trevor searched the northern horizon. 'Can you see him?' he asked the others.

'There he is,' Eccles replied, pointing.

'Right. We're gonna set up here. You fellas get started, eh?'

The trucks pulled off the road. Over the next thirty minutes they unloaded the panels, crush and crates of equipment they'd need for the first mob. Meanwhile, Trevor, in his ute, the boys and three of the crew on their own bikes, headed north.

Trevor drove ahead of the others. He had a good feeling. After everything that had happened since the last muster this gathering would mark a new beginning. Things would improve. Money would flow in. The boys would settle, and learn to love Gaby.

He came across Bill, flying low, sweeping arcs, encouraging the herd southwards. All they had to do was come around behind the mob and move them along the road. As they went, and as the boys criss-crossed on their bikes, he estimated there were eighty or ninety head. There were plenty of calves and slow-moving steers, their shoulders hunched, their pop-eyes watching the helicopter and bikes. Occasionally some of the mob would drift to the side, seeking quiet, or grass, but Harry would be there, calling to them, guiding them.

He checked his temperature gauge. Running hot. Decided to go back. The others could handle the mob – they were quiet and content to keep moving. He moved towards the front of the herd. An animal ran off, breaking the flank – then a few more, trying their luck. He planted his foot, heading west into the desert. He knew he was faster, and they'd probably change their minds. He took a longer line, bouncing across the landscape, turning in on the animals to make his intentions clear.

Then he saw a bike coming up beside him. It clipped the front of his ute and its rider tumbled across the sand and grass. The bike skidded and spun a few times. He braked hard, stopped in a cloud of dust and got out. Chris Eccles was walking towards him. 'What were you doing?' he asked.

'I was cutting them off.'

'You nearly killed me.'

'I was in front ...'

'Fuck.' He just stood staring at him. 'You were comin' up the back.'

'I moved.'

The stray cattle had returned to the mob. Aiden, Harry and the others kept moving them south. As they went, they looked back at the pair and wondered what was going on.

Eccles returned to his bike, still running, picked it up and said, 'You came outa nowhere.'

Half an hour later the yards were ready. Trevor, Bill and the others waited as the mob, controlled by Aiden on the left flank, and Eccles on the right, moved towards them. Trevor watched as his son guided the first few animals through the opening, moving back and forth, squeezing them in, never rushing, never calling, never worrying when a few heads turned as though they might break away.

The yard was soon full. The animals bunched and pushed against the panels but within a few minutes they'd calmed and were looking about to see what it all meant.

'Nice work,' Trevor said to his sons, as the gates were closed and bolted.

Harry and Aiden got off their bikes and climbed and sat high on the fence around the stock.

'You did well,' Eccles said to them.

'Won't all be that easy,' Aiden replied.

They stopped for tea and mud coffee and Harry gave them a demonstration of his whip work. When he sat down he asked, 'Can anyone beat that?'

Eccles said, 'You're doin' well.'

'I practise on my bottle tree.'

'Right.' He pointed to something hanging around Harry's neck. 'What's that?'

Harry showed him. 'A hen's tooth.'

'Yeah? Where'd you get it?'

'I found it. Mum put it on a chain for me.'

Trevor could remember finding the bloodied tooth in the yards and giving it to him.

'It's for good luck,' he told them.

'Does it work?' Eccles asked.

'I suppose.'

Trevor had noticed him wearing it again in the months since Gaby had first visited. Prior to this he hadn't worn it for a year, perhaps longer.

'When I was in hospital,' Harry told them, '5B had a show-and-tell morning. One day I showed them this.' He displayed the tooth again, although he wouldn't remove it from around his neck.

'You told them it was a hen's tooth?' Eccles asked.

'Yes.'

'And did they believe you?'

Harry could remember the seven or eight faces, the gowns, the cold legs and feet. And one of the girls saying, 'That's a big tooth for a hen.'

'It was a big hen.'

'How did it fit in its mouth?'

Shrugging.

'It'd have to be a mouth the size of a cow.'

He could remember thinking: the cattle yards, the blood, his father's smile. 'Hens have only got a few teeth,' he'd told the girl.

'No ... none.'

He could remember studying her face and disliking her

270

immensely. *What do you know? Do you live on a farm?* As she gave him a sort of *you-country-kids-are-so-stupid* look.

'So, what were you doing in hospital?' Eccles asked.

Silence.

'We had a car accident,' Trevor said.

'Ah,' Eccles said, looking at him. 'I don't think we should let you behind the wheel.'

Bill Clarke just stared at him. His smile faded and his eyes settled on his mug of tea. The other men were silent.

'I screwed up my leg,' Harry said, patting it. 'But it's better now.'

Higgsy, the mythical Susan, sat forward. 'Hasn't kept you off your bike?'

'No.'

Aiden was looking at his father. His eyes were saying, Aren't you going to tell them? About Mum? The road marker? The paint? The kangaroo?

Silence. Nothing but the cattle moving and shit slopping in the sand.

Harry hid his tooth under his collar. 'It's not really a hen,' he said, and this time none of them argued.

Then Bill Clarke asked, 'Where's Banger?'

Trevor emptied his tea into the sand. 'Yanga. Too old. Sleeps all day.'

'Pity. She was a good cattle dog.' He shrugged. 'Takes an old dog for a hard road, eh?'

Trevor agreed. 'Yeah ... but she'd need a cracker up her arse.'

Harry smiled. 'Like Mrs Amery. She's seventy, but she's still teaching.'

'Christ,' Aiden said.

They all looked at him.

'I forgot to tell her we'd be absent.'

Harry didn't seem to care. 'She'll work it out.'

'Aiden's become Harry's home supervisor,' Trevor told them.

'Ah, Herr Professor?' Eccles said. He looked at Harry. 'What's he taught you?'

Harry stopped to think. '*Schreibe, was für Fächer du hast, was für Fächer du gern oder am liebsten hast, und was für Noten du gewöhnlich bekommst.*'

They all looked impressed. 'Might come in useful one day,' Higgs said.

And then Bill Clarke stood up. 'Righto, come on, let's get these bastards done.'

The mob was funnelled through a draft into two other pens: one for the steers, heifers and old cows (as Trevor carefully looked them over, aware he needed a heavy cull) and another for the calves. Higgs was in charge of separating them, opening and closing a spring-loaded gate that decided their fate. He sat on a fence operating a handle, hovering over the bottleneck like some sort of bovine god. If he worked too fast the other men, receiving the cattle in the yards, would call, 'Wait up, Susan.' He'd look at the next cow and say, 'It's not your lucky day, is it, old girl?'

The cattle were becoming agitated. Dust rising, forming a talcum-cloud, spreading out and settling on their boots. Each of the yards had been supplied with a trough and each of these had been filled with water from a tank. The cattle were bunching, pushing, using their mass to gain proximity to the water.

'Okay, keep 'em coming,' someone called, and Susan started feeding the cattle through again.

Trevor and Harry had set up for the big animals. The second pen, half full of heifers, cows and steers, had another draft where each of them could be vaccinated and drenched. From there, another gate, operated by Eccles, would separate the culls from the animals destined to return to the paddock. Harry was already set up, standing on a box, holding his drench gun, waiting. On the other side of the race, Trevor stood with a bottle of 5-in-1 vaccination hanging around his neck. From the bottle, a long tube fed into a syringe.

They were ready. Two men entered the yard and pushed the cattle towards the draft. They moved, but then shied away. The men hit their rumps with lengths of rubber pipe. When the first went the others followed. Soon they were bunched, pushing harder along the race. A big steer moved forward between father and son. Harry slipped the drench gun into its mouth, pulled the trigger and felt the measured dose. Trevor reached behind its ear, grabbed a fold of skin, drove the needle home and injected. It jumped, but settled. 'Looks like he needs a good feed,' he said to his son.

Harry picked up a piece of chalk resting on an old lump of timber. Made a mark. 'Next.'

Eccles opened the gate and the animals pushed through into the bigger of the two holding yards. It was aligned with the road so the trucks could back up to it. A loading ramp sat waiting. The first steer ran a small circuit around the yard. It worked the panels with its head but couldn't move them.

In the other yard, Aiden and Bill had started on the calves. Harry could smell the stench from the dehorner: keratin, flesh and hair. Bill's hands were red and he had a bucket full of balls.

Harry's tally continued – his first group of five, ten, twenty. His trigger finger was sore.

'Cull, keep, cull,' his father's voice droned.

Sometimes Eccles would ask, 'Sure you don't want to keep that one?'

'Cull.'

Of the fifteen or so heifers in the keep paddock, one animal pushed its rump against a panel, realised it was loose and started forcing it.

'Hold on,' Eccles said, jumping down from his spot, putting his shoulder behind the panel and pushing it back into place.

'Who did that?' Trevor asked.

'Buggered if I know.'

Trevor had seen what a loose panel could do. Years ago. A hundred animals in the yard. A bull had pushed back on a fence and knocked it out. Within seconds there was a stampede around the trucks and cars, Murray running for his life, dropping his clipboard, almost tripping and falling. Later he'd asked, 'Who put that fence up?' Threatening to sack the idiot who'd nearly killed him. They'd had to return to the desert to start again. But this time the animals were spooked, running, fanning out in every direction.

Soon Harry had marked off sixty-five. He wanted to ask for a break but dared not. No one else was tiring. He refused to be the first.

'Cull, keep,' his father said.

The road train appeared, slowly moving along the track. Trevor looked up. 'Just gonna tell him where to back in,' he said to Eccles, before making for the road.

Eccles didn't need to be asked twice. He climbed down from his spot, lit a cigarette and stood watching Trevor talking to the truck driver.

Harry, meanwhile, thought he'd get ahead of his dad. He worked his way along the draft, drenching each of the crammed-in animals. Half-way along he dropped the drench gun. It fell inside the race at the feet of a big cow. Without thinking, he climbed the panel and lowered himself between the steel mesh and a sweaty, head-high rump.

The cow shifted. He couldn't move. The other animals pressed forward and he was trapped, half-kneeling, half-standing. He tried to push against the cow but it wouldn't budge. Then, he could feel the pain on his arms, his torso, his legs. The pressure increased until he felt himself unable to breathe. He tried to call, but couldn't.

Aiden saw him and sprinted over. He climbed the panel and dropped into the race, taking him under the arms and pulling him up as Bill, hanging off the opposite panel, pushed the cow back with his foot until there was enough of a gap for Aiden to retrieve him.

He took him around the chest and climbed out. Then he laid him in the sand and cradled his head in his lap. 'What were you thinking?' he said.

Harry was still trying to get his breath.

'You know you don't do that.' He turned him on his side, lifted his shirt and saw the red indentations from the mesh. 'That's gonna be sore.'

Bill ran his hand across his back. 'You won't do that again.'

'I didn't think,' Harry said.

Trevor looked over and noticed the group. He came running. Saw his son on the ground, leaned over and noticed the indentations. 'You went in?'

'I dropped the drench gun.'

Aiden was looking at his father. 'Who was meant to be watching him?'

Trevor knelt on both knees and took his son's hand. 'I can't do six things at once.'

'It was my fault,' Harry said.

'Shit happens,' Bill Clarke added, sensing the accusation, noticing Aiden's eyes. 'He's alright, and he's learnt his lesson, haven't you, Harry?'

'I didn't think.'

'We all do stupid things.'

Trevor looked at Eccles. 'Where were you?'

He shook his head. 'Don't look at me.'

'You were meant to be – '

'He's your kid. I'm not here to babysit.'

Bill moved between them. 'Enough. What's it matter? Shit happens. Lesson learnt, eh, Harry?'

'Yes.'

Trevor was still looking at Eccles.

'Get someone else if you want,' the stockman said.

Trevor turned to Aiden. 'Back to work. And you,' looking at Harry, 'you can get the water on for smoko.'

22

Surprisingly, Murray was the most nervous. Sitting in reception, pressing the folded margins of a piece of paper, looking at his son. 'Very generous of you.'

'What choice have I got?'

Seeing how the bank had called them in at short notice, asking them to bring their accounts. 'It won't hurt giving them a day off,' Trevor said. 'Even Bill's getting stroppy.'

'They coulda kept on.'

'It's my call.'

Murray looked at him, as if this was further proof of his incompetence.

Trevor thought it best. Higgs and a man named Ackroyd had been working on each other – something about the way Higgs always gave orders when it was Bill who was meant to say what needed doing. There'd been heated words, and then nothing, for three or four days; just a *do it this way* or *not like that*. Then Ackroyd had looked at Higgs the wrong way and Higgs had told him to fuck off and Ackroyd had said *you get fucked* and it had nearly come to fists. Bill had told them to stop acting like pricks and Trevor, sitting, watching, wondered how they'd make another four weeks.

'More lost money,' Murray whispered, loosening his tie.

'Either I'm running it or I'm not,' Trevor said. 'Which is it?'

'Won't be any better tomorrow.'

Trevor guessed it could always be worse: a mother in frayed track pants and an old boob-tube, a cellulite midriff and pierced belly button, or what could be seen of it. 'Bush pig,' he whispered.

Murray looked at her. 'Fuckin' disgrace.' And her four chil-dren: shoeless, mop-haired, writing on withdrawal slips, screwing them up and throwing them at each other. 'Oi, cut it out.' The mother turned to him. 'They should be sittin' down,' he said, and she replied, 'You should be minding your own business.'

One of the children, a boy in long pants and a singlet, smiled at him and raised his finger.

'You think that's okay?' he asked the mother, but she just turned and walked off with a teller. The kids trailed after her, the boy slapping his arse.

'Maybe I should go fishing,' Trevor said.

'Maybe you should.'

'It'd be a lot more fun.'

'Well, if you don't wanna be there.'

'You know what you're doin', you tell 'em.'

No response.

'That way it gets done right, eh?'

Murray shrugged. 'Wait till you're nearing eighty.'

'Eighty? Seventy-five. How's that nearing eighty? You're expe-rienced. They'll listen to you.'

He shook his head. 'Why you so contrary these days?'

'You're the one tellin' me – '

'Cos it's costin' us so much bloody money.'

Trevor was sick of arguing. 'All I'm sayin', if you're not happy – '

'I'm happy! Fine. Give 'em an extra day off. Just stop goin' on about it.' He leaned forward, studying the carpet. 'I agree … it was needed, especially with Bob's back.' Strained, as he'd lifted a calf, dropping it, breaking its leg. Trevor telling him to put it aside for fresh meat.

Trevor just looked at him, wondering, waiting for the caveat.

They were greeted by a dark-suited twenty-something and taken into an office. Sat down on the wrong side of the desk. The loans officer (and assistant manager) offered them a coffee and apologised for dragging them in at such short notice. 'I've just been looking at your loan,' he said. 'About a year ago we agreed we'd have a review, but we must have let it slip.'

'We were waiting to hear,' Trevor said.

'Well, that's my fault.'

They both looked at Murray, but he didn't move. He was wondering if this kid knew anything, and how the bank had the nerve to make them sit and listen to him. 'You local?' he asked.

'No,' the young man replied. 'But eight years of rural finance. Farms. We keep 'em all going.' He smiled.

'Keep ours going?'

'I hope.'

Murray just looked at him. 'I've done some sums.' And laid his piece of paper on the desk. It was covered with figures in rows and columns, ruled off, added up, one number subtracted from another. Some of the calculations had been crossed out and rewritten and other parts were just scribble. 'Here,' he said, indicating, 'is what I reckon we'll earn this year. And here, this is what it will cost us.' He used his finger to highlight the numbers. 'As you can see, there's a bit of a gap, which is where the bank comes into it.'

The young man studied the numbers, tried to make sense of them, shifted the paper, picked it up and held it close to his face. 'We gotta get you a copy of MYOB.'

'What's that?' he asked, as though this boy was planning some sort of trick.

'Business software.'

'That's clear enough, isn't it?'

'No, it's not, Dad,' Trevor said. He looked at the assistant manager. 'We tried, but all the details are kept in a shoebox ... *his* shoebox.'

Murray glared at him. He wanted to ask who he was really with.

'So, this figure here, this is the shortfall?' the young man asked. Murray looked. 'Yes.'

'Fifty-eight thousand … this year?'

'Yes.'

'And that's because …?'

'Prices are down. After seven years of drought the animals are in poor condition.'

'Well, for a start,' the officer explained, 'I'm not exactly sure how you came up with this figure of fifty-eight thousand.'

Murray couldn't see the problem. 'Money in and money out, and that's what's missing.'

'Right.' He studied his screen and sighed. 'It's not just that amount. It's the sixty-two thousand last year, the thirty-eight the year before, and going back, twenty-six, seventeen … Then there's the interest.'

Murray shrugged. 'Like I said, we're in the middle of a drought.'

'I understand that. But it's the overall level of debt. You're in a position that's probably not … viable.'

Viable? Viable? 'What do you mean?'

The officer sat back in his chair, suddenly philosophical, as if he were a doctor telling them about a malignant tumour. 'Even if it rained tomorrow and kept raining and there was all the grass the animals could eat … and they put on weight and you started making money, and this column shrank and this one grew …' He referred to Murray's scribble. 'There's just so much debt. The interest is killing you. That's all you're paying … interest.'

Silence.

Trevor wanted to say it: My thoughts exactly. What are we working for? Why are we killing ourselves? 'Only ones smiling are the shareholders,' he said.

'They'll always make money. Problem is … Bundeena. If you were a café or shop you would've closed years ago.'

'Well, we're not a shop,' Murray growled. He tapped the desk, his sums. 'It's simple. You give us that, we keep going. Everyone gets a roast, we keep our farm.'

'And if you were us, Murray, would you keep forking over?'

'Too bloody right I would.'

The officer folded his arms. Now he was studying Murray's face, his flaring nostrils and his fingers clawing at the desk. 'Another five years, then you decide to walk away. And we're left with the debt.'

'Things'll come good, they always do.'

'Things are different now. We're a business. We manage risk.'

Murray had no response. He knew the figures didn't lie. 'Fifty-eight thousand,' he said. 'Another two years.'

'It won't be up to me.'

'Who then?'

'The big boss.'

He couldn't take this silliness any more. 'Who the hell's the big boss?'

Trevor could hear it even if Murray couldn't. The young man, he thought, was doing a decent job of telling them. 'We've had an offer to sell to an equity firm,' he said, without meaning to.

Murray turned on him. 'Leave this to me.'

'No.' He looked at the officer. 'It's a decent offer. It'd keep you guys happy and solve our problems, but ...' He turned to his father.

'A hundred and seventeen years,' he said to him.

'So what?'

'Over my dead body.'

'It will be.' He picked up the sheet of figures. 'Then Aiden can have a go, and Harry, and we can all kill ourselves, and be bloody miserable till Judgement Day.'

Murray was silent. 'It's how we live,' he said.

'Bullshit.'

Murray turned to the young man. 'Don't the government give you money to write off debt?'

'I want you to – '

'They do! Or if you lot could stop charging interest for a year. What did you make last year? Five billion? Why can't you give us a break? Two years? We can draw up some sort of plan.' He took a pen from his pocket. 'You got a bit of paper?'

'That was pretty bloody disappointing,' Murray said, sitting with his arms crossed, as they drove through Port Augusta.

Trevor didn't respond.

'You had to bring it up then?'

'It was relevant.'

'*Relevant?* While I'm tryin' to get more money?'

A roundabout, and more grey roads, as Trevor retreated further into his own world.

'We're meant to be a family,' Murray said.

'Meant to be.'

'It's our place. You got given it, your kids will – '

'*I got given it?* When? I'm just workin' for you.'

'Bullshit.'

'Well, hand it over. Where's the deed? Under your bed?'

Murray guessed there was no point arguing. 'What I mean is … the only way we can move on …'

Quiet. The indicator. A small Gemini roaring past.

'We can't move on, Dad.'

'Don't be so dramatic.'

'They're just lettin' us stay cos they wouldn't get nothin' if they sold it.'

'Bullshit. It's been worse.'

Lives, crumbling, but the land still yielding. Murray could see it – every minute of every day for the last hundred years. The small and big tragedies. Bill arriving home from town, placing Mary's packages on the bench and saying, 'Next time we'll get someone to drop 'em off.'

Mary looking at him. 'Why?'

'No reason.' Although there was – the stares, as he walked down the main street of Port Augusta, whispers, Bill Wilkie, wasn't his boy on the Cowards' List?

Bill saying, 'I've heard.'

'What?'

'They're willing to meet us.' Calling for the stranger, going to the sleep-out, finding a freshly made bed, and a note.

> I'm sorry, but I've never been to no war. They said in town about John – I needed work. Seeing how your farm was so big. I been stupid. I know. I wish you all the best with John. Your good people. I made up a name – I hope you can forgive me.

Sitting on the bed for a full five minutes. Noticing a box of John's old books the stranger had been looking through. And on top of this, three- and four-year-old newspapers with references to John's battalion underlined.

Trevor pulled into Gaby's drive. She was quickly at the door, waving, struggling with a case she'd packed for her next stay. He got out and helped her. Murray remained in the car, watching as his son kissed her lips.

Back at the muster the next morning, Gaby helped Harry make scones. He spent ten minutes mixing the eggs and sugar until there was a froth of almost-dissolved crystals. Then he placed the bowl on the table and asked, 'Ready?'.

She looked at the mixture. 'Will that be enough for fifteen people?'

'I suppose.'

Fay, who'd come with them earlier that morning, walked over, looked in the bowl and said, 'That'll be fine.' She tried to smile at Gaby. 'As long as it looks like food they'll eat it.'

She returned to her spot beside the fire, splayed her legs and rubbed her scaly thighs and knees. She watched Gaby working and noticed how she was never quite sure – what to use, how to mix, where to find what she wanted. She saw how she handed the flour to Harry before putting her arm around his shoulder. 'About half of that, I reckon.' Before looking over. 'What do you think, Fay?'

'No, all of it. There's fifteen people.'

Harry tipped all of the flour into the mixture. He looked at Gaby. 'What next?'

She handed him the milk. 'You tip slowly as I mix.'

Fay watched how they'd become a unit. How they worked without speaking; seemed to rely on each other; how he'd accepted her, for now. 'I used to enter my scones in the land competitions,' she called.

'Sorry?' Gaby replied, looking up.

'The CWA. Years ago, before I lost interest. They were a bunch of old chooks, really.' She stopped to remember. 'Sultana cake. Sultanas evenly spaced. Fifteen-inch tin. No rack marks, top or bottom. Golden brown exterior. Shouldn't crumble down your chin.'

Gaby stopped for a moment. 'You must think we're a pair of amateurs.'

'No, that's the thing. They all had something up their arse.'

She almost laughed, sharing the moment with Harry, who said, 'Aunty Fay!'

Fay looked over at the men. The untucked shirts, half-beards and greasy hair. Ripped jeans and crushed boots. And Murray, ear-tagging the calves, telling Aiden what to do. 'It's just a cake, isn't it?' she said, and Gaby and Harry looked at her. 'Just something you eat.'

Harry tasted the mixture. 'Is it ready?'

'A few more lumps.'

'You'll never get them all,' Fay said. She watched her brother stand and straighten his back. 'I used to be camp cook,' she said.

'Really?' Gaby replied.

'First few years after I arrived. Of course, it was a bigger crew back then – you could have eighteen men at a time. And I had Chris running around bothering them.' She focused on her brother's stony face and remembered Chris having a go at the vaccinating, accidentally injecting himself, crying and screaming as he watched his arms turn red. As Murray said: 'It'll pass.'

Her. 'Should we get him to a doctor?'

'No, it'll pass. What, I gotta drive him to town *again*?'

She was still watching her brother. 'That job nearly killed me,' she said. 'I had four big roasting ovens and they were going all day. The men had to have meat and veg. I started at four and finished at nine. Then they'd want something before bed.'

Gaby couldn't see the frail old thing slaving away all day. 'Quite a job,' she said.

'Yes, for no pay.'

'And why did you stop?'

'My brother said I wasn't keeping up.' She remembered the men waiting for their tea at 8 pm, looking at her, decent enough not to say anything. 'He sacked me,' she said.

'No?'

'As much as you can be sacked, by your own family.'

And again, she could hear him, on the phone to the stock agent, asking if he knew any decent camp cooks, and pronto, today, tomorrow – as theirs had just walked out on them.

'I don't know what they're gonna think of our scones,' Gaby said, looking at Harry.

'We should start.'

She sprinkled flour on the chopping board and spread it with her fingers. Took the lump of dough from the bowl and slapped it down. 'Off you go,' she said, messing his hair.

He knew what was expected. Started kneading the dough, rolling, flattening and ripping off chunks that he formed into scone-sized balls. 'Okay?' he asked.

'Good.'

Fay looked at the way she dressed. The boots that weren't suited to a farm; the horse-riding pants, although there wasn't a horse for miles; the vest, with its sewn panels, fresh from someone's needlework class. Still, she guessed, these habits could be changed. Would be. If she ended up staying at Bundeena things would be different.

'Righto,' she heard Murray call, and looked to see him picking up a calf, load it across his shoulders and walk from the yard.

He came towards them, watching Gaby, smiling, saying, 'Fresh meat.' He knelt down, put the calf on the ground, took a knife from his belt and cut its throat.

Gaby turned away. 'Jesus.' She almost stumbled and fell. Harry held her.

Murray sliced through the trachea. He waited as blood drained from the artery and the calf kicked a few times, stilled, kicked again, and relaxed.

'Not there,' Fay said to her brother. 'You'll bring in the flies.'

But he wasn't listening. He was watching Gaby, and the way she walked away, her head low, her groans accompanied by Harry's fussing.

Part Three

2006

23

'Harry!'

Trevor walked the perimeter of the compound searching for his son. It had been hours since anyone had seen him. 'Where are yer?' He looked through the sheds, his carving nook, the veggies, Fay's garden. 'Harry!' The native pines, the branches of every tree, the crew hut, even inside the old tank. Then he went back to the house and looked through every room. His bed was made. He searched for a clue – a game, a letter, a toy. Then back out to the living room. 'Stuffed if I know,' he said to Aiden and Fay, sitting at the dining-room table.

'Is his bike there?' Aiden asked.

'Yes.'

'He's probably off diggin' for wombats.'

'He knows better.'

'He's a shit-head.'

He went out to the front porch and sat on the edge of the verandah, scanning the desert, trying to think of a hiding spot.

'Harry!'

The country had returned to desert. After the road trains had left, the crew rolled up their swags and driven off, life had returned to its usual drudge of jobs to be tackled and avoided. Then there was Christmas, and a circle of bodies sitting in the same spots saying the same things, giving the same gifts. Roast pork. Apple sauce. Tissue crowns.

Chris had distributed the gifts. He'd given everyone his usual coat-hanger in a crocheted cover. They'd all given their well-rehearsed thank you. 'That's great, Chris, I needed a new one.'

This was the template, and it sufficed, mostly. Gaby stayed for a week and gave them all expensive gifts. Murray knew what she was up to (again) but this time didn't care.

'Harry!'

'He won't be far,' Murray called from his sleep-out.

The grass had died over the first few weeks of summer. The cattle had slowed, revealing more bone, rib, hip, spending more time sniffing for something green. And now, he'd found two dead animals: a young steer and a cow, their hides collapsed onto a scaffold of bone, flies in their eyes and ears.

'Prob'ly kickin' a ball somewhere,' Murray said, tuning his ukulele, singing:

> Oh! wilt thou think of me, Eileen,
> When I am far away ...

'Not again,' Trevor said.

'Your great-grandfather used to sing this one.'

'And you remember it?'

'I remember everything.'

He listened for the sound of a football, a boot, a bounce, a dribble. 'Harry!'

'Shut up, will yer.'

The scuffed Sherrin football, dug up from the bottom of Harry's wardrobe every December in time for the School of the Air staff versus students football match in Port Augusta. This year it was just him, standing on the outer as the other dads formed a chorus of good blokes, laughing at each other's jokes, slapping each other's arms, encouraging each other's boys. All of whom were fighting for the ball, pushing and shoving men twice their size as Harry dragged his leg across the turf, called for the ball (which no one ever kicked to him), tried for a mark (but fumbled) and finally attempted a left foot kick for goal (the ball veering off in the wrong direction, dribbling, stopping, as the chorus fell silent).

He screwed up his leg in an accident, he'd wanted to tell them, but realised it wouldn't make any difference. Instead, he'd shouted, 'Nice try, Harry.'

Harry had looked at him and shrugged, as if to say, Save your sympathy for someone else. On the way home he'd said, 'I just gotta practice my kicking.'

'That's it. You could train your left leg, couldn't you?'

Upon the stormy sea, Eileen,
Each sad and dreary day?

'Dad!'

Murray stopped. 'I can never get this chord.'

Trevor sat up, squinted, his head jutting forward. He stood, walked across the yard and down steps that led to the low part of his property. Five minutes' walk to the Wilkie plots. 'There you are,' he said to his son, sitting with his back against a tree.

Harry just looked at him.

'I've been looking for you for ages.' He opened the rusted gate and went in. 'What you doin'?'

'Just sittin'.'

He sat beside him. 'I've had to listen to Pop all morning.'

'I shouldn't have shown him that site.'

'No, you shouldn't have.'

Music Hall Song Albums: Complete Lyrics, Guitar and Ukulele chords, with biographies of all the great singers.

'He's workin' his way through every one of Albert Chevalier's songs,' he said.

'Some of them are okay. Some of them are funny.'

'Some. I blame that doctor …'

'Remember?' Harry asked, *'Tell me, darling, that you love me …'*
As he remembered Murray, sitting in front of the computer,
playing for the Year Five and Six assembly. The applause. The
other kids asking for more. 'Why you sittin' out here?' Trevor
asked.

No response.

He knew it was a stupid question. 'Get out of the mad
house, eh?'

Harry looked at him. 'It's not a mad house.' He couldn't
say why he'd come. He'd brought his sudoku book but hadn't
done any.

'Strange,' Trevor said. 'All this space, and it's hard to find a
quiet spot.' He looked across the desert. Longed for it. To walk,
to keep walking, in a long, straight line; until his feet or body gave
out. 'You missed this morning's lesson.'

'Aiden wasn't there.'

'So?'

'It's just maths.'

'You like maths.'

Harry rested his head against the trunk of the tree. 'It's the
same stuff as last year. Fractions. Lowest common denominator …
blah, blah.' He watched a small mob of roos pass in front of them.

'We should go hunting,' he said.

'We should do fractions.'

Trevor looked at the urn. He noticed someone had shifted it
from its spot under the tree. 'What are we gonna do with the
ashes?' he asked.

Harry shrugged.

'What do *you* want to do?'

It was nearly lunch. Trevor's stomach gurgled. It was getting hot,
on its way to forty-two, but this didn't bother Harry-in-the-shade,

a baseball cap low over his face. 'It's up to Aiden, too, isn't it?'

'Perhaps … but I'm sure, if you decided …'

'Do you think she'd like it here?'

'I do. It's cool. She'd get the breeze.'

Harry stood, brushed his pants, took a few steps and picked up the urn. He walked through the gate, out to where the grass started. Trevor followed him. He saw that he had decided, that he was determined. He saw how he tried to unscrew the lid, but couldn't. 'You lift it off,' Trevor said.

He did this. Stopped, waited and looked back at his dad. Then he lifted the urn and sprinkled the ashes and watched them fall. Although he wanted them to scatter, to blow across every inch of desert, there was no wind. He replaced the lid. 'I didn't want her in there, with the others,' he said.

'Why not?'

'She wasn't like them.' He walked back. 'It's funny how people go … forever.'

They walked back to the house. Trevor put his arm around his shoulder. Soon they could hear Murray.

Tell me, darling …

They laughed. As they climbed the steps, Harry asked, 'What should we do with this?' He held up the urn.

Trevor thought for a moment.

…that you love me …

'Should we keep it for Pop?'

Trevor stood in front of the fridge. The door was crowded: one of Harry's assignments (87% – he knew he could do better, if only Aiden would spend more time with him); a cheque: $1200. Payable to Trevor Wilkie. From the account of Lifton-Padfield

Salvage P/L. And a note: 'I've calculated this for two days work. Hope all improves. Regards, T.'

T for Turner.

He'd been surprised when it arrived. Not so much for the money, but the salvaging of faith. Turner, he guessed, was only a put-on arsehole: someone who acted tough because he thought that's what was expected of him.

The door was heavy with junk: a plaster dinosaur Harry had made; his laminated certificates from the past three years (a few with the paint not quite cleaned off the edges); Carelyn, with her arms around her boys, attempting a crooked smile.

He heard a noise: metal on concrete. Walking outside, he saw Aiden on the ground in the shed, playing with his trail bike. 'You just had a shower,' he said, as he walked over.

'So?'

'Why didn't you do this first?'

'I didn't think.'

He could see grease stains on his son's new jeans. 'What's wrong with it?'

'The chain slipped.'

He'd completely stripped the bike: chain, brake pads and nuts. The back wheel sat on the ground and he used a rag to clean the spokes, to wipe grease-soaked sand from the frame and engine. 'I was talking to Tom's dad,' he said.

'Yeah?'

'He has his own garage. He said there's a job for me ... if I want.'

Trevor wasn't at all surprised. 'What, an apprenticeship?'

'Yeah.'

It was what he wanted, but didn't want, for his son: a future away from the farm. A new beginning; a new life. It was happening too quickly, but not fast enough. 'And you're interested?'

'I suppose.'

'You either are or you aren't.'

'Well, I am.'

'And where would you stay?'

'They got a spare room.'

Where he'd already been staying. The room left behind by an older sister who'd moved to town to study medicine. A pink room with shag carpet and a white tallboy full of girls' clothes.

'So, why didn't he take on Tom?' Trevor asked.

'He wasn't interested.'

'I would've thought – '

'Dad, they don't get along.'

'Right.'

Trevor stopped to think. Was it generic? Fathers and sons? 'So, you'd stay there, pay board?'

'Yeah.' Aiden looked at him as if he were stupid. He couldn't understand how he couldn't grasp something so simple.

Trevor was trying to see the big picture. He knew what the boys got up to. Knew Tom had a ute with spotlights and air-horns and, he guessed, spent his nights trawling the streets of Port Augusta. But he knew the father was cautious and didn't, wouldn't, take any shit. 'Tom, he's sensible?' he asked.

'Yeah.'

'No burn-outs ... speeding?'

'I'm not gonna end up wrapped around a tree, Dad.'

'I know how boys that age – '

'No, just cos you see ...' He looked at him. He wanted to say it, but couldn't. The kangaroo. There was no kangaroo, was there, Dad? But we can *choose* to believe, can't we? You can say it, and we can agree with you.

'No whoopee weed?' Trevor asked.

Aiden put down his rag. 'Dad.'

'No little pink pills?'

Eyes. Glaring. 'You haven't even met him. Ten minutes, you'd see what I mean. I don't hang around with fuckheads.'

'Idiots.'

He continued working. Trevor was in two minds. He waited, opened the door to the EH and sat down. 'Still ... I've got a farm to run.'

'Well, George, Tom's dad, said I could do it part-time, so I could be here for the muster, and whatever needs doing.'

'Right.' He waited. 'Might work.'

'It'd work. You don't need me all the time.'

Trevor was arguing with himself. Testing the water, throwing in sodium and watching it glow, splutter and explode. 'Pop will hit the roof.'

'Do you care?'

'After all these years, you'd be the first to opt out.'

'I'm not opting out. I'm just trying something different. It's not like I'm goin' to Adelaide, and not coming back.'

'Well, you can tell the old bugger.'

'He's your dad.'

'Your grandfather.'

Aiden slipped the wheel back in place. Adjusted it, secured it with a couple of nuts and started tightening them. 'Can I remind you of something?'

'What?'

'You said I shouldn't feel obliged to stay on ... if there was something I wanted to do.'

'Did I?'

'Yes. You know you did.' He smiled.

'Well ... I might've said something along those lines.'

'That's *exactly* what you said.'

Trevor was starting to like the sound of it. Aiden and George obviously got along, and had a *sensible* relationship, and George had made a *sensible* proposition. He, this old mechanic, searching for someone to fill the gap his son had left, had obviously seen that Aiden was a *sensible* boy. 'And what about Harry?' he asked.

'Well ...' He started feeding the chain onto the cogs. 'He can look after himself.'

'Can you imagine him here, without you?'

'He'd be ecstatic.'

'No, he wouldn't. You know that.'

'Well, he'd have to get used to it.'

He'd seen it. In the last six months, especially. How Harry watched his older brother, waiting to hear what to say, how to think, how to be smart, and sarcastic, and *sensible*. How he'd always stay behind him when they rode off on their bikes; how he'd occasionally overtake him, but then drop back. 'No, he'd be okay,' he said. 'Then, when he starts at Mercy, you'd be close, to keep an eye on him.'

'Hold on. I never said I was gonna do it. I just said he'd asked. It's like you've already decided.'

'No ... it's up to you, son.'

It was Chris's fault, of course. Always was.

You're the one left the doors open, Murray had told him.

For four months, since the muster crew had left. Sand blowing in. Bird shit. Kangaroos. Rabbit droppings.

So he'd been sent to the crew quarters. Murray had followed and stood giving orders, telling him to run the long hose from the house, wash the floor, scrub it with a broom and hose it out again. Then he'd gone back to the house for lunch.

Chris stood in his gumboots, working. He could feel gluey water between his toes. Looking out of the window, up towards the house, he saw Harry practising his whip in the compound. 'Harry,' he called.

Harry looked to see who it was. 'What yer doin'?'

'Cleanin' up.'

Chris had had Murray up to his eyeballs. Telling him to move when he was halfway through a meal; saying things like, *You're puttin' on the pounds, old boy*; throwing his videos and DVDs in the bin (*I warned yer, if I found them on the floor*); grunting at him as if he were a dog (*Go on … get off …*) He hoped the old man would die, and soon. He imagined looking at the dead body, minutes after the heart attack; the ambulance coming and the men in green overalls rolling him onto a stretcher; sitting on a hard bench at the funeral, staring out of the window, mouthing the words of hymns, planning his new Murray-free life. He wondered if he might feel sad for a while, but then thought, no.

He stopped to catch his breath. 'I hate you,' he said. Then he repeated it, louder. 'I hate you … I hate you.'

'Who?' Murray asked, appearing in the doorway.

He just stared at him.

'You hate me?'

'No.'

'Who?'

He continued working. Picked up the hose and squirted the floor, careful to avoid Murray's feet.

No, he thought. I can't wait till he dies. It could be another ten years. Twenty, perhaps? Maybe I could help bring it on?

Murray sat on a chair in the corner. As he watched him work he took out his tobacco and rolled a cigarette. Lit it, placing the pouch, papers and matches on a ledge.

Chris was looking at him. What do you want? Why are you just sitting there? Do you enjoy watching other people work?

'It was you,' Murray said.

'What?'

'If you remember, after the muster, I said to you, gather all the rubbish, sweep the place out and close the doors. Remember? *Close the doors.'*

Chris could still hear Harry's whip. He turned to Murray, hose in hand, finger on trigger. 'I remember cleaning it,' he said. He kept working. Murray continued smoking, occasionally saying, 'You missed a bit' or 'Make sure you get it all.'

Chris was fermenting, slowly summoning the courage. The skin on his feet had softened. He could smell himself.

'Do you remember that first year?' Murray asked. 'When was it? 1969?'

'Seventy.'

'You wanted to help out on the muster.'

Murray was smiling, but he guessed there was something else behind it.

'So we took you. And there's your mother saying, *Oh, watch out for him!* You don't remember, I suppose?'

Why, he wanted to ask, are you telling me this?

'So we got you doin' the tail tags. And everything's alright until … remember?'

He could remember, but only because he'd been reminded so many times. Of how he'd sat on a calf and tried to ride it, but how the animal had thrown him against a metal panel. How he'd been kicked in the head and knocked unconscious. How Murray had come into the yards, picked him up and carried him out, laying him under a tree, saying, 'This is what I thought would happen.'

'Remember?' Murray asked, inhaling.

'Yes.'

'And the next day when I wouldn't let you come back with us, you had a tantrum.'

Chris could tell he was enjoying it.

'Mummy, make him let me.'

'Quiet.'

'*Uncle Murray's mean to me!*'

'You are!'

Murray sat forward. '*Mummy!*'

'Why do you keep telling me that?'

'Cos it's funny. I can still remember you, in the outfit your mum had bought yer, lying there in the dirt.'

'Why do you hate me?'

'And all the fellas were laughing. Remember?'

'Why?'

Murray stopped to think. The boy seemed to have grown unusual claws. 'Cos I gotta get you movin',' he said.

'I always help.'

'I haven't got time to hate you.' Then he tried again. 'You're just lucky it didn't kick you in the temple.'

Chris was staring at him. 'It's cos you never wanted us here.'

Murray spat tobacco from his lip. 'I've always done my best by yous … Forty years. Maybe you should be a bit grateful?'

Silence.

'What woulda happened if I'd turned yers away? Where would you have gone? What would she have done with you?'

Nothing.

'You'd have ended up in a home. No way she could've brought you up alone. She would've given you to the nuns.'

'She wouldn't!'

'If that's what you think.' Murray finished his cigarette, threw the stub down and stepped on it. '*Why do you hate me?*' He stood. 'Think about what you're sayin'. Forty years …' And walked out without looking back.

Chris couldn't stand it. He clenched his fists and stamped his feet. Mentioning his mother, and the nuns, was too much. He'd done it before. Once, he'd said to him, I saw a letter your mum's written to the Sisters of Mercy. And do you know what she's asked?

No.

If they'd look after you.

It's a lie.

I saw it on her dresser. I persuaded her not to send it. I said, Come on, Fay, blood's thicker than water. You two can stay here as long as you want.

Rubbish.

It's true. I'd show you the letter but I made her burn it and promise never to mention it again.

He threw down the hose, walked out onto the porch and sat on a pile of old crates. Then he took off his boots and threw them up towards the house. 'It's not true,' he called, but Murray had gone.

He'd asked his mother about the letter, and the nuns. Is it true?

Who told you that nonsense?

Uncle Murray.

Nuns, he reckons?

Yes.

Well, there was no letter. As if I'd even think about it.

And she'd held him close.

You just be careful. Murray is a troublemaker.

You never wrote askin' if they'd take me?

No. I love you. I'd rather chop off my own legs.

But he wasn't convinced. Perhaps she had written something, and changed her mind? This, in the end, was Murray's curse. To plant seeds. To play with the truth. To muddy the turkey-nest water. Perhaps, he wondered, it was just his way of amusing himself. Or perhaps some people were just rotten?

He looked in the crates. Milk cartons. Bottles. Old newspapers and magazines.

The thought occurred to him.

He went back in, found the cigarette on the floor, and studied the tip.

Too late. It had died.

Then he noticed the matches on the ledge. He picked them up, went out, struck one and held it to the old newspapers. It only took a few seconds for them to catch, a minute for them to make a small fire in the junk. He stood back watching, waiting, smiling. The flames licked the wooden porch. The uprights and lengths supporting the iron roof caught. Within a minute most of the hut was alight. He clenched his fists with excitement, feeling the heat on his face, and liking it. Soon there was enough fire to make a decent amount of smoke. There was no wind so it moved up and dispersed. Still, he guessed, there'd be enough to find Murray's nostrils.

The front walls and main roof beams were burning. He looked up at the house but no one had noticed, yet. Turned to the fire. Beautiful. Burning his face. But he didn't move. It was a pleasant pain. The pain of Murray, still alive, crying out for help, but succumbing.

The front wall collapsed and, with it, the roof. As the dry wood met the wet a plume of smoke rose from the ruin. The fire was burning the remaining walls. Now there was a roar, crackling. The heat drove him a few steps back.

Murray was first, running down the hill. He stopped and looked at him. 'What happened?'

'I burnt it down.'

'You … idiot.' He glared at him. 'Get the hose.'

'No.'

'Go on!'

'No.'

Murray grabbed the hose and pulled what remained of it from the fire. The nozzle had burnt off and water was spraying from the stub. He trained it on the fire but there was no point. Most of the shack had gone and what remained fell into the hot core.

By now the rest of the family was standing behind them. 'What happened?' Trevor asked.

Murray pointed to his nephew. 'He burnt it down.'

Chris just smiled at them.

'Why?' Harry asked.

'Cos he wouldn't help me,' Chris said.

Murray dropped the hose. He looked at his sister. 'See, I told you, he's gettin' worse.'

'Chris,' she called.

'He's gonna kill the lot of us ... he'll do it again, when we're all asleep.'

24

Days passed, with Chris locked in his room, Fay bringing him meals, finding a time when it was clear (of Murray) and ushering him into the shower. She asked him why he did it but he only replied, 'Because Murray wouldn't help me.'

This got her worried. Despite everything, there was always a certain logic to Chris's behaviour: he danced naked because he loved music; he marched because he was a soldier; he ironed and folded handkerchiefs because he'd been taught this was the proper thing to do. But burning down the crew quarters? There was no logic to that.

There was a table near the steps at the bottom of the hill. Trevor was sitting on an old seat, Harry standing beside him. He'd just finished mixing plaster of paris, pouring it into a tray of leaf-shaped moulds and adding magnets. He was wiping his hands on a rag and explaining the leaves he'd been studying in science. He said, 'See, this is the venation.'

Aiden came storming down from the house. He jumped three, four steps at a time. Then he stood staring at his father. 'You got something to tell us?'

Trevor looked confused.

'About Gaby?'

'What are you talking about?'

Harry could feel the volcano rumbling. He lowered his head and started popping the mostly set fridge magnets from their moulds.

'I've just been taking to James,' Aiden said, hands on hips, eyes on fire.

'James who?'

'Banville. He was in my Year Eight English class … remember?'

'No. Why would I remember?'

'His mum used to work at the pharmacy … with Gaby.'

Trevor stopped to remember. Took a deep breath and said, 'No.'

'Well, she remembers you.'

He stood. 'We should take this stuff in now, Harry.' He started gathering the bowl of dried plaster, the moulds, the bag of powder.

'So, James says, My mum reckons your dad used to come in and take Gaby out for lunch.'

'So?' He had the gear, and stepped away from the table.

'Says, That was *at least* three years ago.'

He shook his head. '*She reckons?* Bullshit.'

'Then James says, I didn't know your mum had been dead that long.'

Harry looked at his brother, then his father.

'So, you know what I told James?' Aiden asked.

Silence.

'The December before last. That's when we had our accident.' He seemed to relax. It was as though he was glad it was out, and done with.

Trevor was lost for words. A year, two, three – it was too big a gap to explain. 'I don't know where she got three years.'

'That's what she said.'

'It was only after the accident.'

'Was it?'

'Yes.'

Harry put down his bits and pieces. Now he wasn't so sure.

Aiden was relaxed. 'How could you do that to Mum?'

'What … we had a few coffees?' He clung to the hope of an explanation. 'Mum knew her for years. I'd known her for years. The three of us would go out. We went to her place a few times. Then, if I was in town …'

Aiden waited. 'James's mum didn't say that. She said it was always just you and Gaby.'

Harry was staring at the plaster splattered across the table.

'You wanna believe that bullshit?'

Aiden turned and walked off, moving slowly up the steps.

'Who the hell is this mother anyway?'

Harry didn't know where to look or what to say.

Trevor took a deep breath. 'Some of these women … they're determined to make trouble,' he said, with almost no conviction.

Harry looked at him then back down at the table.

He'd had enough. He turned and walked away. Into the desert. The emptiness he wished would open up and swallow him.

When Harry went into his room his brother was lying on a mess of shirts, his hands behind his head, his thoughts caught up in the webs that covered the pressed-tin ceiling and the single, naked globe. He sat on his own bed, on his hands, looking at his brother.

'What?' Aiden asked. He turned towards the wall.

Harry took a moment. 'I don't believe it's true.'

'Believe what you want.'

'Dad wouldn't have …'

Silence.

Aiden was forensically examining the last few years. He was trying to remember how often his father had kissed his mother; how often he'd gone to town *for business*; how often he'd said: I'll be back Tuesday.

Fine … I'll call you tonight.

Don't worry, I'll call you. I'm stayin' with Sid.

Sid Porter, the stock agent. Or perhaps: Smithy'll give me a room at the pub. With what he owes me …

He tried to remember, but couldn't. Still, he thought, he must have offered some explanation, and his mother must have accepted it.

'Dad's always got business,' Harry said.

No reply.

'He has to go see people.'

Aiden turned and looked at him. 'Are you completely bloody stupid?' Again, the wall.

Harry lay down on his bed. Stretched out and put his hands behind his head, like his brother. 'Maybe they were just friends back then?'

'Yeah, right.'

'Why not?'

'That's not how it works. When you're married you don't hang around with other women.'

'Why not?'

'Because people will think …'

There was a wait, and the sound of Chris in his room watching television, singing a theme tune.

'I don't see why …' Harry was trying to form thoughts, words. 'If they just went out for coffee?'

'They didn't just go out for coffee.'

He was juggling words; whether he should even say them. So, Dad went to Gaby's place? So, Dad *stayed* at Gaby's place? And he knew, if he'd stayed, there were other words. 'Why would Dad lie to us?'

No reply.

'He's never lied to us before.'

Aiden sat up. 'You reckon?'

'No.'

'That's a little naïve, *brother.*'

'He wouldn't.'

'No? A kangaroo, remember? That's what jumped out in front of us. That's why we swerved. That's why we had the accident.'

Harry studied his brother's face.

'Well, I was lookin' and I didn't see no kangaroo.'

'You couldn't see from the back.'

'I could. I did. He was falling asleep, then he woke up.' He could see it, as clear as anything: his father's head slowly dropping; a start, a jerk, grabbing and pulling at the wheel; the feel of the car lifting, the tumble, the paint, the screams, the certificates, the impact, the dust, the crushing, the silence.

'You shouldn't say it if you don't know it,' Harry said.

'There was no kangaroo.'

'Dad says there was.'

'*Dad says, Dad says* … He didn't deny he'd been in the chemist.'

'*So?*'

Harry took another moment; juggled more thoughts, more words. 'So what if he did fall asleep? Doesn't change anything.'

'It changes what he said.'

'Mum's still dead.'

'Yeah, and it's *his* fault.'

'Why? That could've happened to anyone.'

'But it didn't. It happened to him, and he said it was a kangaroo.'

This, Harry realised, was something he couldn't argue with. Like the thought of a man, and a woman, getting about together.

'Maybe Mum knew about Gaby?'

Aiden was still dissecting memories. He wanted to recall words, any words, between his parents. He tested and rejected every explanation. Maybe Mrs Banville had a grudge against his dad?

'Dad kept her pretty well hidden,' he said. 'You don't remember ever going there?'

'No.'

'The pharmacy? Anywhere?'

'No.'

Chicken for lunch. Dressed and roasted, sitting in the middle of the lunch table. All of the Wilkie men except Trevor sat waiting.

'What's wrong with you two?' Murray asked his grandsons.

Aiden looked at him. 'Nothing.'

He wasn't happy with this. 'Usually can never shut you two up. You're not even arguing.'

'There's nothing to argue about,' Harry said.

'That doesn't stop you.'

Fay brought a pile of plates. Laid each in its spot before picking up a knife and starting to carve. Gave everyone a wing or leg and white meat. 'Where's your father?' she asked Aiden.

He shrugged. 'Dunno.'

Murray studied his face. He could tell it had something to do with Trevor. Something he'd forbidden them to do; somewhere he wouldn't take them; or perhaps something to do with the girlfriend. 'When did you last see him?' he asked.

'Earlier.'

'What was he doing?'

'He was helping me with my fridge magnets,' Harry said.

Murray looked at him. 'And then?'

He shrugged.

'God, you two are a lot of help.'

Both boys reclaimed their vacant stare. Murray looked from one to the other. 'I don't know what's going on.'

'Nothing,' Aiden said.

'What, did he growl at yers?'

'No.'

Fay approached with a tray of honey-brown chips. She used a spatula to serve them.

'Salt?' Murray said, without looking at her.

She went into the kitchen, returned with the salt and almost threw it down in front of him. '*Please*,' she said.

'I said please.'

'You did not.'

Harry picked up the sauce bottle and started covering his food in a trail of red.

'Not so much,' Murray said.

He kept going.

'Not so much.'

And stopped. 'That's how much I always have.'

'It's too much. Sauce is for taste; it's not part of the meal.'

Aiden stared at him.

'What?' Murray asked.

'What does that mean?'

'What?'

'*It's not part of the meal.*'

'It means you don't use half a bottle.'

'He always does that.'

'Well, he's gotta cut back.'

Fay walked into the hallway and knocked on the door to her son's room. 'Come on,' she said. 'Lunch.'

'Not here,' Murray said.

She returned to the dining room. 'Don't be stupid, Murray.'

'He can stay in his room.'

'It's been three days.'

'I don't care.'

They all heard the door opening and Chris asking, 'Can I come out now?'

Fay turned to him. 'Come on.'

Chris entered the room. Murray stood up and thundered, 'Get back in there!'

'Murray,' Fay said.

'Go on.'

'He can't stay in there forever.'

'Pop,' Aiden said.

Murray looked at him. 'Thank you.' His hand was up, his finger pointing to the room. 'Go on,' he said.

Chris retreated into semi-darkness. Fay walked over to the table, gathered cutlery and one of the meals and took it in to her son. When she returned she looked at her brother. 'It's not just him, is it, Murray?'

He was picking at his chips.

'He told me how you been workin' on him.'

He didn't reply; wouldn't look up.

'Tellin' him how hopeless he is …'

'He burnt down a building.'

'After so many years of it? Miracle he didn't do something worse.'

'That's what I'm worried about.' He picked up a drumstick and started ripping at the meat. 'This is hard,' he said, looking at Harry.

Harry didn't respond.

'You gotta kill 'em quick. Before they know what's going on.'

'I did kill it quick.'

Fay sat down and they all started eating. Aiden turned to Murray. 'One chop and it was dead,' he said. 'He can't do it any quicker than that.'

'I was just sayin'.'

'You should know the facts.'

'Pardon?'

'Why accuse him of something …'

You've always, *always* hated Chris, he wanted to say. But couldn't. Instead, he managed, 'Don't worry, Aunt, he can come out and help me after lunch.'

Fay smiled at him. 'What are you doing?'

'There's some welding.'

'He can stay in his room,' Murray said.

'That's cruel,' Aiden replied.

Murray flared. 'When you start runnin' the place you can decide.'

'You don't run the place. Dad does.' He lifted his head and straightened his shoulders. 'It's cruel.'

Murray slammed his fist on the table. 'Cruel? Who's the one burnt down –?'

'Because you treat him like a dog.'

Murray was fuming, his shoulder and neck muscles trembling, his heart racing.

'You wanna send me to my room?' Aiden asked. 'I'll save you the trouble.' He stood, gathered his meal and went into his bedroom.

There was silence. Harry studied his plate: the chips, the sauce, the lumps of grease and flesh. Although he hadn't eaten much he didn't feel hungry.

Murray started on a wing. 'I don't want you to end up like that,' he said to Harry.

'How?'

'Disrespectful.'

Harry refused to look at him. There was so much to say but no way to say it. There was no point arguing, and there was no way of escaping. He looked up and his dad was standing in the doorway.

'Come on,' Fay said to him. 'Your lunch is getting cold.'

Trevor sat down and looked at Harry, but he wouldn't look back.

'Where you been?' Murray asked.

'Out.'

'Where?'

'Nowhere.'

'Eat up,' Fay insisted.

He ate some white meat, but felt like he had to chew it for hours.

'It's a bit tough,' Murray said.

'It's fine.'

'I said to Harry, you gotta kill 'em quick.'

'It's fine,' Trevor repeated, looking at his son. 'You did a good job.'

Harry still didn't look at him, or answer.

'Harry?'

'Thanks.'

They continued, faces down, the sound of cutlery, and Murray's clunking jaw.

'I can help you with maths after lunch,' Trevor said to his son.

'I've finished it.'

'Good.'

Silence.

'There's dessert,' Fay said.

Trevor smiled at her. 'Thanks, Aunt.' He sliced off more meat, cutting it in half, quarters, eighths, before eating it. Before looking at Harry. 'You okay?'

No reply.

Aiden appeared from his room. He noticed his father and walked slowly towards the kitchen. Put his plate on the bench.

'You need to talk to your son,' Murray said.

'Why?'

'He thinks it's okay to be rude to me.'

Aiden scraped his plate. Put his dishes in the sink and started washing them. 'Nice chook, Aunt.' Looked at his brother. 'Tender, too.'

Murray shook his head. 'See.'

But Trevor was just staring at Aiden. Aiden could feel his eyes, but refused to look at him.

'He's tellin' me it's *my* fault Chris burnt down the hut.'

'I didn't say that.'

'You did.'

'Dad!' Trevor growled.

'Dad nothin'. He's your son. Teach him a bit of respect. If you don't …'

'What are you gonna do about it?' Aiden said. 'Put me in my room?'

'Aiden,' Trevor said.

Aiden looked at his father. 'You're the worst of all.' He dropped his plate into the sink, turned and went outside.

25

Trevor looked towards the highway. Gaby's car appeared over a ridge, grew bigger, slowed and stopped. He approached her window. 'How are you?' Kissed her, and their lips lingered.

'What are you doing out here?' she asked.

A few moments later they were sitting in the car. He told her about Mrs Banville and her son, ruining everything. 'I thought I better warn you.'

She remembered. 'Bitch.' She could see her looking up as he came in; approaching him and asking if he needed help. 'Does Harry know?'

'Yes.'

'And …?'

'Well, I'm just gettin' the look. No words. Nothing.'

She stopped to think what this might mean. It wasn't that they'd done anything wrong, particularly; it wasn't like Carelyn had known. It wasn't like anyone had been hurt. 'Harry is …?'

'Don't expect too much from them this time.'

'This time?'

'They'll get over it.'

But she wasn't so sure. She feared the boys would see it differently; that she'd become more monster than replacement mother.

They drove towards the house. 'Maybe I should drop you and go,' she said.

'They know you're coming.'

'Great.'

Most of the time she drove over the corrugations. 'We've got nothing to be ashamed of.'

He didn't respond.

'Have we?'

They arrived at the house and he helped with her bags. When they went in they found Harry lying on the couch watching *The Simpsons*. 'Haven't you got some homework?' Trevor asked.

He sat up, turned and looked at them. 'I've finished everything.'

'Hi, Harry,' Gaby said.

'Hi.' He stared at her robe, her scarf, the clear squares of plastic hanging around her neck.

'How have you been?' she asked, coming around, taking his head in her hands and kissing his cheek.

'Fine.'

Yanga was sniffing her dress; he licked her shoe.

'Go away,' she said.

Go away, he thought, sinking into the lounge. Who says that?

Trevor said, 'Gaby's staying a few nights.'

'I know.'

'That okay?'

No reply.

'Harry?'

He looked at his father. 'I suppose.'

Trevor refocused on Gaby. 'Coffee?'

'Thanks.'

She sat down on one of Chris's food-stained rugs. 'I like *The Simpsons*,' she said.

No reply. Harry folded his arms and dropped his head onto his chest. He felt like he'd already conceded too much. This woman deserved nothing. Less than nothing. Contempt. She had no opinion about *The Simpsons*. Another one of her tricks.

'Lisa,' she said. 'That's me as a child.'

'Yeah, right,' Trevor said.

Harry looked sideways at the woman. He wondered whether

he should just go to his room. Or perhaps tell her, both of them, what he thought of them. They continued watching the cartoon without speaking. A few minutes later Trevor came over with the coffees and sat down. Gaby turned to Harry and asked, 'So, what have you been up to?'

He looked at her and thought: Not much. What about you? What have you been up to?

'We went on a bore run this week, didn't we, Harry?' Trevor said.

No reply.

'That sounds like fun,' Gaby said.

He hated the way she played with words. *That sounds like fun.* Like a four-year-old. *That sounds like fun.* He looked at his dad. It's time to go, he thought, but couldn't do it.

'And what else have you been up to?' Gaby asked.

'Nothing.'

'That doesn't sound like you, Harry.'

How, he wanted to ask, do you know what I'm like? I'm not your son, you're not my mother. You're no one. A body my father drags into the house every few weeks.

'How's school going?' she asked.

No reply.

'You'll be boarding soon, won't you? You can stay with me if you like.'

He met her eyes. 'You have to stay there,' he said.

'Not necessarily,' Trevor explained. 'If there's another option. It'd save a lot of money.'

'I want to board.'

'Fine.'

'Aiden got to.'

'*Fine.*'

'You really don't like me,' Gaby said, grinning.

No, he thought. Five years of hell? How could you even think of it? After what you did to my mum.

Silence. More gags. He dropped his head.

'You're a funny one,' Gaby said, sipping her coffee.

'Funny?' he asked.

'The other day you're out on your bike, now …'

'There's a reason.'

'Should we talk about it?'

He even hated this about her. The way that everything, no matter how shitty, could be talked about, resolved, made good. But life wasn't like that. Pop was right about one thing: talking didn't fix anything. 'What's the point?' he asked.

'Perhaps …'

She stopped short again. Aiden had emerged from his room. He stood in the doorway studying the scene.

'Hi, Aiden,' she said.

'Harry, wanna go for a ride?'

'Gaby said hello,' Trevor insisted.

'Harry?'

'Okay.' He slipped on his boots.

'Aiden,' Trevor repeated.

Aiden ignored them. Harry was the only one in the room. 'Ready?' he asked his brother.

'Aiden!'

Gaby looked at him and shook her head. Trevor sank into his seat.

The two boys went out, Aiden squeezing his brother's shoulder. Trevor looked at her. 'Well …'

She smiled. 'You reap as you sow, old man.'

The shed was hot but he was used to it. He could sit sweating for hours and not notice. He'd wipe his forehead with a linseed-rag;

unbutton his shirt and pull out his tails. He had a fan but the motor had fused years ago.

So he just sat, sanding, using the crease in the paper to sculpt the final folds of skin on Harry's hand; the little valleys around the fingernails; the webbing between the fingers. Until he decided it was finished. He laid it on the desk and studied it; moved it so it picked up light and shadow from the globe. It looked like a hand: the blood vessels, the wiring between the wrist and fingers.

Now was the time to take it inside, present it to his son and study his reaction. But, of course, he couldn't. He'd just look at it and give it back. 'That's good, Dad, thanks.' Or not even that. Just a shrug as he placed it on his bedside table.

So, he continued. He used the tip of a nail to deepen the criss-crossing lifelines.

The phone sat beside him. And a scrap of paper with a number and the words: Malboona Rural Equity. The handset was still warm from his conversation with an assistant manager in Perth.

Yes, I've read the letter, and the offer seems generous ... my father is against it, and he has the deed on the place ... so?

Trevor Wilkie was at a dead-end. He could feel every gram, every tonne of the farm collapsing on top of him. Every steer, every cow, every calf. Every person: Murray, wheezing, distantly; Fay, clutching her perch; Aiden, who was still a long way from finding his path. And Harry, unsure what to think about anything.

It was always going to come to this, he thought.

Since the first time he'd gone to the chemist to fill one of Fay's scripts. Since he'd said, 'Yes, I remember you, you came to Carelyn's birthday ... when was it?' Since that first half-hour they'd spent talking, and the next time, a few weeks later, when they'd gone to the Commercial for a counter lunch.

They'd gone from friendship to companionship, hand-holding to a kiss; coffee under a pepper tree in her backyard to the twenty minutes it took on the couch. Later, when he'd come to love her more, things had changed. Part, or most, of what he'd sit thinking about in the shed was the impending disaster he'd manufactured. There was no explaining it away or mitigating it. With the rebuilding of a new Trevor came the pulling down of the old.

She was at the door.

'Finished?' he asked.

'Yeah. Fay's a nice old biddy, but she likes to do things her own way.'

In this case, lavender bags, sewn on the Singer, finished with a ribbon, deposited in drawers full of musty underwear and unwashed shorts.

She approached the desk and ran her fingers through a carpet of shavings and sawdust. 'She's very shaky,' she said.

'She's probably just nervous. Living with Murray all these years.'

'Probably. She has that little tic with her head, doesn't she?' She demonstrated.

He'd noticed it and the thought had occurred to him. 'If it's Parkinson's,' he said, 'it's very early, and she's very old.'

'You should take her to see someone.'

'I will.'

She took the hand from him. 'It's excellent.'

'It's ready.'

'Why don't you give it to him?'

He just looked at her.

'God … they'll get used to it.' She studied the hand. 'Exactly proportional. Nice long fingers, just like his. Come on, we'll go give it to him.'

'No.'

'Come on.' She pulled his arm.

'It needs more sanding.'

How, he wondered, could he give it to him? How could he make up for what he'd done? Reclaim his first lesson with the whip, or the afternoon at the Port Augusta Rock and Roll Muster where they'd all danced to some awful country singer, up to their knees in mud, falling over, picking up handfuls of slosh and throwing it at each other. All before Gaby.

She leaned against the bench, playing with Harry's fingers. 'This is just gonna go on and on,' she said. 'It's silly.'

'It's my fault.'

'Listen, this is what we do. Get them together, explain everything. You say, Yes, I ... we, did the wrong thing, but humans do, don't they?' She waited for a response.

'That'd just make it worse.'

'If you explain ...'

'I don't think so.'

'And then say, We're sorry.'

This much he did agree with. That's what it would have to come to: Sorry. 'I can't do it right now.'

'You can.'

'They need a while for it to ... sink in.'

'Nonsense. The longer you leave it the worse it will get.'

He was tightening into a ball, again. Wanted to push her away, to stand, walk out. 'But I have to,' he said.

There was a long wait. She returned the hand. 'You're gonna have to face it, Trevor.'

'What?'

'*I'm* getting tired of all this.'

Murray still didn't know. As he sat on the porch he told Gaby about Bill. 'He walked out of this door to the stables (it's the shed now), saddled his horse and rode off.'

'He was quite upset?' she asked.

He didn't hear her. 'He rode all the way to Number one. Then you know what he did?'

'No.'

'Let his horse loose. His best horse. *Skedaddle*. It ran into the desert, never to be seen again.'

She felt like a child; Murray-the-storyteller; fairy tales; half-truths (although he swore every word was true). 'I think I know what comes next,' she said.

But he didn't care. 'Bill couldn't accept that his boy was a coward. Never had, never would. Couldn't accept what the school had done, what his neighbours said. *He* knew John was no coward.' He tapped his armrest with his fingernail.

'Things might be different today,' she said, but he still ignored her.

'So, he goes inside the building. He knows what's in there: food, fencing, wire, ropes …'

She shook her head. 'No?'

She studied his face, but was caught up in a thought.

'Apparently,' Murray said, 'there were bolts, screws, nails sitting around, and he filled his pockets. He'd strangled plenty of animals and must have known it wouldn't be quick.'

'How awful.'

'So … he moves a chair under the rope and puts it around his neck.'

Aiden walked past without looking at them. 'What are you up to, Aiden?' she said, but he just looked at her and kept walking.

'She asked you a question,' Murray said.

Aiden stopped. 'Not much.'

'What's your problem?' Murray asked.

'*My* problem? I don't have a problem.' He looked at Gaby. 'Well, one, really.'

'Grow up,' she said to him.

Murray sat up.

'She hasn't told you?' he asked his grandfather.

'What?'

'About her and dad?'

'What about 'em?'

'How long they've been seeing each other?'

Murray turned to her. 'What's that all about?'

'I'm sure he's gonna tell you.'

'Three years. Three years.' He glared at her.

Murray didn't know what to believe.

'All those trips to town … what do you think Dad was doing?'

'Aiden,' Trevor said, appearing beside them.

Aiden didn't care. 'All of that time they were together and none of us knew. Me and Harry, we were just kids.' He looked at his father. 'We thought he was off paying bills, or buying wire. We were busy learning. Ancient Egypt. What was the point of that?'

Murray said, 'Jesus, Trevor.'

'That's what you were doing, wasn't it, Dad?'

Trevor couldn't speak.

'While Mum was home helping us.'

Gaby had had enough. 'This is not particularly helpful, Aiden.'

'It's very helpful. You were the one …'

She waited for Trevor to respond. He dropped his head, lost.

'Typical,' she said, standing and going inside.

Murray, meanwhile, was waiting for his son to respond. 'You better clear this up,' he said.

'There's nothing to clear up, Pop,' Aiden said. 'They'd been seeing each other behind Mum's back.'

Trevor broke away. He went into the house and found her throwing the last of her things into her case. 'Don't go,' he said.

'When you're ready to deal with it, tell me.'

She closed the zip and stood up.

'I will.'

'Bullshit.'

Harry emerged from his room. Stood in a shadow, watching. She looked at him but didn't say goodbye. Walked from the house, nearly collecting Yanga with her case. Trevor followed. 'We'll go back in. We'll talk to them now.'

'You talk to them. When someone's ready to treat me civilly ...'

She threw her case into the back of the car and got in. 'This is a disaster. You sort it out.' She started her engine and drove off without even looking at him.

26

The following morning Aiden drove the Commodore into the middle of the compound. He used a bucket of Fay's grey water to wash it. For the next thirty minutes he scrubbed, rinsed and chamoised each gravel-chipped panel until it shone.

Trevor came out and stood waiting, thinking. 'I'll pay you to do it each week if you like.'

'I don't want to get paid.'

Not far away, Harry was sitting up his tree. He'd been reading, but had stopped, and was straining to hear. *I'll pay you to do it … I don't want to get paid …* He wondered why his brother was talking to his dad. Perhaps he'd reconsidered.

'I've been thinking,' he heard him say. 'I've decided to take this apprenticeship.'

Trevor waited. It explained the clean car. The eye contact.

'Right,' he managed.

'I'll stay and help for a few months, get everything cleaned up.'

'Why wait? Nothin' much needs doin'.'

'I've arranged to come back for the muster. I can have six weeks.'

'Good.'

Harry slowed his breathing and shut out every sound, bird, rustle of leaves, so he could hear them. Aiden was off. He'd leave and hardly ever return. He wouldn't be a home supervisor anymore; a trail bike opponent; a friend; a pain in the arse. He'd just be gone. Like everyone.

'I didn't mean for this to happen,' Trevor said.

'It's got nothing to do with that. I've been thinking about it. We talked about it, didn't we?'

'Yes.'

'And you said, You might be better off out of it.'

Harry wondered how things could possibly function without him. Who'd lubricate the rubbing parts of his family? Tell him about the foul-breathed, nasal-haired teachers at Mercy? Stand up for Chris when Murray got the shits on? Explain improper fractions?

'Gonna stay at their place?' Trevor asked.

'Yeah.'

'Well … that'll work out okay.'

'The good things is, in a year or so when Harry goes to school, I'll be handy, to keep an eye out.'

Harry's eyes lingered on his father. It wasn't being said, but it was obvious: his brother was leaving because he hated him.

'If you're sure it's what you want,' Trevor said.

'It is. I like taking things apart and putting them back together.'

Harry couldn't believe his brother was letting him off the hook. He jumped down from his tree, walked up the road and stood looking at his dad. 'He wants to go because of you.'

'Harry,' Aiden said.

'Cos you've made it horrible to be around here now.' He was clutching his book. 'I don't want to be here either,' he shouted.

'Harry,' Aiden said. 'It's cos Dad thinks the farm – '

'It's not! Go on, tell him the truth.'

The conversation he'd had with his brother the previous evening. When Aiden had said: *This is bullshit, he can't even look us in the eyes. He can't say sorry … he won't tell us when …*

And he'd said, *How do you think he hid it from Mum?*

Lots of lies.

What are you gonna do?

Nothing. I've gotta look after you, y' little prick.

Harry turned from his father to his brother. 'You didn't even tell me.'

'I wasn't sure.'

'You tell me everything.'

'I was still thinking.'

What, he wanted to say, am I gonna do here by myself? You're meant to be my brother. *My brother.* He turned and ran. Around the house, to the porch, where Murray was busy rolling a cigarette.

'What's wrong with you?' he asked.

'Aiden's leaving.'

'What?'

'He's got an apprenticeship in Port Augusta.'

Murray soon found him, alone, polishing the car window. 'What's this about an apprenticeship?'

'I've been offered – '

'Stupid bloody idea. This is yours – ' He used his hand to describe the desert, the grass, the cattle. 'I don't know what this is all about. No one's told me.'

'My mate's dad runs a garage in town.'

'Why can't your mate work for him?'

'He's got a different job.'

He waited. 'No discussion … that's it?'

'I've discussed it with Dad.'

'Who's gonna run this place? It's a family farm.'

'No, it's not,' Trevor said, appearing from the laundry. 'It's your place.'

Murray could feel his heart racing. 'It's your responsibility,' he said to his son.

'It's not. None of it's mine. None of it.'

To Murray, this was the ultimate betrayal. The future. He could handle death and a lack of fidelity. Even rudeness, stupidity, incompetence. But not this. 'I forbid it,' he said to his grandson.

'You've got no say,' Trevor said.

He wanted to hit him. 'This is all your fault,' he said. 'No wonder the boy wants to go.'

'I want to be a mechanic,' Aiden said.

He wasn't finished. 'You know what will happen? He won't come back. Once he's got a taste of it – he won't come back.'

'I will,' Aiden said.

He wasn't interested. 'Well, what have you got to say?'

'It's all organised,' Trevor said.

He returned to Aiden. 'We're not gonna lose all this ... so you can change people's air filters.' He turned and went in, his hands shaking.

The following days, Trevor retreated. There was nowhere for him to go where there wasn't a pair of eyes, and Murray's constant comments. 'Where does this leave us now?'

It was all silence, television, Bruce Willis in his tower, as Chris just stared, oblivious to their own siege. Fay, holding the middle ground, cleaning the oven, asking Harry to shower. 'And why are *you* so miserable?'

No response. Slippered feet dragging across carpet; the door quietly closing; silence. Then his afternoon lesson: clipped responses (*How did the Egyptians move their building blocks?*); Aiden sitting beside him with the answer sheet; Mrs Amery saying, 'Aiden, what did Harry write down?'

'He hasn't done it.'

'It's due.'

'We've been busy.'

Trevor couldn't stand it any more. Four days after Aiden's carwash he got in his Commodore and, without telling anyone, set off down the highway.

A few hours later he pulled into the Belalie Roadhouse. He sat in his car studying the building. It was orange and brown; striped awnings and acres of glass radiating hot days and cold nights into a plastic dining room. He got out and went inside. The walls were spray-on concrete, decorated with Trev's Tractors calendars from the nineties; a few snake skins nailed up under a clock that tried to tick, but couldn't.

He approached the counter and noticed food sitting in bags in the bain-marie – drying out, festering, waiting: spring rolls, dim sims, corn jacks and a grey-looking yiros. 'I'll have three spring rolls,' he said to a girl, although he knew he was making a mistake.

He found a table and sat down. Didn't feel hungry. Even if he did, couldn't eat this shit. Still, it gave him a reason to sit and stare out of the greasy windows and listen to the travellers' conversations.

Once, this had been a special place. He could remember when he was a kid, Murray saying, 'Right, a treat for tea!' He could remember knowing what that meant. The Belalie. Like the Savoy or the Windsor. *The Belalie.* He could remember getting dressed in his best cords and desert boots and arriving in expectation of some grand experience: T-bone, mashed potato and peas, or maybe the cabbage-laden chow mein or Bombay curry. There was a Fisherman's Basket, of course, six types of seafood straight from deep-freezer to deep-fryer. But that was fair enough. It was a four-hour drive to the nearest beach. Or maybe a schnitzel, or fancier still, a parmy, or if you wanted to play safe, the roast of the day.

He sat in the dining room for almost two hours. At one stage the manager asked, 'You okay?'

'Yes, thanks.'

'Anything else I can get you?'

'No.'

He wondered if he really had to go home; keep working; deal with his father, and sons. He wondered if he should keep driving to Port Augusta and see Gaby. Explain. Apologise. Negotiate. But there was no point; he wasn't welcome there either. The Belalie was the only place that would have him.

Towards evening the diner filled up. People were looking for a spare table. The manager looked at him a few times and eventually came over and said, 'If you wouldn't mind?'

'Fine ... I was just leaving.'

So he went, depositing his bag in the bin by the door. He drove back to Bundeena. When he arrived it was dark and the lights were on inside. He sat in the car for another ten minutes deciding whether to go in. When he did (still wearing his boots) they were all sitting at the table eating Fay's tuna casserole. She looked him over and said, 'Sit down, I'll get yours out of the oven.'

'I'm not hungry.'

'Where you been?' Murray asked.

'The Belalie.'

'Why?'

He didn't respond. Harry wasn't looking at him, but Aiden said, 'You should have some – it's good.'

'No, thanks.'

'Don't worry, I've been holding the fort,' Murray said.

He went to his room and lay on his bed and listened to them eat. Didn't even take off his boots, but could hear Carelyn growling at him: *Not on the bed.*

So what?

Look, you're getting shit everywhere.

He listened for another hour: television; Murray spitting on the front porch; the tinny ring of Aiden's iPod. Then Fay came in.

'You okay?' she asked, switching on the light.

'Turn it off.'

She could only see his outline: 'Want a beer?'

'No.'

She stood staring. He wanted to tell her to go away. 'I'm fine. Just tired.'

'I worry about you.'

No reply.

'Everything going on … it'll all clear up eventually, won't it?'

'Of course.'

He turned towards the open window. 'I'm fine.'

'I've told Murray to keep his nose out of it. I told him Aiden can do what he wants.'

'And what did he say?'

'You know, made a big production, but so what? I just ignore him. Just a lot of noise. And bluff.'

'Yeah.'

'That's the thing … don't listen to him. Now, do you want some food?'

'No.'

'I'll keep it in the oven.'

Then she was gone, back to her son, telling him to turn the television down, Trevor was trying to sleep.

Just after 10 pm, when the house had settled, he stood and went out to his shed. Left the door open to the night and worked by the yellow light. Continued sanding Harry's hand – every line and wrinkle. Guessing that it was beyond finished. Despite everything, he was happy with it.

It was nearly 11.30 pm when he stopped working. Putting the hand on his desk, he wiped his own hands clean and found his phone in his pocket. He started writing: *hi gaby. ive been sorting things out. spoke to the old man. is it possible to come and see you tomorrow. we need to work this business out.*

Send. He felt better. Until he heard his father's footsteps coming from the front of the house, shuffling, stopping in the doorway. 'What the hell you doin' at the Belalie?'

He picked up the fine sandpaper and the hand and kept working. 'A little excursion.'

'What was the point of that?'

'There was no point. I felt like doing it, so I did.'

Murray just looked at him. He still couldn't work him out. Didn't know why he was so moody. 'What are we gonna do about Aiden?' he asked.

He just looked at him. 'What do you mean?'

'This apprenticeship. How are we gonna stop him?'

'We're not.'

Fine dust filled the air.

'I don't understand you,' Murray said. 'He's your son. You gotta make him see sense.'

'Why? It's what he wants to do.'

'He's always known, he always *said* he'd stay here.'

The phone lit up and jumped about on the desk. He picked it up and read the message: *not convinced not coming back for more of the same that old cunt will never change.* He faced his father. 'Why would he want to stay?'

'He used to love getting out with the animals.'

'Why? I don't want to. Harry doesn't want to. Fay never wanted to, but she never had any choice.'

'If you hate the place so much, leave,' Murray said.

'The boys were getting along with Gaby – but you weren't going to have that, were you?' He stood and walked from the shed; the compound; down the hill into the night. Murray called after him. 'If you won't do it, I'll call this fella. I'll tell him there won't be no apprenticeship.'

He was gone.

'Then I'll tell your son.'

The phone lit up and jumped about again.

Murray went in, looked around the lit-up lounge room, saw

Chris asleep on his chair and muttered, 'Christ!' He went into the boys' room. Harry had kicked off his sheets, as usual, and his long legs lay over a pile of clothes and books. He sat beside Aiden, stripped down to his boxers, covered in a single sheet. He studied the three or four days' growth on his face, the few pimples, the edges of sharp teeth in his open mouth. 'Aiden,' he said, taking his elbow and shaking it.

He turned away, pulling his sheet up over his shoulders. 'What?'

'You listenin'?'

'I's asleep.'

'I want to talk.'

'*What?*'

'This apprenticeship ... I don't think it's a good idea.'

'I's asleep.'

'You might *think* it's a good idea, but I don't understand why you want to leave.'

'Tomorrow ...' He slipped back into his dream.

'I have a plan.'

'Pop.'

To sell off some land, the old man wanted to say. To pay down the debt. To restock. To make the place viable. So there's a future, for you and Harry.

'While I got it in my head,' Murray said. 'I'll explain.'

But he was asleep.

27

It was already hot by eight. Harry – wearing his boots, shorts and a T-shirt – walked away from the house. He was pulling a small, flat-topped trolley. Sometimes it sank into the sand and he had to yank it out. It held toys. Stuff, he figured, he didn't need any more: a few action men, a Bionicle, a couple of dinosaurs and a container of Lego.

He walked until the house was a small bump on the horizon. Stopped, took a bottle of water from the trolley and drank. Replaced it and cursed himself for not wearing a hat. On, for another hundred metres, until he came across a dead cow, the last of its skin stretched across its bones. There were others, plenty, across the farm; cattle that had strayed too far from water, or couldn't get what they needed from the grass. He examined the ear-tag and saw that it was only three years old. What did it matter? It was his dad's, or Murray's, or someone else's fault.

He moved on and, a few minutes later, stopped at a lone gidgee tree. Taking a small spade from the carriage he started digging. As he did he heard a trail bike. He looked up and saw his brother approaching. When he arrived he said, 'What are you doing?'

'Digging.'

'Why?'

No reply.

Aiden looked at the trolley and noticed the toys. 'What you doin' with those?'

'I don't need them any more.' He continued, deepening and widening the hole.

'Why'd you come out here?'

He shrugged. 'Just did.'

'Why didn't you put them in the bin?'

'Didn't want to.' He reversed the trolley up to the hole and tipped the toys in. Aiden kept watching, wondering if the whole ritual had some hidden meaning. 'You might want them sometime.'

'No.'

He picked up the spade and slowly, carefully, filled the hole. When he was finished he walked over the sand, compacting it.

'Done.'

'You got anything else buried out here?'

'No.'

'A dead body?'

He sat down against the gidgee tree and used his T-shirt to wipe sweat from his face. Reached for his water and drained the rest of the bottle.

Aiden got off his bike and sat down next to him. 'Why did you bury that stuff?'

'No reason.' He looked back to the house. Took a few moments and said, 'Are you really going to leave?'

'Yes.'

'Why?'

'Cos that's what you do when you're my age.'

He felt the contradiction; knew his brother should go, knew he should stay. 'I'll have to deal with Pop.'

'You can do that.'

Silence.

'At least *she* won't be back.'

Aiden felt the contradiction; that she was bad; that their father still needed her. 'Dad, he's the one you're gonna have to look out for.'

'I know.'

'You'll have to … forget all the other stuff.'

'I know.' He looked at him. 'I'm the cripple, I know.'

'Cripple? You've just got shit for brains.'

He looked at him and felt happy. 'At least I've got a brain.'

They rode back with the trolley hitched to the bike. Harry guessed it would be okay. There'd still be tuna casserole, and Pythagoras.

Another hour, on his bed, Trevor was lost, jumping from one solution to another. All he could really take was silence; his dark room; curling up beneath the sheets; entering a trance where there was no thought, no concerns, no connection with other people. He could hear them, of course. Chris, who would live his life in this one unchangeable mood; Harry, telling Aiden to stop wearing his slippers; Murray in his lean-to, *she had a pair of fine daughters* ...

At 3 pm Fay came in. 'You okay?'

'Fine.'

'You tired?'

'I think ... I got some sort of bug.'

'Just rest.'

Soon he couldn't hear the noise; he was awake but didn't know what was going on. Felt warm and secure. Gathered his legs in his arms.

At 4 pm he stretched out, dropped his legs to the floor and slipped on his boots. Walked from his bedroom. The television was on but there was no one around. He went out through the laundry, across the compound, to the shed. Yanga followed but he didn't acknowledge her. Sitting on Aiden's trail bike, he turned the key in the ignition. And waited. For someone to come and stop him, or at least ask what he was doing. But no one came.

So he rode across the compound, down the hill, into the emptiness of his, or Murray's, top paddock. He didn't try to find the road or a trail or firm ground. Went over the grass, down hills and back up before seeking a straight line and following it. Rode like this for an hour – slowing, quickening, stopping, setting off again.

5 pm. No darker or cooler. He kept moving in some direction towards some destination. He was grateful that thoughts had stopped forming. It was as though by leaving things behind they ceased to exist. By refusing to argue, there was no argument. By refusing to explain himself, he was no longer at fault.

He stopped and realised he was only a few hundred metres from Number one, with its water, fuel, ghosts. He decided he needed to move beyond any straight line, any join, any joist. So, he turned and rode away from the shack.

A few minutes later he ran out of fuel. He dropped the bike in the sand, stood, and thought. Started walking away from the bike, the shack, Bundeena itself (although there were thousands of hectares in front of him). His boots sank into the sand so he kicked them off and walked in his socks.

At 8.30 pm Fay stood outside his door. 'Do you feel like something yet?' she called.

No reply.

'Trev?'

Nothing. She knew he was withdrawing, something he'd always done, ever since he was a boy. Running and hiding in his tree when Murray growled at him, but then moping about for days; going into the shed, sawing pieces of wood, nailing them together. She'd find him and ask, 'What's that?'

'The *Titanic* ... but I need some round bits for the funnels.'

She waited, but guessed he wouldn't respond. 'If you want something later, tell me. I'll warm it up.'

Everyone assumed he was asleep. It wasn't unusual. He was often asleep by 7 pm during the muster, or after a long drive from town. Snoring by 8 pm; his light and radio left on.

The next morning it took a while to notice. Fay opened his door and saw the made bed with its single indentation. The thought occurred to her, she dismissed it. There were a hundred places he could be. She went out to the lounge room. The rest of the family was gathered around the table. 'Anyone seen Trevor?'

No reply. Just slowly grinding jaws; Murray reading the *Stock Journal.*

'His bed hasn't been slept in,' she said.

'Prob'ly gone to see his girlfriend.'

Aiden looked at him. 'The car's still there.'

Silence; as they all looked at Murray. 'What about the bikes?' he asked.

Harry jumped up. Ran outside and was back in a few seconds. 'Just the one.'

'He's off on some job?' Fay asked.

'No,' Murray replied. 'I've been awake since five. I haven't heard a thing.'

Unusual, since it had always been an unwritten rule (even if you were in a shit) that you told someone where you were going.

Aiden stood. Walked outside and they heard him calling, 'Dad?' Heard him walking around the house and into the sheds. 'Dad, where are you?'

Fay was worried. 'What do you reckon, Murray?'

He took a few moments. 'Mighta just took off into town.'

'He always says something.'

'Well, maybe he didn't.'

But she couldn't imagine it. 'It's not like him.'

'He's been upset,' Harry said.

'Yes,' she agreed. 'He was very ... down last night.'

'What time?' Murray asked.

'When did I go in there ...? Six, seven?'

Murray felt the warm breath of history. 'Maybe we should call the girlfriend?'

Aiden came back in. 'Nothing,' he said, standing in the doorway, waiting. Then Fay noticed his keys and wallet sitting in their usual spot on the end of the bench. 'He would've taken them,' she said, indicating.

'Right!' Murray knew this was another problem he'd have to fix. 'Harry, hop on yer bike, ride down towards the highway. Fay, get Chris, go through the house, the sheds, all around. The bike track. The old airstrip. The yards. And take a phone. Aiden, you come with me.'

Ten minutes later they'd separated and were travelling around and away from the house. Aiden was driving the ute at full speed along the bore run. It jumped, dropped, settled, followed the low land, spun out in sand, gripped the earth and carried on. Murray was holding his door, his feet planted on the floor. 'He knows better,' he said.

Aiden didn't reply. He was searching the distant flats and gibbers for his broken-down or out-of-fuel father. That's all it could be, he thought. Something technical, something mechanical.

After a silent drive they arrived at Number one. They got out and Aiden said, 'Have a look inside. I'll go for a walk.'

Murray waited. 'You go in.'

'Don't be stupid ... I'm gonna climb some of these dunes, get a good look.' He was gone, sprinting across the sand, climbing the highest of the hills in the mid-distance.

Murray looked at the small shack, its door left open to the desert. Come on, you silly old cunt, he said to himself. Come on.

He approached and slowly climbed the steps.

Come on. If he's done something he wouldn't do it here ... why would he?

He kept walking, stopped at the door but then went in. It was dark. His eyes took ten or fifteen seconds to adjust: the spare jerry-cans; the containers of water; the first-aid kit. Then he looked up at the few inches of wood he'd been avoiding for so long. It was rough, but there were no marks, no signs, or at least nothing he could make out in the semi-dark. 'Shit,' he whispered, feeling his heart race.

Aiden was behind him. 'Pop, come on, I've found him.'

They went out, climbed into the ute and Aiden started it. He pumped the accelerator a few times and said, 'I can see his bike.' They set off across the flats. Murray took out his phone and said, 'I'll call Fay.'

'Wait. Let's see what's happened.' He imagined the scene; the accident; the result of their desert chase.

'Christ knows what he was thinking,' Murray said, refusing to believe, even now, there was more to his son than Bundeena.

'He was just trying to get away.'

'From what?'

He just looked at him.

They stopped beside the bike. Aiden got out, looked around and called, 'Dad?' He waited. Louder. 'Dad?' Then lifted and shook the bike. 'Empty.' He noticed tracks heading west. Walked over and stood beside them. 'I'll follow them, you drive.'

They continued for ten minutes, Murray keeping the ute in second, sinking, revving, driving on, Aiden with his head down. The tracks started deep but shallowed. They came across his boots. Aiden picked them up and showed them to Murray.

They continued until they found his shirt; his pants; his socks. Until Aiden said, 'He's going round in circles.' He pointed to Number one, a few hundred metres to the east. 'Dad!' he shouted. Louder. 'Dad!'

The tracks continued into another depression. Now, Aiden was running and Murray was in third, fourth.

'Dad!'

As it dawned on him how little time they had.

'Dad!'

The tracks were unevenly spaced, blurred, where his father was dragging his feet. He came over another rise and there he was, lying near-naked under a gidgee tree. 'Dad!' He knelt beside him. 'Dad …' He gently shook him but there was no response.

Murray got out of the ute and came over. 'How is he?'

He could see that he was alive, moving, stretching out on the hot sand. 'Get some water.'

Murray returned to the ute, fetched a bottle of water and returned. Aiden sat his father between his legs and lifted him so he was mostly upright. He took the water from Murray and tried to make him drink. At first he wouldn't take it, but then started swallowing. Then he kept going until the bottle was empty.

Aiden stood, lifted his father and slung him across his shoulder. He didn't feel the weight. He carried him towards the ute, waited until Murray dropped the back panel and lifted him onto the tray. 'Right, you get in, I'll drive,' he said to his grandfather. He unbuttoned and slid off his pants and rolled them into a tight cylinder. Then he propped them under his father's head.

28

When Aiden carried his father inside, Fay knew she'd been right. As he laid him on his bed she cursed herself for not having done more. Discussing it with the others (although Murray wouldn't have cared). Calling a doctor. Finding Gaby.

But, for now, she realised, they'd have to fix the body. So, she ordered the boys to find extra fans, bring them in, fix them on their father; she washed him with a cold flannel and spent an hour rubbing aloe cream into his red skin. She made him keep drinking and covered him with a sheet as he pissed into a pan from the medical kit. Stayed with him as he slept, or at least pretended to. Said, 'Aiden wants to call for help,' and he replied, 'No, I'll be better tomorrow, Aunt.'

When she started falling asleep she asked Chris to come and sit with him. When she woke the next morning he was still there.

She was soon back at work: bedpan; aloe; flannel. She stared at him, sometimes muttering comments like, 'Get you up and about' or 'See how you feel tomorrow.'

Later in the morning, he got up, walked to the toilet, returned and sat up in bed. 'I'm alright now,' he said. 'You've got stuff to do.'

Instead of going, she just smiled. 'It's always been my job.'

'What has?'

'Looking out for you. Murray was never the father-type, I don't think. I worked that out a long time ago.'

'So did I.'

'You wouldn't remember, but when you were little we all went to the Claradine race meeting.'

He looked up, curious she'd never mentioned it before.

'Murray was off somewhere and you,' and she touched his arm and smiled, 'sprinted across the track in front of the horses.'

He studied her old eyes. Maybe she was making it up. Maybe it had happened. Either way, he sensed, it was the notion more than the memory.

'So there's me,' she continued, 'off across the track after you, these horses coming towards us …'

'What happened?'

She tried to remember. 'I must have got you back.'

He was convinced it might have happened, in some form or another. Perhaps he'd run onto a road and the story had grown. Perhaps it was something Chris had done and she was substituting, like different attachments on her old Mixmaster. Perhaps it was something she'd seen on a telly show, and dreamed into existence. Or perhaps it had never happened at all.

She said, 'A lot of water under the bridge.'

He didn't reply.

'But if it's come to this,' and she squeezed his hand, 'perhaps it's better to move on.'

He waited.

'Sometimes things don't repair … can't.'

He looked down. 'Thirty-eight thousand hectares,' he said.

'Murray's carved from salt. You wait for him to change … even drop off the perch … there'll be nothing left.'

'It's all down to me.'

'So? You ring up, they take some photos, they put them on the internet. Some fella calls, makes an offer, you say, I'm gonna refer you to my father, and if Murray says no …'

He waited. He'd already decided (as he laid awake, bladder-full, during the night). It wasn't so hard; it was just the mechanics of leaving.

'It's all over,' she said to him.

'I know.'

'For the boys' sake … you and Gaby.'

He waited.

'I've been worried about you for months,' she said. 'I knew this day would come. I'm only glad you didn't …'

He stroked the back of her hand with his thumb. She was still chasing him, he guessed, across the track, turning to see how close the horses were.

Harry stood in the shed, looking at the hand, laying his own beside it and comparing them. It was almost a perfect match: the length of his fingers, the curve of his thumb. He ran his hand over the knuckles, between the webbing, along the sharp edge of the fingernails. He guessed it was finished. His father had taken down the photos and burned 'H. WILKIE 2006' on the plane of amputation. He took the sculpture and went inside.

Sitting down between Chris and Aiden, he placed his hand beside his plate. Murray was serving stew from a dish. He looked at the hand and said, 'Not on the table.'

He looked up and said, 'It's finished.'

'Not on the table.'

He made no attempt to move it.

'Did you hear me?' He almost threw a bowl of stew down in front of him.

'I want to look at it.'

'This is the problem, isn't it?'

'What?'

'Causing people grief.'

'Who?'

Murray decided it was wiser to back off, for now. He gave Chris and Aiden their stew and they all started eating.

The next minute was cutlery on china, the whispers of Fay and Trevor from the other room, a radio left on, somewhere.

Then Murray said, 'I did have a plan.'

They all looked at him.

'The Coopers are interested in that land beyond the railway line.'

Again, silence.

'Jeff Cooper, he's been asking about it for years.'

Aiden didn't believe a word he said. More games; more blame shifting. And if things came good, it'd all be forgotten.

'I's thinking of going to see him and asking if he wants to make an offer.' He waved his hand in the air. 'That's what I was gonna tell Trev ... before all this business. I'm still willing, but I don't know how this changes things.'

'How what changes things?' Aiden asked.

'This ... drama.'

'You think he ... got lost?'

Murray stopped eating. He didn't know how to have this conversation.

'You can say it, Pop,' Aiden continued.

He just ate.

'He didn't want to be found,' said Aiden.

'Just eat yer stew.'

'And you know why.'

'Quiet!' He slammed his fist on the table. '*I've* come up with a solution. Ten thousand acres ... even if he only offers a couple of hundred an acre. Next year we restock ... it rains.'

All three looked at him.

'It's a bit late for that,' Aiden said.

'It's not my fault that he – '

'It is.'

Trevor was standing in the hallway. He came forward. Fay

345

came up behind him. 'Alright boys,' he said. 'In yer room … I'll get yer cases.'

They all stared at him. They could see he was tired, but determined.

'Get your stuff packed,' he continued. 'We're going.'

29

Aiden drove towards Port Augusta. He was still in his shorts, T-shirt and slippers. Harry sat in the back, a case in his side, clothes (a small mountain of them they'd just thrown in) under his feet and across his lap. Shoes and boots. Books (dozens he'd pulled from his bookcase and shoved under the seats and in the gaps between the half-tonne of junk they'd salvaged).

As Murray stood on the porch shaking his head, saying, 'Nice performance, son.'

By now, Trevor didn't see the point of speaking to him. He just kept going between bedroom and car, loading, squeezing, telling Harry to get his assignments, his toothbrush, his pyjamas.

'Leave it to me,' Murray was saying. 'Chris can help with the muster.'

Fay had returned to the kitchen to clean up. Her job was done. Things might, in one way or another, fix themselves now. But she would still have to live with her brother. So it was back to the kitchen and the part she'd played for the last forty years. It was back to Bruce Willis and the smell of cheap tobacco, the memory of the Tea and Sugar.

Trevor had put his chair back. As Aiden drove he watched the desert pass, but didn't feel a part of it anymore. It was just landscape. The grass would grow without him. The animals would still fuck and have their own little children (full of spirit and a million possibilities) but he mightn't be there to help them breech.

For the first time in a long time, he was happy. He looked at Aiden and felt proud to the point of crying. Everything was right; everything would work out. This was the realisation he'd had, in the desert, as he heard, but couldn't see, the distant Indian Pacific. Harry, too, would be the greatest man who ever lived. He shuddered when he thought of the accident and what might have happened but fought for breath when he remembered, realised, how much he loved his sons.

There was nothing else now except the three of them, the four of them.

He turned and looked at Aiden. 'I'm sorry,' he said.

'Why?'

He couldn't answer. But Aiden knew it wasn't about Gaby or his mum or his walk into the desert. It was about how they'd been living, for so long.

And then he remembered. *Be!* He felt in his pocket and the small piece of paper was still there. *Be!* He didn't even take it out. He remembered what it said; about the voice of life crying: *Be!*

An hour after they'd gone, Murray went into his son's room and lay down on his bed. He wondered how long he'd be gone. Overnight, at least. A few days at most. He wondered why he'd taken so much gear. But that was Trevor – always the actor. The drawers were all hanging open, empty, apart from some of Carelyn's clothes; the hangers in the wardrobe were twisted at awkward angles.

Then he noticed a letter on the bedside table. The name, Murray, printed on the front. He sat up, took it, studied it. Opened it. It was written on lavender-scented paper. He imagined what Fay had said to Trevor. He knew she would've told him, or at least encouraged him, to go. She had never put down Bundeena roots. She'd never understood the place. But it had been his responsibility to take her in. That's what no one seemed to realise. It wasn't about what you wanted.

Time to sell up. If you put it on the market I'll come back and help you sell it, destock. Then, I take enough to buy a place in town. Somewhere close to Mercy, and the garage. You keep enough for a unit. You decide. My mobile number's on the fridge.

He screwed it up and threw it across the room. It settled in a pile of abandoned underwear.

The Wilkie men stopped at the car-house. They got out, sat on the bonnet and drank from a bottle of flat Coke Trevor had grabbed on the way out. 'It's gonna be hot,' he said to his sons.

'Fucking hot,' Aiden replied, smiling.

'Really fucking hot,' he said.

There was nothing but silence; then a B-triple hurtling past. Harry ran over to the old house, with its bonnet walls, its hub-cap tiles, its wind-down windows. He looked back at them and said, 'This place is so ugly.' Ripping a hub-cap from the wall, he threw it into the yard. And again. Until Aiden joined him, and they had a competition to see who could throw the furthest.

'Ugly!' Harry called. He kicked one of the wall panels, and another. He ripped a few down. He stood on a bucket seat and kicked in a window; another. Aiden joined in. They pulled down tyres and rolled them out towards the highway; they pulled down a row of ornamental carburettors and kicked over a table fashioned from an engine-block. Then they moved away from the house, gathered stones and started smashing windows. One after another, as they laughed, and dared each other, and Harry called, 'Ugly!'

Trevor just watched, wondering if they should burn it down as well; wondering how Chris would keep, as the sole moving target.

… Fay and Chris can live with us, then you won't be bothered by anyone.

The boys returned to the house and he could hear more smashing, more breaking.

Murray sat on the porch, looking out towards the long train. Fay was cooking chops; was always cooking chops. He finished rolling a cigarette, put it in his mouth and lit it. And thought: I can't go. I can't.

Yanga was sitting at his feet. She looked up at him. She twisted her head as though she was confused about something.

He studied the phone number on the scrap of paper on the table beside him.

I can't.

Yanga stood up and walked away. She found another spot and sat down.

I can't.

The undersides of the clouds were red, and he thought it was more beautiful than anything. The land was hot, honey-coloured, breathing. It promised life, a future, income; it always had.

Fay popped her head out. 'You can come in now.' And she was gone.

He could never leave the ghosts: Bill, John. Although, he supposed, his son and grandsons had given up their mother. Maybe that's what it took, he thought. Maybe something had to be given up. Something precious. Something irretrievable.

I can't.

He picked up the number, and studied the digits.

'Come on,' Fay called.

He could smell the chops; but couldn't go in.

It was after nine as they drove through the back streets of Port Augusta.

Trevor was feeling excited; light.

Aiden stopped at a roundabout to let a boy on a dragster pass.

'That's an old one,' he said to his dad.

'Don't think I ever had a bike,' Trevor replied.

'Not much point,' Aiden said, as they drove on.

It was hot in the small houses. People had come out onto front porches to escape the heat. Some of them sat on old benches, some on car seats; others on lounge suites.

As they drove into Gaby's driveway, Harry woke. He looked and saw where they were; remembered why; felt it under his feet; board games, even, on the parcel shelf behind his head.

Gaby was soon out, waiting beside her dead garden, her arms crossed. She could see they'd filled every inch of the car with their crap.

Harry was out first, and he ran over to her; across the dead lawn, catching his T-shirt on her mouldy roses.

He tried not to smile. 'Guess what?'

Then she wrapped him in her arms. She looked up at Trevor, emerging from the car, stretching. 'Come on,' she said. 'I'll make you a coffee first.'

Acknowledgements

Many thanks to Michael Bollen, Angela Tolley, Margot Lloyd, Molly Jureidini, Michael Deves and Julia Beaven.

Songs

'Comrades'	Felix McGleason
'Eileen Bawn'	words H.J. St Leger music M.W. Balfe
'I couldn't even swear to the colour of her hair'	words Harry Hunter music Walter Redmond
'Tell me, darling, that you love me'	John A. Orway
'Underneath the mellow moon'	Wendell W. Hall
'When you and I were seventeen'	words Gus Kahn music Charles Rosoff

By the author of
Time's Long Ruin

Stephen Orr

Dissonance
A novel

What happens when children disappear?

Time's
Long
Ruin

A Novel

'A compelling
page-turner'
RICHARD WALSH

STEPHEN ORR

'His prose lavishly packed with particulars, Orr's characters assume
poignant life as modernity and old-time religion go head to head in
a wonderful period portrait.' Cath Kenneally

HILL OF GRACE
Stephen Orr

DISSONANCE

Stephen Orr

Dissonance begins with piano practice. Fifteen-year-old Erwin Hergert is forced to tackle scales and studies for six hours a day by his mother, Madge, who is determined to produce Australia's first great pianist. To help Erwin focus, Madge has exiled her husband, Johann, to the back shed. Jo is diagnosed with cancer and Madge allows him back inside, but only for long enough to die.

Madge takes Erwin to Hamburg to continue his studies. Erwin prospers in Germany with his new teacher until he meets a neighbour, sixteen-year-old Luise, and finds there's more to life than music.

Meanwhile, Germany is moving towards war. Late 1930s Hamburg forms the backdrop to an increasingly difficult love-triangle, as Erwin is torn between the piano, Luise, and the demands of his love and devotion to his mother. Soon the bombs, real and imagined, start falling. Marriage and parenthood give way to death, and tragedy. Before long Erwin and Madge are drawn into the horrors of a war that leaves little time for music.

Dissonance is a re-imagining of the 'Frankfurt years' of Rose and Percy Grainger. This is a novel about love in one of its most extreme and destructive forms, and how people attempt to survive the threat of possession.

'Compelling … an engrossing novel. Orr is a vivid storyteller.' – Stella Clarke, *Weekend Australian*

'*Dissonance* is a rich, layered and absorbing novel.' – Suzanne Eggins, *Canberra Times*

'Our own Wakefield Press has produced a nicely bound and presented work which ranks as one of the finest pieces of Australian writing I've seen for a long time.' – Peter C. Pugsley, *Indaily*

ISBN 978 1 86254 945 6

For more information please visit www.wakefieldpress.com.au

TIME'S LONG RUIN

Stephen Orr

Nine-year-old Henry Page is a club-footed, deep-thinking loner, spending his summer holidays reading, roaming the melting streets of his suburb, playing with his best friend Janice and her younger brother and sister. Then one day Janice asks Henry to spend the day at the beach with them. He declines, a decision that will stay with him forever.

Time's Long Ruin is based loosely on the disappearance of the Beaumont children from Glenelg beach on Australia Day, 1966. It is a novel about friendship, love and loss; a story about those left behind, and how they carry on: the searching, the disappointments, the plans and dreams that are only ever put on hold.

Winner, Unpublished manuscript award, Adelaide Festival

South Australian winner, 2012 National Year of Reading awards

'In *Time's Long Ruin* [Orr] has conjured up the suburban claustrophobia of the Fifties and added to it streaks of ... darker pigments. His Thomas Street, Croydon – particularly on hot days, when no one has enough to do and everyone gets on each other's nerves – is Adelaide's very distinctive version of Winton's *Cloudstreet*, Malouf's *Edmondstone Street* and White's *Sarsaparilla*; but the quality and vividness of Orr's evocation of those stultifying times ensures he can hold his head high in such illustrious company. *Time's Long Ruin* is a compelling page-turner.' – Richard Walsh

ISBN 978 1 86254 830 5

For more information please visit www.wakefieldpress.com.au

HILL OF GRACE

Stephen Orr

1951. Among the coppiced carob trees and arum lilies of the Barossa Valley, old-school Lutheran William Miller lives a quiet life with his wife, Bluma, and son Nathan, making wine and baking bread. But William has a secret. He's been studying the Bible and he's found what a thousand others couldn't: the date of the Apocalypse.

William sets out to convince his neighbours that they need to join him in preparation for the End. The locals of Tanunda become divided. Did William really hear God's voice on the Hill of Grace? Or is he really deluded? The greatest test of all for William is whether Bluma and Nathan will support him. As the seasons pass in the Valley, as the vines flower and fruit and lose their leaves, William himself is forced to question his own beliefs and the price he's willing to pay for them.

The Barossa Valley of the 1950s is beautifully captured in this, Stephen Orr's second novel. His first novel, *Attempts to Draw Jesus*, was a runner up in the 2000 Vogel Award and published by Allen & Unwin.

'His prose lovingly packed with particulars, Orr's characters assume poignant life as modernity and old-time religion go head to head in a wonderful period portrait.' – Cath Kenneally

ISBN 978 1 86254 648 6

For more information please visit www.wakefieldpress.com.au

Wakefield Press is an independent publishing and
distribution company based in Adelaide, South Australia.
We love good stories and publish beautiful books.
To see our full range of books, please visit our website at
www.wakefieldpress.com.au
where all titles are available for purchase.

Find us!

Twitter: www.twitter.com/wakefieldpress
Facebook: www.facebook.com/wakefield.press
Instagram: instagram.com/wakefieldpress